THE DEADMAN'S TRIBE  BOOK 2

bad ENOUGH

NICOLE CRAIG

DEDICATION

To my high school students from the past twenty-five years...

Yes, I know this is a romance novel, and one that high school students probably shouldn't be reading. But, by the time this crosses any of your paths, you're ok to read it, especially since I'm now retired. But even if you never do (and it's extremely unlikely you would), this still holds true.

It was my honor... It was my privilege...
I love every one of you, no matter how you feel/felt about me.
You were my reason to get up each day.
You made me a better teacher.
You made me a better person.

If you remember nothing else of our time together, remember this:
- You matter to me.
- I see you, even if you think I don't.
- I believe in you.
- I know you can do it, even if you think you can't.
- I am cheering for you every day.

Note that none of these are in the past tense. If you were my student in 1999 on my very first day of class, or if you were my student in 2024 on my very last day, it doesn't matter. I am still your teacher, and I will always think of myself that way.

All the jokes you made about driving me crazy, driving me to drink, driving me to gray hair, driving me into retirement at the tender age of 54... we can laugh about those things. But walking away from teaching is the hardest thing I have ever done. I know I'm not really ready to leave. Maybe you need me more now than ever. I don't know. But what I do know is that YOU are what I am most proud of in my entire life. YOU. No one and nothing else.

Make the choices that are best for YOU, not for anyone else.

Go to college, or not, where YOU want to go, not where someone else wants you to go.

Do what makes YOU happy, not what makes someone else happy.

And if people put obstacles in the way of your happiness, find a way to rip those obstacles down. Find a way around them. Find a way over them. It's YOUR life, not theirs.

If you want something bad enough, make it happen.

1

APRIL 6TH

Sylvan

PING! "You've got mail!"

After clicking into her email and scanning its new contents, she worried the left side of her bottom lip and hissed when she felt herself draw blood. "Go. Away." Hastily, she clicked the box in front of the new, unwanted email, clicked the "delete" button, and then proceeded back to her manuscript.

Fingers poised over her keyboard, she stared at the white page. Her brain waited for words to flow from its dark, creative corners.

A full minute passed, and nothing happened. Her fingers didn't even twitch.

Her eyes narrowed to pour every ounce of her energy into staring down the cursor's mocking wink.

Aw, are you stuck?

"No, I am not stuck."

Hmm. Distracted, perhaps? By anything in particular? Or should I say, "anyone"?

"I don't know what you're talking about."

Oh, I think you know EXACTLY who I'm talking about.

"Please, what would be the point of being distracted by him? It's not like he cares."

See? You knew who I meant. And distractions don't have a point. That's why they're called distractions. They are, by definition, pointless. Besides, he must care at least a little. The two of you texted for hours two nights ago. Not his previous M.O., which was to text you, you replied, and a couple of hours would go by before he responded again.

"Maybe *you* should stop bothering me. You're the one distracting me right now."

Don't blame this on me! Blame it on tall, dark, and broody.

"You don't know that he's any of those things. You've never seen him."

Oh, but I can imagine him that way. And if I can, that means you can because we're the same person. So be a good girl and admit he's distracting you.

She huffed in indignation. "I will admit no such thing!"

Who do you think you're fooling? Do you even hear yourself talking to yourself? Don't tell me you're not distracted.

"Oh, for sittin' on the cat. Are you even listening to me? Us? Whatever! I told you I'm distracted. I'm just not distracted by him."

That's so sweet. You honestly believe that, don't you? Stop lying to yourself. Recognizing the problem is the first step to recovery!

"I'm ignoring you now. Buh-bye."

Sylvan swore she heard mocking laughter echoing inside her head.

Giving her shoulders a quick shake, she settled her fingers in the "asdfjkl;" position on the keyboard once more and returned her eyes to the screen with a new sense of purpose.

Three minutes later? Nothing. Not even a string of gibberish.

"These words aren't going to type themselves, you dumb bunny, so think of something! Forty-seven days isn't much time."

A frustrated sigh expelled itself from her mouth with a force strong enough to lift the stray wisps of hair falling loose from the messy pile on top of her head. In twenty-five previous manu-scripts, she had never experienced this. Writing manuscript one, with no technical understanding of the craft, words poured out of her fingertips so fast even she had been surprised. With manuscript two, she'd worried that her sophomore effort would prove her greatest fear—that the freshman effort was a fluke, and she'd never write another novel. But even then, the words had always come, although they weren't necessarily great ones at first.

Today? Not a floofin' thing.

Her fingers sat atop the keyboard, her eyes gazed on the page, and Sylvan's brain wandered again. Back to those texts from two nights ago when the distracter in question told her some hilarious stories about his co-worker, particularly one where he suffered a bite to the butt by a coral snake. She'd been smiling like a loon through the whole exchange, totally acting like a teenager texting with her first crush, but she was past caring.

Come to think of it, their texting sessions had gotten longer and longer of late. Maybe he was a little intrigued. Then again, he'd been stuck on his recent business trip coming up on fifty days, so he was probably climbing the walls with boredom and texting her to pass the time.

DING DONG!

Sylvan's brow furrowed. "Who the heck is messaging me at this hour of the night?"

She clicked over onto her social media page to see that, sure enough, someone had messaged her on her author page. Before thinking it through, she clicked on the notification. Thinking things through had never been her strong suit. She really needed to work on that.

UNKNOWN

Hello, Red. Miss me?

UNKNOWN

I told you that you'd never escape me.

UNKNOWN

I have to say, you made me work to find you.

UNKNOWN

And you've been ignoring my emails. Can't have that.

UNKNOWN

See you soon…

All the blood rushed from the upper portion of Sylvan's body as the messages began appearing on her screen. When she violently shoved her keyboard, as if that would make the message writer be further away from her, it caught the edge of her teacup, sending the contents spilling. The scalding liquid splashed her hand with stinging bites, and it ran in all directions on her desk, ruining her notes in the notebook she'd been referencing.

She whimpered.

Lock it down. He can't see you. He's not here. He can't hurt you. He may have found you on the computer, but that doesn't mean he knows where you are. You hid well.

Shaking with real fear, Sylvan reached out to hard shutdown the computer. Clutching her burnt hand and ignoring the spreading spilled tea, she sprung from her desk chair, dove into her bed, and pulled the bedspread up over her head just like she used to when she was little and scared. A part of her prayed for the magic that children believed in, that if every part of you was under the covers, the monsters couldn't touch you.

Unfortunately, she knew from experience that some monsters were far more powerful than cover-magic.

It was hours of tears later when she finally fell into a fitful sleep. But even then, she dreamt of shadowy figures who ripped and tore covers to shreds, then covered her with their stinking breath, salivating mouths, and grotesque bodies. And there was no Prince Charming in the background to fight them off.

2

———————

APRIL 10TH

TB

Multicolored lights swung and spun chaotically to shine down on the dance floor. Fog machines flooded the floor with cold mist, enveloping the dancers packed in "The Pool," as it was called, because of its entrances being five steps down from the main floor. The club was hot. Too hot for his liking. Worst of all, his organs felt like they were being shocked with electricity, and his blood seemed to pulse with the synthetic bass line of classic Depeche Mode.

The club's speakers are working overtime tonight. Too loud.

Internally, he sighed. Even to him, his inner voice sounded old. He hadn't wanted to come to The Library tonight, but he was twitchy. Pissed off. Well… pissed off was a constant state for him, so this qualified as more pissed off than usual. Coming to the club should have helped ease the twitchiness, but as soon as he arrived, he remembered it hadn't helped the last few times he'd come here before going overseas.

Same shit, different day. What's the point?

He blamed part of his current negativity on his team leader, Waters, for being the ultimate dumbass. The man was acting completely out of character, leaving his woman while she was possibly still vulnerable to danger, simply on the orders of their boss. The man was going to pay for his mistake in more ways than one.

I love that man like a brother, but sometimes…

Then there was the long-standing fuckery of one of his teammates, Nemo, who irritated him simply by breathing. They'd only been back from Roatán for a few hours, and he'd already been the victim of two confetti cannons, an air horn, and a skeleton popping out of a closet at him. TB wished that the snake the idiot had recently battled with would have bitten him on the dick instead of the ass.

You know you need to stand off to the side when opening any door in the office, dumbass.

Internally, he sighed. Putting on his club persona, Lobo, was usually an easy task. He spent most of his adult life using codenames, nicknames, and aliases in his undercover work in the Israeli military and then again in his self-contractor role over the dark web. Going to work for Tribe five years ago had added another name to the resume. Being someone else was nothing new, but lately, it was exhausting and a little like he no longer knew who he was.

Perhaps the worst part of why he was in a crap mood right now was his current conversation partner. Tilly, the club name for internet influencer Matilda Moll, a young twenty-something from the Valley, had sashayed over to him at the club and tried to flirt with him. She was a regular at the club and overall a sweet thing when she wasn't being a brat, but TB didn't like sweet things.

Flame is a sweet thing. You like her.

Shut up, goody-two-shoes, or I'll throat-punch you right out of my head.

I'm frustrated. I need something to work my frustration out on. Tilly would be perfect in brat mode.

The trouble was, all he wanted was to swat her away like an annoying mosquito.

Sighing internally, he realized he should have skipped the club and stayed home to chat with Flame. That's what he had wanted to do, but he chickened out like a total pussy and forced himself to come here. Flame was too sweet. Too nice for the likes of someone like him. She deserved romance and a man who would be home every night to make love to her. Not a jaded fuck like him. His hands were far too bloody to even think of being in the same room with her.

And yet, it was what he desperately wanted. Through their online chats, he discovered she was harboring such naughtiness in her head, all he wanted to do was muss her up. It didn't even matter that he had no clue what she looked like. He'd honestly fallen in love over a computer chat. Him. The love bug had bitten Mister Asshole, and he was so infected, his brain kept trying to come up with scenarios where he deserved his little Flame in his life every day.

But every scenario he came up with was a bust, and when his team leader threw in the towel on the best thing that ever happened to him? TB knew an omen when he saw one. That was the only clue he needed to remind him that relationships were not for men like them.

Technically, relationships were forbidden. One disastrous project involving Waters' sister, Sarah, brought that on. For a brief while, however, the team had looked on at the off-the-wall chemistry of Waters and the spitfire film director, Kubrick, and had been rooting for them. They'd all been believers for a short while. And then, poof! It went up in smoke.

Internally, he snorted at the direction his thoughts were running. He was such a hypocrite. Not too long ago, he'd been telling his team leader to seize the opportunity instead of turning his back on the possibilities with a woman he'd fallen for. For a brief while, it looked like he'd done it. Now the poor bastard was sulking in his office at Tribe, his tail between his legs, and TB was ignoring the very advice he'd given his team leader.

Well, my situation isn't the same.

Really? Exactly how is it different?

He hated when the voices in his head argued with one another. He always felt like he was stuck in the middle of some weird ménage à trois. It was creepy.

I'm not a nice guy, and Waters is.

Nice? You remember the project in Somalia, right? He's the one who taught you that trick with the handsaw.

And I hope I never have to use it. That even gave me nightmares.

Raising his glass to his mouth, TB took a generous swallow of his water. He never drank while at the club. If he took part in the club's upper-level activities, nothing should interfere with those experiences. But right now, Tilly's never-ending chatter was making him wish for a heavy dose of Scotch and a sharp pencil to stab through his eardrum to his brain and end the misery.

"I desperately wanted to dump my energy drink on his antique desk since he was being such a total prick, you know? Apparently, I didn't set my phone alarm last night, or else I slept through it. I mean, I was up really late helping my friend through her latest man disaster. But what else was I supposed to do? Girl code says you don't let the bestie down, no matter if you have to go to work the next morning or not. So what if I was fifteen minutes late?

"Then the boss was mad because I allegedly misplaced some files he needed for a client today. I found them eventually. He spends the first five or ten minutes shooting the shit with them about their golfing, or their fishing, or whatever stupid old-man hobby they have, anyway. The client wouldn't even have known it had been missing.

"And to top it all off, he claimed I double-booked his lunch appointment today with his mother's birthday lunch date. If he let me merge his personal calendar and his business calendar into the frickin' computer app, I wouldn't have to remember to check both of them before scheduling anything. Who cares if the rest of the staff can see his personal schedule? We're all too damn busy to be poking around in his private life.

"Besides, even if I did all those things, everyone has bad days, right?"

TB didn't bother to reply. He knew she wasn't really expecting an answer, and her dialogue would continue.

"You look a bit like you've had a bad day yourself. I like the broody look myself, so I don't mind. Goes with all the black clothing, the leather jacket, and your dark hair. Totally smokin'. And your eyelashes! I know a lot of women who would kill for eyelashes like yours, so thick and dark. I bet you'd be really hot if you smiled more."

He barely refrained from rolling his eyes.

"I mean, not that you're not really hot now. You totally are," she corrected. "I know you're really built, and I bet you spend a lot of time at the gym. That's hot, too. You don't see a lot of guys your age who take such great care of their appearance. I like that. Normally, I wouldn't be interested in someone so much older than me, but you're different."

Guys my age? I'm thirty-seven, not seventy-seven.

"So, are you?"

He took another swallow from his glass, finished his water, and set the empty glass on the bar. He flicked a finger at Ryleigh, his favorite bartender, signaling he needed a refill. Without looking at Tilly, he asked, "Am I what?"

"Having a bad day."

He nodded at Ryleigh as she pushed his refilled glass toward him.

"No."

"Oh. Wow. I mean, like I said, you've totally got that broody alpha thing going, but you're looking even more grouchy than usual. Do you wanna dance? Might cheer you up. I'm a really good dancer."

"No."

"Oh. Okay. Um... do you wanna go upstairs?" she asked nervously. "Maybe I could make your day better if we did a scene."

TB stood straight and grabbed his glass from the bar top. "I thought you were exclusive with Cosmos." He slammed the water in his glass, set the empty glass on the bar, and slid it toward a smirking Ryleigh, who had overheard Tilly's offer.

She looked properly embarrassed at his rebuke. "I'm sorry, Master Lobo. I thought maybe..." She shrugged. "Everyone's been talking about how you haven't been involved in a scene in a while. The subs talk about how they really enjoyed partnering with you. I just was hoping I might get to see for myself, especially since you haven't been doing scenes with anyone. I figured that meant you were available." She sighed. "Besides, I think Cosmos is tiring of me."

Tiring of the chatter, probably.

"Go on, Tilly."

"Yes, Master Lobo."

Picking up her drink, she turned and began walking over to her friends at their high table along The Pool. On the way there, she began circumventing the bodies coming off the dance floor. Someone bumped into her hard, spilling her drink on her dress and almost knocking her to the floor. The person helped Tilly right herself, and then the river of people from the dance floor was rushing upon and around them, dividing into two paths to avoid the obstacle, much like salmon swimming upstream to spawn. He tried to follow them, making sure she was okay, but he lost them in the crowd.

TB turned to face the bar as he shook his head and sighed in frustration.

"You can't blame her, Lobo. But you could have been a little nicer about the put-down."

"Are you telling me how to handle my business, Rye?"

"Yes."

"I should put you over my knee."

"I'm no one's sub to punish. Just working here to fund my editing costs. BDSM is fun to read, but not really my thing in real life."

"Everyone's got their kink, Rye." TB reached for his wallet and pulled out a twenty. "Even you." Placing the bill on the bar, he winked at her.

JUST BEFORE ELEVEN, Fleur, a newer submissive, and Tripoli, a current dungeon master, approached him. TB was talking with another club member, a tall, blond businessman-type named Loki, one-third of a triad that had joined the club last month.

Loki held out his hand to the former Marine. "Tripoli."

Tripoli grasped his hand. "Loki." He nodded at TB. "Lobo. Sorry to interrupt, but Fleur was just telling me that Tilly is missing. She thought Tilly was heading over to their table after talking to you, but she never arrived. Did she mention going anywhere when she left you at the bar?"

Lobo frowned and looked at Fleur. "I definitely sent her back to your table. I saw her get bumped into by someone in the crowd, and he was helping her regain her footing when the crowd poured in from the dance floor. Are you sure she's not at the bar?"

"No, Master Lobo. I looked. She doesn't seem to be anywhere."

"Is Cosmos here tonight? They're on contract for another month yet. Maybe they're in a scene upstairs?"

"No, Sir. Cosmos is in London until next week on business."

"Where else did you look?"

"I went to the Dungeon, but she wasn't there. I checked the locker room, and her locker was locked, all of her things in it. I know her combination and checked it."

Loki spoke up. "I'll go check with Frost at the front desk. Maybe she signed out and took a rideshare home. Fleur, why don't you come with me, and we can have you call Tilly from your phone. If the rideshare doesn't pan out, maybe she got a ride home from someone."

"Thank you, Master Lobo and Master Loki."

TB and Loki shared a look before the latter led Fleur to the lobby. TB turned back to Tripoli.

"Did you notify Tabitha?" Lobo asked.

"That was my next step," Tripoli replied. "Didn't want to jump the gun, but with each place Fleur told me she looked, the hairs on my neck started standing up further and further. I was going to check with Triumph in security as well. He's running cameras tonight. Figured maybe we could try to run footage to find her, or at least a direction to search."

"I'll go do that," TB offered. "You go check some of the restricted areas since you work here. Maybe she's hiding out, licking her wounds."

Tripoli smirked. "Approached you, and you shot her down, didn't you?"

TB rolled his eyes. "I don't understand some of these newer submissives. Someone's not training them very well. Pretty brazen."

Tripoli shrugged his shoulders. "It's just how these younger girls are. Some Doms like brats. Gives them a reason to dole out some punishment."

TB grimaced. "Too much work." He wasn't into the punishment angle of BDSM. He dealt with it nonstop as part of his job. He didn't want to deal with it in his personal life. "It could be she's hiding somewhere. Or maybe one of the newer Doms convinced her to break the rules and find a restricted area for some entertainment."

Loki returned. "Frost hasn't seen her, and she didn't sign out while she was on her break. Her phone is still in the lockbox."

The men shared another look.

TB stared at Tripoli. "Better check the alley, as well."

Tripoli nodded and took off.

Loki looked at TB. "I've got a bad feeling about this."

TB grunted. "You and me both."

3

____

APRIL 11TH

Sylvan

PING!

Sylvan clutched her silk robe closed at her neck. Heart racing, she sat in the dark of her sanctuary, curled up in her window bed and staring at her laptop screen.

LOBO: Finally home. Hello, little Flame.

Uncertain, she curled up even tighter into a ball.

What if it's HIM? What if he's been posing as Lobo all this while?

Her stomach felt like it dropped to her feet.

LOBO: Flame? I know you're there.

She let go of the breath she was holding.

LOBO: What's wrong?

FLAME: Nothing. I'm here.

She closed her eyes, squeezing them tight. She was so scared. He was the only thing that made her feel safe.

How sad is that? A man you've never met. Never seen a picture of. Only ever talked to over chat and text. How can you trust someone you've never met?

Self-confidence had never been a characteristic of Sylvan's. Every day of her life had been one that either ripped apart what few feelings of success she began to build for herself or prevented any such feelings from forming. Her latest situation had pretty much destroyed her joy in her work. The only thing that seemed to keep her going was her chats with Master Lobo.

His arrival tonight had kept the panic attack at bay.

She curled even tighter against the bookcase headboard, staring at the laptop screen, silently begging him to say something.

After three minutes of nothing, bubbles began to appear, letting her know he was typing. Then they disappeared but immediately started back up.

LOBO: I'm sorry I didn't have time to check in the last few days. We had some excitement here, and I had to focus.

FLAME: Are you ok?

LOBO: Worried for me, princess? Yeah, I'm fine.

LOBO: Another co-worker is, personally, in a tough spot, and we left a friend of his in a bit of a lurch. Hopefully, it will smooth itself out.

FLAME: How's your friend's butt? No more snakes, I hope.

LOBO: No more snakes.

LOBO: How did your writing go the past few days?

Smiling, she unconsciously uncurled from her protective position. He always asked. Like he actually cared. Even if it was just out of politeness or even as a means to move on to why they really chatted, she liked to think he actually cared. Foolish, perhaps, but she had so few people in her life.

Well, that's a lie. You have thousands of fans who love your books and care about your stories.

FLAME: Not great. My deadline is looming, and while I've written, it feels like garbage.

FLAME: I can't seem to think of any new ideas. I feel like I'm repeating what I've already written.

LOBO: Hmm.

LOBO: Have you been incorporating your research?

The writer's block was odd. It wasn't as if she didn't have plenty of inspiration. Fantasy after fantasy of a mystery man who up and disappeared for days at a time.

FLAME: Yes, but it feels weird to write about the things you've told me about.

LOBO: I thought that was the whole point of this?

LOBO: You wanted to learn about BDSM so that you could write a book that was accurate.

FLAME: Yes, but…

She left the text hanging, unsure how to phrase what she wanted to say without giving away her silly crush.

LOBO: Yes, but what?

Jeepers, how do I get out of this?

LOBO: There's no getting out of answering me.

"Yikes! How did he know what I was thinking?" She started to type a response. Erased it. Started again. Erased again. "Oh, Frankenstein! Why is this so difficult?" She bit her lip and scrunched up her face. "Oh, what the heck'um, just do it."

FLAME: It's begun to feel personal. Especially since you started texting me.

FLAME: It shouldn't.

FLAME: You're there, I'm here. It's not like we'll ever meet.

FLAME: But, let's face it, sex is personal. It feels like I'm writing about you and me, and it feels like an invasion of something private. But it shouldn't because we're not really doing anything.

The screen sat blank for a minute. Then two.

"Way to go," she muttered to herself.

FLAME: I'm sorry.

FLAME: I've made this weird now, and I didn't mean to.

FLAME: You just always tell me to be honest, but maybe there is such a thing as too honest.

FLAME: I should just go.

His answer was immediate.

LOBO: No.

She huffed in exasperation. "'No,' what? No, don't write about what we talk about? No, don't get personal? No, it's not personal? No, it's not an invasion? Give me a clue!"

LOBO: Don't go.

Huh. Well. That I was not expecting.

LOBO: Maybe it's time it did get personal.

"Jinkies," she whispered. "What the bleep does that mean?"

LOBO: You're not wrong.

LOBO: It stopped being about strictly research a while ago. Now, we're just using that as an excuse.

LOBO: Are you in bed, princess?

Holy jeepers! Next thing he'll be asking me what I'm wearing.

LOBO: Princess?

FLAME: Yes.

LOBO: Yes, what?

FLAME: Yes, I'm in bed.

LOBO: Good to know, but not what I meant.

LOBO: Yes...?

"Sweet sassafras!" Sylvan sat straight up in her window bed, her back coming off the propped-up pillows. "Does he want what I think he wants?"

LOBO: Flame, I'm waiting. It's never good to make your Master wait.

"Double sassafras," she whispered. "This is either going to be super hot or super embarrassing." She gulped. "Or both."

Here goes nothing.

FLAME: Yes, Sir.

LOBO: There's my good girl.

Sylvan's heart soared. Why was that praise making her so tingly?

LOBO: Tell me what you're wearing.

Flippity-flip-flip! I knew it!

LOBO: Remember. Be honest. A D/s relationship only works when there's honesty and trust.

FLAME: But we're not in a D/s relationship.

LOBO: Oh, princess. We so are. The minute you agreed to my terms for information, it became one.

LOBO: What did I teach you?

FLAME: That it's a Master's job to know their submissive's needs.

LOBO: And?

FLAME: The submissive must trust that the Master will pay absolute attention so that a safe word never needs to be used.

LOBO: Excellent, little Flame.

LOBO: Now. Tell me what you're wearing.

Could she do this?

It's not like you're ever going to meet the man. Just do it! You know you want to.

FLAME: A long nightgown and matching robe.

LOBO: Very nice. What color?

FLAME: Light blue.

LOBO: Is it silk?

FLAME: Yes. And lace.

LOBO: Describe it.

LOBO: In detail.

FLAME: It touches the floor, so I can't see my feet. The top has thin spaghetti straps that connect to a lace torso. That part is very fitted, and the front is very deeply cut.

LOBO: Are your breasts completely covered? Or do they swell beyond the material?

FLAME: I'm covered, but the cleavage makes it appear like I might spill out of it.

LOBO: Go on.

FLAME: The lace continues down the front of the skirt from the waist on a diagonal from my right hip to my left foot. The gown flares from just below my waist to the floor, but the skirt is still narrow.

FLAME: The robe matches. And the sleeves go to the wrist where they button tight, like a man's dress shirt.

FLAME: The top of the robe has a deep V to it that matches the neckline of the nightgown, but it flares down, like the skirt, where they meet at the floor.

LOBO: And underneath?

Sister Mary Francis!

LOBO: Flame? What are you wearing underneath?

FLAME: Silk panties. The same color.

LOBO: Is this something you normally sleep in?

LOBO: Or are you wearing it just to meet with me?

FLAME: I love pretty lingerie. It makes me feel beautiful.

FLAME: There wasn't really any clue you would be back tonight.

LOBO: No. It was a surprise to me, too.

LOBO: Do you always wear pretty lingerie when you meet with me?

She hesitated.

FLAME: Yes.

LOBO: If you'd known I would be here, would you have worn this one?

FLAME: No.

FLAME: I would have chosen a different one.

FLAME: I have one that's black.

LOBO: Why black?

FLAME: It reminds me of a wolf. A black wolf.

There was a pause after her admission.

Finally, a message appeared again.

LOBO: What color hair do you have?

FLAME: Red.

LOBO: Ah. The name. I should have guessed.

LOBO: How are you wearing it?

FLAME: It's all piled on top of my head.

LOBO: Pins?

FLAME: Yes.

LOBO: How long?

FLAME: Past my waist. I've never cut it.

LOBO: Very nice.

LOBO: Dare I hope for green eyes and porcelain skin?

FLAME: Yes.

LOBO: Kryptonite.

LOBO: Take it down.

As if hypnotized, Sylvan began to pull the pins from her hair, the long tresses falling to her shoulders and down her back.

LOBO: Is it down?

FLAME: Yes, Sir.

LOBO: Such a good girl. Put your computer off to the side, but where you can still see the screen.

LOBO: Remove your robe.

Oh, freakin' Frankenstein!

4

———————

APRIL 11TH

TB

What the fuck am I doing?

This was possibly the dumbest thing he'd ever done. But was he going to stop?

"Fuck, no," he said to no one.

TB shifted his six-foot-seven, two-hundred-forty-pound frame in his desk chair. His hand swiped through his dark brown, mussed hair and scratched the back of his head. That same hand came back to cradle his face, palm holding his chin, and he leaned his elbow on the desktop as his green eyes stared intently at the screen. Absently, he used his other hand to adjust his hardening cock at the thought of what he was about to do.

Sitting up straight, hands flying over the keys, he went back to typing in the chat box.

LOBO: Is it off?

There were a few moments before she replied.

FLAME: Yes, Sir.

LOBO: Lie on your side, facing your computer.

LOBO: Get comfortable.

LOBO: Are you ready?

FLAME: No.

LOBO: Relax, princess. I promise to take good care of you.

LOBO: Being a submissive is about freedom. When you give your pleasure over to your Dom, you allow yourself to just feel. You don't have to worry about making things happen, what speed they happen at, or anything else.

LOBO: If something becomes too much, use your safe word. I will stop immediately. We'll talk. Discuss why you needed to use the word. Honestly.

LOBO: If you use your safe word, once we've talked, then we discuss if we're to proceed and in what direction.

LOBO: The word is not to be used lightly. It's for you to use when you're feeling distress beyond nervousness or embarrassment. When something is truly beyond what you can handle.

LOBO: This is an honor situation as I'm unable to see you, but I trust that you will use it if needed.

LOBO: I'm going to tell you exactly what I would do if we were in your bed together right now. Your hands are going to be my hands, so I want you to do as they do. Can you do that?

FLAME: Yes, Sir.

LOBO: Excellent.

LOBO: Imagine that I'm lying behind you, and your head is pillowed on my bicep underneath you.

LOBO: You're pulled so tightly to me, you can feel my hard cock between your ass cheeks.

LOBO: I slide my top hand across your collarbone, trailing my fingers down into the valley between your breasts.

LOBO: My fingers scrape ever so gently across the skin.

LOBO: I slowly slide my fingertips between your breast and the material that covers it.

LOBO: Cupping your breast, I squeeze firmly but not painfully so, kneading your warm, soft flesh.

LOBO: My hand slides to the underside of your breast, taking its weight in my palm, and my thumb brushes back and forth across your nipple until it comes to a hard point.

LOBO: I turn you on your back, lowering my mouth to your breast.

LOBO: The tip of my tongue reaches out to taste your nipple, and I swirl it all the way around the nub before covering it with my lips.

LOBO: The scruff of my closely shaved beard rasps against the soft skin of your breast, turning it a light pink.

LOBO: My teeth gently bite down on the nub, giving you just a bit of pain. I can taste your skin beginning to perspire, a combination of your arousal and our body heat.

Oh, yeah, this is a terrible idea. I'm hard as a rock.

LOBO: Letting go of your breast, I trail my hand down the center of your body. My teeth let go of your nipple, and I swipe my tongue gently across the tortured nub, softly blowing air across it to ease the sting from my love bite.

LOBO: My fingers drag down to the warmth between your legs. They slide flat against your mound, cupping you through your nightgown with just a bit of pressure to let you know where my hand really wants to be.

LOBO: Slowly, I inch the skirt up your legs, taking one handful of the material at a time, prolonging the anticipation as I pull until your panties are exposed.

LOBO: I rise up from your side on the bed, slipping to my knees between your legs.

LOBO: I slide your panties slowly down your legs, dragging them to your knees, raising your legs straight up in the air.

LOBO: I keep dragging that scrap of silk over your calves, past your ankles, over your toes, then drop them to the floor beside the bed.

LOBO: Resting both of your legs on my shoulder, I smooth my calloused hands up and down your calves and thighs, each time getting closer and closer to that pretty pussy that you've shaved smooth for me.

LOBO: I bring your legs down, and I lie down behind you again, dragging your top leg over mine, spreading you wide open for me.

LOBO: My long, thick middle finger slides inside of you to feel the walls of your pussy squeeze around me.

LOBO: Then I curve it up to find your G-spot, the palm of my hand firmly against your clit, the heel of my hand putting pressure on your pelvic bone.

He groaned out loud. Normally, he could engage in any sort of dirty talk without letting his control slip, but there was something about tonight that was different.

You were stuck with no one but Nerdboy and Demon for the past fifty-two days, guarding your boss as he got his freak on with Kubrick. Of course you're horny. Any woman would have brought about this reaction after that long. You just need some release, and everything will go back to normal.

He ignored the other voice in his head, telling him he was an idiot if he believed that nonsense.

LOBO: I add a second finger, thrusting in and out of your channel, groaning at the sounds of your slick insides, readying for your orgasm.

LOBO: I start to whisper in your ear. I tell you how beautiful you are. Praise you for trusting me. Compliment you for being such a good girl, letting me please you like this.

LOBO: I describe how slick you feel to me as I slide in a third finger. I can smell your arousal in the air. Your skin is flushing, and you feel warm from the inside out.

LOBO: I feel your body start to tighten, but I'm not ready for you to come yet, so I slide my fingers from your body and drag your fluids up to your clit.

LOBO: My touch is barely there as I tease it out of your hood with light circles.

LOBO: You arch your back to try and get more pressure to the spot, but I keep you pulled tight back against me, my other arm around your waist, my hand splayed against your stomach, keeping you in place.

LOBO: I can't resist. I dip my fingers back into your sweet pussy, capturing more of that sugar on my fingertips, and then I bring my fingers up to my mouth.

LOBO: I reach out my tongue to taste you on my hand.

LOBO: You taste so good. The flavor explodes on my tongue, your scent traveling up to my nose and weaving around me.

LOBO: I need more of you.

LOBO: So after I've sucked you clean from my fingers, I return my hand to between your legs and start all over again.

LOBO: This time, though, when your body begins to clench, ready to release, I bring my hand up to your mouth, painting your lips with your wetness. Your tongue slips out to lick yourself off of your lips, and then you suck my fingers clean, your tongue laving the pads of my fingers.

LOBO: You moan my name, and I know it's time to give you what you need. Your breathing is rapid. Your breasts are heaving.

LOBO: My cock is rock hard against your ass, and you can feel something wet against your skin.

LOBO: My precum is leaking from my tip in anticipation of your orgasm.

LOBO: My hips start to thrust against you from behind, twisting slightly to get friction as I move.

LOBO: I thrust my fingers inside you one more time, a bit more pressure, a bit more speed, rubbing against your G-spot, and finally, your body lets go for me.

LOBO: As I feel your muscles squeeze me, my cock erupts on your ass, my cum painting your skin.

He pulled his hands back from the keyboard and used one to squeeze his cock through his jeans again, trying to ease the unbearable pressure he'd created while typing to her. His skin felt overheated, and he knew a cold shower was in his future.

I wonder what she looks like right now.

He took another moment to collect himself before typing again.

LOBO: A Dom knows his submissive, little Flame. He knows what she wants. What she needs. He knows what will please her. More than that, he knows what her limits are at all times and knows what will bring her the most pleasure, even if she herself does not know it.

LOBO: Remember that, princess.

LOBO: Sweet dreams. And happy writing.

And then he logged off.

He shut down his laptop, turned off the light, stood from behind the desk, and crossed to his bedroom and his bathroom.

After a very long, very dissatisfying shower, TB lay in the dark, reliving their conversation. It had been a bit cowardly to sign off without asking her if she was okay. He should have provided some sort of aftercare to her, although damned if he knew exactly what that would be. He'd never engaged in cyber-play before. He'd always played in person.

She unsettled him. He wasn't sure when exactly it had changed between them, but he knew he was drawn to her. That wasn't good considering the current circumstances, but he was man enough to admit that his body didn't seem to care.

And now, despite the cold shower, his dick was hard again, and he wanted to get back on the computer and do it all over. Maybe this time with video.

Already, his brain was running with new scenarios to bring both her and himself to release.

Sighing and turning over onto his stomach, he punched the pillow a few times before closing his eyes. It didn't take long for exhaustion to take hold and pull him under.

It was the first decent night's sleep he'd had in fifty-two days.

5

———————

APRIL 12TH

TB

Come on. Where are you? In two minutes, I'll have to log out because you're not showing up.

The arrangement they had made for their computer chats was that they logged in at ten p.m. If one of them didn't show up by ten minutes after, they wouldn't be available that night. That way, neither of them was waiting and wondering. She was always here when he logged in. He assumed that was because she was on her computer most of the day writing. Today was the first time he had been first online.

TB was known for his unfailing people-reading skills. It was what made him a superior interrogator.

Correction. Information Specialist. What a nice way to title someone whose specialty was torture techniques.

Had he read her wrong? It wasn't impossible, as no one was perfect. But he'd been so certain. Had he gone too far, too fast last night? Had he scared her away?

All day today, he'd found himself consciously willing time to pass so that he could get home to talk to her. He knew they were both already emotionally invested at some level. Him? He'd be... uncomfortable... when it was over. He was used to people leaving, even when it was unavoidable. But her? She was going to get hurt in the end, and the truth was, he didn't know how to avoid it.

He grunted. Since when did he care if someone got hurt?

Since Waters fell in love with Kubrick, that's when. You went from total bastard to total pussy with the first swear word that came out of her mouth. Each and every member of the team is a little in love with her, too. Jealousy sucks.

The computer dinged, and in the upper left corner of the chat box, a flame avatar appeared.

LOBO: Good evening, little Flame. Thought I was going to get stood up tonight.

LOBO: Did your writing go better today? Was I suitably inspiring?

FLAME: Sorry. Time got away from me.

FLAME: Yes... and no.

LOBO: Yes, your writing went better today, and no I wasn't inspiring?

LOBO: I'm going to have to try harder.

FLAME: You certainly gave me a lot to think about.

LOBO: Ah. So I distracted you.

FLAME: Yes. I spent a lot of time staring off into space.

FLAME: I sat at my computer for seventeen hours. Only managed six pages.

LOBO: You've been sitting at your computer since five o'clock this morning?

LOBO: We got offline before eleven. Even if you went to sleep right away, that's not enough rest.

LOBO: You should have been more relaxed after we chatted. I failed you last night.

FLAME: I couldn't shut my mind off.

LOBO: Tell me why.

The screen remained blank.

LOBO: You can tell me anything, princess. That's the beauty of online chat. Anonymity.

FLAME: This is kind of personal.

FLAME: Embarrassing, actually.

LOBO: Consider me intrigued.

FLAME: I've never done anything like that before.

Oh, fuck. And now I'm hard again.

LOBO: You've never pleasured yourself? Or you've never had cyber-sex?

FLAME: No matter which I answer, it feels awkward. But I meant the second.

LOBO: Did you do what I described?

FLAME: I thought I was supposed to.

LOBO: Oh, yes, little Flame, you were.

LOBO: Did you enjoy it?

"Come on, say yes," he whispered.

LOBO: It's a simple question, princess.

LOBO: Don't overthink it.

LOBO: Did you enjoy it?

LOBO: Use your words, little Flame.

FLAME: I don't know.

LOBO: You don't know?

LOBO: Then I definitely didn't do it right.

FLAME: No, it's not that!

FLAME: That came out wrong. I didn't mean it like that.

FLAME: At the time, it was very enjoyable.

FLAME: But all day today, I second-guessed myself.

FLAME: Should I have done that?

FLAME: Were you laughing at me, knowing what I was likely doing?

LOBO: I would never laugh at you, little Flame.

LOBO: I wanted to make you feel good.

LOBO: It was also a lesson in Dominance/submission.

LOBO: If I can command you online, imagine what I could do if we were in person.

Neither of them typed for a few minutes.

LOBO: Do you trust me?

FLAME: No.

LOBO: That's a very good girl. I appreciate the honesty. But in this, you can.

LOBO: My job was to teach you about BDSM.

LOBO: However, I've done about as much of that as I can over chat.

FLAME: Does that mean we don't talk anymore?

LOBO: Would you miss me, little Flame? I'm flattered.

LOBO: No, it doesn't mean we don't talk anymore.

LOBO: I would miss talking with you, too, if we stopped.

LOBO: Last night was a practical lesson. That was the next logical step.

LOBO: Are you ready for the next step? As in an in person, practical lesson?

There was no reply. He waited a few minutes, feeling like he was holding his breath.

LOBO: Flame?

LOBO: Answer me.

Finally, an answer came.

FLAME: I don't know.

LOBO: Why don't you know if you're ready?

FLAME: I don't know you.

FLAME: But meeting you feels too intimate to not know you.

LOBO: Meeting someone physically doesn't necessarily mean you know them.

FLAME: Logically, I know that.

LOBO: I bet I know you better than anyone else does.

FLAME: It's difficult.

FLAME: I don't trust people.

LOBO: You mean men.

FLAME: No, I mean people. People are cruel. They rarely worry about anyone but themselves. They rarely truly care about others.

Somebody has done a number on this girl.

LOBO: That's the whole crux of a D/s relationship, sweetheart. The Master cares about the sub.

LOBO: Because a good Dom gets his or her pleasure knowing that their submissive is taken care of and happy.

FLAME: I don't think I'm ready. I'd make a fool out of myself.
LOBO: Not possible.
LOBO: But that's why you'd go to the club with me as my guest.
LOBO: Think about it.
Another pause.
LOBO: Goodnight, princess.

6

———————

APRIL 13TH

TB

THWAP! THWAP! THWAP! THWAP-THWAP!

The sound of leather on leather filled the room. Each sound was punctuated by a male grunt at the expended effort, and a spray of sweat traveled from TB toward the bag. The bag jerked on its chain, but it didn't swing more than a few centimeters as it was being held in place by another set of hands encased in sparring gloves.

"C'mon, the boss never lets me get away from that fuckin' box. Pretty soon, I'm going to be stroking off to Siri's voice and sending out birth announcements for our daughter, Alexa. I gotta live vicariously through you."

"There's nothing to tell."

He worked hard to portray a sense of nonchalance and prayed that his sparring partner didn't go digging through his chats on a whim. In a moment of weakness, he had casually shared his invite to his "research buddy" job with his teammate, Midas, and now was wondering if he should be concerned that he had. Midas was an excellent hacker, and he could probably easily get into TB's private system and read what had really happened two nights ago.

And just remembering what we did, there goes my dick again.

"Well, what did she say to your invite?" the spotter asked.

"Nothing." A smack and a grunt. "I logged off." A series of quick jabs and grunts followed as TB let loose a succession of hits.

"No hint of yes or no?"

TB pulled up from his fighting stance and wiped the sweat from his forehead with the back of his arm. "I just told you, I logged off. There wasn't a chance for a declaration of intent."

Letting go of the bag, the spotter rolled his eyes, putting his hands on his hips. "I didn't ask for a declaration. I just asked if you had a sense of if she would agree to go or not."

Walking over to the lockers along the wall, he threw over his shoulder, "Midas. Listen to what I'm saying. I. Logged. Off. I didn't hang around to see what she'd say."

"You really do live by your nickname. You are a Total Bastard today. Almost as bad as Waters."

"Waters has no one to blame for that shitshow but himself."

Midas snickered. "Yeah. The supervisor of Operation Shitshow." He sobered quickly. "Demon texted me and said that Kubrick actually overslept yesterday. She's kept it together in public, but he's pretty sure he's heard her tossing and turning all night. Yesterday, she looked like she'd been crying. Said she's barely eaten since he left. Had to force her to at least eat a Zinger."

TB's gaze bounced to Midas' in surprise. "She loves chocolate. Like, she loves it better than sex."

"I don't know about that part. I've seen some shit on the surveillance video I can't unsee. Shows how gone the guy is that he forgot to give the signal to turn the cameras off. Let's just say our team leader is... thorough, and she's reaping the benefits." Midas shifted uncomfortably. "Anyway, when Demon handed her the Zinger, she burst into tears again. What a mess."

Both men walked over to the gym lockers, built extra-wide to hold bags of gear, extra changes of clothes, and other individual items specific to the team members' workouts. Midas pulled off TB's gloves, then threw them in the bin for sanitizing. Both men unwrapped the tape around their knuckles. Midas sighed in exasperation. "I still don't get it. Why did he leave her? It's not like we're leaving *tomorrow* for Egypt. We don't have enough information to do that yet. I told God I still have a lot of research to gather before we can do that."

TB grunted in agreement and sat down on the bench to untie his shoes.

Midas froze mid-unwrapping, his eyes open, but his mind was obviously somewhere other than where his sight pointed.

TB looked at the cyber-geek with a frown. "What's wrong?"

Midas looked at him, then let his muscles relax with a shake of his head. He continued to unwrap his hands. "Nothing, really. I just wondered if maybe it was a test. You know, the boss ordered him back. To see how serious Waters was about Kubrick."

TB snorted. "I doubt the boss has the time, or the inclination, for that kind of game playing."

Opening the metal door of his locker, Midas reached past the huge gym bag hanging up and grabbed a white towel. After a quick rub down of his skull, trying to take off the worst of the sprayed sweat from TB out of the barely-there brown hair, as well as what he had accumulated himself from working diligently to keep the bag from swinging, he reached into the back of the locker again, grabbing a second towel.

Throwing the used towel in the laundry bin nearby and beginning to strip, he continued his argument. "I wonder if your Flame's really who she presents herself to be. I mean, I wonder if she's really a hottie, or if she's just a normal chick, or if she's, like, three hundred pounds and seventy years old. Maybe that's why she won't commit to meeting you."

TB scrunched up all of his facial muscles. "Since when did you become as shallow as your twin?"

"I'm not," he defended himself. "I'm just trying to figure out why she wouldn't jump at the opportunity."

"Kink makes a lot of people nervous," TB countered with a

shrug, returning his attention to his shoes. "Publicizing their interest takes a lot of courage. Even when they're in a safe space, like The Library, a club that's designed specifically for people in the scene, new people struggle with the worry of being judged. The fact that all the people around them are also in the same club often doesn't register. She's pretty shy and probably obsessing over what others will think about her." His shoes unlaced, he moved to pull his sweat-drenched T-shirt over his head and snapped it at Midas. "And not that it matters, asshole, but the club owner told me she was very good-looking."

"Yeah, but you know women. They stick together. And I looked up your research pimp, Mistress Tabitha, and that woman is smokin' hot. There's always that pretty-girl's-best-friend thing."

Shaking his head in disbelief, TB stood and lifted the latch on his locker. As the metal door opened, a loud bang went off, and projectiles flew toward his face with no time to get out of the way. TB dropped to the floor face first, and seconds later, after his ears cleared, all he could hear was cackling, whooping, and hollering. Turning his face back toward the locker, his eyes traveled from the floor of the locker, where he saw a pair of Under Armour running shoes, a pair of well-worn jeans, a tight blue tee exposing full tattoo sleeves and neck, and finally, the face of one of his other teammates. Nemo, the jackass, had stuffed himself tight into the locker and now stood in there with an empty confetti cannon in his hands. Pastel rectangles of paper floated through the air and covered TB, Midas, the floor, and the bench.

Midas, Nemo's fraternal twin, was shaking his head but laughing.

"You fucking prick!" TB yelled at the man in the locker. "That's the third time in two days. Just fucking stop already. What are you, five?"

Inside the locker, the young South African was still laughing so hard he was turning red. Nemo was the chick magnet of the group with his killer body, golden tan, blond hair that was in a pseudo-military cut, just too long and glued straight up, and baby blue eyes that were always lit up with laughter. He had a smile that was set with perfect, straight white teeth, and deep dimples on either side. He was also the practical joker of the group, and sometimes, he didn't know when to quit. Like now.

This fucker is going to pay.

"Hope you liked your stay in the locker, Nincompoop," TB growled. "It's going to be your new home."

Before Nemo could get a word out, TB closed the locker back up and put the combination lock on it. Backward. He banged on the locker twice. "Good luck getting out of that."

Then he walked away.

Banging began from the inside of the locker, with its occupant hurling invectives at TB's retreating form. Midas was still laughing, but he was also yelling at TB to get his ass back there to let Nemo out. TB ignored them both and went into the shower room to clean up.

Serves the douchebag right.

An hour later, Nemo was freed from his cramped prison, and the entire team was arriving at the conference room for the daily meeting.

The whole team had taken their seats around the table, minus their teammate, Demon, who was currently guarding Hollywood film director Kai Serrano, also known to them by her nickname Kubrick. Her brother had gone missing months earlier, and Waters had been assigned as a consultant on her current movie project down in Honduras in order to watch over her. The belief was that her Navy SEAL brother, Ka-Bar, had been captured, and now his sister was in trouble due to him passing information to her for safekeeping. Just a couple of days ago, they had learned that the "information" in question was actually Ka-Bar's girlfriend from his teenage years, who was very pregnant with what they assumed was his unborn child.

The big boss, known only as God, because they never saw him and only spoke with him over the speaker, had called Waters and his team back to L.A., forcing them to abandon Kubrick, something that was not sitting well with their team leader, who had fallen in love with the sassy director. Technically, Demon had also been called back, but Waters had refused to leave his lover there completely unprotected. However, their team leader was less than happy, and both parties of the couple were nursing some seriously broken hearts.

Waters stood at the front of the room, remote in hand, next to the oversized telescreen. His normally intense but blank facade was cracking. There were exhaustion lines around his eyes, his mouth pinched, and he looked pissed. Like Midas, he kept his dark blond hair cropped close to his head, but it was a little on the long side right now, and it was easy to tell he had been running his fingers through it in frustration.

Again. His own damn fault.

"Okay, now that we've moved on from high school antics of shoving people into lockers," Waters bitched, "we can get down to business." He pressed the blue button that powered on the starfish speaker in the center of the table, then pressed the red button that secured the locks on the doors, tinted the windows to block anyone from seeing inside, and dimmed the lighting to a slightly red tint around the wall edges. "God is online. Let's start with an update on Zahra."

Steel piped up from his side of the table, his silver eyes boring into Waters' figure up front, where he had his head focused down on a briefing folder. "I ran down all the technicals on the break-ins at Kubrick's trailer. Impossible to track their ingress and egress, so unsure if it's connected to the package reveal or not. No luck yet pinning down a location on Ka-Bar's woman."

Midas' fingers whirred and clacked over his keyboard, and the telescreen on the far wall filled with images. Ka-Bar. News articles about the woman who featured front and center on the screen.

The very beautiful, very pregnant Zahra Kader, seventh child of Pharaoh Kader, the richest man in Egypt. Also, a very subtle picture of Kubrick in the upper right corner.

I'm sensing the boys are sending an underhanded message to the bosses. Sneaky bastards.

"I've got facial recognition running as requested, but so far, no hits. Wherever she is, she's well hidden. I also have no intel on hired hits for Jacques, the French ambassador, or the location of his family since I found their abandoned vehicle. Also, confirmed no hits contracted on Kubrick or chatter that she has a package he sent."

"Dark web?" TB asked.

"Negative there as well," Midas replied.

Waters' gaze had snagged on Kubrick's picture. His jaw ticked, but other than that, no reaction.

His face went back to the folder in front of him that TB would bet his last paycheck had pictures or references related to Kubrick buried at the back.

"So chances are this is happening in-house with the Kader family. Fucking fabulous. I love nothing more than creating an international incident," Waters snarked. "Anything at all about Ka-Bar's location?"

The computer expert brushed his powerful hand over the top of his head, hunching his bulky frame over the laptop on the table. "Not exactly. But, literally about fifteen minutes ago, the computer tracked down the notice he punched his trident through. It's for an international film festival at Cairo University. It was an ad for a showing of *Taken*."

Various expletives flew around the table.

The disembodied voice of God came over the speaker. "So, we know he was grabbed while in that warehouse, and he must have had his suspicions that this would occur if he had the foresight to pull down that poster."

"So where does that leave us, then?" TB asked.

"Hellah, nowhere," Midas admitted. "All we have now is confirmation that he's missing by force, not by choice."

"And now that we know she's pregnant, we know there's no way in hell that he'd voluntarily leave without them," Steel added.

"We don't know for sure if it's his kid. He could be just trying to help an old girlfriend."

Steel shook his head. "Regardless, he wouldn't leave any woman stranded."

Ouch! That was a low blow.

The silence in the room weighed heavier than any elephant. All the men looked around at each other, with the exception of Waters, who refused to look at anyone.

God cleared his throat, breaking the tension. "So, what's next?"

Midas shrugged. "I've got facial recognition running twenty-four-seven, but I'm out of monitor space for possible locations. And to be honest, it's probably a waste of resources looking for him that way if he was captured."

"Well, we know where he was hiding out initially, and we know about when he was there. Can we run what little CCTV footage we have on people who were in the area at the same time and see if we get a hit that way?" TB asked.

"We tried that. Backtracked a week. Didn't even see hide nor hair of Ka-Bar himself, let alone anything truly suspicious," Waters replied.

"Given his skill set, I'm thinking we'd be more likely to find someone that's linked to the snatch and grab than it would be finding Ka-Bar himself," TB pointed out. "It might be a good idea to rewatch those recordings and look for repeating non-repeaters."

"Repeating non-repeaters?" Nemo asked.

TB turned his head to him. "Yeah. Repeat visitors."

"The area Midas narrowed it down to is a frickin' street market. Most everyone will be a repeater," Nemo pointed out.

Sighing, TB asked, "When you two cased a museum, there were always people who came back regularly, yes?"

Both Nemo and Midas nodded.

"People are creatures of habit. They have favorites. They stick to places, people, and things they like and know. The same goes for their entertainment. Guards are trained to watch for people who repeat. The elderly woman who stops at the museum after church on Sunday. The family that always goes to the movies on Tuesdays and orders the same snacks. The mother who takes her baby to the park and meets with other mothers every Friday morning for a play date."

Midas snapped his fingers. "The grocery store!"

TB smiled. "Now you're catching on."

"What are you blathering about?" Nemo asked in confusion.

"Think about it, bro. When you go to the grocery store, what path do you use?" Midas shook his head. "Never mind. I forgot. Unless you're stalking a girl, you don't go to the store."

"None of us go to the store, jackass. Cherry places delivery orders."

"You know what I mean," Midas returned.

"I see where you're going, Midas," Waters jumped in. "People follow the same order of the store. They start almost automatically in whatever aisle is closest to the door."

"Right. And the reason that the frozen aisles are closest to the checkout is because you don't want your ice cream, or whatever, to be out of the cold any longer than it has to be. People don't go to the ice cream aisle, then go shop for bread, soup, chips, etcetera."

Waters made the connection. "So what we're really looking for are repeaters who *don't* repeat a pattern."

"Exactly," TB confirmed.

"Huh? That sounds like an oxymoron," Nemo said.

"Wow. Did you save up all your pennies to buy that word, Nerfherder?"

Nemo grinned. "Nice movie reference. There's hope for you yet."

"The point is," Waters interrupted, "the average person is socially conditioned to patterns in their behaviors. But what happens if you need to do something in a space where you can't avoid cameras, like a store, but need to go unnoticed?"

Midas looked at his brother. "Dude. You know this answer. Walk yourself through the Metropolitan Art Museum job."

Nemo's brow furrowed. "Well, I never went to the same rooms in the same order. I went through different doors if there were options. If I ate there, I ordered something different every time; I tried to never get waited on by the same server. Didn't pay the same way or tip too much, too little. I even went in through different doors from the outside, even if it was just one over from the one I'd normally..." His face cleared. "Ah. Now I get it. Watch for the people who are repeating things, but they're doing them differently every time."

"Okay, so Midas, back on the video surveillance," God ordered. "Other ideas?"

"I can go back and hit the ground again," Steel offered. "Maybe I missed something."

"Unlikely," God barked, "but we need to do something proactive. I'll consider it. Give Midas a week to try and dig up some direction, then take Nemo with you."

"Field trip!" Nemo hooted.

Steel's face was blank, but TB imagined the man wasn't all that thrilled with the partnering. Still, TB did have to admit, when Nemo was on a job and had an objective, he was frighteningly focused and meticulous. He was just annoying when there was downtime. Or he ran his mouth. Or cracked his gum. Or breathed.

"Anything else on Ka-Bar?" There was silence around the table. All of the men were looking at each other, wondering if any of them were going to bring up the elephant in the room— Kubrick.

Waters snuck one last glance at the telescreen, swallowed, and then plowed on as if sensing the direction of their thoughts. "All right, next. The Library."

7

———

APRIL 13TH

TB

TB jerked his head in the direction of Waters.

The fuck?

In the background, Nemo did his best porn music imitation.

Steel smacked him upside the back of the head. "Quit fucking around, this is serious."

Waters checked his watch and read from his notes. "Just over four hours ago, I fielded a client by the name of Nathan Moll, a tech-mogul out of Silicon Valley. His daughter, Matilda, lives with her mother, Brandy, in Los Angeles full time. He travels back and forth for his work. On the tenth, Tilly went to the kink club known as The Library, and as far as anyone can tell, she never returned home."

Tilly's picture flashed up on the telescreen behind Waters.

"Who reported her missing?" TB asked, his gut rolling. When he hadn't heard differently, he had hoped that meant she had been found.

Obviously not.

God piped in over the speaker, his speech distorted by the ever-present caramel apple sucker in his mouth. "Their head of security contacted her father when no one could find her after several hours of looking. Even a complete search of the premises after it had closed for the night yielded no clues of any kind. One of my informants tells me four additional women, all members, have gone missing over the past five months."

Five pictures of young women flashed up on the screen in order of their disappearance. A slither of unease traveled down TB's spine, his mind reviewing the last moments he saw Tilly two days ago. The stranger. The spilled drink. The crush of people. No trace of her. He, along with Loki and Tripoli, had spent several hours looking for her, which included the after-hours search Waters had mentioned. Eventually, the head of security at the club, a computer whiz kid named Triumph, had taken over and was combing through security footage, trying to establish when she'd left the club and with whom. Last he knew, he'd made no progress. Obviously, the man took the next step when he ran out of search options.

"How did the father know to come to us?" TB asked.

"Word of mouth. Friend of a friend kind of thing," Waters replied.

Waters picked up the thread. "The previous disappearances have been unpublicized until now. No one has been pressing the police for results, so they've kept it quiet. According to the most recent police report, even the club owner appeared to be in the dark until the police were called in."

Midas joined back in. "Since I just found this out with all of you, I haven't had a chance to delve deep. My initial look into the police records just now shows that no one has seen any of the other four for a while. Common thread is the last place any of them was confirmed being seen was the club."

Steel muttered something in Spanish under his breath. "Everyone see what I'm seeing?"

Nemo piped up. "All in their early to mid-twenties. Red hair. All short and stacked."

"A little respect, dude," his brother hissed.

"What? They are."

Midas shook his head and looked back at his screen.

"Are any of the others who are missing high flyers?" Steel asked.

"They come from money since the club membership pretty much guarantees an exclusive clientele, but nobody of the same stature as Tilly."

Steel followed up. "No ransom call?"

Midas shook his head. "Not even a hang-up call. There's nothing connecting the five missing girls other than all were allegedly last seen at The Library, and there's been no suggestion that this is related to Tilly's father's work."

"And no ransom call means it's not money-related," TB added.

"Correct," Waters confirmed. "So with ransom out of the picture, we're left with the usual round of reasons someone is kidnapped. Stalkers, sex trafficking, or the possibility that she disappeared on purpose."

Midas scanned his screen and answered the questions about to be asked. "Family and friends report that Tilly was her normal self prior to her disappearance. No depression, paranoia, or tension. No change in spending habits, no excessive purchases in the days or weeks prior, which her bank account and credit cards support. No current boyfriend, and the ex-boyfriend claims it was an amicable split over six months ago when he took a banking job overseas. And before you ask, the ex has an alibi. He's in France on business, which is also where he was the night she disappeared. No police reports of any kind. The worst thing she had going on was a reprimand from her boss that day, and his alibi checks out as he was at a business dinner that night. Seen by a whole restaurant of people. She was known to be partnering with another regular at the club, a Dominant named Cosmos. He is also out of the country in England. They weren't dating but were on some sort of club exclusivity contract."

"That takes care of the stalker and planned disappearance angles," Steel said.

"Affirmative," Midas agreed. "So, we're left with the sex trafficking angle."

Waters continued, "That appears to be our direction. Once Midas does his magic, I expect we'll see that the first four women were all pretty much loners, possibly all from other states originally. Also betting that there will have been no close family or friends they talked to recently or on the regular, so it wasn't really concerning when there was no word from them. I was able to confirm that missing persons reports were filed haphazardly and not by people close to them. One report came from a letter carrier when she saw the mail piling up and told a police officer whom she happened to see on her route."

TB scowled when he looked at the girls. "These girls were targeted. But what's more concerning is that Tilly is famous, at least in certain circles. People would have noticed very quickly that she was missing. Why the change in his type?"

"Got tired of no one recognizing what he was doing?" Demon offered.

Midas nodded. "Classic narcissist would want people to see how clever he's being. Would want the recognition. If he's not getting it, taking someone more recognizable would certainly get attention paid to him sooner."

"Perhaps it's more about the location than the girls themselves." Waters closed the folder in his hands and set it on the table, then folded his arms across his chest. "Anything you want to share with the class, TB?"

TB looked his team leader straight in the eye. Then he looked to his right at Midas.

Midas shrugged. "I didn't tell him. Spidey senses, man, I'm telling ya."

Well, shit. Here we fuckin' go.

"This is the first I've heard of missing girls. They're all regulars. I know all of them, but not... well. I actually spoke to Tilly on the night she disappeared."

Nemo squinted at him. "What do you mean you 'know all of them, but not... well'?"

Inwardly, TB sighed. He was never going to hear the end of this. "I'm a regular at the club."

The silence was near deafening until Nemo leaned forward on the table and asked, "Come again?"

God, their boss, crunched something hard, uttered an expletive, and mumbled something about calling the dentist, while over the speaker, everyone heard the sounds of more crinkly sucker plastic being torn through. Distorted articulation due to something in his mouth, the man said, "Well, this has been dumped in our lap now, so while Midas is working his voodoo on the Ka-Bar situation, we'll be working on the disappearances of the women. TB, is there anything that you've seen there that might pertain to what's going on?"

All eyes turned in TB's direction. "Being in Roatán for fifty-three days makes it difficult to know what's been going on. I didn't even know any girls were missing."

Waters prodded. "You have the best angle here. I need you to talk with the owner." He reached down and flipped open a second file folder. "Tabitha Winchell?"

TB nodded.

"Okay. Talk with Ms. Winchell today and collect whatever information she has, both in terms of the police investigation and the missing girls. Discreetly," he reminded TB. "I'd prefer we stay unexposed for now. Mr. Moll signed the NDA. I stressed to him the importance of remaining quiet, or we will fade away. He's frustrated, but he'll toe the line."

Nemo leaned back in his chair, tipping it on its axis, his eyes twinkling with mischief. "I'd like to hear more about your connection to the club."

Of course you would, dickhead.

"It's not pertinent to the investigation," he replied evenly.

"Oh, I think it is. I need the full lay of the land. For background purposes, of course."

Fuck.

"Okay, let's get this all out in the open so I only have to say it once, and everyone's curiosity is put to rest. The owner and I have participated in scenes together in the past. I haven't played at the club in months, although I have been in there when we've been home to have a drink. I know nothing personal about the owner. That's it. Nothing more."

"I'd say you know some pretty personal things if you've played together," Nemo corrected.

Waters cut in. "We have more important shit to get done than you two assclowns bickering over this."

TB noticed him wince at his swear word.

Yet another reminder of Kubrick.

"TB, while you've been at the club, *in hindsight,* have you seen anything that now looks like it might have any bearing on our missing women? Anything that might raise a red flag of any kind?" Waters asked.

TB shrugged. "It's a kink club. There are red flags everywhere. Just not the kind you're referring to."

"What kind of red flags are you seeing?" God asked.

"It's rare, but sometimes the lines get blurred between long-time couples, and they tread into domestic abuse.

"The Library has a strict drugs and alcohol policy, which they enforce to the letter since safety's such a huge part of the BDSM world. But like anywhere else, there are still issues. There's an employee who was caught dealing, mostly Molly, just before we left for Roatán. He was let go."

TB looked up at the screen again. "But my gut is telling me that something there isn't right. Why aren't the police treating this like a serial killer? There are certainly enough grounds here, flimsy though they might be."

"No bodies equals no killer," Waters confirmed.

While Waters continued to brief the room on what little the police had found, TB's cell phone vibrated in his pocket. His cell phone never rang unless it was one of the guys, but they were all here with him in the meeting.

Except Demon. Shit.

He slipped just the screen out of his pocket and gave it a quick glance.

CHERRY:Someone named Tabitha called your "work" number. I

informed her you were out of the office but you would call her when you returned.

He slid the phone completely out of his pocket and rose from the table. Waters' eyes lifted from his notes.

"Cherry texted. The owner called my work line."

Waters frowned. "Why would she be calling you?"

"I don't know. She never has before. It can't be about this, so it must be personal. She must have pulled it from the application to the club that Midas put together for me back when I joined."

Waters considered quickly then hit the blue button on the starfish, and the room went back to normal mode.

All talking ceased while the other men around the table glanced at TB curiously, but no one said anything as he left the room.

Once he had exited the room, TB heard the security protocols go back in place as Waters sealed the room.

He texted Cherry to let her know he got the message, then he entered the code on his phone to make it look as if his call was going through his fictitious work number.

She picked up on the second ring, but he barked out, "What's wrong?" before she even had a chance to say hello.

"Hello, Lobo, I'm fine. Thanks for asking," the voice purred teasingly on the other end of the call. "Nothing's wrong. I have some news, and I apologize for sneaking into your application to get your number, but I assumed you'd want to know this right away." She paused, then dropped the bomb on him. "Flame called me. She wants to come to the club. Said you invited her."

His mouth went desert dry instantly, and he nearly swallowed his tongue. When he finally was capable of responding, he had to clear his throat twice so that his voice sounded normal when he spoke. "When?"

"Tonight at ten o'clock."

Closing out the call, he let his arm drop to his side, and he stood in the hall staring into space.

Tonight.

He was going to *see* Flame tonight.

Lost in thought, TB knocked on the conference room door. The security measures kicked off, he went into the room, and the security measures went back on as soon as the door closed behind him. His eyes caught the screen, and that's when it hit him.

TB had never believed in coincidences, higher powers, serendipity, fate, or anything like that, but today, he was not going to look this gift horse in the mouth.

I am never going to live this down, but here goes.

"I may have us a gateway to gather some intel the police can't get."

He sat back down at the table.

"What's that?" Waters asked.

"A while back, Tabitha, the owner of The Library, asked me for a favor. She had an author friend, a woman who writes romance novels, who wanted some research for writing a BDSM romance novel. They're all the rage right now, apparently. Anyway, over the past couple of months, she's been interviewing me about the lifestyle. I've never seen her, but Tabitha just called to tell me she's coming to the club tonight for the first time."

"Fifty Shades of Total Bastard." Nemo started up the porn music again.

"Shut it, Neanderthal," TB warned.

"What are you suggesting?" Waters asked.

"She's new to the scene. I've laid out the foundation of the lifestyle to her, but seeing it in action is a whole other thing. She's going to have more questions. As my guest at the club, she could be the key to getting information from other club members that I can't easily get."

"So, you're suggesting you use her as a cover story," Steel connected the dots. "You're a regular at the club, and people know you, so you're not out of place. But if you asked about people's personal lifestyles, activities, connections to the missing women, and so on, it would be a red flag that something was out of the natural order."

"Correct," TB confirmed. "For a first visit, a new member has to either go with a mentor, or they have to be a guest of an established member for more than six months."

God chimed in. "And if she goes in as your guest, you can introduce her to people and features of the club that will allow you to potentially check out members you normally wouldn't come into contact with. She can ask a lot of questions of members that won't seem out of place."

"Yes," TB acknowledged. "She's always got another question to ask, and since she's new, if it's improper, they'll let it slide. It will pass off as a newbie error, and they'll know I'll correct the behavior as her Dom. They'll never know anything hinky is going on."

"Hinky?" Nemo asked. "Is that the technical term? Thought it was 'kinky.'" He cracked his gum with a smart-ass grin.

"Watch it, mister, or I'll put you back in that locker, and this time I'll solder the lock," TB warned.

"All right, children, settle down," Waters urged.

"So, the current plan would be that TB has his author friend as his guest and squires her around the club. He becomes a repeating non-repeater," Midas summarized.

"Exactly," TB confirmed.

Nemo sat up straight with an exaggerated, innocent schoolboy look on his face, his hand raised. "I have a question."

Waters looked at him warily. "What would that be?"

He looked up at TB with an evil twinkle in his eye. "Would you rather... be tying people up or be tied down?"

There were snickers all around the room. Even Waters was having difficulty keeping the corner of his mouth from upturning.

Nemo shrugged. "Inquiring minds want to know."

"Shut the fuck up, Nymphomaniac."

"It's a serious question." Nemo held his hands out, palms up, to his left and right. "Gentlemen?"

There was a chorus of "tying people up" in perfect harmony from around the table.

Nemo's expression was squared up and serious, but his blue

eyes sparkled just a bit too much for TB's liking. "After all, we need to be read in on all aspects of the project."

TB looked at Waters for saving, but no such luck.

Waters shrugged. "He's not wrong. I'd be lying if I said watching surveillance of your sex life doesn't fall into the TMI area, but we should at least have some idea of what the plan is so that we can discuss contingencies if this doesn't work out as you propose. I mean, you're going to be forced to interact with her in public. Are you up for that?"

Nemo muttered, "Oh, I'll bet he's 'up' for it."

TB bristled. "You want to find out how good my knots are? Keep this shit up, and I'll tie you up in unreleasable knots and string you up in the gym like a pinata to use you for punching bag workouts. Even an EMT's scissors won't be able to cut you loose."

"Kinky," Nemo sniggered. "Are you going to use that on her when you interact at the club? Cuz I want a video."

"For fuck's sake, what is the matter with you people? There won't be any video. I'm not interacting with her one-on-one. That would raise eyebrows as I've not been participating in scenes lately."

So, what would you call the night before last, if not "interacting" with her?

"You've been chatting with her online. That's definitely an interaction," Steel pointed out.

"Also not wrong," Waters agreed.

TB rolled his eyes. Waters just couldn't resist getting in a reciprocal jab, could he? Fucker. "I'm not interacting with her *publicly*," he emphasized the last word.

Which, technically, is not a lie because it was cyber-sex and in private.

"I'll give you five hundred bucks for a copy of their chat transcripts, bro," Nemo begged his brother Midas.

"No," Midas firmly replied. "But for a thousand, you can ask me again when I get video of inside the club."

"Cool. This is going to be educational."

TB exploded. "Are you two brain damaged? Did you kick each other in the head while you were in the womb together?"

Waters tried to get them back on track. "All right, ladies, let's be professional about this."

"The point is," God interrupted from over the speaker, "the introduction of this woman—" A clang on the other end of the speaker preceded the crinkling noises of a new sucker being opened. "What's her name again?"

"No clue. Her online name is Flame."

"Okay, Midas, see what you can dig up on her just to cover our bases. In the meantime, this Flame woman facilitates TB being able to move freely and talk to members he wouldn't normally be seen talking to. Will you be able to get her to the club frequently as part of your cover?"

"Actually," TB reluctantly admitted, "I think my recent disappearing act has helped the situation. She's a bit more…" He searched for a word.

"Eager?" Nemo taunted.

"For lack of a better word, yes."

"Awww, she missed her big, bad Dom," the jokester teased.

The irony of the Big Bad Wolf reference was not lost on him. There was no way Nemo could know TB's club name, Lobo, but the teasing remark still hit the target. "My being gone has held up some of her work, so yes. I'd say she's eager to get moving in that direction. It has nothing to do with me personally."

That almost sounded convincing.

Waters concluded, "Okay, so TB will continue down that pathway. Next up…"

8

——————

APRIL 13TH

TB

He was sitting at the bar in his usual seat to the right of the service station when Tabitha sashayed up to it. She was waiting for the bartender to hand her a champagne bucket and tray of glasses, but for some odd reason, she didn't look at him.

He fit in with the rest of the men in the club, but he was not like them—a thin, black leather jacket, black button-down shirt, black jeans, black cowboy boots. His dark hair was cut short but was long enough on top to be mussed, and his beard had probably two days worth of growth, all of which made him look cleanly disheveled. Some people might think he was catering to the broody type that women saw as a challenge. He wasn't. The outfit was his standard go-to ever since he abandoned the Israeli army ten years ago.

"Pretend I'm not talking to you," Tabitha said as she continued to face forward. "She's about twenty feet behind you at the high table. Cream-colored outfit. Lots of red hair."

TB took a long swallow of water. His right elbow propped on

the bar, his fingers dangled the tumbler glass, and then he began a casual perusal of the club's bar area from near the door. He rested a few places as if he were checking out the women, then finally fell on the woman Tabitha described.

Whoa.

She was all softness, curves, and sugar. Someone, somewhere, was offering him a reward that he didn't deserve, but damn them if he wasn't going to take it anyway.

He should move his glance on, but he couldn't pull his eyes away. Then her eyes met his, and even from this distance, he knew her pupils had dilated, and her heart rate had sped up. Inside his head, he heard her soft gasp.

He knew he was too intense for most people, and right now, he felt like he had her trapped, as if she were a butterfly pinned inside a shadowbox. He raised his glass and drained it dry, his eyes never leaving hers. Finally, he turned his attention away from her, placed his glass on the bar, and pulled his wallet from his back pocket. "Thanks," he said to Tabitha, his back to Flame. He removed a bill from his wallet, flagged Ryleigh with it, and laid it on the bar.

She winked at him as she set the bucket down on the bar for Tabitha and pocketed her tip before heading over to a customer waiting to order.

"Lobo," Tabitha warned. "This wasn't part of the original bargain when I connected you two together for her research, but I am granting you this meeting because I know both of you well, and she assured me she was okay with it. Don't make me regret it."

"I got this. Not my first rodeo," he reminded her.

"Overall, that's true, but you've always detested being with new submissives, so—"

"She's different," he interrupted. "I don't know why, but she is."

Tabitha's mouth pursed. "Don't catch feelings, Lobo. She's too innocent for you."

He didn't dignify that with a response. He knew his Flame.

Without another glance at the beacon in cream, he walked through the throng of people pouring off the dance floor when the DJ announced she was taking a break. He made his way to the back of the club where Tripoli, tonight's doorman, let him through to the more private portion of the club.

Christ, I am so fucked. Not interacting with her, my ass.

He shrugged out of his jacket and hung it in the wardrobe cabinet. Unbuttoning the sleeves of his shirt, he then rolled the cuffs, exposing his forearms and the wide leather bands around his wrists that bore wolf heads centered on silver plates.

His brain drifted into plans for the evening, and he realized that he was feeling greedy. He wanted one night where he wasn't working an angle. One night to just *be*. He deserved that, didn't he? Tonight, he would make it all about her needs.

Don't you mean yours, asshole?

Fine. It'll be about us. No job. No missing girls. Just us.

Next time. Next time would be soon enough to begin utilizing her for cover around the club. Damn right, he'd enjoy himself for once. And he was justified in doing that because making tonight about her needs would cement the trust she'd developed for him online into trust for him, the person, which would ultimately set him up for the assignment.

Which means you're going to betray that trust. Classic dick move. Just tell her the truth. She'd be all over that shit. Probably make it the plot for her next book.

He shook the thought away. It went against all the etiquette of a Dom/sub relationship to have ulterior motives, but in this case, it couldn't be helped. Besides that, it was too dangerous to get her involved. He needed to think of it as a project with her as a mark and him as the facilitator. Tribe had been hired to find Tilly Moll and the other missing women. The job always came first, and everything else was second. As his team leader was fond of saying, "Tribe always wins."

You're an idiot. Whether she knows she's involved or not, it's still dangerous to her. That part doesn't change.

Yeah, but if she doesn't know, then she'll just be curious instead of nosey.

Now you're really being an idiot. You think a kidnapper's going to stop and consider the difference?

That's my story, and I'm sticking to it.

You're not just an idiot, you're delusional.

Shut up.

You're going to lose her! Then you'll be just like your boss and his crabby ass.

He's in love. I'm not. I'm just... intrigued.

I'm not talking to you anymore.

TB snorted. He waited. The voices appeared to have stopped.

Thank fuck his situation wasn't life-altering like Waters' situation was. That man was being forced to choose between love and death. Love, meaning a real shot at happiness. Death, meaning... Well, being without her would suck the life right out of him as sure as if their boss enforced his final edict and terminated him. Literally. Choosing to walk away would just make it a slow, painful death versus whatever method God chose to retire an employee.

Either way, TB promised himself his assignment wasn't going to be the shitshow that Waters' assignment had been. TB would go undercover, using Flame to gather intel and find the missing women. The bonus was that he'd be required to hang out at the kink club and engage in some activities to make it look good, which in turn helped Flame with her research, and he'd be able to work this woman out of his system. A woman who was far too sweet and innocent for the likes of him. When the assignment was over, they'd go their separate ways. Easy enough.

What's that saying Waters used to use? "The only easy day was yesterday." You're going to get burned, buddy.

He closed his eyes and sighed. Apparently, the voices weren't done.

Was his subconscious trying to tell him that he wanted more with Flame? He certainly looked forward to talking to her. Some days, it took every ounce of his control to refrain from taking their conversations past texts and chats.

Was he just feeling pangs because of watching Waters become the happiest he'd ever known him? It was probably natural to see happiness like that and be jealous of not having it himself.

Was he balking at pushing forward because his co-worker was currently drowning in his own misery? It certainly didn't appear that those few weeks of being happy were worth what the man was going through now. His team leader was worse now than he'd been for the previous two years after his capture and subsequent rescue.

More importantly, TB wondered if he was capable of maintaining a relationship, given his proclivities in the bedroom. Relationships meant compromise. Compromise meant giving up control.

Just the thought of that gave him the chills.

He wasn't so ignorant to think that a committed relationship couldn't utilize elements of BDSM to make it function better. But in his experience, there had never been anything romantic about tying someone up, spanking them, or any of the other aspects of the lifestyle. He had to admit, there were probably Dominants out there who believed that a submissive surrendering control to them brought some elevated level to the relationship.

TB had never wanted a relationship before. Never even gave it a thought based on his disaster of a past. His damage wasn't the same as Waters' had been. Similar, maybe. People left. Even when they didn't want to.

The slithering snake of unease he'd been feeling before burst into an explosion of baby snakes going every which way. He closed his eyes and took a deep breath. After holding it for a few seconds, he let it out in a controlled exhale.

Time enough to worry about this later. Stick to the plan. Enjoy tonight. Proceed with the job tomorrow. Maybe tonight will give you a better perspective.

He opened his eyes and looked closer at the room. It looked like a French salon out of Louis XVI's era. A chaise lounge in cream upholstery and gilded wood. A pink and cream striped matching chair, wider than a typical armchair. A pink velvet loveseat. All three pieces were in a semi-circle around the edge of a square, cream-colored floor rug that lay in front of a three-paneled standing mirror.

He knew Flame was nervous about tonight based on their conversation the previous night. An all-over romantic atmosphere would probably help turn her nerves into arousal on the sharp point of a knife. Themed rooms were too close to role-play for him. He was very clear on what he needed, and he didn't need to be someone else to achieve it. However, he did recognize that it might be easier for her in this environment. She needed permission to let go, and while he'd managed to create that online for her, in person would be more challenging. If the themed room helped, who was he to argue?

A knock came at the door.

He rolled his neck from one side to the other, allowing some of the tightness to leave his shoulders. He crossed to the door. Before opening it, he took in another deep breath, then exhaled.

When the door opened, Tabitha was one step behind and a half step to the left of her charge. His eyes met Flame's, and he heard the swift intake of breath. It was stunning to watch her emerald eyes widen in shock and her pupils fog in desire as she recognized him from the shared glance on the main floor.

"Lobo, I bring you Flame," Tabitha said.

"Thank you, Tabitha." TB opened the door wider, and Tabitha waited for Flame to make the choice to enter the room. Neither she nor TB would urge her to do so or give her an out. The choice was hers, as all choices ultimately would be.

He watched the indecision cross her face. Her lungs filled with air, then she expelled it with a small shudder, and she stepped over the threshold. Once she was clear of the door, TB nodded at Tabitha as he closed it gently yet firmly.

Flame stayed rooted to the spot, eyes to the floor, clearly remembering his online lessons.

TB observed her from behind. She was incredibly tiny. She stood about five feet, over a foot and a half shorter than him, but she was wearing what appeared to be five-inch heels. Her long braid's tail was tied off with a cream-colored ribbon that matched her outfit. She looked virginal and angelic.

He walked around her so they were facing each other. "Hello, Flame."

"Hello, Master Lobo."

Wow. Her voice is like music.

His inner grouch smacked him in the back of the head.

Like music? Seriously? Just because you've decided you're not going to be an asshole doesn't mean you have to turn into a pussy.

"I don't require an honorific. You can simply call me Lobo."

Her eyes were still downcast.

"Look at me, Flame."

She raised her eyes to his.

"I prefer to see your eyes. They help me to know what you're thinking and feeling."

She smiled shyly. "I much prefer looking at you. You're handsome, even if you scare me a little. That's not right. I'm not afraid of you. Your stare is... intense. Dangerous. Every woman secretly loves a bad boy, even if it's just to look at. Despite the bad boy look, you still make me feel safe."

She stopped abruptly.

Reading her expression and her body language, he realized she'd said something she hadn't meant to. One of those baby snakes of unease skittered into his brain.

Safe? Interesting word choice.

"I'm sorry, I'm babbling. I don't even know what I'm saying. This is all a little... overwhelming, even though I want to be here."

"There's no need to apologize. A little nervousness is to be expected. Normal, even." As difficult as it was, he moved away from her to sit in the single-seat chair. "Come to me, Flame."

She stepped shakily in his direction but without pause.

When she reached his knees, he spread his legs wide and tapped the top of his right thigh. "Sit, princess."

She sat gingerly, and he tagged her around the waist and slid her up his thigh further to also be touching his torso. Her body was literally vibrating.

She looked at him, her eyes wide with anticipation but also with naked attraction to him. He had to admit to himself he had the same feelings. It felt good to finally have his hands on her. It felt right.

"Before we begin, we need to discuss a few things."

"Okay."

"First, you already know I've been vetted extensively by the club. That means not only have I had a thorough background check, I've had no complaints from club members, which is what allows me to remain here as a member."

Okay, so my background check was "created" by Midas, but I'm no threat to her.

"Second, safe words. We'll use the traffic lights. Periodically, I will ask you for your color. Green means 'continue.' You should never need to use that one, as I should be able to tell if you are enjoying something or are comfortable. Yellow means 'slow down.' At that point, we take a break. We talk about what's making you uncomfortable. We determine whether to continue or adjust. Red means 'stop now.' Whatever we're doing is so far out of your comfort zone that we stop the scene immediately, and we do not return to it.

"Normally, I shouldn't need to ask your colors because I'll be paying very close attention to your reactions. But because you are new to this, and we've not scened in person, I will ask occasionally so that you get into the routine. Do you understand the system?"

"Yes. Green means 'continue,' yellow means 'slow down,' and red means 'stop.'"

"Excellent. Third, Tabitha shared your limits list with me, but we're going to take this slow since this is your first in-person foray into BDSM. For tonight," he emphasized, "tell me what your limits are."

"I…" She swallowed, her eyes locked on his.

He stroked a hand down the side of her face to soothe her. "Remember, princess, communication is key."

"I'm nervous."

"I know. I can feel your body shaking. That's why I'm asking you to voice what we can and cannot do tonight. This is part of the power exchange facet. After negotiation, I will control what happens, but tonight, this is all about your needs. This should be enjoyable, not uncomfortable."

"I guess I'm a little embarrassed."

"You have nothing at all to be embarrassed about. Trust me. I've seen a lot and probably done most of it.

"Maybe 'insecure' might be a better word. What if I ask for something I shouldn't? What if the things I want aren't what you want? I'm new to this. Way too… 'normal.'"

"Okay, Miss Author, define 'normal' for me."

"What's usual. Acceptable."

"Usual or acceptable to whom?"

"To everyone."

"Hmm. But this is usual for me. It is acceptable. And while everyone's BDSM experience is personal and unique to their needs, that in itself makes this usual or acceptable to all of those people in the club. So who's 'abnormal'?"

She huffed slightly. "You know what I mean. What if I'm too vanilla for you?"

That's kind of cute. She's worried about not being the "bad girl" stereotype.

Instead of laughing, he gave her an encouraging smile and a reassuring squeeze of his hand to her waist. "If you weren't what I wanted, just as you are, I wouldn't be here. You never have to worry about pleasing me, little Flame. My pleasure always comes from the power dynamic of giving my sub what she needs." He smoothed a stray tendril of hair back behind her ear. "Right now, you need me to reassure you that this is okay for you to want so that the experience can be positive. Am I right?"

"Yes."

"See? A Dom pays attention, reads cues, and works to know what he needs to know. Anything you want is okay, Flame," he reassured her.

Eventually, the tension in her spine began to ease. "Feeling better, princess?"

"Yes. Thank you."

"All right. Now, we'll start with the easy ones. Red is red. We're not worried about what's already on that list. What's red for you tonight that is otherwise yellow or green?"

Her face burned pink. "Mistress Tabitha said conventional sex was red for you."

"She is correct. No conventional sex with a partner I've just met. But that leaves room for a lot of other things that still qualify for pleasure and release."

Tension seemed to release from her body. "Good." She took a breath and released it before continuing, "Nothing anal. No whips." She looked down at his chest. "I don't know that I'm ready for any toys tonight, or paddles, or anything like that. Yellow on those."

He raised her chin with his fist so she could see his face and he could see hers. "All right. Anything else?"

Relaxing a bit further, she sucked her bottom lip under her top teeth, which he quickly rescued with a brush of his thumb out of fear she would bite into it and draw blood in her nervousness. He waited out her answer, no expression on his face. "Spanking," she whispered.

He nodded in response. "Plenty of other punishment options, but I somehow doubt they'll be needed. Anything in particular you do want to experience tonight?"

She was blushing again, but her breathing had elevated, and her pupils were dilating. She swallowed hard. "I'd like to be blindfolded. Tied."

Oh, definitely.

"Nudity?"

"Yellow." It came out as a whisper, just barely heard.

Hmm.

"No judgment, princess, but why are you unsure about showing your beautiful body to me?"

"There are parts of my body I'm not comfortable with."

"You're exquisite, princess. I knew you would be."

She blushed. "Thank you for the compliment, Lobo."

"Can you tell me what part of your body it is you aren't comfortable with?"

Her eyes gazed into his. "My arms. I don't like them to be bare. It's silly, but... just don't remove the sleeves. I can handle anything else."

Okay. That's a new one.

He nodded. "Sleeves are red; all else is green. Got it."

"You're not unhappy? I mean, my limits tonight are pretty boring, I'm guessing. Wouldn't you rather be playing with someone who is open to more?"

He brushed her knuckles with his thumb, eyes never leaving hers. "I'm here tonight only because you are, and I want to give you what you need."

She smiled shyly at him. "I'm flattered. You didn't say tonight, and I should have asked first in case you had plans. I'm sorry. Not particularly good submissive behavior."

"Well, I did intend for my invitation to be whenever you were ready, so we'll let it slide. This time," he warned her. "And I was planning on texting you, anyway, to see what other mischief I could convince you to get into." He winked at her, producing that nervous giggle in her again.

Her face sobered as she stared at his chest. She began to reach out her hand to touch him, then stopped, remembering that she shouldn't without permission.

"I worry that I won't please you."

And that's my cue.

Without a pause, he swept her up into his arms and took her

toward the mirrors. He slid her down to stand in front of him so that she could see herself with him behind her. "Look at yourself in the mirror, Flame. Your eyes are never to leave us and what I'm doing to you. You are not to look at me other than through the mirror. You are not to look away or close your eyes, even briefly. Just watch us in the mirror."

He pulled her tight against his front. Her eyes went wide again, and there was a quiet gasp. Their eyes met in the mirror.

"Do I seem displeased?"

"N-n-no."

"Exactly. My body is the easy part. You already pleased me when we were doing no more than chatting over the computer, so you have no worries there, little Flame. Now..." His hands slid to hold her upper biceps lightly. "Let's begin."

9

———————

APRIL 13TH

Sylvan

Sylvan tried to remain calm, but her heart felt like it was pounding so hard that her chest actually ached. She could see her pulse battering the skin of her neck like it was something caged and trying to break free. Lobo had also seen it because he let go of her arm and brushed the back of his hand against it. Then, he replaced his hand to its previous position.

She watched his hands as they slid up and down her arms from shoulder to elbow, barely skimming the surface. His fingers felt warm through her clothing but sent sparks throughout her body when he grazed her bare skin at the shoulder. She wanted the sleeves removed so that she could feel the tingles and flares the entire time he touched her, but then she worried she would combust and become a total pile of ash if they did.

And she didn't want him to see her arms. She didn't even want to see them.

His right arm came across her chest, just above the bodice of her bodysuit, the fingers holding onto her opposite shoulder. The other arm slid to cover her waist where the boning of it met the silk wraparound skirt.

"What do you like best about yourself when you look in the mirror?" he murmured.

"My hair."

"Mmmm." She felt his chin resting on top of her head. "It is very beautiful. You should be proud of it. I love how it contrasts with your pale skin and your emerald eyes." She saw the hand that had been across her chest now playing with one of the loose, wispy curls she had allowed to remain free of her braid. "It feels like silk." He lowered his cheek to lay flat against her head, his nose buried just above her ear. Then she heard and felt him take a deep breath and then exhale. "It smells like roses." He inhaled deeply again. "I bet all of you smells like roses."

The hand at her waist pulled her to him even tighter, the hardness of his cock nestling tight against her ass. "I love this color on you." The hand playing with her hair let the curl go, and then both hands drifted up to trace the boned edges of the corseted bodice. "Why did you pick this outfit?"

Why is he asking me these questions?

"I like the contrasts. The corset keeps me feeling restrained, but the skirt and sleeves make me feel like I'm floating, and the bare skin makes me feel exposed, yet I know that I'm not."

His fingers were still lightly tracing the edges of the corset, just teasing her exposed skin with barely-there brushes. The back-and-forth motion of his fingertips abraded her skin while creating a pleasurable ache.

Her fingers wanted to glide over his powerful arms, feel the braided leather and silver at his wrists, feel the heat of his tan skin, slide through his mussed hair.

"May I touch you, Lobo?"

"No, princess. Not tonight. This is about you."

His hands stopped tracing the edges of the top of her corset and slid down the sides of her torso's hourglass shape until he reached the flare of her hips, then crossed over to the ties of her skirt that held it together in front.

He pulled the ties and stepped back just enough so the skirt fell loosely behind her. One of his hands had retained hold of the silk, and he pulled it clear of her and dropped it to the floor off to the side. His hands went back to her hips, moving back up against her. "Look at how beautiful you are." His voice was giving her an order, but it felt like he was marveling at his luck at being in her presence. It made her feel powerful that this gorgeous man could find her attractive.

His hands moved to the tail of her braid, then stopped. "We didn't discuss your hair. May I unbraid it?"

"Yes," she whispered, her eyes frozen to where his large fingers played with the tail.

Deftly, his fingers untied the scrap of silk tying her braid closed. Once it was removed, he tucked the ribbon into his pants pocket and began to lazily slip the strands free from the single plait. Once it was all undone, he took his time combing through her hair until it fell loose and soft down her back.

He brushed all of her hair over both shoulders so that it covered her front. His hands rested at the top of the hooks to the corset bodysuit from behind. "Color?"

"Green."

Her voice was so quiet she wasn't even sure if the words had actually passed her lips. They must have, however, because she began to feel him loosen the hooks of the garment so painfully slow that she could anticipate each action. Every snick of the metal pieces unhooking was like a gasp of breath in the room. Once all were undone, his hands slid inside the garment to rest along her hips, where they settled for just a moment, as if allowing her time to change her mind. Then he pushed down the sides of her legs, taking the garment in its entirety off of her body. When it fell around her ankles, he crouched down to lift first one foot and then the second out of the clothing.

With care, he picked the garment up, as well as the discarded skirt, and took them to the chair they had been sitting in earlier. He laid them gently over the back so that nothing touched the floor, then returned to stand behind her. His hands perched on her shoulders, slipping beneath the waterfall of hair that covered her from the top of her head to the rounded undersides of her ass. "Don't move. Keep your eyes focused on the mirror."

She felt his hands leave her arms, and he stepped around her body to walk to the mirror. It was odd watching him in the reflection when he was right in front of her. It felt like what was happening to her was happening in synchronization with watching someone on television or in a movie, making it just a little bit naughty to think she was playing along with the entertainment.

Like on the computer, when he told you what he wanted to do, and you acted it out on your end.

"Oh!" It was more of a soft gasp of understanding rather than the speaking of a word. In the reflection, she saw him smiling to himself as he grabbed the two swaths of cloth draped over the top of the mirror. He knew she'd made the connection to what he was doing.

He pulled the pink silk swath. It slithered down from the top of the mirror, and he draped it over his shoulder. His hand raised again, but this time to the cream tulle swath, and pulled its end. The rasp of the tulle was quiet, but it filled the room. Once he held it in his hand, he turned to face her.

His measured steps took him back to her. She was still watching in the mirror, her hungry eyes fixated on the material hanging from his fingers, barely trailing along the floor. Her chest rose and fell rapidly, a growing flush of pink stretching across her bare skin.

Behind her once again, he took hold of both her hands and drew them loosely to the small of her back. She inhaled sharply as he wound the tulle around her wrists, effectively binding them.

His mouth went back to the shell of her ear, his eyes meeting hers in the mirror. "The knot will be tight enough to keep you from being able to use your hands. If you feel trapped, just say 'red,' and I will pull it free. If you feel panic at any time, or I don't undo it quickly enough, use your left hand to pull the tail, and the whole structure will fall apart."

Eyes holding his fast in the mirror, she closed her fists. "Thank you."

He tested the tightness of the restraint by sliding his fingers between the material and her skin. "Are you in any pain? Losing feeling in your fingers?"

"No pain, no tingling, no numbness."

"Good. That means it's tight enough without restricting blood flow. It's extremely important that if at any time your fingers begin to tingle and go numb, you need to let me know immediately."

He reached to his shoulder and slid the pink silk from where it hung, grabbing it in both hands. Slowly, as if he were concerned about startling her, he brought the material over her head and stopped for a second in front of her face, then covered her eyes completely with it, tying it off in a large bow at the back.

His hands settled the blindfold a little more securely, then smoothed down the sides of her face, neck, shoulders, torso, and waist, and finally rested on her hips. The position of her restrained arms automatically pushed her breasts forward. She could feel that her skin was flushed, and she bit her lower lip, her breathing elevating further.

"The restraint is to keep you from touching me," he explained, his breath warm in her ear. "The blindfold will allow your other senses to dominate. Both will cause you to experience the other three senses more intensely in order to compensate for the loss of your hands and eyes. I want you completely focused on my touch, no matter how it comes to you."

Her high heels helped shorten the distance between them, but she was still a foot shorter. And while she was curvy, she still felt incredibly delicate compared to his hulking frame. Standing behind her, his groin was pressed into her backside, directly at the same level as her tied hands. Her fingers twitched, but she didn't reach to grab him when clearly the impulse was to do so.

"You're doing so well, princess. That deserves a reward." His hands reached around to cup the undersides of her breasts, his palms taking their weight, his thumbs barely brushing her already puckered nipples. Her skin broke out with goosebumps.

She swallowed tightly. "Your touch feels good."

He dragged a fingertip in a circle around her left nipple. The moan that came from her was soft but from the back of her throat.

"Does it feel better now than it did a couple of nights ago when I had you touch yourself as if it were me?" he whispered.

He lightly squeezed the hard point of a nipple.

She sighed. "So much better. Your skin is rougher. Your hands do more physical work. Mine are softer. I sit at a keyboard all day."

"How else?"

She considered his question. "You're more aggressive. More confident. You know what to do. What pressure to give and when to pull back. I was more hesitant. It was awkward. I'd never done some of those things before."

"Never? You've never touched yourself? Never brought yourself to orgasm?"

She shook her head, then remembered to speak. "Yes, I've touched myself before, but I..." She whispered, embarrassed, "I could never have an orgasm."

"So you've never orgasmed before the other night?"

"No," she admitted.

His touch didn't stop. "Princess, I'm going to ask you a very important question, and you need to be honest because it determines how I proceed. Not if, just how." He paused. "Are you a virgin?"

How do I answer this question?

"No. It's just... this is just new. My... I wasn't considered before."

"Lean back, little Flame," he whispered. "Give me your full weight. I won't let you fall."

Her head drifted back so it nestled against his chest. Eventually, she felt her body begin to relax as he continued to run his hands lightly over her skin.

"Your trust is a gift, Flame. Just be in the moment. You're here. You're with me. You're safe."

His thumb and forefingers plucked her already distended nipples, working to create a sharp pinching sensation that caused her to inhale sharply. After each pluck of the buds, he lightly brushed his middle fingers across their surfaces to soothe the sting.

"It's time for you to feel what you're capable of."

His hands traveled down her body, one resting on her hip, and the other slid down her side, over her hip, and toward her smooth mound.

Giving it a gentle stroke at the top of her outer lips, he murmured, "Spread your legs shoulder-width apart, little Flame."

She inhaled, bit her lip, then followed his instruction.

"Exhale, princess. If you feel faint at any time, you need to tell me. Can't have you passing out on me."

Once she had settled into the new position that opened her to his touch, his fingers drifted to cup her sex, sliding his middle finger between her folds to find her slit soaked with her arousal.

She gasped and tensed in his arms.

"Easy, little Flame."

She shivered.

After several strokes through her wetness, her hips bucked gently into his hand.

He withdrew his hand. "Don't move unless I tell you to," he reminded.

She stilled and bit her lip. Her head turned toward his mouth as if searching for him. "Please, Lobo," she begged. "I ache."

His voice entered her ear, lips brushing against the shell as he spoke. "Where do you ache, princess?"

"Between my legs. Please. I need more. I need you to touch me."

"You beg so pretty, little Flame. Keep that up, and I might just give you what you want." His hand smoothed down to her sex again, resting at the juncture of her thighs, his touch light. "But not yet," he taunted, withdrawing his hand. "I say when and how much."

In a sweeping gesture, he gathered her in his arms again, walking just a few steps to their left, before he slid her body down his front, setting her on her feet, making sure she was steady before removing his arms from around her. With his boot, he pressed between her two feet to get her to slightly widen her stance. Ever so gently, he placed downward pressure to her back, causing her to bend at the waist until she lay with her head on a velvet throw pillow, her hips canted over the arm of the chaise lounge.

His hand stroked feather-soft against her spine. "Anything pressing uncomfortably or causing pain?"

"No. No pain."

His hand brushed up and down along her spine, neck to waist, where her hands were bound. She shivered, but her skin flushed.

He began the same back-and-forth motion from her lower back to the underside of her ass cheeks, his blunt fingernails lightly scraping over the creamy swells. When his touch met the backs of her thighs, he traced around the curve to her far hip, then returned to the small of her back just below her tied hands.

His hand continued its circular strokes, first to the leg at the inside of the chair, the next pass to the outside leg. After several rotations, he switched the pattern to lazy figure eights until finally, his hand slid down to her lower back and then to between her legs, separating her inner and outer lips from her channel. "Color, little Flame?" he whispered.

She whimpered. "Green."

His hand continued its quest through her slick folds and found her clit already extended from its hood.

"I want to hear you, princess. I want to hear every moment of what you feel."

His middle finger skimmed over her clit, causing her to inhale and tense, then he placed the slightest of pressure as he dragged the digit back down over it, causing her to groan on the exhale. His lazy circles around the button sensitized the nerves so much that, without thought, she pressed her shoulder against his leg, her head resting against his thigh, almost as if she were a kitten rubbing against its owner.

His hand froze.

After a moment, she mewled in frustration. Actually mewled! And she pushed against him, trying to get his hand to move again. "Please, don't stop," she begged. "I feel like I'm going to jump out of my skin if you don't keep touching me."

He pulled his hand from between her legs. "What's the rule?"

"I don't get to determine how much or where. Only you do," she replied. "I'm sorry, I can't seem to control it."

"You can," he assured her.

He returned his hand to her backside, retracing circles, clearly starting the whole process over. Her vocalizations were incoherent whines. He'd reduced her to a whimpering mess.

"That's it, little Flame. Who makes this little kitten purr?"

"You do," she gasped out in a pained exhale.

"That's right. I do." He slid his fingers down to between her legs again, brushing through her folds and tapping lightly on her clit. "I own this pussy until I say otherwise."

Her core was hot and slick, absolutely no resistance as he slid his fingers across her skin. She was on the verge of an orgasm, so when he pulled his hand away from her clit, she wailed in agony and frustration, but she didn't beg him to put his hand back.

"Sssh, I'm here. You're doing so well."

He swept his palm up and down her back, turning the wail into a moan. Finally, he lightened the caresses until her breathing gentled, and she stayed in position, her legs trembling.

Moving behind her, he bent over her body, his chest to her back, nestling his groin against her backside so that she could feel his rock-hard cock against her. The fingers that had been teasing her clit snuck around her right hip. His thumb unerringly found the pearl, and two fingers plunged into her pussy, pumping inside her walls.

She screamed and bucked against his chest, but his sheer height and width kept her pinned in place.

She felt her body begin to tremble. Without stopping his strokes, his other hand swept her hair to hang over the shoulder closest to the couch back. Then he slid his palm around her throat, placing pressure, but not dangerously so. Just enough to restrict airflow, not cut it off.

His mouth latched onto the skin just to the left of her spine where her neck and shoulder met. The circles on her clit stopped, and instead, he placed pressure against it while he filled her with a third finger. He pushed them inside as far as he could, dragging them across her walls. She began keening in the back of her throat. Between the pressure on her clit, G-spot, and throat, she was ready to explode for him.

His mouth let go of her skin, a slight stinging radiating from the spot. He groaned. "Your cunt feels like it's on fire. Let go, little Flame. Burn me."

As the first convulsion began, he used powerful strokes inside and outside her sex, and he eased up all the pressure on her throat, although he left it there as a support. She screamed, and her passage flooded. His fingers pumped in and out, and her release began to squirt in force from her.

HER ORGASM SEEMED to go on forever. When her screams eased down to gasps and she went totally limp, it felt as if her body slid into a liquid pool of bliss. She was so tired, she couldn't do anything but exist. Her eyes remained closed, and her body relied upon her cheek on the pillow, her hips over the arm of the chaise lounge, and her feet on the floor to hold her up. Nothing mattered except just being.

Abstractly, her brain registered as he gently slid his fingers from inside her and took his other hand from around her throat. From a long way away, she heard him whisper in her ear, "I'll be right back. Don't move."

Couldn't move if I wanted to.

Minutes later, or maybe it was hours, she felt his presence next to her, but she was still too tired to do anything about it. There were sounds around her that she had no clue what they were, and she didn't care anyway. There was a soft, warm sensation smoothing along her skin between her legs. This was followed by the repetition of a cool sensation on her forehead and across her face. Inwardly, she was smiling, but it took way too much energy to make her facial muscles move into the actual position on the outside.

More cool sensations followed. Her arms. Her back. Her center. Her legs.

Her brain wanted to fight and swim up to consciousness, but she was far too comfortable to actually do it, so she remained as she was. She felt weight on her hands, then nothingness. Something held her wrists, a gentle rubbing of the flesh causing circulation to burn sweetly in her veins. She hadn't been in pain, so this was more like a low-heat burn moving through her, tingling sweetly, and spreading throughout her body. As that sensation soothed her, warm hands settled on her shoulders, massaging lightly. The darkness lightened as well, but she refused to open her eyes. Something told her that if she opened them, the pleasant thrumming in her veins might go away.

A deep voice coaxed, "Come on, princess, time to stand up."

She whimpered, her head turning on the pillow as she began the slow climb back to reality. The person behind the voice reached to stand her up like a doll, draped something around her shoulders and back, and then scooped her up into his arms. Her eyelids fluttered open, then back closed, as her rescuer moved them sitting elsewhere in the room, her body gathered against a wall of muscle.

Rescuer? What do I need rescuing from?

Her body began to rise closer and closer to the surface of lucidity. An arm held her tight from underneath while a second tucked a blanket around her. If she had wanted to have any say in what was going on, she wouldn't have been able to. Her breath evened out to slow and soft, feathering across his neck as he tucked her under his chin. She felt him brush his chin up and down the top of her head.

10

———————

APRIL 19TH

Sylvan

"It's been six days, and he hasn't come online? Hasn't texted you? Hasn't called you?"

Sylvan stared out the window of her sanctuary, barely registering her friend's voice over the phone.

"No, he hasn't. I've gone online each night, I've waited the prescribed amount of time, and he hasn't shown up."

"You didn't text him or call him either?"

"I thought about texting, but I've never initiated that before. Besides that, he left without saying goodbye. I'd say that's pretty conclusive he doesn't want to speak to me again." She'd really wanted to, though. "I assume he had to leave for work again. That's usually why that happens. Look, Tabitha, it's not a big deal. You hooked us up for research, and I'm forever grateful. The scene was a bonus. I went, I got to experience it, and he was great. But I'm not exactly the kind of woman he's going to play with on a regular basis. I'm just a tad vanilla," she said with sarcasm.

"Vanilla is not the issue, and stop calling yourself that. I hate that term. I happen to love vanilla."

Sylvan snorted. "I'm not talking about the oil being poured all over your body and then licked out of your belly button."

"Neither was I. Although, it does sound good right about now." The clicking heels stopped, and an icy pause occurred before Tabitha's suspicious tone came over the line. "Did he do that with you?"

That brought a genuine laugh to Sylvan. "You almost sound jealous. No, he didn't. And even if he had, I wouldn't tell you. I don't think I'm supposed to share that information. Doesn't that violate some sort of club or BDSM code?"

The heels began clicking again. "Nope, nothing in our rules about that. Your experience to share as you two agreed upon," she answered a bit grumpily.

"Well, we never discussed it, so I'm putting that on the 'Do Not Share' list. And none of this matters, anyway, since it wasn't a date. It was research." It physically hurt to say that. She actually felt a sharp pain where her heart was and a lurch in her stomach.

"Yeah, well, no 'research' I've ever done has left me so blissed out that a friend had to drive me home. You were so gone I couldn't even put you in a rideshare."

"In his defense, it was probably awkward. I don't think it's supposed to take that long to come back to life."

"Hmph. It's called subspace. And if you were there, he did his job well." She paused. "Looking back, I guess I should have answered your questions instead of sending you to Lobo. After we chatted, I just thought a pure Dominant would be better than a switch. I should have connected you with a submissive. It literally never occurred to me that you two... that things would end like this."

"Again, Tabitha, it's okay. I definitely wasn't expecting a relationship out of it. Not even a repeat performance." She needed to get off the phone before she broke down. "Look, you have to get to work, and I have a deadline looming, so I'll talk to you later. Don't whip anyone too hard."

"Ha! As if. I can't remember the last time I picked up a flogger."

"Bye, Tabitha."

"Bye, Sylvan."

Sylvan disconnected the call.

For the next six hours, she tried to write, but no words would come. Her characters still weren't speaking to her. She tried everything she could think of to get back on track. She ate a whole pint of ice cream. She tried taking a nap. She tried watching an episode of *Firefly*. None of it helped. She didn't write a single word —just stared at the mocking cursor on the page. When ten o'clock rolled around, her hand hovered over the keyboard to open the private chat room, and then she simply shut down her computer, crawled into her bed, and stared out the window into the darkness until she fell into a fitful sleep.

11

—————

APRIL 19TH

TB

3105552376

What the hell is wrong with you?

3105552376

We need to talk.

TB ACTUALLY WINCED AS HE LOOKED AT THE MESSAGE FROM HIS FAKE text account. He knew exactly why she wanted to talk.

He wasn't surprised she knew about him ghosting Flame. What surprised him was that she hadn't discovered his dumbassery sooner because he'd been to the club every night. Then again, he had been doing an excellent job of avoiding the club owner.

While avoiding her, he'd started conversations with the other Doms. The ones on contracts or in permanent relationships had few observations to add on the single subs. The ones who played around with a wide variety of subs had little knowledge because they were trying to remain unattached and didn't often repeat with partners. Since Cosmos was overseas, it would have been a while before he'd known something was wrong.

He'd chatted up the submissives. That had been painful. Every one of them thought he was looking to play.

He talked to staff members who knew everyone and most of the gossip that people thought was private—after all, staff were often invisible as human beings unless a member was actively in need of one, and that was by design. However, members did come and go in waves, so no one thought anything of people they hadn't seen in a while. Even Ryleigh hadn't thought much of not seeing the girls in question.

Currently, he sat at the conference room table at Tribe Corporation, rubbing a piece of cream ribbon between his fingers, totally tuned out to the conversation around him. He'd found it in his pocket when he got undressed that night after being with Flame. Without thinking about it, he'd pocketed it every day, not able to leave his apartment without it.

Waters was briefing them on the upcoming trip tomorrow to Egypt to search for Zahra and Ka-Bar. Hell knew how long they'd be gone this time because he didn't think they'd be coming back until they found at least one of them.

He didn't owe Tabitha anything, but out of respect for her relationship with Flame, he would meet with her.

He owed Flame an explanation. And an apology. He wasn't good at those. Most of the time, he didn't give enough fucks to apologize for any of his actions. In fact, he couldn't remember apologizing to anyone for anything. Ever.

Maybe it would just be better if you delivered your head on a platter. Or both of them.

It was then that he realized the meeting was over, and it was just him and Steel at the table. While the men worked interchangeably amongst each other to suit their strengths, Nemo and Demon tended to partner together, as did TB and Steel. Because of that, Steel was very attuned to his moods. Sometimes, it felt like he could even read TB's thoughts.

Fan-fucking-tastic.

"What do you want, Steel?"

After a couple of moments, he nodded at the ribbon in TB's fingers. "She's really got your guts in a twist, doesn't she?"

TB pocketed the ribbon, got up from the chair, and gave it a shove toward the table as he tried to head to the door.

Steel called out, "I'm just trying to figure out when the angle became a thing."

TB had reached the door, his hand on the knob, but he turned back to face the man still sitting, relaxed as could be, at the conference table. "There's no 'thing.'"

"Call it whatever you want, but there's definitely a 'thing.' You don't usually sit through meetings completely tuned out to what's going on and contemplate pieces of frilly material."

"I have a lot to do to get ready for tomorrow. Is there a fucking point somewhere here?"

"Between you and Waters this past week since you got home, it's like trying to navigate a minefield."

"My problem is nothing like Waters' problem."

"At least you admit you have a problem," Steel muttered. He continued, "Does your grouchiness have anything to do with the text you just got?"

"No."

"You know, for an expert interrogator, you can't lie for shit. C'mon, seriously. What is going on?"

"Why do you care?"

Steel shrugged. "Do you blame me for not wanting to work in an office full of cranky men? Glad Demon's not here because then it would be all doom and gloom."

"Whatever." He headed through the door. "I have to go."

"Have you learned nothing from the bossman's mistake?" Steel called out again.

"What is it you want?"

"I want to know if you're going to learn from his mistake and fight for what you want?"

"You talking about Flame? The author and her research?"

"That may have been how it started, but that's not how it

ended. Or, ended prematurely, should I say. It did not go unnoticed by anyone that you went to the club with her, and then for the past five nights, you've gone alone, and you've not been home in time for your nightly chats with her."

"Fuckin' Midas," TB spat. "Is he following my chats? I'll fuckin' kill him."

"No, TB, he's only checked the connection. He would never look at your

communications, no matter how much Nemo begs. You would have known that if you'd been listening in the meeting. He said it out loud, and he was right next to you. You didn't even flinch."

"Look," TB tried to explain, "it became very clear that she's too innocent for this. It's not fair to lead her astray. She's going to get caught up in the whole role exchange, and then I'm going to hurt her. When we get back in town, I'll have Cherry partner with me. Same scenario—a newbie able to ask questions."

"Yeah, that won't look odd at all, you bringing *another* new girl in." Steel shook his head. "And good luck getting Cherry into that club dressed like a sub. We'll be lucky if he only raises the roof and doesn't burn this building to the ground."

"He who? God? He's sent her undercover before."

Steel mumbled under his breath about the best and brightest being the most oblivious.

TB frowned and shook his head. "No idea who or what you're referring to. Regardless, if in a week I haven't found anything, there probably isn't anything to find. Maybe the club has nothing to do with it directly. Maybe it's just a vulnerable location to hunt. I'll talk to the security team there. One of the dungeon masters is a former Marine."

"Waters says his spidey senses are telling him it's connected to the club, so that means it is ninety-nine percent connected. He just hasn't figured out how he knows it. I think... maybe... just maybe... you got too close to Flame and got burned." Steel stood, stretched, then walked past his friend and headed out the door. "Figure it out, big man, or you're going to end up like Waters."

TB sank down into the chair closest to the door. He sat alone and in silence, contemplating what Steel had said to him.

It wasn't that he didn't like her. He did. Way more than he should.

But no matter which way he looked at it, he couldn't see any sort of a future between him and Flame. His job wouldn't allow it with someone like her. She'd be crying and demanding he stay home and spend time with her within two project stints.

She hasn't complained in the time you've been chatting.

We weren't a couple. We were just researcher and interviewer.

Keep telling yourself that bullshit. Someday, you might convince yourself.

Even if she never complained, it's not fair to her. I am not relationship material. I'm selfish and don't like answering to anyone else. Besides that, I don't want to change the way I live my life for someone else.

Yeah, because living in your sterile apartment upstairs and spending all your time working is such a fantastic life.

Fuck off. To top it off, relationships require compromise. I don't compromise.

How would you know? You've never tried.

This is a pointless argument. I'm not relationship material.

Again... how would you know? You've never been in one.

Relationships are fine for people like Waters. He still has some humanity left in him. I do not.

Right. Humanity. We've talked about the handsaw, right?

"Ugh."

Okay, Waters did have some dark spots. He had some shady as fuck shit in his past that was part of why he'd been on the verge of a dishonorable discharge before he got his insides rearranged by a member of the Taliban. Stuff that rivaled TB's methods. Despite that darkness, he had started a relationship everyone had been rooting for. He was genuinely in love with that woman. If Waters could do it, who was to say he couldn't?

TB snorted at the stupidity behind that idea. He could play the role of an attentive partner if he had a reason to do so. He could even sustain it for a while if the project needed it. But he couldn't *be* that person. He'd gotten to know Flame too well, and he couldn't unlearn who she was and later, when it didn't work out, put her in the same category as some stranger that he cultivated in order to get to his mark. It would be cruel to put her in that position. She deserved better.

What could it hurt to try? It would be so easy to put her first.

Nope. You did the right thing. You just went about it the wrong way. Just officially cut the cord, and you'll feel better about it.

ENTERING through the external door into the marble foyer, TB approached the information desk. Frost, the receptionist, sat behind it, her sleek blonde hair up in a bun so tight, it looked like it was painted on her head. Her tortoise shell framed glasses covered ice-cold blue eyes. "May I help you?"

He leaned on the high countertop. "Mistress Tabitha called me."

Without a flicker of emotion, she keyed in an extension on her phone.

"Mistress Tabitha, Master Lobo is here."

He heard a clicking noise, which meant the hidden door had opened that went to Tabitha's office. He knocked once on the high counter he'd been leaning on and strode over to the wall, where he slipped his hand into the crack that appeared and pulled the door open enough to move into the inner sanctum, shutting the door carefully behind him. On this side, it functioned as a bookcase.

The room he was now closeted in had the appearance of a Victorian library in an English country estate. Leather furniture in deep browns, floor-to-ceiling bookshelves, complete with the rolling ladder to reach the uppermost shelves, cut crystal decanters and glasses at the bar trolley, and the soft glow of fake gaslights lit the deep-colored hardwood floor and Oriental rugs. Behind a Victorian desk in a pool of light from a green, shaded lamp sat Mistress Tabitha, owner of The Library.

She stood up from behind the desk and crossed over to the bar trolley. Deep chocolate brown hair that curled slightly beyond her shoulders, dark brown eyes beneath perfectly shaped eyebrows and thick, sooty lashes, and pink, glossy lips over perfectly straight white teeth complimented skin that glowed with a healthy tan. Her body was tightly encased in a black leather corset that had a velvet collar and sleeves attached to it, a keyhole cut out from throat to armpit. Not a speck of cleavage showed, but it didn't have to. The cinching of her waist and the tight fit of the corset gave rise to more than enough imagination, helped by the tailored fit of the black leather skirt that molded to her backside and fell to below her knees, plus her signature heels, with ribbons tied perfectly around the ankles.

He could admire her looks and her business savvy, but she had always reminded him of a cobra. She could be venomous to people who pissed her off. He remembered one particular instance where she'd bordered on cruelty with a female sub, and it had never sat right with him. The pretty candy coating didn't always agree with the inner bitch. They had scened in the beginning, when he had first joined the club, always with her as a submissive, but those days were long gone.

She poured herself a whiskey, then went back behind her desk and sat down, ignoring him.

Nothing like a power play between a Dom and a switch.

"Thanks, I'd love a drink, Tabitha."

"You don't deserve my expensive whiskey," she explained without looking up at him.

He crossed to the drink trolley and poured his own drink, then moved to the bookshelves behind her desk, perusing the titles as he sipped, feeling the burn of the rich liquid as it hit the back of his throat. Her pen continued to scratch over the page on her desk, letting him know she was still not paying attention to him. He let the warmth flood through his veins as he continued to study the book titles. "Why did you drag my ass down here just to give me the silent treatment?" he rumbled.

"I didn't drag your ass anywhere."

"Tabitha—"

She sighed loudly. "Sit down."

Under normal circumstances, he would never follow her orders, but this wasn't exactly normal. In an effort to try and take some of the wind out of her sails, he humored her.

Not the hill you want to die on. Lose one battle to win the war.

Moving to the seating area in front of her desk, he lowered himself into the right-hand leather armchair. He leaned back, his expression blank, as he waited for her to make her move.

Setting her pen down, she picked up the glass of whiskey she had poured herself. She leaned back against the cushions of her high-backed leather desk chair, the arm not holding her drink folded across her middle, and she looked over her glass's edge at him.

She sipped again, watching him closely.

He simply returned her stare.

"It's unlike you to ghost a woman. Put her down harshly, maybe, if she's not getting the message. But that's not what I saw a week ago." She pointed a long, lacquered nail at him. "And don't bullshit me that you were out for work because I saw you on the security cameras. You were here every damn night. So what happened?"

"I wasn't aware that I was under any sort of agreement to talk to her unless I wished to."

She probed, "So you don't want to talk to her? Don't want to see her?"

"That's not any of your business, Tabitha."

"It certainly is, Lobo! I chose you specifically to help her. You were supposed to answer questions, maybe demonstrate some of our activities. I certainly didn't expect you to send her so far into subspace that she took an hour and a half to come down. And based on my conversation with her earlier, no matter what she says, she's developed feelings for you."

Tabitha leaned forward, put her whiskey glass off to the side on her desk, and then folded her arms in front of her on the desktop. She looked at him deeply. "I have to admit, I'm not surprised she was attracted to you. She lives with her head in the clouds, romanticizing everything. But you catching feelings? That was a surprise. I couldn't believe you, of all people, were attracted to her. She's so innocent. Considering our sessions in the past, I wouldn't take you for the vanilla type."

"She's not vanilla. She's definitely submissive. More so than you," he murmured.

She held her glass against her bottom lip, her fingers grasping her glass so tightly, they were white with the pressure. "You need to tell her it's over."

He stood up and crossed over to the bar trolley to put his empty glass on the lower level so it would get washed for the next day. When he turned around, Tabitha was right behind him. He'd been so wrapped up in his own head, he hadn't heard her leave her desk chair.

Her hand stretched out, her eyes following it as it ran down his shoulder to his elbow and continued to his wrist, where she traced the wolf's head on his cuffs. "I'm sorry. She's my friend. I feel responsible for her, as well as the clusterfuck this turned into. You were supposed to be a safe option." Her eyes looked up at his. "I would never hurt you purposefully. What can I do?"

Drawing his arm back from her touch was the best he could do since there was no way to back up with the trolley at his back. "I'm fine, Tabitha."

Her hands went to lay flat on his chest. "You don't look fine. Maybe a session with me and the spanking bench would help? An opportunity to punish me for my bad choice?"

He took both of her hands in his and gave her a nudge to step back so that he could escape his hemmed-in position. "Tabitha, there's nothing to punish you for, and besides that, you know I have no plans to scene with you again."

With that, he strode to the door, clicked the mechanism to open it, passed through, and went home.

HE'D DONE everything that needed doing before tomorrow. He'd packed his gear. He'd cleaned his personal weapons.

There was just one thing left to do.

He sat in front of the laptop at the breakfast bar in his apartment, dreading the upcoming conversation. Tabitha was right. Sylvan deserved at least a final conversation, as uncomfortable as it would be. She'd done nothing wrong except be herself.

What was worse was that Steel was also right. She'd definitely burned him. And it had scared the fuck out of him. As he'd held her in his arms while she struggled out of subspace, he'd felt panic rise.

What would she say?

What would she do?

What would she expect?

How could he be anything even close to what this beautiful woman deserved?

The truth was, he couldn't. Pure and simple.

So, he'd made sure he'd provided the initial aftercare she'd needed. Then he left her with Tripoli in the Resting Room, letting Tabitha know where she was.

Then, like a coward, he'd run. Metaphorically, anyway.

So, here he sat in his apartment, at quarter to ten, logged into the private chat where he waited.

Ten o'clock.

Five minutes after ten.

Eight minutes after ten.

Ten minutes after ten.

By ten thirty, he realized how badly he'd screwed up. She wasn't ever coming back. Now, there was no choice for him to make because his actions had made it for him.

Self-sabotage much, idiot?

He decided to leave her a message through email. His heart pounded loud and hard with each word he typed.

Flame -

I owe you an explanation for not showing up for our chats this past week. The truth is, there really isn't one.

I'm going out of the country tomorrow, and I don't know when I'll be back, but I do think it's safe to say that I've given you everything I can give you. I hope it was enough for what you need. Be well, princess.

Lobo

He shut down his computer, locked it in his personal safe, and trudged downstairs to the armory. There was no way he was going to sleep tonight, so he might as well do something useful before they left.

I'll sleep when I'm truly dead.

12

——————

JUNE 15TH

Sylvan

SYLVAN UNLOCKED THE DOOR AND OPENED IT TO SLIDE HER HAND INTO the mailbox to collect the envelopes inside. Walking away from the door, she sorted through the mail. In the middle of the bills and junk mail was a plain lavender padded envelope that was the size to hold a 5×7 photograph. Her name was front and center in calligraphy. No address. No stamp. No return address. She frowned. Squeezing it, it was clear that there was something solid, something squarish inside. Stopping in her confusion, she put the other mail under her arm and opened the envelope.

Her stomach dropped as she took stock of the contents, and she broke into an instant cold sweat, stumbling into the wall next to the stairs and sliding down onto the floor.

No, please, no! How? Why?

Perhaps she'd known it was just a matter of time before he'd find her at her home. Wasn't that how it happened on all of those crime shows?

Sylvan fumbled for her pocket and pulled out her phone. Her hands shook as she tried to pull up her best friend's number.

"Hello?"

"Kai?" Sylvan whispered.

"Syl? What's wrong?"

Sylvan was so petrified she couldn't get words out. Eyes wide, all the blood drained from her face, a death grip on the mail in her hand. Even if the lavender envelope had been on fire, she couldn't have let go of it. She just sat there and shook.

"Syl?! Syl! Answer me!"

"Kai," Sylvan wailed. "He found me."

"Are you in the house?"

"Y-y-y-yes." Her teeth began to chatter.

Sylvan could hear talking in the background, but her fear blocked out any understanding of what was being said. Then Kai's voice came through loud and clear like a lifeline to a drowning victim. "Lock the door. Stay right where you are. I'll be there in ten minutes."

"Don't hang up!" Sylvan pleaded.

"I won't, sweetheart. I'm staying on the line." There was a murmur in the background again, but now it was Sylvan's sobs that were counteracting her ability to hear. They sounded loud and chaotic to her, almost echoing off the walls surrounding her. "We're on our way, Syl."

The quality of the call changed with Kai's last words. Tin-like. As if she were speaking from a long, man-made tunnel. She was on speaker so that whoever Kai was with could hear the conversation. Sylvan curled tighter into herself and lay on the floor in a fetal position, still clutching the mail and the phone.

Even with Kai's continual crooning in her ear, ten minutes felt like ten hours. When Kai physically arrived at Sylvan's door, she pounded on it. "It's Kai, Syl! I'm using my key!"

From her place on the floor in the corner, Sylvan stared at nothing, heard the key turn the lock, and shrank further into herself. Maybe if she didn't move, didn't breathe, no one would know she was there.

"Oh my God, Syl!" Suddenly she heard a terrible clatter as something was dropped on the hardwood floor at the door. She felt herself being raised from the floor to an upright sitting position, then hugged tightly to another body. A strange keening sound could be heard in the distance, along with muted voices as if they were background actors on a TV show. "Jesus Christ on a crutch!"

"Kai, your creative swear words and phrases do not induce calm reactions," a low rumble replied.

"She looks like a fucking vampire drained her of all of her blood. How do you expect someone to react?"

"She's clearly in shock. I'll call 911."

"No!" Kai shouted to her companion. "We can't take her to the hospital. She'll get worse when she comes out of it if we do."

"Fuck... Kai, she needs help. We have to call someone." Sylvan, still locked away in her head, could hear the companion Kai had brought with her, and she retreated a step further into her brain to avoid the stranger. "Double fuck. God's going to fucking kill me if he finds out."

"Then don't let him find out."

Sylvan heard muttering that moved further away from her out onto her front porch. "Demon. Ping me. We need emergency medical attention for someone, and we can't call 911. Whatever you do, don't tell anyone else."

She felt herself being rocked gently, a soothing voice cooing nonsense in her ear, a cool hand stroking her hair. And yet, she felt herself drifting further and further away, the sounds and touches fainter with each moment.

Then she felt herself gently fall back toward the floor, her head leading the way. Her chest began to feel less restricted, cool hands touching her neck and chest, followed by a warm weight that seemed to cover her from neck to toes. And then blessed nothingness.

Sᴠʟᴠᴀɴ ʜᴇᴀʀᴅ ᴀ ɢʀᴏᴀɴ. Opening her dry and heavy eyes was a near Herculean task, and her mouth tasted like it was full of cardboard. She realized the groan had come from her and that, for some reason, she had passed out.

"That's it. Come on. Wake up a little more." Sylvan tried to clear the blurriness from her eyes, but her vision just wouldn't clear out. The deep Irish-lilted voice was nice to listen to. It must belong to the shadowy figure leaning over her, touching a hand to her forehead, then pressing against her wrist at the pulse point. "Do you think you can sit up?" A pair of strong arms wrapped around her shoulders from underneath and helped her rise to a sitting position on the couch.

"Syl?" It was Kai's voice. "Syl, oh, thank God."

"Kai?" she asked weakly.

A wrecking ball plowed into her side on the couch, and a cat-o'-nine-tails smacked her in the face. Slowly, Sylvan's vision started to clear. Now, she could identify the wrecking ball as her best friend, Kai Serrano, and the cat-o'-nine-tails as her long blonde ponytail. The woman appeared to be both gasping in relief and shaking with anger. "Dammit, Syl, don't you ever, ever, ever scare me like that again!"

"For fuck's sake, Kubrick, let her breathe, or she'll pass out again," a deep voice rumbled from across the room.

"Fuck you, Waters."

"Seriously?" the Irishman griped. "You two say 'feck' more than I do."

"That's because you don't say 'fuck,' you say 'feck.'"

A grunt, one that Sylvan supposed might pass for a laugh, came from the slicked-back, shoulder-length, dark-haired stranger kneeling in front of her who was wearing a tank top, board shorts, and flip-flops.

She had a terrible headache. "What's going on?" Sylvan asked weakly, a hand raising to her forehead as she glanced around the room.

"You called me in a panic. All I could get out of you was, 'He found me.' I raced over here and found you near catatonic in a corner." Kai stroked the side of Sylvan's face, attempting to smooth the damp hair back into her hairline. "What happened, Syl?"

Sylvan's eyes skittered to a blond man with a worried stare standing in the background, then to the dark-haired man still on one knee in front of her. She looked at her friend and whispered, "Who are these people, Kai?"

"I'm sorry, Syl. I know how you feel about strangers in your home, but I didn't know what else to do. I was having breakfast with—" Kai looked over at the blond—"with him when you called. When we got here, you needed medical attention, and I knew you wouldn't want me to call an ambulance, so he called his friend over, who has some medical training."

"Thank you," she whispered, dropping her gaze. "I'm sorry she had to bother you both."

The dark-haired surfer shrugged. "I was close by."

"Going into shock is concerning. What happened?" the blond asked.

"Just something stupid. I must have had a panic attack."

"Syl," Kai admonished, "this was more than a panic attack. You went into shock, and we couldn't wake you. Now what the fuck happened?"

"I don't want to be a burden, Kai."

"Oh, sweetheart." Kai's tone instantly became softer and more big sister-like as she framed Sylvan's face in her palms. "You are never a burden. You're my friend. Does this have to do with that bastard that's been bothering you on your author page?"

Sylvan's eyes filled with tears, and she nodded before dropping her eyes to her clasped fingers in her lap. "He started messaging and emailing while you were filming. I've been ignoring him. Deleting his letters and messages. Today, I went to get the mail. There was an envelope in the mailbox with no address or stamp. Just my name. I didn't think fast enough, and I opened it."

"Where is the envelope?" the blond man asked.

"I don't know. Last I knew, I was still holding onto it."

He reached into his pockets and pulled out a pair of latex gloves. He stepped out into the foyer and returned, holding up the purple padded envelope and matching piece of paper, along with the rest of her regular mail. "Is this it?"

She nodded.

Who in this world carries latex gloves in their pockets like it's an everyday need?

When the blond man came back into the room, he had a frown on his face as he looked at the envelope in his hands. The frown then transferred in his gaze to her. He scrutinized the two women, then turned his attention to the bookshelves along the wall. He had an odd look on his face as if he were solving complex math equations in his head. "Your name is Sylvan Jones. The romance novelist."

"How do you know that?" Kai asked.

He waved the envelope at her. "I'm not just another pretty face. I can read."

"I meant, how do you know she's a romance novelist, Kraken-boy?"

"Babe. One of her books is on your nightstand, and there's like eighty gagillion more of them on your bookshelf."

Sylvan leaned over to her friend and whispered, "How does he know what's on your nightstand?"

Kai grimaced.

He set down the mail on the sofa table behind the couch and went through it, piece by piece. He then sized it into piles of the same types of envelopes and stacked them neatly off to the side.

"Jesus, Waters, you have issues," Kai grumbled.

He grunted. "Says the woman who couldn't find her favorite bra this morning because she doesn't put laundry away, let alone color-code it."

Interesting. He knows what's on her nightstand, she was having breakfast with him, and she couldn't find her bra? We definitely need to talk.

Waters glanced at Kai, muttering, "Why am I just hearing about this now?" He gestured at the envelope.

Kai gave Sylvan's arm a squeeze, then gave a slightly exasperated glare at the blond man. "Why would I have told you? She's not exactly in the market for a…" She gestured at the two men. Lost as to how to finish the sentence, she continued, "For you and your co-workers. Annoying direct messages and emails are a police issue. Besides, if somebody would let me up for air once in a while, I could share personal details in my life that aren't in the huge file you compiled on me."

His glare became a little less irritated and a lot more wicked. "I haven't exactly heard you complaining."

Whoa. I'm not sure if that's hot or scary.

Kai stuck her tongue out at Waters, which earned her a raised eyebrow and a strange comment of "Rule six" from him.

"Okay, okay," she spat back rather than apologizing. "When it first started, I didn't know you, and by the time it had begun escalating, we were in Roatán, and then we weren't together. When I was back in your orbit, I had slightly larger concerns, remember? So when was I supposed to tell you? Last I knew, which was the middle of May"—a sharp glance was thrown at Sylvan—"she hadn't mentioned anything, so I figured maybe the assnozzle had gotten bored and moved on. Apparently not."

Waters snorted. "You think?"

He examined the purple sheet of paper first, reading the words on the page and frowning. He turned it over, saw nothing there, then held it up to the light, again finding nothing but the shadow of the ink from the front side.

While he was examining the note, Sylvan whispered to Kai, "Who is this guy? How does he know you couldn't find your favorite bra? How does he know which one is your favorite? What haven't you—"

The ponytail-wielding blonde looked at her with another grimace of chagrin. "I've been a super shitty friend and have been keeping secrets, but... some of it is because I didn't have a choice. Do you remember when I came back from filming, and I was so upset?"

Sylvan nodded, then her eyes widened, and her mouth opened into an "O." "He's why?"

Kai nodded. "His name is Waters. He was the consultant I told you about for the Navy SEAL movie I just filmed. We hooked up while working on it, some things happened, and we ended up separated for a bit. A few weeks ago, we were sort of forced together again. It's a long story, but basically, we're back together."

Both women turned their attention back to the man in question. He was totally focused, looking over the envelope with the same intensity as he had the note.

Sylvan felt a tremor go through her as she watched him. She turned her head to Kai and mouthed, "Wow!"

Kai grinned, mouthed back, "I know," and then gave a dramatic shiver.

"I saw that," he mumbled.

"Of course you did, G.I. Joe," Kai retorted.

When he looked up, there was no smile on his face, but he winked at Kai, and there was definitely something funky going on with his eyes.

Was that what the authors meant when they wrote about heroes whose eyes sparkled with lust? Dayum.

Waters turned his attention back to the envelope and looked inside. "What the ever-loving fuck?" he growled.

He dumped the contents of the envelope out onto the coffee table and started pawing through what appeared to be photos of Sylvan in a variety of local places, including inside her home. There were also pictures of her in the main bar area of The Library.

The Irishman whistled.

A glance at Sylvan showed Waters' concern. "This is a bit more than annoying messages and emails. This is the first time you've gotten something like this?"

"I've gotten direct messages and emails, but not with… extras."

"And this came to your house? Hand-delivered?"

"I saw the letter carrier come up the walk about twenty minutes before I went to get the mail out of the box. Technically, I have a post office box, but… the letter carrier empties my box each day and brings it to the house. I don't like to go out if I don't absolutely need to."

Waters glanced at his watch. "That was just under an hour ago. He'll be long gone by now. How long have you been having problems before today's delivery?"

Kai looked at Sylvan, who nodded encouragingly at her. "Tell him."

Sylvan shifted slightly on the couch, Kai's arm around her shoulders, head leaning comfortably against Sylvan's. She didn't deserve this woman as a friend.

"The freaky stuff started around Christmas time. I remember because I was running a Christmas card exchange with my readers, and he was sad because he missed registering for it."

The Irishman stood up, hands on hips, and he looked at Waters. "What are you thinking?"

The two men's eyes were locked in some sort of psychic connection. Waters shook his head and looked at the floor. "Shit, this is going to be a cluster. Walk with me."

The two men stepped out onto the back porch, closing the door between them and the women. They watched Waters tell the other man something, then he showed the dark-haired man something from the envelope, and then both men turned to look at Sylvan for a moment.

"The other guy, they call him Demon," Kai said. Sylvan's brow furrowed. "It's a nickname."

Looking at the men on her deck, she could tell that Waters was worried about something. Demon didn't look much happier, but he didn't appear to be arguing against whatever Waters was saying to him.

Demon looked over his shoulder at Sylvan and Kai, then

turned back to Waters, clearly asking a question, and Waters shrugged his shoulders as he replied.

I hate knowing I'm being talked about.

"What's going on, Kai?" Sylvan asked. "Who are they?"

"I don't know what I can tell you, Syl. It's... complicated. All I can tell you is that I'm involved with Waters, but no one can know."

Sylvan's frown went deeper. "No one can know? Jeepers, Kai, what is he? An assassin or something?"

Kai mumbled, "Or something," and then shut up as the sliding door opened, and the two men returned to the living room.

Demon began packing up medical supplies into a backpack while Waters looked long at Kai, then at her. "Sylvan, I know you don't know us from anyone, but based on just what little I've seen, you have a serious problem. Add to that how you reacted to receiving this, and it's probably even more serious than you think it is. I'm guessing you haven't gone to the police?"

"I tried, but the police can't help me because he hasn't actually done anything toward me except send messages. What am I supposed to do?"

Demon glanced long at Waters, then took his backpack and himself out the front door. Waters then looked back at Sylvan. He sighed. "Why do I feel like I'm in that movie about the high school kids you made me watch?"

Kai frowned. "What movie?"

"With the singing and the dancing."

"Oh! You mean *Grease*."

"Yeah. My spidey senses are telling me I'm about to live out the bonfire scene." He shook his head. "Fuck my life."

13

JUNE 15TH

TB

W: Kubrick needs a favor. Conference room stat.

"Already? You two have barely been back together for two weeks," he mumbled to himself.

TB hated favors. They made his skin feel like it was sliding over his bones through oil. He could already sense this was going to be messy.

Unfolding himself from his Humvee, he sauntered through the underground parking garage to the elevator that would take him up to Tribe's offices. As he pressed the up button, a Bronco came careening around the corner and slid across two parking spaces. Rolling out of it from the passenger seat came Nemo, and his fraternal twin, Midas, came bursting out of the driver's side. Arguing, as usual.

"All I said was one of these days, you're going to get caught. Fuck in a bed like the rest of the world," Midas yelled.

"Why?" Nemo corrected him, "That's boring." Both were

booking it toward the elevator where TB stood. "Morning, Godzilla! How's it hangin'?"

The elevator doors opened, and TB walked in, completely ignoring the blond twin who threw himself in the door, trying to escape his brother's tripping foot. TB looked at the dark twin. "You know, assknockers, there's a reason for those yellow lines in the garage."

"Dude," Nemo interjected, "eight of us work here. Even if Kubrick showed up with her 'vette, that's nine cars maximum. There's gotta be thirty spots easy."

"What he said," Midas greeted as he spun through the door and punched the button for the lobby. "Morning, TB."

"It's after two o'clock," TB corrected.

"Well, I just rolled out of bed"—Nemo shrugged—"so it's morning for me."

"Try 'car lot,' not 'bed,'" Midas groused. "Remind me why I left here and went to pick you up? I'm not an Uber."

"God won't let me bring girls back to this fortress of solitude, so if I choose to sleep elsewhere, that's my issue, not yours. Mom!" He pushed.

"Picking up an accountant from a car dealership, then going back to the lot to test drive the backseats of numerous new cars is not sleeping."

TB looked at Midas. "That's a new one." Switching mental gears, he smacked Nemo up the backside of the head. "Be respectful to your mother."

Midas smacked him as well. "Listen to your father."

"Look, I like the challenge; I can't help it. You're all so frickin' normal in your sex." He glanced at TB. "Well, I guess you're not. You need to tie people up, and that is definitely not normal."

"I don't *need* to," TB told him. "It's a kink, not a fetish, you narrow-minded toad."

"Call it whatever you want, Mothra."

Midas lectured his twin. "The real point here is that God's told you not to sleep with all these different women who can identify you, but you just keep on doin' it."

"No worries on the identification." Nemo padded his cargo pocket. "Double wrapping prevents DNA accidents."

"Eww. Do you take it with you when you leave?"

"Hell, yes. I just find the nearest dumpster after I'm at least a mile away."

"What the...? Who the hell taught you that? I know it wasn't me, and it sure as hell wasn't Mom."

"Definitely wasn't our sperm donor," Nemo muttered. "Nah. Came up with that on my own."

"We're dead. Your DNA doesn't exist in any system worldwide. What a fuckwitch."

"Yes, but no point letting it slip *back* into the system somewhere, somehow, now is there?" Nemo reasoned.

"Speaking of fuckwitches," TB interrupted the brothers, or they'd snipe at each other for hours, "any idea what this favor is for Kubrick?"

Midas had a terrible hero worship of Waters' woman, Kubrick, and her language skills. He still hadn't erased the whiteboard tally of her creative swear words, and TB doubted he ever would. If anyone knew what was going on, her evil minion would know.

"Not a clue," Midas admitted. "Waters called, said she needed a favor, here we are."

"And I needed a ride from Carlsbad before the dealership opened, and Cynthia had to go to work, so it worked out perfectly."

TB looked at Midas, stunned. "You drove ninety minutes to pick this loser up?"

"And back," Midas confirmed.

Now it was Midas' turn to get whacked in the back of the head.

After flipping TB off, Midas looked at Nemo with confusion. "I thought her name was Cicely?"

Nemo cracked his gum. "Cynthia, Cicely, Ci-something."

The elevator door opened into Tribe's lobby. TB rolled his eyes. "You are such a whore."

Pointing his finger at him, Nemo informed him, "I do not charge! But I probably should."

Cherry, their handler, was standing there waiting for them. "Perfect timing. You have your physical after this meeting, plus a blood and urine test."

"Bet Demon's excited about that," TB muttered with a look at Cherry.

"So very excited," she agreed. "I believe he requested a hazmat suit from God after the last one. Said he was worried he'd catch something just from looking at him."

"Hey!" Nemo yelled. "That's not nice."

"Then stop sleeping with everything that has a vagina," Cherry snarked.

"I haven't slept with you," Nemo teased.

TB cuffed him around the back of the neck and steered him down the hall, Nemo's arms flailing all the way there. "And you're not going to, Nanoid, so pipe down. Get in there." Midas opened the conference room door, and TB propelled Nemo into the room where Waters was already waiting.

Just as they were sitting down, the door opened again, and the stragglers, Demon and Steel, appeared.

They were an odd group, TB had to admit. None of them looked like they belonged in the same room as each other, let alone working together. But for the past five years, they had done exactly that and did it well. There were moments when he wasn't sure that he liked all of them, especially Nemo, but despite their vast differences, they did work like a well-maintained machine.

Midas had his Oakleys flipped upside-down and riding the back of his head as he booted up his laptop at his seat.

Demon threw his first aid backpack down the length of the conference room table, then threw himself into the chair it landed in front of, making enough room between the chair and the table so he could put his flip-flopped feet up on the edge, crossed at the ankles. He had clearly been out with the waves this morning. While his board shorts were dry, and he wore a tank top over his torso, TB could see that his skin still bore the sheen of salt water on it, and his shoulder-length brown hair was damp, although thrown up in a man-bun, sporting the tangled look of a surfer. He was surly and was quick to throw a punch. Or a chair. Sometimes even a knife if you really pissed him off. The medical bag was not a normal addition at a meeting, however.

Waters must have called him in off the waves. So, the favor involved someone who was hurt.

"Kubrick in an accident?" TB asked, nodding his head toward the backpack.

Waters didn't look up from the papers in his hand. "No, not Kubrick. Someone else needed medical attention."

Steel slunk into the seat between Nemo and Demon. Steel rarely spoke. TB wasn't a chatterbox, but Steel was downright mute. His gray eyes were an oddity in his otherwise Latin features and cold like a snake. And like that same snake, you never knew when he would strike, which made him an incredibly deadly assassin. Together, TB and Steel had made more than a few subjects piss, shit, faint, or vomit after only a few short minutes in their presence.

Waters stood in his usual place at the head of the table and turned on the starfish speaker at the center of the conference table. The telescreen on the far end came to life, connecting to Midas' laptop.

God's voice suddenly boomed through the speaker. "What's going on, Waters?"

Waters looked around the room. "Sorry to drag you all in on what should have been a rare day off. A friend of Kubrick's is in trouble, and while the situation is not normally something we would get involved in, ironically, it connected itself back to our office, and we need to deal with it."

He glanced at TB, an odd look on his face. The best he could describe it would be pensive.

"Remember when I said normal was never going to occur again?" the disembodied voice over the speaker reminded him. "This is what I was talking about."

Waters shifted his attention to the starfish and flipped his middle finger at it, to which their big boss grunted, "I saw that."

"You were supposed to."

"What happened, boss?" Steel interrupted.

"Kubrick got a call just after eleven this morning. A friend of hers was having a panic attack on the other end of the phone. Immediately, Kubrick made me drive over to the woman's house. She was in a catatonic state, and I wasn't allowed to call 911. So, I called Demon in for medical assistance. He treated her for shock, and when she came to, we managed to learn that she's being stalked. It started online, but now her admirer has raised the stakes and brought it to her in person. She received an envelope with numerous photos of her, many of them while she was in the privacy of her house. They were hand-delivered—dropped off at her door sometime after yesterday's mail. Possibly as recent as twenty minutes before she took the mail out of her mailbox. We'll need to check with the post office as to whether or not it was in the mailbox when the letter carrier arrived today, but I'm guessing no."

Tingles started again on the back of TB's neck. He didn't like this feeling. Oily. Cold. Messy.

The conference room door opened, and a very nervous and pale redhead dressed in a mixture of Victorian and Bohemian styles walked in with Kubrick right beside her, an arm around her shoulders as if holding her upright. The pale woman's green eyes darted all around the room, never landing long on any of the men at the table, and then they landed on TB.

Her eyes went round. If possible, she got paler. And then she passed out.

Yup. Things just got messy. Fuck my life.

14

―――――――

JUNE 15TH

Sylvan

For the second time that day, in a matter of a few short hours, Sylvan was waking up to the soft brogue of the Irishman. While his face and voice were certainly pleasant to wake up to, it was rather embarrassing to be doing it again.

Standing from his crouch next to the lounge's sofa, he reported, "She's awake."

"Sylvan, are you trying to kill me?" Sylvan closed her eyes and tried to block out the worried anger of her friend, but it was no use. Kai wasn't going to let this go, but Sylvan honestly wasn't sure how she was going to explain this. After all, what was she supposed to say?

Sorry, I didn't realize that one of these people you claimed could help me had recently blindfolded me, tied me up, and caused me to orgasm so hard that I basically launched into space.

Instead, Sylvan reverted to her usual apologetic self, hoping that would make this whole situation disappear. "I'm sorry, Kai. I don't mean to be a bother to you."

The indignation of her friend was overrun by a deep voice rumbling from the doorway. "Maybe instead of worrying about being a problem for others, you should be more concerned with who's being a problem for you, little Flame."

She closed her eyes as a shiver and a wave of nausea swept over her at that voice.

How the hell does someone get turned on and sick to their stomach at the same time? Only me.

"TB, what-the-ever-fuck is wrong with you?" Kai hissed, her focus temporarily diverted. "Why is my best friend passing out at the sight of you? And what's this 'little Flame' hipposhit?"

Without looking at the woman, Sylvan could feel Kai's eyes bouncing back and forth between the two of them, and the tone of voice suggested she was pissed and suspicious all at once.

This is going to be more embarrassing than waking up to the doctor guy again.

"Kai, you know I love you, but could you please stop shrieking?" Sylvan begged, her hand over her eyes. "My head is killing me, I don't feel well, and I've had way too many shocks today."

"I am not shrieking," Kai emphasized each word on its own. "You have yet to hear shrieking, although that may be coming."

"Kubrick, Demon. I need to talk to Flame. Alone," TB added.

Please, someone say no!

Demon spoke up. "Can you open your eyes for me, sweet colleen?" His hand brushed her forehead. Sylvan opened her eyes and looked at the handsome surfer-doctor whatever he was. "I want you to stay lying down for a bit yet. Don't move until you feel strong enough to support yourself. Do not, under any circumstances, allow anyone to bully you into doing otherwise." He looked pointedly at the two other people in the room. "There's bottled water and a chocolate bar on the table. Both will help with recovery. You cannot leave this room until both are gone." Demon stood, picked up his gear, and looked pointedly at TB. "If she gets lightheaded again, prop her feet up a little higher. More water couldn't hurt. If she's cold, there's an extra blanket." Then he was gone, his flip-flop slaps echoing down the hallway.

She closed her eyes again, her hand still covering them.

"Syl, are you sure you don't want me to stay?" Sylvan actually heard Kai's body vibrating through her voice. Whether it was out of concern or curiosity, she had no idea. Probably both.

"I'm fine, Kai."

Sylvan could hear the glare on her friend's face as she rounded on TB. "I don't know what's going on here or how you know my friend, but I want answers. She's too weak right now, and I refuse to bully her after all she's been through, so get ready, Total Asswad, because I'm coming for you later." Sylvan registered her friend's tone change completely when it turned to her on the couch, that sisterly-bestie thing coming on again. "I'm just down the hall if you need me, hun."

Without lowering the shield she had created with her hand or opening her eyes, Sylvan waved goodbye to Kai. The light hurt her eyes even when closed, but looking at him would hurt much, much worse, so the hand over the closed eyelids served as double protection.

No words were exchanged, but Sylvan heard her friend purposely shoulder-jack the giant man in the doorway. He said nothing in response. All she could hear was the hum of an appliance and the soft whirring of the air conditioning as it came through the vent.

Gradually, the brightness of the lounge they'd taken her to dimmed. When she peeked beneath her fingers it was to find that TB had dimmed the lights and then turned the blinds downward so that the bright sunlight from outside was mostly blocked. He stood over by the window, staring out through a gap in the blinds, shrouded in partial shadows, saying nothing.

She licked her lips. "Which name is the correct one? TB or Lobo?"

"Lobo is my club name. TB is my nickname."

"And what does TB stand for?"

"Total Bastard."

She blinked. "What's your real name?"

"I don't have one."

Her hand tilted up, and she looked at him with one opened eye. "Excuse me?"

"The only name I know anymore is TB." He shrugged. "I'm selfish, cruel, often sadistic, impatient, vulgar—"

A pain hit Sylvan behind her right eye, and she winced, rubbing her forehead above the orb. "I get it, I get it. You're a total... you know."

Gently swinging her legs over the edge of the couch she lay upon, she sat up gingerly. She reached for the water bottle, cracked open the cap, and after a small swallow of water, she straightened her spine. Exhaling, she asked the question she didn't want to ask. "What do I say when people ask how we know each other?"

He shrugged. "The truth."

She huffed out a laugh. "Yeah, I don't think so."

"It won't be news to my team, so the only one who might be shocked will be Kubrick. Waters will give her a demonstration."

She refused to process that. "Why would your team know about us?"

"That conversation is for another time." She opened her mouth to protest, but he held up a hand and cut her off. "I promise. I will explain, but not now." He crossed over to her seated form, his arms crossed over his chest. His entire body was tight with tension. "Start talking."

Elbows to her knees and body hunched over, her fingertips massaged her temples. "Do we have to do this right now?" she asked. "I don't feel well."

"Why didn't you tell me what was going on? I would have helped you."

Okay, I guess we're doing this now.

Did you really think he was going to let you avoid this?

No. But a girl can dream.

"How was I supposed to know you could help me? I didn't even know what you did for a living. Still don't. How could I possibly know that my research subject could help me when we weren't sharing personal details per your request?"

"Why didn't you at least go to the police?"

"You think I didn't? How stupid do you think I am?" He opened his mouth to reply, but before he could get a word out, she snapped at him. "Don't answer that. I can guess."

"You can read minds? Excellent. That will save us a helluva lot of time."

"It's written all over you like graffiti on the sides of train cars," she muttered.

She watched his jaw muscle tic before he spoke, "I do not think you're stupid. Don't put words in my mouth. You have every right to be scared, and you can be as pissed at me as you want for our history, but it was an honest question."

She felt herself getting angry, her body and mind equating his smart remarks with the police officers' lack of sympathy for the whole situation. Her whole body tensed. "I went to the police," she ground out. "They said he hadn't done anything except talk to me, and while I maybe didn't like what he said, he hadn't actually made a threat of any kind. Apparently, a woman needs to wind up beaten in an alley or murdered in her own home before someone takes this kind of thing seriously."

After another swig of water from the bottle, her fingers began plucking at the label on it. "And to top it all off, the one weasel even suggested that since I 'write pornography' for a living, I'd invited his attention, so I really didn't have a reason to complain. Told me I was teasing the guy. Leading him on, so what did I expect? I mean, great gravy—" She looked up at him. "What?"

On the outside, his body hadn't changed, nor his face, but something was definitely different.

"Go on. Let it out. Be pissed," he rumbled. "I'm pissed, so you definitely should be. No one has the right to treat you as less than."

She couldn't hold back the bark of laughter. "No one, huh? Not even you?" She sighed, waved off the questions she had asked, then closed her eyes and rubbed her forehead like she was in pain. "Ignore that. Not even sure why I said it."

When he replied, his voice was softer. Almost apologetic.

"Nope. Not even me." He turned and began walking away. "We're not done here. For now, rest. Someone will be back in a bit to let you know what's going on." He stopped in the doorway and looked over his shoulder at her. "We're not going to leave you stranded, little Flame. I promise we're going to make sure we catch this asshole for you."

With that, he exited. Sylvan lay back down on the couch, her hand back to shielding her eyes.

Only I can get myself out of a mess, think I'm safe, and then get myself into another mess. If it weren't for bad luck...

15

JUNE 15TH

TB

Wʜᴀᴛ ɢᴏᴇs ʙᴇʏᴏɴᴅ ᴛʜᴇ ᴛᴇʀᴍ "ᴄʟᴜsᴛᴇʀғᴜᴄᴋ"?

He felt a headache coming on, and he didn't get headaches. In fact, he couldn't ever remember having one.

TB thought about returning to the conference room, but he needed a quiet place to think. His brain was in chaos trying to figure out how he was feeling, and it was a state he didn't remember being in since that day in the Dizengoff Street diner when his entire world had been upended, never to be righted again.

October 25-30th, 1994
Micah

. . .

"I FOUND *him inside the restaurant, hiding in a supply closet. Tried looking for his parents, but no luck. I wasn't sure what else to do."*

Standing in the entryway of the dilapidated building, Micah's eyes were round in fear. He held the hand of the man in the police uniform. The din of what sounded like hundreds of children in the building was overwhelming. Where to look? He couldn't focus. His eyes drifted up toward the ceiling as he stood in the center of a vertical tunnel of stairs that rose what felt like thirty stories. Those same noisy children were staring at him over the rails and through the spindles. He wanted out of here. The last six days had been confusing enough with the boom, the fire, the smoke, the ground shaking, the building walls tumbling, the screams of people, and the sirens. Then the shuttling back and forth between the police station and the man's home.

When the explosion occurred, he and his parents had been sitting at a table in a restaurant on Dizengoff Street having a late breakfast. A bus had pulled up just outside the window, and Micah had been watching when it burst into flames and flew straight up in the air. The shock blew out the windows of the restaurant, and debris blew into the building. Years later, he would still be haunted by his first memory after the explosion—lying stunned on the floor next to his mother, her eyes wide but otherwise unresponsive to his cries and his small hand touching her face. His tiny fingers had come away slick with the blood that covered the side of her face.

He rolled over in the chaos, seeing people attempting to crawl from the wreckage. Finally, his eyes fell on a brown dress shoe. His father's shoe. Micah crawled on his belly to where his father's body sprawled awkwardly. A large shard of glass protruded from his chest, and several smaller pieces were embedded in his face. His father also did not respond to Micah's attempts to wake him.

His ears hurt, and he was frightened by the muffled sounds that made it sound like he was underwater. Micah crawled to a table in the back of the restaurant that had somehow remained intact and set for the next guests to sit at. Crouched as tight as he could to the wall, hands covering his ears as if that would reduce the pain, he watched as people picked through the rubble, helping loved ones and strangers from beneath the debris. After a while, rescuers arrived to assist the injured. Micah watched those same rescuers examine his parents on the floor beside their window table and then cover them with tablecloths.

No one noticed him.

Much later, Micah watched as the rescuers removed the bodies of his parents from the restaurant in what looked like garbage bags with zippers. He stayed hidden under the table. Somehow, he remained unfound. When people came to investigate the restaurant, he hid in a supply closet behind a tower of boxes. At night, he crept out and raided the cupboards for food. On the third day of his hiding out, he was finally found by a nice man who tried to ask him questions. Micah stared into his eyes, but he refused to answer.

The nice man took him to the police station, but that was more overwhelming than the restaurant had been. There were so many people rushing here and there. At the restaurant, he had been invisible because he'd been hiding. Here, he was invisible even though he was in plain sight.

A lady in a navy blue dress with a briefcase came to visit him. He just looked at her as well, refusing to answer her questions. The lady talked to the man about him, and there seemed to be a disagreement about what to do with him.

For two more days and nights, he traveled back and forth with the man between the police station and the man's home. The man had a pretty wife and two children who were older than Micah. They were all very nice to him, but it wasn't home. They weren't his family. He wanted his mother and father.

On the third day after he'd been found, the man took him in a police car to the building they stood in now. All Micah could do was look around in confusion. In six days, he hadn't cried, hadn't spoken. Somehow, he knew his life had changed irrevocably, and not for the better.

The man crouched down to Micah's level. "Are you sure you can't tell me your name? Where you live? I don't want to leave you here. I'd like to get you back to your family."

Micah simply stared at the man's face.

The man sighed. He reached into his pocket and pulled out a little card. "This has my name and phone number on it. If you change your mind, or if you remember anything about yourself or your family, have the orphanage call me." He put the card in Micah's jacket pocket. When he rose, he also handed a card to the woman he had been speaking to when they arrived. "Hopefully, someone will come forward for him soon."

The man ruffled Micah's hair. And with that, he turned and left.

The woman took him by the hand, and they began to climb the stairs. It felt like they had been climbing forever before she made a left turn and took him down a long hallway to a room that had four beds in it. Each bed had a small table next to it with a big drawer and a single cubby space. She brought Micah to the farthest bed in the room and sat him on the edge of the bed. She removed his jacket and shoes, then tucked him in under the scratchy sheets and thin blanket. "Get some sleep, young man. You've had a rough time of it. Hopefully, the police find your parents, and this is only for a few days."

Even at seven, Micah knew that no one would find his parents. It would be eleven long years of living at the orphanage before he could leave its walls legally and make his own way in the world.

TB SHOOK himself free of the past. Within ten minutes, his team leader found him.Leaning against the door jamb, hands in his pockets, Waters quipped, "I didn't know you remembered you had an office." He looked around at the bare walls, bare desktop, and the computer monitor that wasn't turned on and likely never had been. "Do you even have anything in those cabinets and drawers?"

TB rolled his eyes.

Clearing his throat, Waters entered the office, closed the door, and sat down on the couch against the wall, stretching an arm across the back of it. "We were just discussing how you are going back to your side project."

"We?"

"Well, God and I were. The twins were snickering and reverting to middle school girl behavior, Demon fell asleep, and Steel looked like he was plotting ways to kill everyone in the room, so I kicked them out to continue angles on the Ka-Bar project."

TB grunted. "So, I'm guessing this isn't a social call."

"Nope," Waters replied.

I hate it when he pops that "p" when he says that word. Fuck. Now what?

TB rubbed the back of his neck and stared at the dark computer monitor as if it was going to magically hold answers to his dilemma. After a few moments, he decided to just rip off the duct tape. "Going back to that project might be tougher than we originally planned. I cut her loose when we went to Egypt looking for Zahra and Ka-Bar," TB admitted.

Waters tapped his fingers along the back of the couch as he scrutinized him. "Why?"

TB rolled his eyes. "What I'm about to tell you does not leave this room, or I walk, and you'll never find me in order to kill me."

Waters sighed and shook his head. "Should we pinky promise on that?" he snarked.

"You know that you and Kubrick are melding into the same person, right? It's hot and creepy all at the same time."

"Deflection. Shut up and tell me your deep, dark secret. And no, I won't tell anyone, a.k.a. Nemo."

TB took a deep breath, held it a moment, then exhaled. "We'd been talking online for a while. I figured it would be a couple of conversations and done. But somehow, it turned into every night I wasn't on a project. Then, while we were in Roatán, something changed. I started texting her. The gaps between texts got smaller. The conversations were no longer about the research. It began to get more personal, I guess."

Elbows propped on the desktop, TB ran his hands over his face, over the top of his head, and laced his fingers behind his neck, his face turned down. Gathering himself, he willed his body to relax and return to an upright position in his chair. "I knew within an hour of getting home I needed to get out of here, or I was gonna pound you to a pulp for your dumbassery, so I went to the club. I was twitchy. Thought maybe a scene would help me work out whatever was poking at me. I realized I'd been going to the club for months but never left the bar area. It just didn't hold my interest anymore, and within minutes of being there, I knew that I wasn't going to be participating after all."

TB continued, "By the next morning, I finally admitted that what I needed was to talk to Flame. It was so strong I couldn't have denied myself if I'd wanted to. And then shit got out of hand."

"How so?"

"I engaged her in an online practical application of BDSM. That led to an invitation to meet at the club, which she agreed to the next day."

"That was the phone call you got when we were in the meeting."

"Right. We met up, we had a scene..." TB couldn't say it.

"Ahhhh." Waters connected the dots. "'Out of hand' meaning it went *too* well."

TB looked at his boss with surprise.

"Don't look at me like that. I'm an analyst. It means I take shit apart and look at the pieces to see how they work as a whole." He counted off the evidence on his fingers. "One, based on her reaction to seeing you, she was obviously shocked. Two, Demon said she couldn't even look at you when you appeared in the break room, which suggests that she was embarrassed. Three, she did agree to talk to you, but only if people weren't in the room—so, hurt, but not angry. And four," he added with a shrug, "because I know your defense mechanisms."

Waters stared at TB. Instead of tapping, now Waters' thumb and first two fingers were rubbing against each other. TB didn't know how long they sat there in silence, but as he watched the spidey senses take over Waters' brain, TB diverted his attention back to the blank computer screen.

I know that look. Shit. Here it comes.

Finally, Waters asked the question that TB was trying to figure out himself. "How do you feel about her?"

And that's the million-dollar question, isn't it?

For the briefest of moments, TB considered playing dumb. However, he respected his team leader too much to start now. "I don't know," he admitted.

"Well. Not what I was expecting to come out of your mouth."

"I'm pissed that someone's terrorizing her. I'm thrilled to see her, even if it's for fucked up reasons. I'm..."

"In a panic because when you look at her, your lungs won't inflate? Can't think clearly because you're torn between wanting to kiss the hell out of her and wanting to spank her ass because she doesn't realize just how bad this situation is? In a blind fury because you want to use your bare hands to strangle the shitweasel who's terrorizing her? Should I go on?"

Closing his eyes, TB pinched the bridge of his nose and groaned. "I fucked up. Majorly." TB took a breath and let it out. "I didn't talk to her for a week afterward. Well, technically, I never talked to her at all. Eventually, I thought better of my stupidity. I went back online the night before we went to Egypt to explain why I did what I did or what I'd convinced myself was why I did it, but she never showed up. So I left her an email telling her that I'd given her all I could and that she was good to move on with her research with others, basically. I should have texted her. Called her. Had Midas find her. Anything but what I did."

Waters nodded in commiseration. "Yeah. Know the feeling well." Waters exhaled, moderating his frustration and leaning against the sofa back again. "I wish I could tell you those feelings will pass quickly, but I'm guessing it's going to take a while for you to get your shit straightened out."

"Nothing to straighten out. I'm not good for her."

"Yeah. I had that conversation with myself, and a couple of the team members, as well. Remember?"

"It's not the same."

Waters shrugged. "Yeah, it is, but I get why you feel that way right now. It's going to be a bumpy ride, and the guys, including me, are going to give you no end of shit, but you'll figure it out eventually."

TB grunted.

Shifting gears, Waters gave him the bad news. "In the here and now, we have a connection between Flame and the disappearances, and it's not a pretty one."

"Steel said your spidey senses were tingling."

"Several of the pictures inside the envelope she received were of her at The Library the night you two met up."

TB pushed so hard on the desk, it skidded a couple of inches in Waters' direction, and his chair overturned when he stood up out of it in his rage. He started to make his way to the door, but Waters stood between him and it, placing a hand on TB's chest when he got within range.

"Dude, she's still in the break room. She's safe. Relax."

TB's chest was heaving, like he'd run a marathon across the desert.

"There's more. You need to sit down."

TB glared at him.

"You either sit down, or I won't tell you, and I'll lock your ass up. I can't have you going on one of your typical rampages on this one."

"Motherfucker, I swear to God I will—"

"Sit. The Fuck. Down."

Waters was smaller than him but scrappy. TB knew better than to test his team leader when he went into operator mode, despite the fact that he hadn't been one in truth for almost two years.

TB began grinding his teeth, then whirled around, smashing his hand against the in-out trays sitting on the corner of the desk, shattering them on contact. Standing at the window, hands on hips, he tried to rein in his anger. It was several minutes with Waters standing in front of the door, waiting for TB to collect himself, and TB clenching and unclenching his fists as he stared out at nothing on the street below.

Get your shit together. She's inside Tribe. No one can get to her here.

No place is impenetrable.

No one here is going to hurt her.

Damn straight.

Finally, TB turned, picked up his chair, and sat back down behind the desk. It was another minute before he was able to unclench his teeth and speak.

"What else?"

Waters sat back down on the couch but on the edge of it.

Whatever it is he's about to tell me, I'm not going to like because he's ready to cut me off at the door again.

TB could feel the cold coming over him. It was in these moments that he knew he was most dangerous. Because when he felt cold, there was no compassion, no faith, no mercy, and no justice. Only revenge and retribution.

"There was also a note inside the envelope."

TB felt his heart pounding. His fists were clenched on top of his thighs. His upper teeth were grinding down on the bottom ones.

"He called her a whore. Said he always knew she was one. That participating at the club proves he's always been right about her."

"I know how your mind works. You think he's someone she knows. Do you think she knows who it is?"

"Can't tell. Too much fear there to cut through right now. That suggests to me, yes, she knows who it is and is legitimately scared. Midas is compiling a file on her while he waits for Cyclopes to do its A.I. thing on the photos, looking for shadows, reflections, whatever."

"Fuckin' computer program scares the shit out of me," TB

murmured. "Pretty soon, we won't need Midas anymore. That or he and Cyclopes will meld."

Waters pulled a photograph out of one of his cargo pockets and threw it across the desk. "Right or wrong, I held this one back. I don't think she saw it, as it was stuck inside the envelope down at the bottom. Demon and I, and now you, are the only ones who've seen it. I'll hold off on showing it to anyone else until I absolutely have to."

16

JUNE 15TH

TB

TB REACHED OUT FOR THE PICTURE AND TURNED IT SO THE IMAGE WAS square with his vision. It was him. Carrying a blissed-out Flame wrapped in a blanket and taking her into an elevator. And there was no mistaking the look on his face in that picture. Tenderness. Care.

Way beyond care.

His fingertips held the photo down on the desk, almost gently. But inside, he was seething.

Answering Waters' unspoken question, he murmured, "That elevator goes to the Resting Room off of Tabitha's office. She has it in case of any sort of incidents. Sometimes Doms and subs need to be separated, or someone has an involuntary reaction to something or needs medical help."

Waters stood and came over to the desk. He leaned down on the top of it with his fists. "Who else was around you when you took her to the elevator?"

"I don't remember."

"Think. The area doesn't look very crowded."

TB closed his eyes. A deep inhale, a slow exhale, and he reconstructed the scene. "There were several people there. Tabitha, one of the dungeon masters named Tripoli, and a sub named Medusa was just coming out of one of the rooms with her Doms, guys known as Loki and Gilgamesh." TB opened his eyes to meet his team leader's gaze. "Maybe a couple of other members. I honestly don't remember. I just needed to get Flame to the Resting Room. I was focused on her and her only."

"I thought you said she responded well to you."

"She did. I've never had a sub respond to me like her. Once the scene was over and my brain had a chance to register what had really happened..."—he swallowed—"I freaked out. I had to get away from her. I needed somewhere safe for her to be so I could bolt." TB ran his hands through his hair and leaned back in the chair, tilting it off balance. "The fucker was there, right fucking there, and I don't remember."

There was silence in the room for several minutes.

It doesn't matter that you didn't know. You left her vulnerable. You made the same mistake as Waters did with Kubrick.

Waters stood up. "You had no way of knowing."

"Doesn't matter."

"You're sounding like me from a few months ago," Waters warned him. "Let that shit go right now. Blaming yourself will only get you an extremely high tab at the bar and one step closer to a twelve-step program. Trust me. I know from experience."

Waters perched his ass on the edge of the desk. "There's something else. Steel made the connection while you were out of the room."

TB looked up at him. "What?"

"When did you start talking to Flame about her book?"

He considered the question. "About seven months ago, I think. Sometime in December. Tabitha would know the exact date she asked me if I'd talk with her, and then I connected with her online a day or two after that. I'd have to check my chat records."

"The first girl that went missing? It was December seventeenth. Midas was able to confirm by the check-in records from The Library."

"Okay. So?" TB knew there was something he was supposed to be understanding, but his thoughts were in complete chaos.

"TB. Think about the pictures of the girls," Waters encouraged. "Now. Picture Flame."

It took a nanosecond for TB to remember Nemo's observations. "Flame looks similar to all the girls who have been taken."

"Yes," Waters confirmed. "Red hair. Small. Curvy. Based on what small pieces of info I have from Kubrick, the superfan escalated to stalker around the time she discussed with her readers online about writing a BDSM-themed novel. And the first disappearance, according to Midas, occurred just a couple of days after you hooked up with her for research purposes, something she talked about with her readers online as well."

"What are the fucking odds?" TB whispered.

"Really? Probably not that high. Stalking behavior doesn't just start. It evolves. He's likely been building to this for a while, staking out her home longer than she thinks. My guess is when he discovered you entering the picture, it pissed him off. Couldn't get to her with you around, so he settled for replacements. I bet each girl he took can be linked somehow to something you did in connection to her. Something that upset his plans."

"What do you want me to do?"

"Go hang out at the club with Flame. Talk to people. See what you can find out."

TB was conflicted. If the stalker and the kidnapper were the same person, flushing the bastard out this way would work the fastest. But it put Flame at an awful risk.

"Talk to me, TB," Waters pushed.

"She's not safe at home alone."

"No," Waters agreed. "She's not. So, we've got two choices. Option one, we set up some security at her house since she has none. You can stay inside, and we'll set up a rotation outside for extra coverage."

"You think it's a good idea to put the two of us in a confined space?"

"Who would you recommend instead? Nemo?"

"Like hell, you'll put him with her."

"Option two, she stays with you in your apartment here at Tribe. That is unless you'd like Nemo to house her."

"What did I just say about him and her?"

Waters just smirked.

TB drummed his fingers on the desktop. "Who's going to give her the good news about me watching her?"

Waters got up from his seat and moved to the door. When he got there, he opened it and turned back to TB with a shit-eating grin on his face. "Why you are, big guy." He rapped on the door frame twice, and then he sauntered down the hall toward his own office, whistling.

It was at that moment that TB realized karma had chosen today to hit him all at once because taking Waters' place in the doorway was the worst possible person: Nemo. He, too, was smiling, and he was chewing his ever-present bubble gum with great vigor, like a cow chewing cud, followed by blowing a big bubble he then sucked back into his mouth.

"What do you want, Nuisance?" TB growled.

"Nothing, Jolly Green Giant. Well, except to say that, you know, if you're too old and tired to wield the flogger, I'm up for it."

"You so much as try to get within spanking distance, I will break your hand."

Like Waters, his grin got even bigger. "Very nice. We just set up the bets in Midas' office over how long it takes you to admit that you've fallen ass over tea kettle for her. God is pissed that you're following Waters' lead. Didn't keep him from placing a bet, though."

Oh, fuck. She cannot learn about those bets.

"Get that down from the board. You idiots need to grow up."

"Oh, gimme a break. We bet on everything in this place. Even you bet on Waters and his relationship. You're just pissed because it's you on the board."

TB shoved back from the desk. "I don't want you within a hundred feet of her." He then barrelled past Nemo, heading toward the break room.

Nemo called to his retreating back, "No can do, Andre the Giant. We need to go sweep her house. That's what I was stopping by to tell you. So get your ass in gear, go grab your sub, and we'll meet you there."

Without warning, Nemo pulled an air horn from his cargo pocket.

There was a loud blast. TB stopped dead, shrugging his shoulders up to his ears and holding them there as he tensed up from the surprise. Slowly, he relaxed his body and, without turning to look at Nemo, continued on his way, Nemo's cackling echoing in his ears.

I hate my life some days.

17

JUNE 15TH

Sylvan

When TB returned to the lounge, she was sitting hunched over, forearms leaning on her knees, a tissue being crushed and worried in her hands. Kubrick was sitting next to her, an arm around her shoulders, whispering in her ear, assuring her everything was going to be okay, but to be honest, Sylvan wasn't really listening.

Were things really going to be okay? She had a stalker and writer's block, and now the man who'd given her the greatest experience of her life, then unceremoniously dumped her, was suddenly back in her life.

Kai got up from the couch with a squeeze to her hands, then crossed the room to TB. She fisted his tee, twisted it tight, then pulled him out into the hall, and Sylvan realized that TB was about to get the lecture of a lifetime. She was glad she wasn't him. Those one-sided discussions never ended well. You spent the next day or two feeling like you'd disappointed a parent and that you'd been sent to stand in the corner with a red-hot spanked bottom until you apologized and promised never to do whatever stupidhead thing you'd done to make her lose her ever-loving mind.

A nervous giggle boiled up from inside as she imagined Kai spanking TB and then standing him in the corner.

She was just trying to figure out how to stop Kai's temper tantrum when there was silence except for angrily clicking heels down the hallway. TB entered the lounge looking for all the world like he had not just had a run-in with Devil-Kai.

"Waters has assigned me to protect you from your secret admirer. I'll be staying with you until he's caught."

Stunned, Sylvan's mouth opened and closed several times like a fish, no sound coming out. No kind remarks asking if she was feeling better. No illusion, even, of her being involved in the decision-making process. Just threw the information at her like she would go along with it, no questions asked. "What do you mean, 'staying with' me? Like guarding the outside of the house?"

"No, Nemo will be outside at night, watching the house so that I can get some sleep. I will be inside the house. Twenty-four seven."

"But you can't do that!" she exclaimed. "I have work to do. I have a deadline, which I am severely behind schedule on. I can't have you underfoot, in my space, and interfering with that."

"I won't be in your way. I'll leave you alone to your deadline. I just need to be inside to protect you in case the fucker manages to sneak inside."

"But aren't you busy looking for Kai's brother? She told me that's part of how she met all of you. That's far more important than my problem."

"If I'm needed, I'll be pulled, but right now, we're in a holding pattern with that. If I have to leave, then you'll come stay in an apartment at Tribe where we can lock you down."

She scrambled for another excuse. "But my deadline—"

"Flame, you work from home. A laptop is all you really need, and you'd have one here if need be. But admit it. You'll be much more comfortable at home around your own things."

I hate being talked about instead of to!

"Why was all of this discussed without my input?"

"I wasn't there for the initial conversation, so I can't say. Apparently, it's been determined that my judgment on what's best in this situation is cloudy."

"But it's okay for you with your *cloudy judgement* to protect me? That doesn't make sense."

He rolled his eyes. "I'm the best choice for a number of reasons. One, we have an established relationship. Your stalker has been watching you, and he already thinks we're a couple. So it wouldn't surprise him.

"Two, we think my presence could provoke him into acting. When guys like this get angry or upset, they tend to make mistakes, making them easier to catch.

"Three..."

She prodded him. "Three?"

He looked pained that he'd gotten himself caught in something he didn't want to talk about.

"You said earlier that there was something you'd talk to me about later. Does that have to do with number three?"

He turned his head and looked out the window. "Yes," he finally answered. "But that's probably a discussion best left for a time when you're less overwhelmed, and I—"

There was an awkward silence before she asked, "Won't staying with me be uncomfortable for you?"

"I'm not any happier about this than you are, princess."

Well, that wasn't what I wanted to hear.

After a moment, she nodded and looked down at her hands. "I get it. I'm sorry you all got dragged into this. I should never have called Kai and just sucked it up and not acted like such a ninny."

"His behavior is escalating. No one enjoys their privacy being invaded. And besides, there's no possible way you could have known that calling Kubrick would have put you back in my orbit."

Her eyes searched TB's, then she took a deep breath.

"Tell me the truth. Was it all nothing? Was it just teaching me BDSM language and philosophy? Or was there something else there? Because it felt like there was something there."

His lips pressed tightly together as if he was trying to keep words inside. She swore she saw a flare of regret in his eyes, but then it was like a shield dropped down over them.

Avoidance. If he says nothing, he neither admits nor denies. But really, it tells me exactly what I need to know, doesn't it?

She could feel tears wanting to come forward, but she vowed not to cry in front of him.

As if she hadn't asked those questions, TB informed her, "The guys are going to head over to your place ahead of us to sweep for cameras and microphones. They're also going to install some of our own cameras, inside and out, for extra protection."

She gathered herself together, stood tall, and masked her emotions as best she could. Two could play that game. "Won't that look weird if this guy is watching my place?"

TB shook his head. "No. In fact, it's what most people would do if they were having this kind of an issue or felt threatened in some way. And again, maybe it will piss him off enough to make a mistake."

She gave an involuntary shiver at the thought.

He headed for the door. "Come on. I have to head upstairs to my apartment and pack a few things. Then I'll take you home." He turned back when he reached the doorway. "I'll keep you safe, Flame. I promise. With my last breath, if need be."

Without acknowledging his vow, she stepped toward the door and followed him through the hallway to the elevator.

I'm not worried about you keeping me safe. I'm worried about you breaking my heart.

18

———————

JUNE 15TH

TB

No one had ever been inside his apartment at Tribe. No one. He didn't even invite the team in. One more first she was bringing into his life.

Squash that shit down. Don't think about it. If you don't think about it, it's not an issue.

The other voice in his head just snorted in derision.

He had expected it to feel weird for her to be inside his space. It didn't. However, he did watch her like a hawk as she wandered around checking everything out. Her long skirts dragging at floor level made her look as if she were floating. When her arms raised to run along blank shelves and furniture edges, her delicate fingers extending from the ruffled long sleeves, she reminded him of that elf princess in that movie Nemo had forced him to watch.

The apartment was relatively bare. The furniture had come with the place, and he hadn't bothered to make a single change in the space. The reality was that it was just a place to maybe eat some takeout and then crash at night. He'd never even used the kitchen other than the refrigerator and the microwave.

He tried to look at the room from her perspective.

There was a brown leather couch and chair, a loveseat, a coffee table, and a large-screen TV.

The kitchen was all stainless steel. A couple of stools at the breakfast bar. No dishes in the sink and very few items in the cupboards and drawers. Even his refrigerator was bare except for a couple bottles of beer and bottled water.

Eventually, she floated down the hall.

His bedroom was just as utilitarian as the rest of the space: bed, nightstand, dresser, and chair with gun magazines stacked on it. A plain navy blue comforter on the bed with lighter sheets. Blackout curtains over the floor-to-ceiling, bulletproof window.

He had a second room across the hall, a carbon copy of this room, except it had a green comforter, matching sheets, and no gun magazines. No one had ever slept in it.

And the bathroom had all the standard amenities. Nothing was on the countertops, no towels hung on the towel bar, just a bottle of shampoo and a bar of soap inside of the shower.

He was just packing his laptop into his duffle bag when she finished her tour. "Very you."

He frowned at her. "That didn't sound like a compliment."

"Oh, it wasn't," she admitted truthfully. "Very clean and precise. Sterile. Unemotional." She trailed her fingers along the wall to the small TV table underneath the monitor, which held a DVD player. "Decorate it yourself, did you?"

He grunted, zipping the bag. "No. This is how it was when I moved in. Minus my stuff."

"You mean the gun magazines addressed to the office? And the closet contents of six pairs of jeans, ten Henleys, two pairs of boots, and a leather jacket, all in shades of black and gray. Easy matching, I commend you. Add to that, roughly half dozen sets of gear in various environmental camouflage. Then there are your drawers with about two weeks' worth of socks and underwear, a couple pairs of sweatpants, and some T-shirts and tank tops. That takes up two of the four drawers. That stuff?"

"You went through my things?"

She shrugged. "Well, I figure you're going through mine right now, or your team is, so turnabout should be fair play."

The tic in his jaw was the only sign of emotion on his face.

She gave a cynical smile. "Look at it this way. I refrained from going through your bathroom drawers and the nightstand. I was actually afraid of what I might find there."

His brain tried to inventory the contents. "Only use the top right drawer of the bathroom. Nightstand? Probably better that you didn't. Ka-Bar knife at the ready, gun in the false bottom."

"Darn. You really are no fun. Thought maybe I'd at least find the sex toys."

He would not have been surprised if his eyes were bugged out like a cartoon character right now. "I don't need sex toys."

Then it hit him.

She was teasing him.

Huh. Forgot she was sneaky-funny, didn't you?

One of the things I love about her.

Love?

He smacked aside that slip.

Instead, he said to her, "So I'm depressing and lacking, is what you're saying."

Her lips moved to one side as she considered her response. "Depressing? No. Lacking? Oh, yeah. There's a total sense of someone who has no emotional attachments to anything. I mean, walking in here, I can't even tell where you usually sit. Like you don't even have a butt imprint on a favorite chair."

"That's just... weird."

She shook her head. "No, it's you that's weird." She shrugged. "But that's okay. At least you're clean."

He leaned a hip against the breakfast bar. "And what will I see when I come to your home?"

"I don't know. I mean"—she gestured to the room—"it

doesn't look like this. But knowing you? I guess you'll see what you want to see."

He felt a twinge inside. He wasn't sure what that meant, but it didn't sound good.

19

JUNE 15TH

Sylvan

WHEN THEY ARRIVED AT SYLVAN'S HOME, SHE SAW A BLACK VAN OUT front with a fictitious security company name on it. Two of the guys she'd seen at the office, Nemo and Steel, were hooking up cameras on the far corner of the building. The nosey next-door neighbor was out watering her flowers along the fence line, her ankle-biter dog barking up a high-pitched storm.

The guys must have picked the locks to get inside and hacked the alarm. Given what she'd seen and then heard from Kubrick today, it had probably been child's play to them.

Once inside, her shoulders sagged, and she sighed in part relief, part despair.

A hand reached out to give a gentle tug on a wispy curl hanging loose from the braid. "What's wrong?" TB asked.

"Nothing." Sylvan shook her head. "At least nothing I can control. Elphaba"—she gestured in the direction of the woman outside—"will have it around the entire block that I've just returned home, that there are several hunkalicious men working on putting up a security system, and later on, it will be noticed that a Humvee that has never been here before is sitting in my driveway."

"So?" His expression was puzzled.

A smaller sigh this time, she shrugged.

He went to the window, glimpsing behind the partially pulled curtains at the woman at the property line, not even trying to fake spying on the activity. He turned and looked at her over his shoulder. "Is she really a witch, or do you just call her that because of the dog?"

Sylvan laughed. "You know who Elphaba is? Wow. That's sort of frightening."

"Nemo's fault," he grumbled, looking back through the sheers. "Claims he's a cinephile or some shit. We all have to watch these ridiculous movies; otherwise, he doesn't shut up."

"To be honest, I have no idea what her real name is. But the first day I moved in, she was wearing all black and had this huge sun hat on, and that dog was barking away. It doesn't help that she rides a bicycle everywhere, either."

"With the dog?"

"With the dog. Baby goes everywhere with her."

"Fuck."

"Mmm hmm. Every time I see her on the thing, I hum the music to myself. Then I can't get it out of my head the rest of the day. Total earworm."

She caught a glimpse of Waters at her kitchen island, blueprints spread everywhere and a laptop open in front of him. At the moment, though, he was talking to Kai on his phone. The look on his face was much softer. His inflections were low so that Kai could hear them, but not the men around him. Then he smiled, and she swore she saw his pulse tick rapidly in his neck.

From directly behind her, a warm breath murmured, "What put that look on your face?"

The smile on her face was wistful. "Him. He's so in love with Kai. He radiates it." Her smile disappeared. "I wish I could have that someday. Their story should be a romance novel. But"—she drew herself up—"that's not in my future. No point longing for things that will never be." She turned to face TB. "I'm exhausted and want to crash, so what do you need from me before that happens?"

"Nosey neighbor. We start there." He tapped his watch. "Nutcase, go chat up the neighbor lady. Flame basically said she's the neighborhood watch. Maybe she's noticed if anyone's been around who doesn't belong."

"Roger that. Charm time, it is," the voice echoed over the speaker.

"I take it he's the ladies' man of the group?" Sylvan asked.

"Well, given that we're all 'hunkalicious,' I could have sent anyone. But yes, he's the one that could charm a nun out of her habit, as the saying goes."

Sylvan wrinkled her nose. "Huh. Wouldn't have been my first choice, but whatever."

No way would I subject my first choice to her. She'd take one look at TB and melt like someone threw a bucket of water on her.

"Come on, I'll quickly show you the house. Obviously, downstairs. Kitchen opens up to the living room through the far door. You can also access it down this hall. Parlor on our left." She began to walk from the foyer down the hall. "Stairs to the second floor."

She began climbing the darkly varnished stairs, using her right hand along the balustrade to the first landing about halfway up, then turned right to climb the second half flight of stairs. When they reached the second-floor landing, she gestured left. "My room and bath. I guess you'll be across the hall." She gestured to the right. "There's also an attached bathroom. Closet with extra sheets, towels, etc., next door to your room at the bottom of the stairs to the third floor."

He looked up and down the hall. "What stairs?"

"Oh, sugar! Sorry. Right here." She crossed to the end of the hall, where there was an oddly shaped alcove with a Victorian armchair and table. They stood next to an inlaid bookcase at the end of the hall. When she got to the bookcase, she pulled on the handle recessed inside the third shelf. The door swung open to reveal a flight of spiraling stairs to the third floor. She blushed. "I always wanted a house with a hidden staircase."

"What's upstairs?" he asked.

"Sanctuary."

"Sanctuary," he repeated.

She huffed. "Yes, my safe space. It's where I write." She swiped a hand across her forehead and felt herself slump. "I'm super tired. I don't suppose we could hold off looking at that until later?"

He dropped his duffle bag along the wall and shook his head. "Hang on. If the team didn't clear it, then we don't go up." He tapped his watch. "Waters. Did you clear the third floor behind the bookcase?"

"Steel cleared it. You're good," came the reply.

"Copy." He gestured to Flame. "Just let me take a real quick look, too. Then I'll know if there's anything else I want the guys to do before they leave. You can rest while I help them finish up."

She nodded reluctantly, then moved to climb the stairs. "Hopefully, you'll fit. It's kind of narrow."

"Maybe I should go first so that if I get stuck, you can give me a shove?" he suggested.

"Right now, I'd rather push from the other side," she shot back.

He grunted.

When they reached the landing, Sylvan immediately went to the circular window bed and climbed onto it to pull up the shade. She remained there, sitting cross-legged, clutching a pillow, too exhausted to move.

He had said he wanted to look around the space, but his attention was caught by her in the bed. His next words sounded stuck in his throat. "You should try and stay away from the windows as much as possible."

She watched as he stared at her there, his Adam's apple going up and down as he swallowed. She wondered if he was imagining her there on the night he directed her masturbation sequence.

Serves him right, if he is.

"So"—he cleared his throat—"do you sleep up here or in your room?"

Crawling to the edge of the bed, she put the pillow off to the side. She stepped down to the floor and stood next to the bed, her left hand crossed over, grabbing her right elbow. "Most of the time, up here. When I get deep into my writing, I tend not to leave. The stairs seem like too much effort. So I just curl up in that bed, nap, and when I wake up, go back to work. I live by myself, and I don't usually let anyone in except for Kai, so no one really cares. It's just easier."

"You've locked yourself away."

"Excuse me?"

"That's what your house tells me. Layers of protection. The downstairs level is worthy of a glamor magazine. Everything is perfect and in its place. All laid out to the best viewing options and functions. And like those pictures in the magazines, it's too beautiful to touch."

He turned to face her full-on. "The second floor is utilitarian. Neat. Still looks nice, but it's not like downstairs. Functional. But it's a facade of normalcy. A firewall."

"This room, though." He looked around it again. "This is the heart of you."

Holy Snapchat!

He took slow steps until he was directly in front of her beside the bed. "It's like the clothes. All the unrestricted, flowing window dressing that creates an image. Then the boning and shaping to keep everything that's real trapped inside. Strip that all away, that's when I find you."

Their eyes met. She felt something trying to escape from inside her.

A yelling of "Yoo-hoo!" from the second floor and a clattering of heavy feet as they came up the winding staircase broke the moment.

"Jumpin' Jo'Burg, you climb these stairs every day?" Nemo

asked Sylvan. Then he turned to TB. "And you? How the hell did you fit up that thing, Incredible Hulk?"

"What do you need, Nauseous?"

"Nothin'," Nemo answered. "Just letting you know that Henrietta hasn't seen anything out of the ordinary except for us." He grinned at his teammate, all teeth and gum-chewing, as he smiled and rocked back and forth on his heels.

"Henrietta?" Sylvan asked.

"Yeah, your neighbor. Nice lady. Said I was very handsome. Said the other boys were, too, but that you"—he clapped TB on the shoulder from behind—"looked like you weren't feeling so good and maybe needed some castor oil to lighten your mood. Get things moving again."

Sylvan put her hand over her mouth, but she couldn't keep the giggle back.

Nemo winked at her. "You need anything, Rapunzel?"

"Rapunzel?" she asked.

"Yes. Beautiful long hair. No other name for ya."

TB coughed to interrupt the conversation. "Thank you for the update; now go away," he told Nemo.

"You sure you don't need anything, Rapunzel?" Nemo directed at her. "Hair brushed out? Shoulders rubbed? Glass of wine?" He looked over at TB, who looked like he might actually be smoldering. Nemo looked at Sylvan and said in front of his hand with a fake whisper, "Need me to help you research any sexy scenes for your books?"

She suppressed a laugh, but just barely. "Thank you, Nemo, but I think I'm fine."

"Oh, darlin'," Nemo said. "You are definitely F-I-N-E fine, but this lug? He is not. Henrietta's right. He really does look like he's got an upset stomach." He fake whispered out of the side of his mouth to TB, "I told you not to eat those tourists for breakfast." Then, to Sylvan, he added, "Maybe I should go get that castor oil Henrietta offered up."

TB just rolled his eyes.

"He does that a lot," Nemo told Sylvan, pointing a thumb in

TB's direction. "So grumpy. Very cruel to me in particular. We tried to house-train him, but... they wouldn't let me put a shock collar on him. Said it was cruelty to animals."

"Get the fuck out of here, asshole," TB groused.

Nemo looked at Sylvan with a sad little boy face. "See what I mean? Really only suitable to be a junkyard dog." He took hold of her hand. "If you need anything that Frankenstein can't supply"—he winked lasciviously—"you just let me know. I'll be happy to oblige." He gave a swift kiss to the knuckles of her hand he was holding.

"Fuck off," TB growled.

Sylvan tried not to encourage him, but she felt her smile get even bigger. He was good for her ego, she'd give him that. "Thanks, Nemo. I'll keep that in consideration."

Nemo let go of her hand, clasping his to his chest where his heart would be. With an exaggerated sigh, he turned and clattered down the stairs, singing "As Time Goes By," the voice getting fainter with each step he took back downstairs.

"I'm pretty sure his mother dropped him on his head every day for the first ten years of his life. And I warn you now, never, and I mean never, engage in a game of 'Would You Rather?' with him. The man is a menace."

"He sounds fun."

"He's a pain in my ass."

"Well, you don't like to have fun, so he would be."

With that, she swept down the stairs and closed the door behind her after entering her room.

"I always had fun with you," he whispered to the empty room.

20

JUNE 15TH

Four hours later, the cameras had been installed and tested. For now, TB would be in charge of arming, disarming, and maintaining. In a few days, after things had calmed down a little and Flame was less fragile, he'd teach her the system. He wasn't leaving her here alone, so technically, he didn't need to, but he wanted her to have that element of control if it made her feel better.

Flame reappeared as everyone was leaving. Nemo was last out the door since he'd be on night watch. He gave TB several rapid bro punches to the shoulder, flashing him a teasing look, suggesting all kinds of high school insults he was getting ready to say.

TB simply swatted him away like he was a pesky fly.

With his best Hollywood smile on his face, Nemo sauntered over to Sylvan at the foot of the stairs. Hand held out to her, she slipped her palm to lay against his. Walking backward, he pulled her with him to the front door. Smoothly, he swept her up against the door jamb as he stood in the open doorway. His outside arm was straight up along the doorjamb above her head, his best book boyfriend lean-in going on, her face turned down and toward TB with Nemo's lips inches from her ear. Making sure TB had a clear look at his actions, Nemo took one of the stray curls hanging loose from her braid and wound it around his finger, bringing it up to his nose to sniff. "Mmm. Roses. Very nice."

There was a low rumble in the room.

What the hell is that noise? Was that me?

Nemo brought the curl wound around his finger to his cheek and stroked it against his skin. "Nice and silky."

TB heard the rumble again, a little louder this time.

So, what did the fuckknuckle do? Nemo took a half step closer to her so there was no air visible between them.

A whispered invective beneath his breath this time.

Suddenly, he was thrown for a curve when Flame slid her hands behind her back, one on top of the other against the door jamb. She turned her head to face Nemo, opened her eyes wide, and bit her lower lip.

She looked swept away by Nemo's attention. Innocent and vulnerable. Mesmerized.

Nemo put his forehead to hers. It would take next to no effort for the asshole to kiss her.

He saw Nemo's cheek twitch for a moment, and he leaned in so that his lips looked like they were actually against the shell of her ear. He whispered something to her that caused her to blush, then smile and nod.

This time, Nemo whispered loud enough for TB to hear him. "Remember, if something goes wrong, do what he tells you when he tells you to do it. No joke, Rapunzel."

"I promise."

The curl dropped from his finger, which he raised to draw a soft caress down her cheek, then used to pull her bottom lip free from the teeth worrying it. She closed her eyes when he leaned in to kiss her cheek, then opened her eyes as he pulled back.

The growl this time was clearly heard. Nemo turned his head in TB's direction and winked.

Yep. Nemo's dead. Gonna chop him into a million pieces and send one to each of his conquests. No one will ever find him, and no one will miss him.

Nemo ignored the imminent threat of TB and reached for her hand. He kissed her knuckles again, then he went out the door, pulling it shut behind him.

She immediately locked the door.

"What did he whisper to you?" TB growled.

Staring at their reflections in the glass, even he could see he looked pissed. She shook her head. "Nothing important." They continued to stare at each other via reflection, neither knowing what to do next.

Finally, he started to stomp up the stairs. Flame called after him, her voice cracking with something like worry. "TB…"

He stopped mid-step and turned his face to her. "Yes, princess?"

"I don't think the two of us alone in a confined space is a good idea."

His eyes locked with hers. "It isn't."

"If that's the case, why can't someone else protect me? If you don't want to be around me, why doesn't Nemo stay? He doesn't seem to mind being around me."

Slowly, he turned back to her and descended the three steps he'd gotten up before she spoke, his gaze never breaking from hers. When he was so close to her that they nearly touched, her breathing became labored. He kept his expression tight as he towered over her. "This might be the worst idea ever, but no one —and I repeat, NO ONE—guards you but me."

"I see."

"Do you?" He perused her face, starting at the top of her head and surveying every feature down to her cleavage that was near heaving out of her corseted top. "I wonder." And then he turned and started walking up to the second floor.

Upstairs in his room, TB threw himself on top of the bed and leaned up against the headboard. He grabbed the file folder Waters had left behind hidden amongst the security system plans. Both agreed it would probably be disastrous if Flame saw it, hence why he was working in the bedroom. He was going to have to tell her about the club sooner or later, but he wasn't sure how or when he was going to do that. In the meantime, he'd review Midas' file on her.

Most of it was boring, although there wasn't much there. On top of that, she was such an innocent. What the hell could they possibly find on her? Midas had started it back when the plan was to use her at the club as a shield for questioning but had to quickly drop it due to the intel they began getting on Zahra and the need to get overseas to collect her. Midas had been back at it the last couple of hours. All TB could see was the usual information. Name, social security number, birthday, banking information, tax returns, identification card, billing history, itemized lists of where she spent money and what she purchased. The standard questions.

One thing he had avoided was the information about her romance writing. Midas had compiled a list of the twenty-five romances Flame had written in the last five years. Each title had a picture of the cover next to it and a synopsis of the book pulled from the back of the book. He looked at the first one on the list, her most recent book, *Nature of the Beast*.

Book 25 in the Primal and Prejudiced Series

. . .

BLURB: Paris is in the throes of celebration for the upcoming marriage of Prince Henri to Princess Carlotta until a series of brutal killings puts the city in lockdown. The victims? All are recently wedded couples of the elite class who used the services of Sasha Orlov, a sable shifter with an uncanny knack for making perfect matches.

Desperate to protect his new bride as well as the citizens of Paris, Prince Henri hires Antoine Deveraux, wolf shifter and private investigator, to find the killer. Is the primary suspect, Sasha Orlov, a violent murderess collecting large legacies left to her by the happy couples? Or is there a serial killer hiding in the shadows of the city?

When Antoine meets the Wicked Woman, as the newspapers call her, he discovers that Fate can be a cruel mistress. Sasha is his fated mate. Antoine desperately wants to believe Sasha is innocent, but it's difficult to trust her when the evidence is mounting against her.

In order to clear her name, together they race through the streets and against the clock to catch a killer. Will he be able to prove his fated mate is not the killer before she is arrested and sentenced to the gallows?

BIOGRAPHY: Sylvan Jones, USA Today and New York Times bestselling author, is the author of twenty-five books in the Primal and Prejudiced series. She is the recipient of the Best Debut Romantic Novel Award, the Best Historical Romance Series Award three years in a row, and has topped nearly every "Best Romance" list since her debut novel. She is the top-grossing female writer in her genre.

. . .

INFLUENCED by the diabolical mysteries of Agatha Christie and the gothic thriller romances of Victoria Holt, she writes about the paradox of historical eras gone by with the paranormal, following the sweeping family saga of the Deveraux clan, a family with the ancient curse of shapeshifting in their blood and the primal drive to find their fated mate.

"WHAT THE HELL IS A FATED MATE?" TB murmured.

He pulled out his laptop to look up the term. He read aloud, "A romantic trope that brings two people together that are cosmically bound to one another. This trope guarantees a happy ending as the couple cannot subvert nature's plan for them to be together." He rolled his eyes. "Good grief."

He went back to page one of her file and began to read. One page later, he was done reading the file, other than looking at the bank statements, bills, and book synopses.

He went back and reread the two pages again. Then, he did a cursory flip-through of the appended documents. A frown began to appear on his face.

On the third read-through, he was digging in his bag for a pen, a pad, and a highlighter. The frown was now full-blown, and he was mumbling to himself.

An hour later, he was done. He threw the pen down on top of the legal pad. He flipped one more time through the file, scanning the notes he'd made in the margin and the highlighting he'd done on the appended documents.

What. The. Fuck? This isn't possible.

21

———

JUNE 15TH

TB

JOGGING DOWN THE STAIRS, TB GLANCED AT HIS WATCH AND SAW THAT IT was around ten o'clock. Over the monitor, he could hear some music playing softly in the background and up closer, a swift clicking. Obviously, Flame had made her way up to her sanctuary and was working toward her new release. If he went up, he wouldn't be waking her up, at least.

He heard a rustle over the monitor and a sigh. The keys had stopped clicking, and she'd shut the music off. She must be going to bed.

All he could picture was her in that window bed, moonlight shining down on her as she slept. Internally, he groaned.

There was a creak of a floorboard. Fading into the shadows, he reached for his weapon behind his back, unholstered it, and pointed it down at the floor next to him.

Fingers trailing along the banister, hair up in a messy top knot, she had on a purple silk kimono tied tight around her without any skin showing other than her neck and hands. His throat went tight and his mouth dry at the sight of her. He honestly hadn't expected her to come back downstairs tonight, so he wasn't prepared. Although, what that meant was beyond even him. But he did know one thing.

She was stunning. There was no other word for it.

I want to pull down her hair and make it flow down around her shoulders and back. I want to wrap it around my fist, pull it back so that her neck arches, and then I want to lick her from shoulder to ear. I want to whisper the dirtiest things to her. All the things I want to do to her. With her.

So? What are you waiting for? Nothing's stopping you.

If I touch her, there's no staying away. I'll make her mine, and we'll both be ruined for anyone else.

Surreptitiously, he reholstered his weapon.

"What's wrong, little Flame?"

She startled at his voice, her hand covering her heart.

"Jiminy Cricket!" she exclaimed. One hand clutched the neck of her robe, the other curled around her stomach like she was trying to protect herself. "I'm sorry," she apologized. "I didn't realize you were down here. I'll go."

He stepped out of the deep shadow he had moved into. "It's your house. Why should you leave the room just because I'm here?"

Her hands clasped each other in front of her at the waist, and she began twisting them, picking at her nails, then twisting again. "I just don't want to be in your way."

He walked toward her frozen form at the foot of the stairs. "You're not in my way. I'm the one in your way. Having a near stranger in your house isn't comfortable, I'm sure, even if you know they're here to keep you safe."

"You're not a stranger." She blushed. "Well, I mean, I guess as TB you are, but I obviously know the other side of you, the Lobo side." She glanced away.

He cleared his throat. "So, why did you come down here?"

"Oh, yeah, I got distracted." She blushed again. "I just came down for ice cream. Do you like ice cream? I have lots of different flavors." She started to move into the kitchen.

"It's not something I eat a lot of."

She glanced at him, looking at him from head to toe. "No," she sighed, "looking like that, I wouldn't guess you do." She opened the freezer and took out a pint, then grabbed a spoon out of the island drawer. She looked at him again, worried her bottom lip, then went to put the ice cream back in the freezer.

"Hey," he called out. "What are you doing?"

"I don't need it."

She went to put the spoon back in the drawer. Suddenly, he found himself standing next to her, pushing the drawer closed and holding her hand with the spoon to keep her from putting it away. "If you want ice cream, eat it." He went to the freezer and opened it back up.

Whoa.

She did have a lot of ice cream in the freezer. And she did have a lot of flavors.

"Which one did you pull out of here?"

"It was the chocolate fudge brownie. But I really don't need it," she rushed to assure him.

"Bullshit. It's not about need. You obviously want it, so eat it."

He grabbed the pint out of the freezer, closed the door, then opened the carton. Seeing it was a brand-new pint, he pulled the seal off of it, threw it in the garbage, then went to the drawer she had tried to put the spoon back into and took out another one. Once he had the extra spoon, he grabbed her hand and pulled her to the couch in the living room. Then he glanced at the patio doors.

He tilted his head to the door. "Want to sit outside? I saw you have a porch swing."

What the hell am I doing?

You're trying to give her some normalcy, dumbass.

She looked longingly at the door.

"What is it?"

Her arms hugged herself. "Is it safe?" she whispered.

"Nemo's watching, and I'll be with you. It should be fine as long as you let me sit on the outer side, with you closest to the house." He watched her pale at the reminders that she truly was in danger. "It's okay, little Flame. We can stay inside. I just thought—"

"No," she drew out the word. "Since you're here, I can do it." Her voice was quiet and shy in its delivery, but she clearly wanted to go out there.

But I don't think it's because she actually wants to go outside.

Sliding the patio door open, he ushered her outside and slid the door shut behind them. "Okay, inside seat on the swing. Park your butt."

They sat in the dark, the only sound the cicadas and crickets, him gently rocking the swing with one foot planted on the porch. For several minutes, they ate in silence.

He noticed she was taking tiny dips of ice cream from the pint and decided to broach the uncomfortable topic again. "So, why do you think you shouldn't have ice cream?"

She shrugged. He could see her desire to avoid the question, even in the dark.

"Flame." He broke out his Dom voice as he knew it was the only way he was going to get an answer to the question. "Why do you think you shouldn't have ice cream?"

"It's not healthy."

"That's a bullshit answer."

"Well, you said you don't eat a lot of it, and you're incredibly fit. I'm guessing you're big into protein shakes, kale, granola, and unprocessed food in general. I'm clearly not."

He sucked the spoon in his mouth to clear all the ice cream off of it and chewed around a huge piece of brownie in his mouth. "Kale is not a food. It's pure evil. And I eat a lot of takeout, primarily because I don't cook and have zero desire to learn how. That means I work out a lot harder, and I need to be fit for what I do. But how does what I eat have to do with you eating ice cream? I'm not connecting the dots here."

She sighed. "I'm not exactly thin or in shape."

"Everyone has a shape."

She thunked him in the forehead with her spoon. He was thankful it didn't have any ice cream on it.

"What?" he questioned with a laugh. "It's the truth." He dipped his spoon into the ice cream pint. When it came out, the chunk on the utensil wasn't small, but it certainly wasn't as large as the ones he had been digging out. He held the spoon up to her mouth. "Open," he ordered.

Their eyes locked over her sliding the ice cream off the spoon. He watched her savor the chocolate, chewing the chunk of brownie. When she was done chewing, she looked away. "I guess I feel—"

"Don't you dare say 'fat.'" TB's voice was low with a touch of anger to it. "You're beautiful, Flame. You're all soft and curvy in all the ways you should be. A real man does not want a woman who's rail thin and will break if he spanks her ass or grips her hard around the hips when he's sexing her up." In the time that they'd been out in the dark, TB's vision had adjusted, and he could see that her eyes went soft again. "That was the whole point of what we did at the club. You needed to see how beautiful you are. How can you possibly write about BDSM if you aren't comfortable with your body? And how can you possibly own your sexuality if you can't love what you are? There is absolutely nothing wrong with you. You are perfect exactly how you are, and anyone who loves you will feel the same way."

She reached across her waist and grabbed her right elbow. He'd noticed the gesture happened a lot, signaling she was uncomfortable and trying to protect herself. This time, the expression on her face changed to one that looked like pain. Someone had really done a number on this woman's self-esteem. He couldn't believe she couldn't see how gorgeous she really was.

Sylvan shrugged again, looking out across the expanse of her backyard. "It's been my experience that most men are much more impressed with women whose clothing is not in the double-digit category. Unless it's their breasts. Then the higher, the better."

TB took the spoon out of her hand and put it on the table to his left.

"Stand up," he ordered with a grab-hand motion at her.

Brow furrowed, she stood.

He turned himself in profile to her, one leg up along the seat back of the swing. Before he could overthink about what he was doing, he took hold of her arms and half twisted, half pulled her so that she was sitting on the swing with her back to his chest.

"Feet up on the swing, Flame." Rigidly, she complied. When her back didn't quite touch him, he put his inside arm around her middle and tucked her up tight. He reached for the ice cream and one of the spoons, then brought both in front of them. He scooped another mouthful of the chocolate gooeyness onto the spoon, then held it up to her. "Open."

Timidly, she reached forward with her head to clean the spoon with her lips and tongue. Then he helped himself to another spoonful. "Well, I'm not 'most men.'"

"No, you're not," she whispered.

"I like my women with porcelain skin, emerald-green cat eyes, auburn hair that's so long I can wrap it several times around my fist, and curves everywhere."

He heard a soft moan, one he was sure she didn't even know had escaped her.

I'm so fucked. Oh well.

He realized it was all true. He did like her just as she was. She checked all his boxes. He was not used to being this conflicted. He analyzed. He did what needed to be done. And as long as it didn't have long-reaching consequences, he did exactly what he wanted.

So then, why the conflict?

Because I need information. If I give in to what I want and what she wants, when I have to force the information out of her, she's going to think I manipulated her for it.

What if I just laid everything out for her? Told her the straight-up truth about how I feel about her.

The voices in his head paused for a moment.

Are you saying you want a relationship with her? A permanent one?

I don't know about permanent—

Good, because you'd suck at that.

I could do it.

No, you really would suck at it. Like worse than suck. So stop thinking about it right fuckin' now.

Who made you the knower of all things? I've been listening to you for so long, I've never stopped to consider that I might not suck at it.

His brain briefly flicked back to a conversation with Waters a couple of months ago when TB advised him to go after Kubrick despite the obstacles. He wished he could take his own advice, but he knew that he couldn't for several reasons, the first being he couldn't ever give her the stability in a man that she deserved. There was no "desk" version for what he did.

More importantly? He knew that you couldn't count on people to stay, even when they loved you. Dizengoff Street proved that.

"I have to be honest with you, princess. It's not in me to be any other way." He put the ice cream container on the table and wiped his cold hand on his jeans to get rid of the condensation. Laying his cheek against the top of her head, his inner arm hugged her tightly to him again, and his outside hand picked up her hand closest to it. "I meant it earlier. I'm not a nice person. I've done some really awful things in my life."

"Like what?"

He studied her perfect manicure, the white tips against the clear beds. He stroked her soft skin with his thumbs. "Do you understand what I actually do for Tribe?"

"You protect people. You solve problems that other people can't solve, like rescuing people."

"That's part of it, but I mean what my specialty is."

"What do you do?"

He paused.

"I know you can't tell me specifics. And I'm a big girl, TB; I won't run screaming from whatever so-called terrible things you've done."

"I was recruited because I'm an 'Information Specialist.' Prior to working for Tribe, if you had something you wanted, I could get it. That might mean a client would want me to question someone, put pressure on someone to do something, retrieve someone or something for them, or even make someone or something disappear. Do you understand what I'm getting at?"

He watched her try to process what he was telling her. "You're saying that you've been an interrogator, you've hurt people, you've kidnapped people, even killed people."

"Yes. And it didn't matter why they wanted it. In fact, I always told them I didn't want to know. As long as they could meet my price, it didn't matter."

She turned in his arms and tilted her head to one side as she considered his explanation. "If you were ashamed of what you did, why did you keep doing it?"

He kept hold of her hand, but he leaned back a bit straighter at her words. "I'm not ashamed of what I did. Of what I still do, Flame. That's still my job with Tribe. I just don't make the choices of which projects anymore. That's God's and Waters' job now."

"But you are ashamed of it, TB."

"How do you figure that?"

"You said it yourself. You told them you didn't want to know why. If you knew why you were doing it, then you probably wouldn't have taken some of those jobs."

"Sweetheart, I don't think you understand exactly how awful my job was. Is."

"I understand, TB. I think the misunderstanding is with you. I think you believe that I'm this naive girl who has no concept of the evil in the world because I've shut myself away in this beautiful, old house. I have all these lovely things that are nostalgic to other times mixed with the modern day, and you see someone who has a romanticized vision of what the world is. And I know for a fact that you believe my head is filled with romantic nonsense about love and relationships because of what I do for a living. But nothing could be farther from the truth."

Surprised by her words, TB didn't fight her when she pulled herself from his grip and crossed to the patio door. After sliding it open, she turned her head to look at him. "I write happily ever after stories where people seek the greatest prize of all—love—because I'm more than aware of the evil in this world, TB. For it is love that has the power to raise us to our greatest heights or to lower us to our farthest depths.

"I've seen evil up close, and it is ugly because it lives in the people who sometimes we should trust the most." She looked to the interior of her house. "It's part of why I love roses. Not because they are the iconic representation of love but because while the roses are beautiful and fragrant, the thorns beneath are sharp and dangerous. That way, I'm always reminded of what lurks beneath the surface." She looked back to TB. "I choose to see the beauty in the world, not take it for granted. I work to create more beauty. And if you'd read my stories, you'd see that there is great evil lurking, waiting to disrupt the unsuspecting characters. Like in life, if they are worthy, they fight their way through. If they are unworthy, they perish.

"You're still here, TB. You're worthy of whatever prize you seek."

With that, she stepped through the patio door, sliding it closed behind her. He sat there in the dark, an arm stretched out along the swing back, thinking about what she had said.

Is she right? What I want is her. There's no denying it now. Am I worthy? If not, can I make myself worthy?

Thirty minutes later, he still didn't have an answer to that question.

He got up off the swing and went inside after her, disposing of the ice cream container in the trash. He rinsed off the two spoons, put them in the dishwasher, and stood looking out the window above her sink.

Something wasn't jiving. Something she'd said triggered his brain, but he couldn't figure out which word or sentence or thought was bothering him. Maybe if he studied her file some more, it would pop out at him. But there was definitely something about Sylvan Jones that was not adding up.

Up in his room, he went back to the top page of her file and began reading again. Meanwhile, the distant clicking on the keys of Sylvan's computer as she typed away at her novel in the dead of night reassured him that physically, at least, all was well in the household.

22

———

JUNE 16TH

Sylvan

HER PHONE BEGAN TO RING. A GLANCE AT THE CLOCK TOLD HER IT WAS just after midnight. There was only one person who would be calling her at this hour of the morning.

Ugh. Kai. I don't want to do this right now.

While being best friends with someone meant you held nothing back, Sylvan was feeling far too raw after the day she'd just had. However, she knew that ignoring Kai's call would not save her from explanations and recriminations for holding out on the bestie code. Kai would just keep calling. And if she turned off her phone, Kai would just drive over.

Perhaps it will be easier to lie to her if she can't see my face?

No, Kai always knew. Didn't matter if they were face-to-face or ear-to-ear, Kai knew when she was fibbing. She couldn't even get anything past the woman through text or email.

She put her phone on speaker. "Hello, Kai. How are you?"

"All right, let's get down to the shitstorm of the last twenty-four hours."

Yep, that was Kai. No pleasantries. Just right to the heart of the matter.

"I didn't want to worry you."

"I'm not talking about your stalker," Kai fumed. "I'm talking about the rhinocer-ass in your house as we speak."

There was a guffaw of laughter in the background.

Must be Mr. Intense.

"That's a new one. Nice."

"Thanks. I thought it was brilliant, myself. Seriously, Syl, you better start spilling. TB just stood there like a freaking monolith when I yelled at him yesterday; Waters won't tell me jack-shit, and all because my best friend can't be bothered to tell me she's hooking up with possibly the scariest man on the planet?"

"He's not scary."

"You have no idea how incorrect that statement is. But don't you dare defend the turd-gobbler. Tell me what's going on, and I mean tell me right this minute."

There was more laughter in the background.

Sylvan sighed. "I don't even know where to start."

"How about starting with how you met the man when you never leave your house?"

"I leave my house."

"Oh, really? When? Tell me when the last time was?"

"Yesterday."

Kai growled.

In the background, Sylvan heard, "She's not wrong, babe."

Sylvan frowned. "Have you got me on speaker?"

"No. He just hears everything. Now. Stop deflecting. When was the last time before yesterday, smartass."

"Better smart than dumb," Sylvan quipped.

"Syl... I mean it. Quit fucking around."

There was a long pause. Kai simply waited her out, knowing she'd need to get her thoughts together. It wasn't like she wasn't going to share. It was just that she needed to put things together in an orderly fashion, like a plot.

"Remember how I told you I felt that the *Primal and Prejudiced* series had run its course, and I wanted to try something new? Well, I decided to do some research."

There was silence on the other end of the phone. Then Kai hesitantly asked, "What kind of research? What did you do?"

"Nothing! I mean, not at first."

"At first?" Kai squealed. "Sylvan Jones, do not tell me you went to a BDSM club and got all freaky."

Sylvan heard a groan in the background and a mumbled, "I need to take a walk, or I'm never going to be able to look TB in the eye again."

"Bring me a Zinger," Kai told the retreating voice. "Okay, we're out of Zingers, so he'll be gone for a little bit while he hunts for something we don't have. Spill it. And I mean everything."

Sylvan pulled her feet up into her desk chair, sitting sideways. Whenever she was feeling frustrated with her writing or got herself stuck, the bunched-up position helped her refocus. Now she used it as a means to settle in to explain what happened. "I got chatting in Messenger with Miss Tabby from the Reader's Group. It got to where we were chatting daily, and then we started talking on the phone. She admitted to owning The Library, that exclusive BDSM club in the city, and that maybe she could hook me up with one of the Dominants who could help me research. I told her I wasn't comfortable coming down to the club, but I'd love to talk to someone online. She said she had the perfect guy in mind because he was gone a lot on business, and that would allow us, potentially, to still talk to one another if he was on a business trip."

"And that was TB?"

"Yes, although I didn't know him by that name. I knew him as Master Lobo."

Kai snorted. "A wolf. How appropriate. Does he know that you write about wolf shifters?"

"I don't know. He's never asked, and I never offered."

"So then, how did you end up meeting?"

"We would talk online every night at ten o'clock. If one of us didn't show up to the private chat room by ten after, then we knew not to expect the other one. Master Lobo, I mean TB, told me that sometimes his job wouldn't allow him to talk to me because of the time zones and duties and stuff."

"Ha!" Kai laughed. "Yeah, it's sort of difficult to talk BDSM when you're stuck in a tree watching your boss get it on with his new girlfriend."

"Huh?" Sylvan was confused. Then it clicked. "Oh. He said he worked security for you. That must have been during the fifty-three-day absence he had."

"But who's counting?" Kai joked.

"Anyway," Sylvan drew out each syllable, "about two weeks into that trip, he texted me. Out of the blue. It wasn't often, but he'd text, I'd answer. Sometimes, it took him a while to reply, but then, all of a sudden, during the last few days, it was more common. The last night we texted, it was several hours. Then I didn't hear from him for a couple of days, and finally, he came back."

Silence.

"Yeah. We had some excitement right before he left. That would explain the missing couple of days. He was probably on high alert." Kai paused before prompting, "And...? Keep going."

Kai swallowed nervously. "He said that we were sort of at a stalemate. That he wasn't sure how much more he could give me online and maybe it was time we met for a practical lesson."

A whistle came over the phone. "So? I'm assuming you went to the club. Did you meet up with him?"

"Yes, but..."

"Syl, it's okay. You don't have to give me any details."

The two friends sat silently on the phone for a long while.

Finally, Kai broke the silence. "Did you like it?" Her question was a whisper.

"It was like flying," Sylvan whispered back. "I've never felt so good in my life. And then..."

Kai sighed. "This is the part that's going to make me want to kill him, isn't it?"

"He ghosted me. For a whole week. No email, no chat, nothing. The stupid part is, the one night I didn't log on in this whole floofy mess is the night he decided to log on and explain. I was so hurt. I mean, I didn't expect it to become a relationship. But I did think I'd see him again."

"What did the total bastard say when he finally contacted you?"

"That he didn't really have an excuse for not contacting me, but that he figured he'd given me all he could for my research, and he wished me good luck. Six weeks later, you and Waters take me to his boss, and there's Master Lobo in the flesh."

"Crap on a cracker and hold the cheese! No wonder you passed out."

"It was just the last straw, Kai. It was too much."

"Are you okay there with him now?" Sylvan could hear the worry in her friend's voice.

"Yes, it's awkward. But there were moments yesterday where we were okay."

"But there were also moments where you weren't," Kai surmised.

Silence.

"Do you want to fuck him again?"

"Shush it, Kai!" Sylvan hissed, then grabbed the phone and took it off speaker. She looked toward the door of her sanctuary, but she didn't see him, or his shadow, or hear him moving below. "I didn't... we didn't..."

"You went to a sex club, and you didn't fuck him? How is that even possible?"

She kept her eyes on the doorway and tried to keep one ear tuned to the floor below.

"It was the first time I'd been there. He said it wasn't usual for that to happen with a new member right away."

"Okay, so no sex, but obviously sexual stuff. Are you going to go again?"

"I don't think I'm going to be let out of the house anytime soon, given the circumstances."

"Hmmmm. Maybe you'll get your freak on there while he's staying with you."

"Reindeer on the roof, woman!"

Kai began laughing on the other end of the line. "Never start swearing. The stuff you come up with is frickin' hysterical."

"I don't need to swear. I'm friends with you. You swear enough for both of us."

"I beg your pardon?" Kai questioned indignantly.

"She's not wrong." Sylvan heard the mumbling of Kai's new boyfriend, along with plastic crinkling. "You sent me on a wild goose chase, so you're stuck with Little Debbies."

Kai snorted. "I'm sure you'll get your revenge." There was more crinkling, some crunching, and then around a mouthful of food, Sylvan heard, "So, back to the freaky monkey sex."

Sylvan interrupted, "Kai, I sincerely doubt there'll be any 'freak on,' let alone 'monkey sex,' here or anywhere else. Besides, what would I say? Please, TB. You were so hawt; I want you to tie me up, spank me, and sex me up like a stripper on the glitter and shame pole?"

"Ugh," came the background voice. "And I'm outta here again. I'll just go get the whole box of Little Debbies. I think we're going to need them."

Kai was howling with laughter. "I dare you," she forced around the wafer, chocolate, and peanut butter. "I so dare you. I double-dog dare you! I triple-dog dare you!"

"Oh, great gravy, you are the worst. I would never do that, and you know it. Just saying it to you was creepy. Especially since Waters overheard."

Kai's laughter subsided. "Well, you are an author, and you were already talking to TB for background material. Just tell him since you're stuck together, you two might as well do more 'research' for your book."

Well. Why didn't I think of that?

Sylvan shook her head to clear the madness taking place in her brain. "I doubt he'd believe me when I ask for a sort of 'research with benefits' kind of thing."

Kai was hesitant with her response. "He might."

Sylvan sat up straight. "Why? What do you know?"

"It's nothing I know. It's just that Waters said TB seemed very insistent that it had to be him guarding you and not Nemo, the resident horndog."

A low murmur came over the background again, and she had a feeling she was about to be saved from the conversation.

For now.

"I've gotta go," Kai told her. "I'm being bribed with chocolate to get off the phone and go to bed."

"Eww. TMI. Go play with your blond assassin. Have fun."

Sylvan hung up the phone with a soft laugh and shook her head at her friend. She stood and stretched, placing the phone on her desk. No sooner had she set the phone down and it began ringing again. Without looking at the screen, she swiped the green button to take the call.

"Kai, I don't want to be a part of a triad with you, even if it's just verbal. If you're calling me to—"

A male voice interrupted her. "I won't share you."

Sylvan's eyes widened and dilated with fear. Looking down at the screen in her hand, instead of Kai's name showing, it said, "Restricted."

The voice continued, "You were promised to me, Jolie. You've always been mine. And soon, you'll be mine to do with as I please. But first I'm going to take care of that new boyfriend of yours. And it will hurt, Jolie. I'll enjoy hurting him. Then it will be your turn."

Dial tone.

Sylvan stood there, chest heaving, whimpers trying to work their way up from deep inside her. She heard screaming.

She just didn't know that the screaming was her.

23

JUNE 16TH

TB

With the first note of Flame's scream, he was out of the chair and up the two flights of stairs. When he got to her, she was a whimpering mess on the floor, her phone shattered from her reflexive throw.

"Flame!" He crossed the room, gathered her up into his arms, and sat down on the edge of the bed with her in his lap. She was clutching him so tightly around the neck he could barely breathe.

"Flame, sweetheart, what happened?" He ran his hands over her body, checking for injuries. Finding nothing, he managed to pry her arms from around his neck and frame her face in his hands. Tears were streaming down her cheeks, her pupils were blown out wide with fear, her teeth were chattering, and her body began shaking uncontrollably. "Jesus, woman," he muttered as her skin turned ice cold in seconds.

He stood up, tore the quilts back on the bed, and slid her inside the bedding, tucking her in tight. Then he hit a button on his watch. "Call Doc." As it rang, he muttered, "And he better not be out on a midnight swim."

After three rings a deep voice went, "Yeah?"

Waves were crashing in the background.

"It's Flame. Something's wrong."

"Symptoms?"

"Complete meltdown. Skin is ice cold, eyes blown out, shaking like a leaf—"

"Shock. Lay her down. Elevate her feet. Loosen her clothing. Get her warm. No food, no water until she's back with you."

"Got it."

"What happened?"

"No clue. She's not speaking. She got a phone call from Kubrick. Then the phone rang again, and she started screaming."

"Call Waters. I'm on my way."

TB disconnected the call and went back to Flame's side. She had curled up into a ball, pulling all the quilts over her like she was creating a cocoon. He sat on the edge of the bed and gently began pulling the covers free piece by piece. She didn't fight him, but she had a death grip on the portion she had pulled over her head. "Flame, let go, sweetheart. I'm here. Nothing can hurt you."

He pried her fingers from the quilt, but then she just curled further into herself. He didn't know what else to do. He rebundled her in the quilt and brushed the hair out of her face as he called Waters.

"Cock-blocker," the grumpy voice came over the line.

"Something happened. Flame went into shock again."

Waters' voice went instantly serious. "She just got off the phone with Kubrick. How?"

"I heard the phone ring again over the monitor after they hung up. I heard her answer, and then she started screaming. I'm guessing the stalker finally dug up her number."

Waters sighed. "You call Demon?"

"Yeah, he's on his way over, but I'm gonna call him off. I don't think there's anything he can do for this."

"I'll call him. Just take care of her. Leave the phone on, but turn the ringer off. I'll have Midas start working on it. Conference room at oh-eight-hundred. Bring the phone."

"Roger that."

TB disconnected. He crossed over to the pieces of her phone, picked them up, and reassembled them. Making sure all the pieces were present and the ringer was turned off, he set it on the edge of her desk.

Returning to the edge of the bed, he could see she wasn't shaking as violently, but she was still shivering. Without thinking about what he was doing, he pulled off his boots, then propped himself against the headboard. He gathered her to him so they were face-to-face, pulling her legs up over his, and tucked her close to his side. She was still in her robe and nightgown, so he didn't need to loosen anything, but he did use his free hand to undo her hair, gently combing through it with his fingers. Pulling the quilt up to her neck, he cocooned her in the blanket as he had during aftercare. He held her close, brushing his chin back and forth across her forehead until she fell into a restless sleep. He thought about getting out of the bed then, but he stayed and stared out the window into the night.

I'm coming for you, asshole, whoever you are. She may not be able to be mine, but I will protect her like she is. With my last breath.

HE FELT it as she drifted up from the depths of sleep and knew the exact moment her body registered that something was off. Groggily, she tilted her head to the bookcase above her to check the clock. It was just after five a.m. "Go back to sleep, princess. You don't need to be awake yet."

She turned in the direction of the voice to see TB holding her close, one arm around her shoulders, the other around her waist. Their legs were tangled together under the comforter. Within seconds, the events of the previous night must have slammed into her memory, causing her to gasp and lock in place.

"Shhh," he comforted her, his arms pulling her tighter to him. "You're safe."

"I'll never be safe," she whimpered.

"You saying I can't protect you?" he rumbled.

"I know you think you can. But he threatened you, and he meant it."

There was a pause as he processed her words. "Breathe, Flame. No one's getting to me. The house is alarmed. Nemo was outside all night. Midas is already working on tracing the call." Lightly, he brushed his chin against the top of her head. "We've got a lot to talk about today, so I need you to rest while you can."

"I don't think I can go back to sleep."

"You don't have to. Just rest."

They lay together in the bed, not talking, not looking at each other, just tangled up in each other, warm and comfortable. He felt one hand slide up his stomach to rest on his chest, the other between their bodies, gripping his T-shirt tightly.

He absently pressed his lips against her head.

She burrowed down further into the mattress and bedding, and TB pulled her closer again.

At six-thirty, he roused her out of bed. "We have to be at Tribe by eight. I'm sorry to drag you with, but after last night, I can't leave you here alone, and the team needs to meet. Bring your laptop. You can work in my office after the meeting."

"You have an office?"

"This surprises you?"

"Difficult to see you behind a desk."

"I didn't say that I used it, just that I have it. My workspace tends to be the armory bench table."

"Now that I can see."

She floated downstairs to her room, and shortly thereafter, he heard the shower start up. Today was going to be a rough one for her. She was going to get asked a lot of questions, most of which she wasn't going to want to answer, and all of them were going to make her uncomfortable.

He jumped in the shower, dressed, then headed downstairs to clean up his mess from before he ran upstairs in the early morning hours. Luckily, she was still upstairs getting ready, or he would have had a lot of explaining to do. In reality, she was the one who had a lot of explaining to do, but he'd rather be on the offensive for the conversation than try to backpedal with her like he would have been if she'd seen he was aware she had secrets.

Files pocketed into his laptop sleeve, security files neatly piled on the dining room table, he began to poke around in her kitchen. "Who doesn't have coffee?" he mumbled.

"Me," the soft voice came from behind him. "I never acquired the coffee craving other human beings seem to have been born with."

"What do you do for caffeine?" he grouched.

She shrugged. "Don't really need it. I live by myself and keep to my own schedule, so when my body wants to sleep, I go to sleep. When it wants to wake up, I get up. Caffeine isn't necessary for that lifestyle."

"How does your body develop a normal sleep rhythm?"

"It doesn't. I know it's not healthy, but to be honest, sleep and I have an odd relationship anyway." She was picking at an imaginary thread on her wrist cuff.

Evasion. File that away, along with the "odd relationship" comment.

The ride into Tribe was quiet. He knew she wasn't thrilled about being pulled out of her home to spend the day at his workplace, but she didn't complain. Meeting as a large group at her house would draw more attention than they wanted, so they needed to meet somewhere it wouldn't, which was the office.

He dropped off her computer bag in his office and then

escorted her to the conference room. Cherry already had coffee and a continental breakfast in the room, so he got her settled in his regular seat, which put her next to Midas.

"Good morning, Rapunzel!" Nemo greeted. "Since your fire-breathing dragon isn't going to ask, what can I get you to eat and drink?"

She shook her head. "I'm not hungry," she told him.

TB lowered his register when he spoke. "Flame, all you had to eat last night was ice cream, and you didn't eat this morning before we got here. You need to eat something. So, either pick something to eat and drink, or I will, and you will eat every bite of it whether you like it or not."

She looked up at TB. "Dom voice, much?"

He leaned closer to her and whispered, "You're going to get more than the voice if you keep this up. And I won't wait until I get you home."

He watched her eyes flick over his expression, almost like she was considering being a brat on purpose. Instead, she rolled her eyes. "Danish, please."

"I know you don't want coffee. Do you want Cherry to make you some tea? I saw that at the house."

Before she could say not to bother, Cherry interjected, "I'm already making some for myself. I'll get you a cup."

She frowned at him.

"She really does make some every day," he reassured her.

TB went over to the side table. He gave Nemo a shove. "I'll get her food, Nutjob."

Midas sidled up next to him. "Cherry picked up the raspberry ones for her special," he whispered.

TB looked at him with a scowl.

"It's on her Facebook page. I finished her book already, and I was bored." Midas shoved a doughnut in his mouth and walked back to his seat.

TB wrinkled his face in distaste. There was way too much there to unpack. He shook his head and put a raspberry danish on a plate, put some breakfast fruit salad in a cup, grabbed a fork and some napkins, and then took them over to her at her seat.

Midas was already at his spot at the head of the conference room table, teasing her about something, and he had a book between them that she was writing in.

"What the hell?" TB asked.

Midas smirked. "Just getting her autograph."

"I thought you were already dating Alexa?" he asked.

"Nope. Siri. Alexa is our love child." Midas winked at Sylvan. "Thanks, Flame. I'm gonna try out pages one hundred thirty-four through one hundred forty-seven sometime."

"Oh, good grief," TB muttered as he went back to the food. Once he got there, he turned back, flashing a look between the two laughing faces. "What's on page one hundred thirty-four through one hundred forty-seven?" he asked suspiciously.

Nemo hopped into the seat on her other side with his own book. "Oh, no, Total Bookworm. You'll have to learn to read first. Then you can read it and find out for yourself." He winked and gave two clicks of his tongue. "Totally worth it, buddy." His attention went completely to Flame. "Good morning, again, Rapunzel. Will you sign mine as well?"

TB watched her smile and turn to the title page. Then he looked around the table. "Am I the only one concerned about this?"

Waters just smirked and tried to hide it behind taking a sip of his coffee.

TB narrowed his eyes at him.

"What?" Waters shrugged. "Page one hundred thirty-four through one hundred forty-seven is fuckin' hot. You should try it. Worked for me." The last sentence was muttered into his coffee.

"Oh, for fuck's sake," TB muttered, grabbed his coffee, and crossed over to the seat beside her. After he put his cup down, he grabbed the chair Nemo was sitting in, pulled it from the table, unceremoniously dumped him out of it, then put it back to the table and sat down with his own butt in it.

Nemo went and sat in his usual seat on the opposite side of

the table, to the right of his brother and directly across from Flame, smiling from ear to ear. "This seat's better anyway. I can sit here and gaze at her without getting a crick in my neck."

Flame was blushing, and TB did not like it one bit.

She's not going to succumb to his shit, is she? I'll kill him.

A booming voice came out of nowhere. "Is everyone here?"

Flame looked around the room. TB motioned to the speaker in the center of the table and mouthed, "Our boss."

"All right, everyone, let's get going." Waters focused everyone's attention. "So, already, we've had an escalation in contact. Looks like our security system pushed him into making a call. Midas, were you able to pull it off the system?"

"Yup."

Flame's posture went ramrod straight, and all color fled from her face. Midas looked at her. "I only pulled your conversation with him, not with Kubrick."

She clearly understood that Midas had heard the other conversation as well. Midas put a hand over hers that were shredding the napkin in front of her. He leaned in to whisper in her ear, "I promise." Midas' eyes glanced quickly at TB.

She nodded, immediately stopped shredding the paper, and withdrew her hands, putting them, tightly clasped, in her lap.

"Okay, here comes the playback," Midas warned her.

"Kai, I don't want to be a part of a triad with you, even if it's just verbal. If you're calling me to—"

"I won't share you."

"You were promised to me, Jolie. You've always been mine. And soon, you'll be mine to do with as I please. But first I'm going to take care of that new boyfriend of yours. And it will hurt, Jolie. I'll enjoy hurting him. Then it will be your turn."

There was a dial tone, a scream from Flame, the thunk of the phone hitting the floor, and then nothing.

"Call lasted sixteen seconds from connect to disconnect. Burner phone, but he was close by. Within a mile," Midas said.

"How did he get past Nemo?"

Nemo frowned. "No one got past me. But I was pretty close to the house in the big cedar tree."

"He didn't necessarily need to be by the house," Midas explained. "Depending on how he's monitoring, a telescope and a clear sightline is all he would have needed. He could have been in a lot of different places. All he needed to know was that her line was clear. We swept for bugs and cameras. Found nothing."

"Well, if his comments are anything to go by, he clearly knows about TB and that he's connected to Flame," Waters observed.

"Play it again, Midas," God barked.

They listened to the recording again.

"He said, 'You were promised to me.' Odd turn of phrase," Steel commented.

Waters nodded. "Like it's connected to something before. Do you know what he's talking about, Flame?"

TB watched her closely. Her eyes were watching her hands twist in her lap.

"No. I've no idea."

Truth.

"Do you recognize anything about the voice? I know it's going through a synthesizer, but anything about the language used or the cadence of the speech pattern?" Midas asked. He played the recording again. "Anything?"

Flame shook her head, eyes still not leaving her lap.

"Flame." TB used his Dom voice. "Look at me."

She looked up into his eyes.

"Do you recognize that voice?"

Her gaze was solid on his, but her breathing was elevated. "That voice doesn't sound like anyone I know in L.A."

Okay, that's the truth, but something's not right.

The men in the room looked around at each other.

"You're sure?"

"Positive."

Answered too fast, and her eyes are still locked. She's working to hold my gaze.

"And you have no idea why he would think you were promised to him?" Waters asked.

She looked at Waters. "I didn't promise to date or 'be' with anyone."

Truth.

"What about before L.A.?"

Her body stiffened, and her face paled further. "What do you mean?"

She's stalling.

"Did you make any promises to anyone before you came to L.A.?" Waters asked.

"What makes you think I haven't lived in L.A. all my life? And even if I had, I've never dated anyone, promised to date anyone, been engaged, or anything similar."

Never dated anyone? She said she wasn't a virgin.

Waters just stared at her. His gaze was like a hawk on a telephone wire, watching its prey in the grass for a while before it struck.

"I know you didn't. There's no record of a Sylvan Jones in L.A. prior to 2017. No driver's license, no tax return, no school records, no medical records."

Waters continued to stare at her for a few more moments, then leaned forward on the table's edge, forearms supporting him on the conference room table. "Flame, we can't help you if you won't tell us the truth."

"I have told you the truth. I haven't made any promises to anyone."

"Who's Jolie?"

The question over the speaker was a bomb in the room. God went right for the jugular.

"J-Jolie?" Sylvan stuttered.

"Ms. Jones," God continued. "Who. Is. Jolie?"

"I don't know."

"You're lying, little Flame," TB murmured next to her.

"Maybe it was a wrong number."

"Another lie, princess. Remember what I told you about honesty?"

She whirled on him, her emerald eyes flaming with rage. "This is not a BDSM scene, TB. Don't start trying to rack up punishments that neither of us has any intention of following through on."

The room was so quiet all he could hear was the hum of the digital clock on the wall.

They stared at each other. She didn't back down, and he certainly wouldn't.

Without looking away from her, TB spoke out, "Midas, put the photos of the girls on the screen."

TB hated this, but rattling her was the best possible option right now.

The five girls who had disappeared over the past seven months blinked into existence on the telescreen behind Waters. She looked at them blankly.

He leaned back in his chair, leaning on his hand, his index finger and thumb forming the arch to keep him in place.

"Do you know who any of them are?"

She shook her head and turned to TB in confusion. "No. Should I?"

Definitely not a lie. A little curiosity but no recognition.

"These five girls have all gone missing over the past seven months."

"That's terrible," she exclaimed. "Are you looking for them?"

"Yes, we are," Waters said. "But we've run out of leads."

"I don't understand. Why would you ask me about them?"

"Look at them again, Flame," TB ordered.

She studied them.

"What do you notice?"

She looked at TB, more confused. "I don't understand."

"Look at them. Really look at them. What do you notice?"

Exasperated, she turned her head back to the screen and looked over the women. He watched her eyes, her mouth, her facial muscles. He watched her hands and her posture.

Her eyes went from jumping from woman to woman to moving more smoothly from one to the next. Her fingertips gripped the edge of the table, and she leaned slightly forward in her seat. She inhaled slowly.

There it is.

No one in the room said a word as they watched her.

"They all look similar."

Waters spoke up. "Describe them to me, Flame. If you had to give someone a description of them as if they were one person, what would you say?"

"I'd say they were all young women, in their early twenties, I'm guessing. They have pale skin. They look... rounder? I don't know what word I'd use. They're not skinny, that's for sure, but not overweight. They all have red hair, sort of auburn, like..." She trailed off. She swallowed, then looked at TB. "The color of mine. And long."

"Yes, princess," he confirmed. "They all look similar to you."

"But I don't understand. I don't know them. I mean, it's a little creepy looking at them, but what do they have to do with me? You don't think I had something to do with them being missing?"

"No, Flame," Waters assured her. "But it does concern us that they look similar to you, given the circumstances."

"I don't mean to sound insensitive, but there are lots of missing women in the world, including L.A. Millions of them are probably redheaded and built a little curvy. Why do they connect to me?"

TB continued to watch her.

Waters explained, "The fifth one, Tilly Moll, disappeared on March twenty-ninth from the parking lot of The Library. The other four, the last place any of them were seen, was at that same club. We can't say for one hundred percent certainty that they disappeared from there, but we're pretty sure."

"But still—"

"The first one disappeared seven months ago," TB interrupted. "Just after you and I made contact. Just after the audio discussion with your readers about your intent to write a BDSM romance with the help of a consultant." TB grabbed one of her hands and gave it a squeeze of reassurance. "The night that you met me at The Library, your stalker saw us. He was there."

Waters handed the private photo to TB, who slid it in front of her with his free hand. "But then I was gone for work. We were out looking for Ka-Bar outside the country. So he must have thought I was out of the picture. He waited. Then something upset him, and he made contact at the house. And then I moved into the house, and he took another step forward and called you."

Her eyes filled up with tears, and she looked back at the photos on the screen. "They're missing because of me."

"Not because of you, Flame," Waters redirected. "He hasn't been able to get to you because you stay inside. There's been no suitable opportunity. So, he's been taking these other girls from the club because they remind him of you. But now his plans are being upset because TB is back in the picture."

One hand went over her mouth, one arm around her stomach. "I feel sick," she murmured.

TB swept her up in his arms and took her out of the conference room and to the ladies' room down the hall. No sooner had he set her down on her feet, she ducked into the stall and vomited everything she had eaten and drank that morning.

He grabbed several paper towels from the dispenser and wet them down with cold water. One he folded into a small, neat rectangle. He stepped around the wall and into the stall, bent over, and swept Flame's hair off to the side to place the rectangle towel on the back of her neck. Making sure to keep her hair out of the toilet and vomit, he began to dab the other paper towel along her sweating brow.

"It's all right, sweetheart. Get it all out."

He handed her a third wet towel to wipe her mouth, then rubbed her back in small circles to comfort her.

After a short while, he heard her make a noise that sounded like a laugh but not a happy one. Then she spoke.

"You're going to ruin your reputation with them."

His hand still rubbing her back, he asked, "Why's that?"

"Total bastards don't comfort women who are vomiting."

"I just don't want Cherry kicking my ass for not doing it," he lied.

She sighed, sitting up on her heels, and looked up at him. "Not exactly how I thought I'd end up on my knees in front of you."

He blinked at her. He thought his mouth might be making fish faces because he could feel it moving, but nothing was coming out.

Did she seriously crack a sex joke? Now?

"Ex-cu-cuse me?" he finally stuttered.

"Well, I mean, you've gotta admit, it's sort of funny." She grinned weakly, a hand moving, gesturing between them. "You're a Dom. I'm a sub. Women's bathroom, I'm on my knees in front of you."

He swallowed. "Nothing funny about it."

She shrugged and started to get up off the floor. Without thinking, he reached underneath her arms and lifted her up to stand. As soon as she was on her feet, he let go and took a step back from her. Then another.

"I'll, umm..." He darted a look around the bathroom. "I'll let you freshen up."

And then he tucked tail, and if he could have run, he would have. As it was, he nearly steamrolled Cherry over as she came through the door with a toothbrush and toothpaste brought from her apartment upstairs.

24

———————

JUNE 16TH

Sylvan

SYLVAN ONCE AGAIN SAT IN THE LOUNGE AT TRIBE WHILE TB FINISHED meeting with the team. She'd started in his office. An hour later and nothing had been accomplished. Perhaps a change of scenery? The office was so sterile, and on top of that, she felt like she was invading his space, which was stupid since he'd already told her he hardly ever went in there. But the uncomfortableness remained, so that's when she'd moved to the break room.

She'd been here another hour and was getting more and more frustrated. She'd tried working on her newest manuscript, but the chair at the table was uncomfortable. She'd tried editing a paper copy of her up-and-coming book, but her brain wouldn't stay focused, and she worried she was making it worse, not better. She'd tried reading a book, but she kept picturing TB as the hero and herself as the heroine, and that wouldn't do at all.

She vaulted herself off of the couch and began frantically pacing back and forth between it and the window.

Sassafras! The man is a menace, even when he's not in the room!

Cherry walked into the lounge to get the new coffee urn and saw Sylvan pacing. On her pass back to the couch, Sylvan swore she saw a grin on Cherry's face, but since she was in profile, Sylvan wasn't one hundred percent sure. She threw herself back down on the couch. Even pacing was frustrating her.

"TB? Or your novel?" Cherry asked without turning around.

Sylvan sighed in response.

"I'll take that as a 'yes' to both."

Out of her peripheral vision, Sylvan saw the impeccably suited Cherry standing with a teacup in her hand. Looking up at the administrative assistant, she saw the teacup being extended out to her, which she gratefully took with a quiet "Thank you."

"May I?" Cherry gestured to the couch.

Sylvan nodded and sipped her tea. Cherry perched on the arm, crossing her perfectly toned legs, one hand laying on top of the other on her thigh. Sylvan stared in silence at the woman's burgundy painted nails, the gold glitter swirl overlay winking in the fluorescent lights. They sat for a few moments like that before Sylvan burst out with, "His name should be Total Butthead! Why is he so... so...?"

"Buttheaded?" Cherry supplied.

"Yes! That! And aggravating! Closed off! Domineering! Frustrating!" She looked at Cherry's sympathetic expression. "Disturbing," she finished.

Cherry smiled. "The puzzle that is our beloved Total Bastard."

Sylvan snorted. "The man drives me kookoo."

"I'm guessing the feeling is mutual."

Sylvan shook her head in denial. She sat hunched over the teacup, elbows on her thighs, staring into its depths as if somehow the answers she was looking for were in it.

"I don't even think he likes me very much sometimes. I thought he did, when we were first getting to know each other online. I mean, he was very polite and helpful with my research. And then when we met at the club..." She blushed as she snuck a peek at Cherry. "I really thought he was attracted to me. Now? I get glimpses of someone who's capable of feeling, like earlier when I was sick, but other times he's pushing me away so hard it's like I'm going over the edge of the Cliffs of Insanity."

"Mmm. Yes, he's definitely more of The Man in Black than Wesley."

They both snickered at the analogy.

"Unfortunately," Cherry continued, "that sounds exactly like TB. You know, he doesn't let others see the softer side of him. But his past has been darker than most of the guys, and he doesn't believe he deserves anything good because of the choices he's made. I'll share my secret." Cherry lowered her volume. "He leaves me chocolate eclairs, my favorite, on my desk on my birthday every year, but he never admits to it. I had to catch him in the act on the security cameras to figure out who it was."

Sylvan melted a little inside. "What happened to him? Why is he so shut off from the world? All he sees is the negative."

Cherry sat up straight, smoothing her hands down the already impeccable skirt of her navy blue suit, clasping her hands in her lap, mimicking a prim school teacher. "Hopefully, someday, he'll share that story with you. Waters is probably the only one who's privy to all of it since he did the intel and recruiting."

She grabbed hold of Sylvan's wrist. Her voice was almost pleading in its intensity. "Don't give up on him. He's a better man than he believes himself to be. Oh, he'll try to convince you otherwise, but he's been different since he connected with you. And it doesn't hurt that he's halfway in love with you."

Sylvan outright laughed at that. "You could not be farther from the truth. He sees me as a silly little girl, living in my castle surrounded by briars and thorns, awaiting true love's first kiss to wake me so that I can live my happily ever after."

Cherry smiled. "I think the prince already did that. Getting to you was the easy part. Unfortunately, he didn't think about what happened after he awakened you with his kiss."

"I have a million creative ideas," Sylvan mumbled under her breath.

Cherry chuckled at that. "Oh, I'm sure you do. And I'm sure he has just as many, if not more, about what to do with you. But now he's a little torn. I don't know a lot about the world of kink, but I'm guessing he's feeling a little vulnerable right now, and that's not normal for a Dominant personality. That vulnerability is warring with his need to protect you, and if he allows himself to be vulnerable with you, my guess is that makes him feel weak. Like he might fail because he's distracted by his feelings for you."

"I've yet to see him show weakness of any kind."

Cherry smiled sadly. "TB has... abandonment issues. It goes back a long way. They'll probably always be with him. They certainly won't go away overnight. He sees his friend fall in love with a strong woman, and it wouldn't surprise me if he's jealous of that. If there's anything that TB needs, it's love. But it's been so long since he's truly had it, he doesn't recognize what's right in front of him or what he's feeling, and he certainly doesn't know how to handle it.

"Knowing TB, loving someone means giving up control. He does not do that well, which is probably why the Dominant factor in his personality is so incredibly strong. And people respond to it, even men."

"I don't want him to give up his control." She looked at Cherry, eyes wide, realizing how that might sound. "I don't mean the Dominant thing."

Cherry full-out laughed. "Oh, yes, you do. But I understand that it's not just that."

She gave Sylvan's arm a quick squeeze, then stood up to return to her desk. "All of my boys are desperately in need of someone to love them. Please don't give up on him." She walked to the door and turned back before exiting. "You're good for him, Sylvan. He needs to balance out the darkness, and you do that. Everyone sees it except for the two of you, which is often how it is in your books. So instinctively, you know this. Give him space to work it out. He'll get there eventually."

With that, she walked down the hall to her desk. Sylvan sat quietly, contemplating the tea in her cup, thinking hard about Cherry's words.

Is she right? Can I reach him?

Suddenly, something clicked in her head. She stood up, crossed to the table, and sat down. She was so focused she didn't notice the uncomfortableness of the chair.

All the elements were there. She had characters. She had a what, where, and when. The how and why might be murky yet, but that's what she was best at—weaving the world of the characters into a story.

So, in her head, like a spider spinning her web, she began to weave a plot.

At the top of a new page in a new document, she centered her title.

Seduction of the Bastard Wolf.

She began to type.

25

———————

JUNE 16TH

TB

TB STORMED INTO THE CONFERENCE ROOM. "HAVE YOU ALL LOST YOUR goddamn minds?!"

The group was sitting around the conference table in the same positions as before when he had hustled Flame out of the room. Folders in front of them, except for Waters, who stood up near the screen between the table and the window, holding his folder open with a page flipped over the top, and looked at him expectantly. "She's not some HVT. She's the client." TB grabbed the remote and turned off the telescreen that had held her photo there, then threw the remote back down on the table.

"Midas," Waters intoned. Midas grabbed the remote and turned the telescreen back on, smiling as he did so but not looking at TB.

That's right. Don't look at me with that smile on your face, douchebag. If you do, I'll knock your perfect teeth out of that mouth of yours.

"Never seen you get all hepped up about a client before," Waters commented without looking up at him.

TB stalked around the top of the table to where Waters stood and snatched the folder from him. "This is bullshit, and you know it."

Questioning eyes looked up into TB's face as he calmly took the folder back from the angry man. "What exactly are you calling bullshit on?"

"Don't, Waters," TB warned.

"Don't what?" he asked innocently. "Don't treat her the same as every other client? TB, you know this is how we operate. We look into everything, including the people we help. Everything." Waters punctuated every syllable of the last word.

"I'm warning you, Waters—"

"Or is it that you don't want me poking the angry bear? Sorry, my friend, but we're long past that. A real bear would just get someone to pull the stinger out of his hide that he can't reach, but no. Instead, you'd rather suffer and stubbornly leave that stinger in because it would hurt your pride as king of the forest to ask for help." Waters gently threw the folder down on the bottom end of the table and faced TB head-on. "We need this information about her life before arriving in L.A., if for no other reason than to discount it as part of her problem. If you don't want us to 'hurt' your delicate little Flame, then go in there and do what you do. Get the information yourself. That's your specialty. Why are you so fucking squeamish suddenly?"

"Waters..." The low-volume hiss had an edge of begging to it.

"You've never been concerned about the feelings or sensitivities of anyone before. Tell me. What's different now?"

"You know what's different now." He spoke softly for only Waters, but the room was so quiet, everyone heard.

"I wanna hear you say it."

TB stood, glaring at Waters, stubbornly silent.

Hands on hips, his face blank, as if he didn't know the outcome already, Waters pushed the final button to send TB into

Defcon 1. "Fine. If you don't do this, I'll let Midas do it. He'll use his 'hypnotism' who-de-ha shit."

Oh, he did not just say that.

TB turned on Midas and visually pinned him to his chair. "You. Will. Not."

Midas' face was blank, but his eyes glinted with knowing humor. "I will if I'm ordered to. I'm a good little soldier."

"You were never in any military, so fuck off."

Midas put his hands up in a gesture of surrender and leaned back nonchalantly in his seat. "Sorry, bro, we're tribe, but you're not my type. That would be a no two-fer."

TB threw his arms up in exasperation. "I'm an interrogator. She"—he gestured to the image of Sylvan on the telescreen—"is not an interrogation subject. And get her off of there, Nemo!"

Nemo looked him in the eye and blew a bubble with his gum. Without breaking eye contact, he picked up the remote, aimed it at the telescreen, and promptly clicked the zoom button, bringing her picture in closer and larger. After he popped the bubble from his mouth, he grinned his classic shit-eating Nemo grin.

"She's an interrogation subject when we know she's holding back information." Waters pointed at TB. "You know that." Waters pointed back at himself. "I know that." His hand swept around the room. "We all know that."

Is everyone in the world but me this stupid? Am I the only sane person left in the universe?

"Fuck," he whispered as he turned back to the windows and dropped his head. Waters waited him out. All eyes were on his back. He could feel it.

I'm so screwed.

A half a minute passed before he growled at Waters, "Seventy-two hours. No calls. No texts. No emails."

And here's where I just jumped onto the crazy train with everyone else. What the hell am I doing?

"TB," God rumbled, "we can't let you off the grid like that, it's—"

His head snapped to the starfish, and his own rumble was

even more menacing. "I didn't say I was disappearing with her. I just don't want to be interrupted. Watch over us all you like. I'm going to have to take her to the club anyway, and we'll stay at her house."

"Why there?" Waters asked. "Why not here?"

"Know Your Enemy 101." His eyes returned to Waters. "She's not an interrogation subject. She's the victim. She'll be more comfortable in her natural surroundings. Bring her to the apartments at Tribe, where she'll be away from her comfort zone, basically in lockdown, and her fear will skyrocket. It will be brutally clear we're corralling her. She'll be hypervigilant. Therefore, nothing I can do here will get it out of her. I need her in a safe place. Somewhere she feels comfortable. Somewhere she'll forget and let down her defenses."

"So, why no calls?"

"After this latest development, she's going to jump out of her skin every time the phone beeps or rings. Hell, a goddamn notification on her social media will probably send her into a near panic attack. I can't afford to run the risk of working my ass off and getting her to have a moment of trust and open up her mouth only to have one of you idiots ruining it with a pointless update."

"Yeah, cuz you're not Terminator-scary, just the phone is." Nemo snorted as he flew a paper stealth bomber down the table at Demon. Steel, who was sitting next to the man, swatted the thing out of its trajectory and kept it from bouncing off Demon's forehead. Nemo flicked a good-natured one-finger salute at Steel and then continued with his own poking of the bear. "Your skills are slipping, big guy. She's a tiny little thing. You've broken some of the most unbreakable motherfuckers we've ever encountered. How come one pretty little woman is going to be so difficult?"

TB's gaze was focused out the conference room window at nothing in the far distance. He knew they were probably grinning like fools, planning on getting their pound of flesh over his obvious attraction to Flame, but there was nothing he could do about that. Maybe if he ignored their attempts to provoke him, they would get bored and stop.

Yeah. Not fucking likely. Even you know you're crazy about her.

When TB finally spoke, his voice was low and haunted. "She's like a drowning animal that will cling to a branch in raging waters, even though its instincts tell it that the end result is inevitable. In her case, she will cling to her misguided silence to keep herself from spilling whatever secret she thinks is so horrible that it cannot be survived. Whatever it is she's not telling us, she's mortified by it."

He heard a discreet cough behind a hand, and Steel's voice spoke to him, no smile behind it. "She'd live through telling us. We mean nothing to her. But you? It's you that she doesn't want to know the secret. She's worried that it will change your perception of her."

"Then we question her without TB here," God interjected.

TB acknowledged his assessment, his gaze still outside the windows. "Yes, you could. But I'd still end up learning what it was that she's so afraid of. If it weren't for me, she would give up what she knows, probably without a second thought. I've got to get her to trust me enough that her shame is more important to let go of than hold onto." He looked down at his feet and came to a decision. A decision he didn't want to make but knew he had no choice. Not really. "I'll get her to tell me whatever she's hiding. It might destroy us both, but at least that way, you can help her."

The silence in the room was heavy with what TB was suggesting. That he wouldn't be around to do it.

God cleared his throat over the speaker. "Well, ladies, I think this conversation is over. TB will get the information we need. Until we get it, proceed as planned. We'll regroup in seventy-two hours." He clicked off without a goodbye.

Papers shuffled. The murmurs between the guys were undecipherable. Waters clapped him once on the shoulder with a brotherly understanding, and he was the last out the door. The silence in the room hung like the gloom of an execution. And that's exactly how he felt. Because once he did this, there was no going back. The damage would be irreparable. He didn't see how it could be otherwise.

When TB turned, it was to see that Steel was still seated at the table, leaning back in his chair, hands laced and resting at his waist, his ice-gray eyes staring at him.

"Flame is stronger than you think."

"Possibly. But it feels like I'm about to destroy her." He looked at his teammate. "Interrogation is all about using the subject's weakness against them. That means I've got only one tool in the toolbox."

Concern fell into Steel's gray eyes. "What are you going to do, hermano?"

"Flame sees me as a hero. I'm going to give her what she wants: her white knight who will save her. I'll use her romantic nature to break her down. Then, and only then, will she trust me enough to tell me what we want to know."

"Just tell her the truth. You think she can't handle it?"

"She'll see it as a betrayal."

Steel shrugged. "I think you see Flame how you want to see her and not how she truly is. For all her 'enchantments'—the hearts and flowers, the unicorns and rainbows—she is remarkably practical. I think she sees reality far more than you believe she does. She's certainly capable of discerning what is reality and what is fiction."

"You're wrong, Steel. She's exactly as she appears. A young woman with her head full of impossible dreams, just like her books."

Steel chuckled. "You obviously have not read one of her books."

TB grimaced. "No. Not my thing."

Steel had a gleeful smile on his face, something TB rarely saw. He groaned. "Don't tell me you have, too."

"Waters brought us each a copy of the newest one last night."

"Seriously?"

"She's a very good writer. I advise you to read one. I highly recommend *Nature of the Beast*, her most recent. I think you will find it very..." He searched for the word. "Enlightening. Page one hundred thirty-four to one hundred forty-seven included. Might help with your 'interrogation technique.'"

TB snorted. "Highly unlikely. Reciting poetry about the color of her hair and eyes or some other romantic notions are not going to help me."

Steel stood up and pushed in his chair. When he got to the door, he turned back to TB, who was rooted in his same spot. "Don't be a narrow-minded ass. Read the book," he reiterated. "You might learn a few things about her that will surprise you."

"Whatever."

"Could be I'm wrong. It happens. But I sincerely doubt I'm wrong when I'm telling you that your querida is more than you think she is. Waters thinks so. You would, too, if your truth radar wasn't so jammed up right now."

"Well, trust me. You're wrong this time."

With a blank expression, Steel asked, "How can I trust in you when you can't trust in yourself?" And with that, he walked out of the room without a backward glance, leaving TB to stare at the quietly shut door.

26

──────

JUNE 16TH

Sylvan

A PAIR OF WARM HANDS CAME DOWN ON HER SHOULDERS, STARTLING HER and causing her to twist around. "Great balls of fire, TB! Don't do that." She quickly reached behind her and shut the lid of her laptop.

"Writing something sexy you don't want me to see?" he teased.

"Hmph. As if you'd actually read it. I wouldn't want to taint your darkness with my sunniness."

His hands left her shoulders. Immediately, she missed his touch, and she was mad at herself for being a grouch to him. Being light on his feet was ingrained as part of his job. "I'm sorry," she apologized. "That was uncalled for." She wiggled in the chair and tried to stretch out. "I'm going to blame this blasted chair. All the money your boss has, and he can't buy more comfortable furniture?"

TB chuckled. "No offense taken, sweetheart. And I think he purposefully bought these back-breakers so that we'd go back to our offices and work through lunch. We learned quickly. Now, to piss him off, we go out to lunch and take extra time. Or we order in and eat in someone's office and don't bring him anything back."

"It's not like any of you ever see him to give it to him," she pointed out.

"Cherry takes it upstairs."

Sylvan frowned. "Why don't you ever see him?"

"No one knows," he answered. "Cherry's the only one he allows in his bat cave. And Kubrick met him after... when she and Waters got back together, but neither one will say a word as to what he looks like. And Kubrick is silent as to why he wanted to talk to her. Maybe Waters knows, but I doubt it."

"I can't call her that name. It just won't come out."

"That's okay, it's our name for her. Job thing. No one else is expected to."

"Does everyone you work with get a name?"

"Yup. We use it in case anyone's listening and don't want them to know who we're talking about. We learned that one the hard way."

She saw his face go dark with a bad memory.

"What's my code name? Hearts?" She felt the acid burn up her throat to the back of her mouth with the word.

He smiled. "No. It's Flame."

"Oh." She blushed. "Do they know...?"

He shook his head. "No. That was the other thing I needed to talk to you about. They know we were talking on the computer and why, but I never gave details of those conversations. Those are private. All of them," he emphasized, knowing she was particularly worried about their last online session, as well as when they met at the club. "And they know nothing about the club other than we met there."

His hands went back to her shoulders and began working on the knots at the base of her neck from being hunched over in the chair over her computer.

Uhm. Okay, this is odd, but I'm not going to question it because then he might stop. I wonder if it's possible to orgasm from a neck massage?

"Are you done being a grouch to them?"

His fingers stopped. "What are you talking about?"

"Your voice registers your various emotions, so they're easy to pick out. You don't yell in the traditional sense, just the attitudinal sense, so I can tell if you're 'shouting' at someone by that. What I should have probably asked is, 'Are you done being angry at them?'"

His fingers began pressing into her muscles again. "No. I'm pissed is more like it," he mumbled.

"Is it something I did?"

He stopped massaging her shoulders and moved to the side of her chair. "I was angry with them, and you assume you did something? I don't follow how that works."

Sylvan heard the irritation in his voice but refused to look up at him. She shrugged and pulled the cuffs of her blouse down to her wrists. "Lately, you have that same tone when you talk to me, so..."

He tipped her chin up with one finger, forcing her to look at him. His face looked pained at her reply. "I have never been angry at you, Sylvan. Not really. Concerned over the danger you've unwittingly put yourself in, yes. Outraged that someone has decided to threaten you, definitely. Those things manifest themselves as 'angry.' It's not right. It's just how I'm wired."

Somehow, she knew that wasn't the end of the story. "So, what's next?"

"We're going back to your house. Hopefully, by Monday, we'll have some answers."

That answer sounded like he had battery acid in his mouth.

"Is being my bodyguard really necessary?"

He quirked an eyebrow at her. "Do all romance novels end with a happily ever after?"

"Not all of them. Especially if there's going to be a direct sequel. Then you have to leave people hanging." At his puzzled look, she replied, "Right. That was sarcasm. I misunderstood and thought that was a serious question. Stupid me."

As she rose and started to gather her belongings, TB grabbed her hand that was reaching up to fix the hair that had fallen out of her clip. "Leave it," he whispered. "I like them. Those stray curls make you look like a fairy-tale princess."

Whoa, Nelly. Butterflies everywhere.

"And you're not stupid," he assured her. "Maybe naive at times, but not stupid."

And now we're back to reality.

She huffed. "Yeah, because naive is so much better than stupid."

She tried to walk away, but he gently pulled her to him, his hands moving to her shoulders. Being five-foot-five in her heels put her at a distinct disadvantage to his six-foot-seven, so he had to duck down to meet her eyes since she was refusing to look up at him.

He tilted her chin up to his gaze again, and for a brief moment, she got lost in the forest green of his irises. "In this case, I mean that you take people as they are. That can put you needlessly at risk, like now. But the truth is, you also see the world in a much more positive light. Sometimes, I wish I was like you. I know too much about the horrors of the world. Horrors you will never see, thank Christ, and that's the way it should be. Men like me are the sacrifice so that the ordinary world can live in blissful ignorance of what evil goes on around them. I will never see the world the way that you do. It's just not meant to be." He framed her jaw in his huge hands, forcing her to keep looking at him. "And I prefer it that way, princess. I want you to have your romance, your ability to see the beauty of this world, and your giving heart. It's what makes you precious to others."

"What about you? Am I precious to you?"

He felt his heart physically ache at her question. "You have to ask?"

Shrugging, she replied, "Sometimes I don't think you like me very much."

"It's not you, princess. Honestly? I like you more than I should. If I were a different man…" He let that thought hang in the air.

"You can be any man you want to be." At his confounded look, she sighed and shook her head. "Take me home. I have writing to do."

27

JUNE 16TH

TB

He was unsure what to do with himself. He needed to come up with a plan. His brain usually worked best when disengaged directly with the planning of a mission and engaged with something mindless. It was one of the reasons why the club was helpful to him: distraction. Maybe watching some television would help. That wouldn't require any of his brain power, so he left the guest room and went back to the main floor.

His one true weapon against Flame was that he knew she was physically attracted to him, and seducing her would take very little work. They had unbelievable chemistry, and it was an easy interrogation tactic for him. After all, he'd used it before with female marks.

Motherfucker, she's not a mark. She's a victim of a sadistic fuck. Quit being a tool. No, you're worse than a tool. You're the whole toolbox. Probably the whole tool cabinet.

He shook his head. He had just known this favor for Kubrick was going to be messy, and sure as shit, it was. He didn't want to hurt Flame the way he was about to. But if she wouldn't give up whatever she was hiding, he had no choice. It was either hurt her to protect her or let her keep back information and potentially let her stalker frighten her to death or, worse yet, take her.

When he got downstairs, he looked around the living room, and did a complete three-sixty turn. He frowned.

"Okay, I can forgive the no coffee, maybe. But who the hell doesn't have a television?" he mumbled.

Flame, that's who. Why wasn't he surprised? She lived in her books. He rolled his eyes. Of course she did.

That's when his eyes caught sight of the curio cabinet tucked into the corner of the room. He crossed over to it. Behind the latticed glass, he saw books lined up along the shelves. Some were on book stands. Others were all lined up like typical books on a shelf. There were also photos, primarily of shirtless men, that were signed by who he assumed were the models in the images.

When he looked more closely at the cover of one of the books on the middle shelf, he noticed that the photo of the model on that same shelf matched the model on the book's cover and his Flame's name in beautiful flowing script across the cover. These were her books that she wrote, and Steel's suggestion rang in his head.

Well, it's not like there's anything else to do. You wanted something mindless. There can't be anything more mindless than reading this.

Grabbing the book facing him, he read the title. *Nature of the Beast.* Underneath the title, in script, it said *A Historical Paranormal Romance.* The cover sported a man in a white dress shirt from a time gone by, the material shredded. There were claw marks scratched into his pectoral muscle, his head was thrown back, eyes closed, and he looked as if he were close to reaching a sexual peak. A woman's arms were around him, her nails at the base of the claw marks as if she had put them there. Her eyes, forehead, and part of her hair were all that he could see of her, peering intensely from behind the man's shoulder, looking straight out at the reader. The eyes were a vibrant, glowing green, and her hair was long, looking like it was blowing wild in the wind, and a deep auburn.

Well, that's kind of hot.

He settled on her couch in the living room, sprawling his large frame on it after toeing off his boots and putting a throw pillow between his head and the arm of the sofa. Still gazing at the cover, something struck him as odd about the female model, but he couldn't figure it out. Maybe he'd seen her in an ad or on a billboard before? He sighed and gave up worrying about it. Resigning himself to boredom, he opened the book and began to read.

Within ten minutes, his mouth had dried up, he could feel his heart beating faster, and there was a fine sweat breaking out of his pores. None of that was even close to the arousal he was feeling. He attempted to adjust his dick, which was painfully hard.

His eyes devoured the pages.

The sex was right out of the gate.

Leather cuffs. Chains. Sensory deprivation. Commands. Just the barest traces of consensual nonconsent.

Hot. Filthy.

In other words, perfect.

And a whole lot of familiar material to certain chat discussions from the last seven months.

Ho-ly fuckkkk.

The pages kept turning until he got to the end. Once the book closed, he lay on the couch, the book on his chest, his eyes staring at the ceiling, and his thoughts awhirl.

But it wasn't just the sex. She had built great characters. The setting was so vivid he felt like he'd been there, in time and space. What really surprised him, though, was how good the story was. He'd read the whole thing straight through. Now he understood how the guys on the team had read it overnight, even if he really wished they hadn't. She was an excellent writer.

He thumbed back to page one hundred thirty-four in the book and reread through to one hundred forty-seven. The book went back to closed on his chest, and his brow furrowed, deep in thought. Maybe...

"No. Way."

He looked at the cover again. Long red hair. Emerald-green eyes. Long, perfectly manicured nails.

My little Flame, who knew you could burn that hot?

A little bit of jealousy raged that his teammates had read her book, getting a glimpse into her dirty, sexy mind.

A little? Try an inferno of jealousy.

No wonder Nemo had been all smirks this morning.

Abruptly, he sat up on the couch, put his boots back on, and strode toward the stairs, leaving the book behind.

The invasion begins now. She is officially under siege.

28

———————————

JUNE 16TH-17TH

Sylvan

"H.R. Puffenstuff!" she muttered, then rested her elbows on the desk's edge, her chin in her hands.

Nope. Don't create new. Recreate the truth.

She wasn't sure this was ethical. This wasn't the same as what she did with *The Nature of the Beast*. That was a recreation of elements of her research.

However, earlier, she'd realized that she did have a story to write. Hers and TB's story. No one needed to know. He certainly wouldn't read it to know, but it still felt wrong.

There should be enough ways to change it, especially since it's a historical, paranormal storyline. Not like our ending will match the book's ending, anyway.

She'd made great progress today, flying through fifteen thousand words and coming up to the first real sex scene. Then, she got stuck because she tried to reinvent the wheel with the characters.

She groaned, then slid her face into her hands. "Sister Mary Francis, what do I do now?"

Sylvan wasn't sure how long she sat there blankly. It felt like minutes, but it was probably more like seconds. Gathering all the energy she could, she uncovered her face to look at her screen. She began dejectedly pressing the backspace key, murmuring, "Delete, delete, delete," with each stroke of the key.

"I doubt it's all unsalvageable."

She squawked, and her hand flew to her chest. Instantly, she realized who it was. "Jiminy Cricket, TB, don't do that! That's three times now." All she could hear was her panting breath as her pulse rocketed beneath her palm.

He leaned against the doorjamb, hands in his pockets, just a silhouette in the dark by the spiral staircase. "I wasn't trying to be quiet. You were lost in thought. You really need to be more aware of your surroundings," he chided.

"Trust me," she grumbled. "I know when you're around most of the time. It's hard to miss you."

She turned her attention back to her screen, one of the hardest things she swore she'd ever done. She never wanted to miss one look, one movement, one word from him. But those wants were far too dangerous, so she tore her gaze away.

With every book I write going forward, he'll be all I'll see. I won't be able to bear it.

The shadow in her doorway was silent so long that Sylvan's heart, which had just returned to normal beats, suddenly ramped back up in panic.

"What is it, TB? Is something wrong?"

He said nothing.

"TB? You're scaring me." Her voice was still quiet, but it rose slightly in octave.

Slowly, he stood up straight, his hands coming out of his pockets. He moved forward with his predatory stealth. Once he stood across from her over the desk, he simply looked deeply into her eyes.

"Was there something you needed?" she asked in a shaky whisper.

All of a sudden, he was between her and the fireplace. Reaching to the back of her head, he pulled out the clip holding her hair up from her shoulders. The red tresses fell loosely down her back and around her face, one strand falling forward over her ear and down over her breast. His gaze lowered to the curl at its bottom edge that fell just before her waistline. He raised her out of the desk chair, reached out, and pinched the curl, loosely winding it around his fingertip. He seemed fascinated by the softness of her hair as his thumb massaged the lock.

"I just finished one of your books."

He did WHAT?! Oh, flippety flip-flip!

All the saliva in her mouth seemed to dry up in that instant. The best she could manage to do was swallow convulsively.

"I thought you were a hearts and flowers kind of girl. Horseback rides on sunset beaches. Champagne picnics along the river. White weddings." His finger began to wind the curl again, only this time, it didn't stop until it came up to her ear. Then he let go, and the curl unwound itself to fall back to its original place over her breast. Sliding his hand along her neck and ear, he cradled her head in his large palm. Of its own volition, Sylvan's face leaned into his palm, her eyes lowering to half-mast, almost drunk with his nearness.

Suddenly, she gasped as she felt a pleasurable sting. His fingers had tunneled to the roots of her hair and pulled tightly so that her head tilted back and her eyes flew open to stare into his emerald ones.

Oh, yes!

The forefinger on his other hand traced the shell of her ear. "I was so, so wrong. Imagine my surprise that my curious hearts and flowers girl likes her sex very dirty, very rough, and very creative." He brought his face close to hers and dragged the very tip of his nose from chin to brow. "I especially liked pages one hundred thirty-four through one hundred forty-seven. You learned your lessons on BDSM well."

Oh, Frankenstein! He read Nature of the Beast. Of all the ones to read!

"Steel warned me I would learn a lot about you if I read one of your books." Suddenly, his lips were touching her skin, not kissing her but dragging down the cord of her neck. "I told him that reading a romance novel was something I'd never be caught dead doing. Besides that, what could some sappy, unrealistic book possibly tell me about you that I didn't already know? But I decided I'd give his crazy idea a try." His mouth lingered on the spot just beside her ear. "Now I know why the guys were buzzing around you like bees among the sweetest roses this morning. Although... I'm thinking I liked it better when we were on the computer and at the club when I was the only one who could see those dirty desires of yours." And his warm breath was replaced by his tongue tracing the shell of her ear.

Her inner self was whimpering. Or at least she thought it was. It took a moment to register that she actually made the soft moan that escaped her mouth. Embarrassed but unwilling to tell him to stop, her eyes fluttered back to half-mast with a primitive need to experience the sensation without focusing on what she could see in front of her. "Again, please," she begged.

"Do what again, princess?"

"Pull."

"Pull, what?"

"My hair."

He tightened his grip on her hair roots and pulled again gently. The slight stinging sensation traveled to her eyelids, pulling them shut. Its path zigged and zagged down through her bloodstream, causing her blood to burn, her heart pumping double time, her lungs expanding to take in more air, her stomach tightening, her womb clenching, and finally sparking her clit, flaming it to life.

"Yes. That's what you wanted." His warm breath exhaled into her ear, and then she felt something pull open the collar of her blouse. Something soft, warm, and wet brushed at the juncture of her neck and shoulder—his tongue—and then she felt cool air blowing across her skin. Sylvan's knees failed, and she gripped his biceps. TB must have felt her body give way because his arm snaked around her waist and clutched her to him. "I've got you, little Flame. Now, let's see how else I can make you burn."

His mouth moved from her ear, and she whimpered as if in distress. "Don't worry, I'm not going anywhere. You couldn't drag me away now. Put your arms around my neck, little Flame." Tentatively, she let go of his arms and slid them up to his shoulders. She was so tiny compared to him that when TB picked her up so that her arms could reach around him, she clasped him like he was saving her from drowning.

"Look at me, princess."

A sting registered as he nipped her lower lip. Reflexively, she tried to pull back in shock. "Open for me," he ordered.

Trusting him, she opened her mouth, and immediately, his tongue slid inside to stroke hers. If she thought he sucked the oxygen out of a room before, now that his lips were on hers for the first time, she felt like he was a black hole. Everything felt like it was spinning, like she was gasping for air, and like she was endlessly falling.

Then she realized she wasn't falling—she was sliding down the front of his body. "No, no," she clutched at him.

"Shh, lovely. Too many clothes in the way. I want to see you." He turned her so that they exchanged places with her closest to the fireplace, and then he backed her up until she was directly in front of the flames. Once she was firmly on her feet, he pulled the desk chair to the edge of the area rug, turning it perpendicular to her desk and just on the front line of the firelight, and sat in the chair. "Start with your shirt. Let it slide down your shoulders and pool on the floor."

Oh my god, oh my god, oh my god, I'm going to faint.

Straightening her spine, she worked to hold back the shudder of anticipation. Sylvan's fingers trembled as, without question, she did as she was told. She raised her fingertips to the silk lapels of the silk overshirt, then drew them slowly up and over her shoulders, letting it slide down her back to around her feet on the floor, revealing the designer loungewear. Her arms drifted back down to her sides.

He leaned back in the chair, his elbow on the arm, his head propped up by his thumb and forefinger. His face was expression-less. She noticed that he had picked up her hair clip with his other hand and was playing with it while he watched her. "Remove your corset."

Reaching behind herself at the waist, Sylvan slipped loose the double knot and gently pulled at each juncture of the ribbons. Then she unhooked each hook on the front, top to bottom, slowly, until it was completely undone. The boned garment dropped to the floor with a barely-there thud. Her body felt abnormal, being so unrestricted. Her nipples beaded at the lace abrasion of the blouse she had worn under the corset. Despite the areas of opaque embroidery, she knew it would be obvious to him, even in the low light.

"Very good. Now..." He shifted in the chair to sit up straight. "Your trousers."

Sylvan reached to her hip and slid the side zipper on the pants down. With a tilt of each hip, she pushed the waist over her hips and let them slither down her legs to pool at her feet with the rest of her clothing. She was left in a long-sleeved lace blouse, her heeled slippers, and completely at his mercy.

29

———————

JUNE 17TH

TB

THIS WOMAN. SHE HAS NO IDEA THE POWER SHE HAS.

TB moved in his seat, adjusting his cock in his jeans. It took everything in him not to groan aloud. He could not screw this up. This was going to be his most delicate operation and clearly his most important ever.

"Unbutton your blouse, but do not take it off. Just leave it hanging open."

He watched her stutter through his instruction. First, her weight shifted from her left foot to her right foot. Then something changed. She paused. He watched her stiffen her spine with determination as her hands rose to the mother-of-pearl buttons. Buttons undone, she allowed the material to gap open as directed and dropped her hands to her sides.

Knew you were smart, princess.

At first, she wouldn't have realized, but as her adrenaline evened out, her brain would have put together the pieces with the position in which he put them in relation to the flames. She now knew that all he could truly see from this distance was a glow along her edges. He had done that on purpose. He wanted to push her boundaries but do so while empowering her. He knew that with all of her research and with all he had taught her before they met in person, she would understand. In this way, she had control and the freedom to experience without feeling threatened.

And then she did the unexpected. She walked toward him and kneeled in front of him, her hands on her thighs, her eyes downcast.

Closing his eyes, he swallowed hard, breathing in deeply through his nose, then expelling through his open lips. The rapid rise and fall of her chest, the slight tremble in her shoulders showed she was nervous but not afraid.

Opening his eyes, he stood, reaching for his gun at his back. He pulled it from his waistband and laid it on her desk.

His large hand cupped the side of her face. "Look at me, princess," he commanded.

Her eyes rose to his from her position in front of him. The tip of her tongue swiped between her lips.

"Unbuckle my belt and remove it."

Her hands shakily rose to the buckle. She slipped the excess length through the buckle, pried the tab from the hole, slid it out of the way, and then released the rest of the leather from the buckle. Her left hand rested flat on his hip, and with her right, she pulled the strap free of his belt loops. When it had cleared his body, she stretched it straight between her two hands and held it before her on her upturned palms.

His hand caressed the top of her head, down the side, and cupped her cheek.

"Keep your eyes on mine at all times." He took the belt from her hands and laid it on the edge of her desk behind him. "Take out my cock."

He watched her chest expand with a heavy inhale that was nothing close to fear and all about arousal.

Eyes locked to his, still on her knees, her fingers reached for the button on his jeans. It slid easily from its slot; then, she used the thumb and forefinger of her left hand to lower the metal zipper at a pace he could only describe as agonizing. She didn't smile. Didn't blink, as far as he could tell. Just held his eyes, suddenly in complete control of her actions.

Once his zipper reached its lowest point, she raised herself off of her heels to kneel in a straight-up position. She reached down into the denim to find his cock. He heard a soft gasp as she realized he was bare beneath the material. She recovered quickly, her hand cool against his skin. When her fingertips grazed his flesh, he felt himself twitch slightly. It was already hard, but now it felt like it was swelling beyond normal. As if she could feel the cool, jagged metal against her own sensitive skin, she dragged his jeans down an inch so that he didn't rub against the zipper.

Her fingers slid around his cock, the tips of her fingers unable to circle him completely. He wasn't outrageously huge, but definitely not small. Her grip was strong and sure but gentle enough that when she removed him from inside the material, he didn't feel scrapes or rasps of the zipper teeth because she kept her hand wrapped around the root to protect him.

This meant that his cock was pointed straight at her very fuckable mouth.

"Take me in your mouth, princess."

The tip of her pink tongue snuck out between her lips, cupping over the top one, then she sucked it back between her teeth, which bit lightly into her bottom lip.

He waited.

She licked her lips again and leaned forward ever so slightly. When her lips met the tip of his cock, her mouth opened automatically and slid down the length of him about halfway. She rolled her tongue along the underside of him, then pulled back so that her taste buds rasped against the vein beneath. When her lips pulled completely off of him, she swirled her tongue around the head, swiping away the precum that had begun to leak from the tip.

Her eyes fluttered shut, and she mewled.

"Eyes," he ordered gruffly.

They reopened languidly, pupils blown.

His hand began to stroke her hair, from the top of her head to the back of her neck. She continued her tentative pattern, each time sliding just a little bit farther along his length and each time using a little more suction as she pulled away.

On the fourth retreat, her other hand rose up to grip him at the root, her two hands holding him steady. Then, she pushed the weight of her hands toward his groin until they applied strong pressure against his pelvic bones. The pull stretched the skin tight, sensitizing it, now all wet and shiny from her mouth, and he couldn't contain the loud groan as she buried him in her mouth all the way down to her fingers.

"Fuck, sweetheart, who taught you that?" His other hand reached out to lightly grasp the other side of her head. He didn't put pressure, just held onto her as she found a rhythm up and down his shaft.

One hand curved around to the back of her skull. Again, no pressure, but she understood his subtle direction when her lips met her fingers, and she held her mouth and tongue in place for a heartbeat.

He felt it before he heard it.

A near-silent hum vibrated along his nerve endings, a hum that was coming from her throat. A hum that would have released like a moan if her mouth had been free.

Saliva pooled in her mouth around him as she held him.

Then she dropped the hand that was closest to her mouth and slid slightly back on his shaft, sucking hard enough that her cheeks hollowed. When she hit the halfway point between root and tip, she slid back down on him until her lips met her other hand.

"That mouth, princess," he groaned. "More."

Without missing a beat, she increased the suction and began to pull back on him again. Slowly, she set her rhythm back up. Her lips slid smoothly down to meet her fingers, still grasping the root of his cock tightly. He felt the tip of her tongue flutter teasingly along the vein on its underside, and he squeezed her skull lightly in the palm of his hand to let her know what she was doing was good.

More than good. Fuck, I'm not going to last long if she keeps doing that much longer.

Then she began to pull back, her cheeks hollowing deeper, her tongue flattening as she dragged it against the vein.

Suddenly, he realized that her free hand was flat on his other thigh, and her nose was buried in the skin of his pelvis. She had relaxed her jaw, and it had allowed her to take him farther into her mouth to the back of her throat. She remained still. He could feel her trying to get used to the sensation of her mouth being that full and trying not to panic about airflow. She was concentrating hard on breathing through her nose, but there was still some tension and unease.

She'll get there, and in the not-too-distant future, will be my guess. So, so good.

"Easy, little Flame. You've done so good. Back off my cock, sweetheart. I want to see those pretty eyes again."

She slowly pulled back, a gasp escaping her open mouth and a thin line of saliva connecting her mouth to his cock. Her eyes were glassy and just short of tears that would have fallen if she'd pushed any further.

His hands curled to cup her face, his thumbs brushing along her cheekbones. "So beautiful." He leaned down and kissed her forehead. "Undress me."

Her attention returned to the tip of his cock, still straight out to her face. She poked the tip of her tongue out just enough to swipe through the slit to catch another drop of precum and took it into her mouth to savor. He watched her, noticing that her tongue was swirling around in her mouth as if trying to make sure every part of the cavern got a taste of him, and then she swallowed.

Her eyes dropped toward the floor to his boots. She grabbed ahold of his left hand and set it on her right shoulder to use her for balance. She coaxed him to raise his foot so that she could grab the heel, pull it, and slide it off his foot, followed by the sock.

She repeated the process with the other side.

Once the socks were neatly folded and tucked inside his boots, she put them together and off to the side.

Her hands went to the waistband of his jeans, slowly pulling them down, her eyes trained completely on his, the fabric bunching at his ankles. Again, she repeated the process she'd used to remove his shoes. Almost reverently she folded the jeans, then placed them on top of his boots.

He moved items on her desk to the far side, then reached down and gripped her biceps gently, lifting her to sit on the desk's edge. She reached for the hem of his tee and began to drag it up his torso. He helped her pull it over his head since he was a foot taller than her. Again, she folded the material, this time lightly tossing it onto the seat of her chair.

Ignoring his nakedness, he reached down for her left leg and began to gently knead the calves and ankles. He had been on his knees a few times in his life for long periods of time, particularly with a gun pointed at the back of his head, and he knew that she would need time for the blood to begin flowing normally again before she could move. Their eyes remained locked in each other's gaze.

When he felt her leg muscles loosen, he gently lowered it and reached for the other to give it the same treatment. When that leg had loosened up, he lowered it to dangle from the desk's edge like the other.

"Let's see if I can't make you even more beautiful."

His left hand caressed the side of her face, and she leaned into his touch, her eyes beginning to drift closed.

"Eyes on me, sweetheart," he reminded her gently.

Her lids opened fully.

"Put your arms in front of you, bent at the elbow."

Languidly, she followed his instruction. With his right hand, he reached behind him to the desk where he left his belt earlier. He put the tongue of the belt in between her hands, palms together as if in prayer, the very first punch hole peeking out at her thumbs. Then he wound the belt around her wrists and the heels of her hands until he ran out of strap. He needed just a bit more room, so he pulled to tighten it, then slid the tongue through the frame of the buckle, caught the prong in the first punch hole, then slid the tongue through the loop.

Sliding his fingers between the belt and her wrists, he checked to ensure that he wasn't cutting off her circulation. "Remember. If you begin to feel any tingling, you let me know immediately."

"I will."

"What are your colors?"

"Green means go, yellow means slow down, red means stop."

"Excellent." He picked her up, his arms around her waist. "Raise your arms straight, princess, and then loop them around my neck."

Once she had her arms where he wanted them, he carried her over to the window bed and laid her down on the comforter.

"Wrap your legs around me. Grip my hips with your knees and thighs." As she complied, he made sure to notch his hips in her cradle, his hands framing her hips. As he whispered in her ear, his hands followed the cues of his voice. "You remind me of a genie from a bottle." His left hand slid along her skin up along the dip to her waist, the curve to her shoulder, then slid his palm beneath the back of her head and threaded through her hair. "That beautiful long hair," he groaned. "Every time I look at it, I want to wrap it around my fist and pull your head back to expose your throat." He tugged gently so that her neck pulled slightly to the side, and he laid an open-mouthed kiss on her throat.

His lips stayed against her skin. "All these gorgeous dips and curves." His other hand slid across her skin to the places he praised. "This tiny little waist with those hourglass hips, strong thighs gripping me so tight." His tongue licked a stripe from shoulder to earlobe. "And you taste all warm and sugary, like vanilla frosting."

She made a purring sound as his mouth traveled down from her ear to her throat, then between her breasts, where he began to nip at her flesh, then soothe the bites with soft licks of his tongue.

He raised his head. "Look at me, Flame." Her eyes, in the

moonlight, were telling him everything he needed to know. "You glow in the moonlight. You're so beautiful. So perfect."

I don't deserve her. But damned if I'm not going to take her anyway.

"I'm going to hurt you," he admitted. She had no idea how true that statement was right now. "I don't want that."

She smiled sadly. "I won't lie and tell you it won't break my heart when you leave. But that's part of life. I may write about fated mates, guaranteeing readers a happily ever after, but that's not the real world. Your leaving won't kill me, and I'm not going to be one of those stupid heroines who vows to never love again or die of a broken heart. There'll just be a small piece of me that's never completely over you, is all." Using her bound hands, she applied pressure to pull him down to her. "Just make love to me. That's all you have to do."

He began to push the tip of his cock into her opening when he realized he was bare. "Shit. Flame, I need—"

"No." Her legs wrapped around him, her thighs tightening their hold so that he couldn't move away. "I'm good. I'm protected. It's been six years since I've been with anyone. And I really want all of you if this is all I get to have."

"It hasn't been six years for me, but it's been a while." He brushed the strands of hair from her face, then traced a perfectly shaped eyebrow. "I haven't even scened at the club since we met online the first time."

He'd never taken a woman bare before. But he wanted to give her this. When all went to hell in about forty-eight hours, he wanted to at least be able to say that he'd made this good for her. And to be honest, he wanted it. Wanted it more than anything he'd ever wanted in his entire life.

He lined himself up with her opening again, and he could feel just how much she wanted him. Her juices were slicking her thighs and making his cock wet and sticky already. Just to make sure she could take him, he backed off her a little and slid a finger inside her channel, groaning at how wet she was. She was definitely tight.

In and out, he worked his finger, pressing kisses to her fevered skin. She moved her hips in countermotion to his thrusts.

When he felt her begin to loosen for him, he added a second finger, stretching her by pressing his fingers against her walls. He was able to work himself in a little farther, and he paid an inordinate amount of attention to her breasts, nipping at the soft skin, laving away the sting with his tongue. She began to mewl with each brush of his fingers against her inner walls.

He added a third finger, curving up his fingertips to find her G-spot. Her breathing became panting and indecipherable begging, her bound hands clenching and unclenching.

Finally, he felt as if she might be able to take him. Slowly he withdrew his fingers, then notched the tip of his cock yet again at her opening. "Flame. I need your eyes, baby. I need to be able to see you so that I can make sure I'm not hurting you."

She opened her eyes, looking straight at him, and nodded. "Please. I need to touch you."

He shook his head and pushed his hips forward so he was barely inside her. "Just feel," he whispered. Then he pushed just a little further. Every time he stopped, he felt her walls squeeze him, threatening to make him release.

My God, this feels so much better with nothing between us. Is it the lack of condom? Or is it because it's her?

He pushed the thoughts aside, focusing on her and regaining control. When he did, he slid back, then pushed farther forward.

"Keep those arms around my neck, princess. Don't move them."

She shook her head. "You'd have to break them and move them yourself."

He stilled inside her, and as he waited for her body to adjust to him, he brushed his nose along her neck, beneath her ear. "Fuck, you're beautiful. The perfect temptation. Sweet on the outside and inside, but this spicy little surprise in between the layers. It's been hell resisting you." The tension eventually lifted from her body, and he began slow thrusts back and forth, making sure to give his hips a twist when he pulled back and another when he pushed in to create friction for her.

"Yes," she hissed. "More. Like that."

"You want more, little Flame?" he asked with menace.

"More," she acknowledged. "Harder."

"Oh, I'll give you harder. Hang on tight."

Her belted hands reached for what hair she could grab at the back of his neck, threading through the longer strands. When she pulled at the roots, he hissed at her. "Minx," he growled, then snapped his hips hard until he was buried to the hilt.

She moaned. "More, please," she begged, sounding like she was in physical pain. But when he looked at her face, she was so far from pain he could barely restrain himself from losing all control with her.

TB began to piston his hips faster, gaining momentum with each thrust. His hands grabbed the frame of the window on the opposite side of the bed, ensuring that if she moved across the mattress with his pounding, her head would be protected from hitting the ledge. It also allowed him with each twist of his hips to not only grind into her but also put his full weight on her hips without crushing the rest of her.

He felt her orgasm coming like a speeding train. She clenched her legs around his waist so tight, her body actually came forward to connect with his above her. The arms around his neck locked, and he felt the edge of the leather bite into his skin. Then her inner walls spasmed like a fist, squeezing the life and his release right out of him, her scream muffled in his shoulder as her teeth actually bit down on him.

He remained where he was, trying to regain his equilibrium but also trying not to crush her with his weight. In the end, it was easier to roll over with her sprawled on his chest, his cock still locked inside her. The damn thing wouldn't come down.

Just like her damn wolf shifters, knotting in place.

Somehow, it didn't seem so corny anymore.

His hand idly combed through her long hair as their heart rates slowed.

"Do you have a hair fetish?" she mumbled.

His mouth formed a genuine smile. "I enjoy yours." He pulled her wrists from around his neck, removed the belt from around them, and tossed it to the floor. He gently massaged her wrists by rotating his thumbs along her pulse points, his fingers on the opposite sides, making sure the blood was flowing to avoid tingles and numbness. He became thoughtful in the quiet.

Normally, you'd be up and out of a woman's bed by now. Are you sure you haven't fallen for this woman?

Yep. Totally have. Doesn't mean I'm still not wrong for her.

She tipped her head toward his, her chin resting on the hand she had laid on his chest. "I can hear the gears grinding and smell the smoke. What's wrong?"

He shook his head, smiling at her. "Nothing. Just having a conversation with myself over something."

She smiled. "I thought I was the only crazy person who did that."

"Hell no. Sometimes, it's the most intelligent conversation I have all day."

"Sometimes it's the most intelligent conversation I have all day," she said in unison with him.

They both laughed.

Sucking on her bottom lip, he watched her make the decision. "What was the conversation about?"

He rolled her over onto her back so that he was leaning over her. His hand drifted down to between her legs, feeling the mix of their fluids on her, knowing that he, too, was covered in them. He'd marked her. She was his. It would take so little for him to just claim her right there and then. To say it out loud. But somehow, he just couldn't do it.

"I really should clean us up. But I—"

She reached down for his cock, cradling it in her hand. "I don't want you to. I like knowing we're covered in each other. It should feel gross, but it doesn't."

With her hand gently stroking him and his hand dragging back and forth on the inside of her thigh, he kissed her forehead.

"I was just thinking," he finally answered her question, "I can't remember the last time I stayed in bed with a woman throughout the night. Not sure if I ever have other than last night."

Her hand stopped moving. "Why did you stay?"

He looked down and noticed her eyes focused on his face. He hesitated before answering her. "You were so scared. I was enraged that the bastard had the balls to reach out to you like that, take away your feeling of security in your own home. I wanted to protect you." He corrected himself. "I *needed* to protect you more than anything else at that moment.

"Part of it, too, I guess, is I'm not easily captivated. Being a part of the kink community, I've seen and heard so many things over and over. But watching you learn it and experience it for the first time was like it was all new again. If I were to really introduce you to that world, I think you'd be at the club every night if I let you. And then I'd have to collar you so that no one else got to you."

Hello? Collar her? Where did that thought come from?

Doesn't sound like the worst idea.

Shut up. It's a terrible idea. You can't. She deserves better. She'll suffer and be miserable. You can't possibly keep her.

You lie like a rug. Worse than that, you're a coward. Take what you fucking want for once.

She hummed in thoughtfulness. "I guess I'll take that as being tempting."

Pushing his inner voices to the deep corners of his head, he kissed her temple again. "That you are, my little Flame. That you are."

Her words were timid as she asked her question. "Will you stay again tonight?"

He felt her holding her breath, waiting for the letdown. "I don't want to be anywhere else."

AN HOUR LATER, TB sat in the darkness, propped up in the window bed against the headboard. Sylvan lay in the crook of his arm on the inside of the bed closest to the window. Her arm lay across his bare stomach, her breaths even and deep as she slept. One of his hands made lazy circles on her bare shoulder. The other lay gently on top of her arm that lay across him.

He stared at the blank wall across from him, not seeing the wall but simply staring into space, his brain processing what had happened tonight. He wasn't sure how he felt about it, let alone how she felt about it.

Well, that's a lie. You know exactly how you feel about it.

On the outside, he was as cool as ever. On the inside, he was in panic mode. Sylvan was stirring up more than just his protective instincts. Emotions better left unfelt. He didn't want them. And yet he did. He wanted them so badly. He wanted her. But taking that final step and taking a sledgehammer to the carefully constructed walls he'd been building and solidifying since he was seven years old felt like a task too great.

What if she leaves you when she discovers you're not enough?

What if I lose her because I don't make a decision at all?

Well, if you never make the decision, then it eventually gets made for you.

And then I'll always be left wondering, "What if...?"

If he gave in to her, made his claim, he knew that his career at Tribe could be at risk. Obviously, God wasn't going to carry through with his threat about executing anyone who tried to leave the corporation over a relationship. Waters and Kubrick were proof that it had been an emotional but empty threat. And in all honesty, even if he had put the order through, no one on the team would have carried out the hit. But still. He'd always worry about her when he was on a project. And the projects were often dangerous. He'd be distracted, and not only would that risk him, but also his team.

He shifted his head and looked down at her sleeping form in his arms. The problem was, she felt right where she was. Like she was supposed to be where she was and nowhere else.

30

JUNE 17TH

TB

HE WAS DOWNSTAIRS IN THE KITCHEN WHEN HIS WATCH PINGED. Glancing at the text, he saw Waters was asking him to check in as soon as possible. A glance at the time said it was just after three o'clock in the afternoon.

Seriously? I told them no contact. For fuck's sake, can't even follow the simplest instructions.

He scrubbed his face with his hands and moved to sit at the dining room table.

After opening his laptop, he clicked on the video chat link. When Waters appeared on the screen, he groused, "Have you forgotten how to tell time, asswipe? It's barely been twenty-four hours yet, let alone seventy-two."

"Another girl has gone missing. Someone named Fleur."

"Shit." He ran his fingers through his hair from forehead to nape, gripping the back of his neck. "That's the girl who realized Tilly was missing. Are we sure she was taken from the club? She hasn't just taken off somewhere?"

"Her shoes were found in the parking lot near her car, and her escort was found unconscious there as well. Got hit in the back of the head with a tire iron. A guy named Tripoli."

"He was with Fleur when she reported Tilly missing."

"What's his connection to the club?"

"He works as a dungeon master and mans the door to the upstairs sometimes. Former Marine. Actually, he might have been Navy. Don't they get their medics from your alumni?"

"Yup. Any idea where he served?"

"No, not a clue."

"Okay, I'll get Midas to give a look-see into him, just for elimination purposes."

"He's a good guy. Pretty sure he comes from money, and I think he's a silent investor in the club. Might even have been an actual doctor, now that I think of it. He's got a tattoo of that medical symbol." TB frowned. "Fleur is blonde."

"Wondered if you'd catch that."

"He's changed his pattern. Something's really wrong." TB looked out into space, not seeing the room around him. "We wanted him to screw up and make a mistake, but I don't think this was one. This actually feels calculated. He left behind a witness of sorts. Is Tripoli awake yet?"

"Demon went in there and did his impression of a doctor, which is how I've got the information I'm giving you."

With a sigh, TB brushed his hands back up his head from neck to crown and tousled his hair. "What are your spidey senses telling you?"

"Same as you. Not a mistake."

TB heard paper rustling in the background.

"We also have other news."

TB felt his heart rate spike. "Another threat against Flame?"

"Yup. And here's the twist. It didn't come through the mail, email, or chat. It was left under Fleur's windshield wipers."

"Fuck. It is the same guy."

"Confirmed."

"Was Midas able to get the security footage from the club?"

"Yes. We caught a huge break on this one. Tripoli followed her out the door after about sixty seconds. Said he was supposed to walk her out, but there was a distraction inside, and he got hung up. She must have felt she was safe because, get this, turns out she's an undercover cop. She was hiding out investigating the missing girls."

"Wow. I wouldn't have guessed that by looking at her. Come to think of it, she's always avoided me like the plague, except regarding Tilly. Must have known instinctively I'd expose her hiding as a sub." He expelled a deep breath. "Well, at least the cops hadn't actually given up. What did the video show?"

"It's difficult to see because it was dark. Assnozzle took out the light by her car. Plus, he's all in black, and he apparently knew exactly where the cameras were because his face was almost completely turned away. Not only that, but he's covered head to toe, likely wearing a ski mask as far as we can tell, and also had gloves on, so not a speck of flesh is visible to even hope for any identifying marks. Midas is trying to clean up the footage, plus he's testing out his fancy measuring program inside Cyclopes, so between the height of things in the lot and the height and weight of Fleur and Tripoli, we should be able to get some sort of dimensions on our guy."

"But that's not particularly helpful. There will be a million men out there that fit the same dimensions," TB groused.

"And not only that," Waters acknowledged, "who knows if that build is even going to be accurate. There are a lot of ways he could make himself taller and bulkier than he actually is, so those millions probably quadrupled in number because we also have to consider smaller variations." There was more rustling of paper. "Nemo made an interesting observation, though. He wondered if maybe we have the wrong gender."

"What? Why?"

"Well, there are a couple of reasons. Number one, the build on this guy is pretty small."

"Trust Nemo to be looking at measurements. He's probably more accurate than Midas' fancy program. We tested him not too long ago. Had him look at an issue of *Hustler*. He got every one of them right. That man is a menace."

"Glad I missed that."

TB chuckled. "Purposely didn't invite you. We figured Kubrick would gouge out your eyes, hand us our asses, then burn down Tribe."

"No shit. Either that or she would have joined in on the bet."

"What's number two?"

"Number two, Nemo pointed out that while there are a couple of guys in her social media following, they don't fit the profile. Several of them have solid alibis for Identity, the LGBTQ+ club."

"Going to a club known for its homosexual clientele doesn't necessarily mean someone's gay. Hell, I've been there."

Waters cleared his throat. "Yeah, I'm not touching that one."

TB sat up straight in his seat. "Would it matter if I were gay?"

"You wouldn't be the first guy I know to walk both sides of the street. And no, it wouldn't matter. Anyhow, while the sites have a few male followers, ninety-nine percent of the members are female."

"Also means nothing. Anyone can be anyone on the internet."

"Yes, we did think of that. Midas has got everyone going through her followers' profiles, lateral reading, and hacking into accounts and back channeling to see if there are any potential candidates. So far, nothing, but there are thousands of them, and it's taking a hot minute to go through them. More than a few women setting themselves up as people they aren't, and a few who are authors with pen names, but none of them are tripping any triggers as stalkers. And, of course, Kubrick is on there, under a fake name, as well as Cherry and Tabitha."

"Makes sense. Flame said that's how she connected with Tabitha in the first place." TB considered Nemo's points. "He's not wrong in his ideas, but I still think our stalker's a male."

"That's our general leaning, too, but Nemo just didn't want us to overlook options. Plus, he can be incredibly astute at times."

"Like we need more work with this."

Waters paused. "I need to ask you to do something you're not going to want to do."

"You want me to go to the club tonight. With Flame."

"Sorry. I know you wanted time alone, but I literally don't think we have time with Fleur's disappearance. Like you said, Flame can ask questions openly that you can't, and no one would probably think twice about it."

"Normally, a Dom would discipline her for doing that. Prying. It's not respectful."

There was a pause again. "You're the one who suggested this line of investigation. Why the flip-flop?"

There was silence as the two men stared at one another over the screen.

Waters sighed and shook his head. "I know you don't want to hurt her. So don't. Dude, we all know you're gone for her, so why are you denying yourself this?"

TB rolled his eyes. "I can't."

"Micah. Listen to me, and listen well. Do *not* do what I did. Because when it gets fucked up, and it will if you proceed this way, you're going to be miserable. You're going to feel like the world could implode, and you'd be happy for it to happen because you need her so badly. Like if she's not there, you can't breathe. When Kubrick and I were separated, it physically hurt to the point I was wishing I'd died in Cairo and never met her. I was willing to do *anything*, and I mean anything, for a second chance, but my pride wouldn't allow me to go find her. Remove your head from your ass right now. Follow the plan. But be real with her. Make use of the club as a couple. Enjoy yourself. Just... please don't tell me about it afterward."

"She's going to feel like I've lied to her. She'll never believe I really feel anything for her once she realizes why we're going to the club."

"Look, I'm not going to claim I'm an expert on women. But I do know this much—tell her the truth. Go do it now. She might get angry, but she'll get over it. She'll want to help, especially after what she learned in the meeting yesterday. I'm telling you straight. Do not fuck this up for yourself."

TB sighed. "I'll think about it."

"As a famous green little alien once said… 'There is no try.'"

"That's not the quote. You need a session with Nemo."

"Thanks, but I have enough movie shit in my life with Kubrick." Waters shifted gears when Midas handed him some printouts. "Okay, back to reality. There are six new members who joined the club around the time this all started, but three of these people seem to show up almost every night, similar to this Fleur woman."

TB was grateful for the subject change. "Yeah, that's probably Medusa, Loki, and Gilgamesh. They're a triad. Came in sometime about six months ago." His neck began to itch. Something was off. "When Flame and I go to the club tonight, I'll watch for them. They'll actually be the perfect cover. It's a bonus that I've already been seen talking with them at the club. Plus, Flame will want to know about triads and reverse harems for her books, I'm sure."

"I'm going to try to forget you mentioned those two things. I've got more than I can handle with just one woman." Waters paused. "And don't think too long about what I said before. You'll thank me for it later." He snapped his fingers. "Almost forgot. Nemo delivered something to the house for you earlier from Midas. A 'just in case' item. It's on the porch."

"Tracker?"

"Yes. He put it in a collar."

TB winced.

"Problem?" Waters asked.

How to explain this?

"A collar at The Library connects a sub to a Dom. It means she's been claimed."

"Okay. Again, problem?"

"It's going to look like a declaration of my intentions to her."

"And?"

TB sighed. "It's going to be out of place. I've never done that before."

"Huh. Well, first time for everything, I guess. Maybe it will send our stalker a message." Waters' voice lowered. "Maybe it even sends one to you."

"This Midas' way of offering his opinion on the matter?"

"Christ, when did you become such a drama queen? Why are you making this into a big production? Just admit you're into her already. You're giving me a headache and a craving for chocolate. That means I'll have to go buy my own because Kubrick doesn't share."

Waters clicked out of the chat.

Shaking his head, TB checked his watch for the time. Three-thirty.

31

JUNE 17TH

Sylvan

She'd heard murmurs from downstairs when she left her bedroom, so she'd stopped at the top of the stairs, shamelessly eavesdropping. After all, if it was about her stalker, she deserved to know. If it weren't, she'd walk away.

When they started talking about Tripoli being in the hospital, she left the top of the landing and climbed the stairs to her sanctuary to revert to her typical avoidance method of diving into her writing to distract herself. Right now, her brain refused to process one more thing about the nightmare her life had become. Maybe it would help her decide what to do about his questions.

She'd been tapping at her computer keys for about ten minutes when the air in the room changed. She hadn't heard a noise, but something was different. She looked up and let out a squeak of surprise.

He was in her doorway again.

"I hate it when you do that. Please stop. You're going to give me a heart attack. I've had all of the surprises I can take lately, and you're going to be what's going to kill me," she muttered.

"Not funny."

"I didn't say it was! I didn't mean to be funny. I meant to sound irritated."

"You can say 'pissed off,' you know." He shifted to lean on the door jamb. "Are you irritated with me?"

She folded her arms in front of her on the desk. "Do I have a reason to be?"

Dragging himself off the door jamb, he walked toward her. Like he was carrying a weight that was taxing. When he got to the other side of her desk, his attention was drawn to her glass paperweight, focusing on the rose that appeared to be floating inside of it. He picked it up and examined it closer.

"We need to go to The Library tonight. Another girl has gone missing. He's escalating." He set the paperweight down. "Flame... it will be dangerous. We have no right to ask this of you. But a replacement won't pass. I swear, I will protect you with my last breath. Every one of my teammates will."

"I know you will. I trust you."

He was quiet for a few more moments, just staring at her. He opened his mouth as if to say something, then changed his mind. "Eight o'clock." He turned and walked down the stairs.

She called out to him. "Should I wear anything in particular?"

He glanced at her over his shoulder from just outside the door at the top of the stairs. She could see his expression clearly in the lit hallway. She saw him consider before he answered her. "Something that might be a little out of character. We need to try and push this guy to make a move. And... wear your hair down."

That is not for the stalker. That's for him.

She nodded. "Okay. I'll find something."

Flame sat for a few moments, considering the upcoming evening. She had no idea what would happen, but maybe it would prevent other girls from being taken, and that in itself was more important than any problem between her and TB.

THIS WAS A CALCULATED RISK.

When Sylvan came down the stairs to leave for the club, she watched as TB nearly swallowed his tongue. It wasn't her usual clothing style, so she'd definitely hit a bullseye.

Good. Two can play the seduction game for what we want.

He'd been one hundred percent correct when he'd analyzed her clothing choices and how they matched her home, something she'd never really thought about. And she knew he liked the funky mix of flowy and binding that was so much a part of her everyday world. Tonight, she still held her typical style, but the choices were all modern.

Up top, she wore a tight white leather jacket that closed with a shiny gold zipper. The jacket functioned much like a bustier would, with a two-inch gap between the bottom of it and the navy blue miniskirt. The zipper tab on the jacket hung open to expose most of the inner swells of her breasts.

The miniskirt hung low on her hips, like a pair of low-rise jeans. A double-strand gold chain ran around her midsection, just below her belly button. It seemed to draw his eyes to the skirt itself. The material was translucent and looked like layered handkerchiefs. If she didn't have the satin cheerleader-style shorts underneath, it would never have covered her decently.

The skirt tails ended right at the curve of her ass cheeks, and then there was a huge expanse of exposed thigh before white thigh-high stockings that adhered to her thighs with pointed lace tops that ran unevenly around her legs in a flame pattern. On her feet, she wore high-heeled patent leather Mary Janes shining bright.

Her auburn hair was pinned up top, but the bulk of it flowed down her back in waves, reaching just shy of the end of her skirt.

She'd been going for a high school boy's Catholic-school-girl fantasy come to life. Based on his stare, she might have surpassed her goal.

Forgive me, TB, for I have sinned...

She stood shyly, one foot on the bottom step, the other on the second, tipped up as if in mid-step, only the toe of the shoe on the stair. Her hand closest to the railing rested on top of the finial.

Slowly, he walked over to her, his eyes never leaving hers until he was directly in front of her.

"Both feet flat on the bottom stair, little Flame."

Once she complied, his palms framed her hips, but the thumbs stroked the bare skin, and she shuddered at the slow movements back and forth. The room seemed to suddenly get brighter, which meant her pupils dilated, her eyes opening wide to adjust to the dimness of the hall as well as the arousal his touch was creating.

"Every man there is going to want a piece of you," he breathed. He perused her face closely as if looking for something. Then his eyes dropped to her throat, and his hands moved to either side of her neck, the heel of his hands resting on her clavicle, the fingers going around her throat as if to squeeze it. But he didn't. Instead, his thumbs stroked the hollow. "Guess I'll have to mark you as off-limits. Don't move," he told her.

She nodded once.

He took two steps back, his hands letting go at the last possible second, and went to a box on the table. He opened it and removed the black leather collar inside it and brought it over to her. In the center, it had a silver wolf charm dangling from it.

"Nemo brought this over. It has a tracker inside it. That way if the absolute worst would happen, we could find you. Never take this off. Even when we're away from the club, you wear it."

A small shockwave went through the air as if his last two sentences were being overrun with extra meaning.

Gently, he turned her to prevent her from falling off the bottom step. He gathered her hair into a thick ponytail and put it over her shoulder, then buckled the collar. After testing the tightness by sliding his fingers between the collar and her skin, he moved her hair back to cover her back, then turned her once more.

His eyes rested on the collar, needlessly straightening what was already straight. A hand went under the charm, allowing it to lie against his fingertips.

"I should warn you," he told her, looking into her eyes. "No one has ever worn my collar before. I've never indulged in a contract of any length, let alone anything that qualifies as a relationship. People there will know that. It's bound to raise eyebrows. I may get some awkward questions, possibly right in front of you. I will be respectful in my answers, but probably heavy-handed alpha, just so you know."

"And if I'm asked questions, how do you want me to answer them?"

"Stick as close to the truth as possible. Less chance of tripping up that way. Give no more information than what's asked. If you're not sure how to answer them, just flash me a look. I'll answer it." He let go of the charm. "I need your help as well. Let your author's curiosity go to work. Ask questions. You can even gossip about the girls. Word will have gotten out, so people will be talking. But gossiping is—"

"Inappropriate submissive behavior, I know."

"It's going to require me to correct you. Publicly. If we have to delve too deep, I'll have to take you somewhere private where it's assumed I'll be doing more stringent correction."

"So I'll be asking questions you can't and purposefully getting in trouble as a cover. And, between the atypical clothing, being there with you, and then being publicly taken away, you're hoping to draw out my stalker."

He nodded. "Yes, that's the plan."

32

JUNE 17TH

TB

ONCE AT THE LIBRARY, HE CHECKED THEM IN, TURNING OVER HIS PHONE. It was a dummy phone, but they didn't need to know that. His watch had his actual phone in it.

Turning to Flame, he held out his hand. He saw her puzzled expression. "Phone. You can't have it inside the club due to privacy rules. It will be safe in my lockbox."

"Oh. Umm… I didn't bring it with me," she told him.

His eyebrows raised in disbelief. "You don't have your new phone with you?"

She shook her head.

"What if there's an emergency?"

"I'm with you. Why would I need it? You're better than a phone in an emergency."

He rolled his eyes.

"You know you do that a lot? One day, they're going to roll right out of your head."

He sighed loudly.

"Oh, don't act so put upon."

"Flame. Go nowhere without your phone. Ever. Especially with your *friend* looking for you."

After signing them in, he guided Flame over to the bar. He ordered her a glass of wine and himself a water. His stomach was rolling. He couldn't tell if it was because her stalker was here, or if he was nervous about tonight's questioning, or if because they'd been here less than five minutes and he already had a list of men to throat-punch for looking at his Flame.

When their drinks came, she took a sip of her wine while she looked around. Then she looked up at him, clearly concerned, as she was biting her lip.

He used his index finger to tap her lips lightly, reminding her to stop hurting herself. "What's wrong?"

"Why would something be wrong?"

"You always bite the left side of your lip when you're agitated. What's wrong?"

She raised a hand to her lips as if she could stop herself from doing it ever again by touching them. "Umm... I told you a fib earlier."

"And what would that be, naughty girl?"

"I do actually have my phone. I know they're not allowed inside, but I didn't want to give it up since, as you pointed out, my *friend* is looking for me."

He scowled. "Where is it? You don't have a purse on you. And that jacket is so tight, I don't see anything in your pockets."

"I have a special pocket in all of my corsets. I sew them myself. All the boning helps keep it safe."

"Why don't you carry it in your purse?"

"It always falls to the bottom of my bag, no matter where I put it, and then I can't get to it. Plus, sometimes a purse is bothersome, so my little pocket has room for my phone, ID, and credit card. That way, if I get stuck somewhere, I can get to it easily."

"Not that easily," he grunted. "You have to reach into your corset to get it. That's got to look weird."

"It's for emergencies. If it's a real emergency, I'm not going to care if anyone sees me feeling myself up to get to them."

You have to give her credit. In a weird way, it makes sense.

"Sometimes your logic defies my understanding."

She snorted. "Make up your mind. Mad I don't have my phone in case of an emergency. Mad I'm breaking club rules by having it hidden on my person. Amused by my hiding place. Besides, it doesn't have to make sense to you. It just needs to make sense to me."

He pulled her close, putting his mouth next to her ear. His hand dropped below her waist and gave her a quick swat on the ass. "That's for lying." He kissed the side of her head and quickly smoothed over where he'd spanked her, his fingers sliding deftly under the layered skirt to tease her skin just below the cheek. "And that's for being prepared. Good girl."

Over the next two hours, TB made sure to introduce Flame to several of the regulars in the bar area. As predicted, he noticed how many people saw her collar, glanced at his wrists with the wolf bands, and registered surprise. Doms and subs alike registered disappointment that both appeared to be off the market. At least temporarily. He managed to keep from rolling his eyes, but just barely.

Just after nine-thirty, he noticed the triad come into the bar and sit in one of the large private booths. The two Doms named Loki and Gilgamesh flanked their sub, Medusa. To the casual observer, nothing would seem out of place. But TB suspected there was something more going on with the threesome. He knew when people were casing a location, and these three were definitely involved in a surreptitious conversation, as well as watching the crowd with intensity, even if no one else knew.

TB double-tapped his watch to activate the communication device so that the others could hear the upcoming conversation. "Okay, Flame. This is a group I need to ask questions of. We're going to go and talk to this triad at the booth. Are you ready to be curious?"

"A real triad?" Her question was breathy. "I won't need to try to be curious. I definitely have questions."

He chuckled. "Something to put on your list for 'research'?"

Ignore that pang in your chest at her answer. It's heartburn from the curry at dinner. Never mind, you've never had heartburn before.

She blushed and shook her head. "Well..." She considered. "Questions, yes. Do, no. I've all I can handle with one partner."

He put an arm around her shoulders and pulled her close. He ducked his head to whisper hotly in her ear, "Never say never. It's always the quiet ones who are the most adventurous."

"Is that..." She bit her lip, and he could tell what the rest of the question was, but he was going to make her ask it anyway. "Have you done that?"

Honesty or lies?

He tilted her chin up and in his direction so that he could see her eyes. "Yes, but I don't share well with others. And I would never, ever share you."

Her mouth opened as if to say something but then closed almost immediately. The blush on her cheeks stained brighter. Rather than make her glow a furious red, he put his hand on her back and steered her toward the booth.

"Loki. Gilgamesh." He nodded at the two men. "This is Flame. She's new here, and I thought perhaps she might like to meet Medusa."

"Lobo." Loki glared at the pair's sub. "I shouldn't allow it. She's in trouble."

Medusa looked at Loki with a cool stare, just short of defying him.

Loki was in what TB called CEO garb. Crisp white button-down shirt, sleeves rolled up, top button undone, dress pants, and dress shoes. He had obviously lost his jacket and tie somewhere along the way. One hand held a drink. The other was resting along the backside of the curved leather booth behind where Medusa sat.

Gilgamesh grinned at his partner. "A little over the top for stepping out into traffic, friend."

The language was lighthearted, but Lobo got the sense that Gilgamesh wasn't nearly as humored by what she had done either.

I wonder what kind of "traffic" she walked out into?

Gilgamesh was slightly older than his male counterpart. He was shorter than Loki and dark to his light. Not only looks-wise, they were opposites in terms of temperament. Loki was forbidding, and Gilgamesh was more fun-loving. He also was more of a playboy. His tight jeans, trendy purple button-down, and generous ink showing from his cuffs and neckline made him a definite favorite topic of conversation and lusting amongst the subs, both male and female.

It wasn't unusual for triads to be so opposing, especially if they were committed groupings that completed one another, but it was the woman who was the enigma.

Medusa was dressed in a tight black skirt and a brown lace tank top that cut off and showed a tight midriff with a pierced belly button. Her shoulder-length hair was a mix of browns, blondes, and reds, giving the illusion to different people what her hair color actually was, and the ends curled up in chunks in different directions. He supposed that was part of the nickname because the ends did look a little bit like forked tongues. For TB, the oddity of Medusa was her eyes. They were violet. It was clear they were colored contacts, but there was something odd about them even then.

And there was no mistaking it. All three of them gave off an aura of "Do not fuck with us," but of the three, he was sure she was the most dangerous of the triad.

She may be dressed like a submissive, but there is nothing submissive about her.

"Flame, this is Medusa. She is the submissive in the triad with Loki and Gilgamesh. They are relatively new to the club as well."

Medusa looked at Loki with exaggerated emotion, clearly requesting permission to speak.

Loki covered her hand on the table with his other hand, picked it up, and, after threading their fingers together, kissed the back of it. "Medusa, don't be like that. I only meant I was worried."

She turned her face from his, the simpering gone. The look on her face now was more natural because she smiled, but TB noticed it was only with her mouth. The eyes were deep and cold. "Flame. It's nice to meet you."

He felt Flame stiffen as she also recognized the lack of connection in the woman's gaze.

"You, also."

To break the tension, TB felt Gilgamesh redirect the conversation. "I don't believe I've met your partner before, Lobo." Gilgamesh stood and held out his hand. "It's nice to meet you." Gilgamesh smiled, raising her knuckles to his lips, where he pressed a kiss.

"Gil, back down," Loki ordered. "My apologies, Lobo. Apparently, his inner Lothario is out tonight."

"*Mi scuso se ti ho offeso,*" Gilgamesh apologized.

"None taken. May we join you?"

Loki nodded, and TB gestured for Flame to slide into the booth on Loki's side. While he knew the three were a committed triad based on their play at the club, he wasn't one hundred percent sure Gilgamesh wouldn't continue to work his Italian charm on her despite the fact he'd never strayed since they'd arrived as members.

Gilgamesh was the one to cut right to the point. "It would seem the lone wolf has finally been tamed." His head gestured from her collar to the cuffs on Lobo's wrist, but his grin was all for Flame.

Lobo smiled. "It would appear so, wouldn't it? Sometimes, I wonder if it wasn't just that I couldn't bear for anyone else to have their hands on her."

It was a subtle warning, but it only made Gilgamesh's grin wider, and a laugh issued from his smiling lips. "A sure sign of a man who hasn't quite realized the prize he has."

Loki injected, "It's been some time since you've been here, Lobo. Thought you'd disappeared for good; you were gone for so long. Is this beautiful woman the reason why?" His eyes flicked over to Medusa quickly.

Odd. He clearly saw me the night I was here with Flame and the five nights after that.

Attention directed at Loki, he led in with a warning, "She definitely is a beautiful distraction. By the way, not that you aren't already, but be on your guard. A girl disappeared from the parking lot last night."

"Yes," Loki replied. "I heard about Fleur and Tripoli. Gil, Medusa, and I will be... watchful."

Interesting word choice.

Loki and Gilgamesh shared a look. Between the two of them and the coldness of Medusa, his skin was itching.

Something's off.

"I didn't know Fleur since this is only my second time here. Did you know her?" Flame asked Medusa.

The young woman nodded. "Yes, I did. She didn't strike me as someone who couldn't take care of herself, though. I would have thought she would have been difficult to coerce into a vehicle or even to take by surprise. Even so, I'm surprised the doorman allowed her out into the parking lot by herself."

"That does seem odd. I would have thought this Tripoli would have been more careful with his sub."

Good girl. Casting aspersions on his character quickly to start the gossip.

"Flame," TB warned.

She looked at him with innocent eyes. "Well, it isn't very safe to allow a woman to go alone into a parking lot. You've told me it's part of your job to protect me. He's not exactly been a ringing endorsement for protective Dom behavior."

"I believe Tripoli was only escorting her to her car. Fleur was uncollared, and I don't believe they had scened together," Medusa added.

Gilgamesh spoke up. "You should have no worries, Flame. Your Dom is one of the most protective men I know. Now that he has finally collared a sub, it would appear the wolf has been well and truly captured. And wolves do fight to the death for their mates, whom they take for life. Or so I've been told."

"Flame knows I would never allow her to be unprotected, don't you, princess?" TB put his hand around the back of Flame's neck and gave it a squeeze, making sure his gesture of reprimand was obvious. Then he whispered loud enough for them to hear, "Never be disrespectful to another Dom by making assumptions about their behavior. It's not done."

33

———————

JUNE 17TH

Sylvan

"I don't mean to be disrespectful," she murmured, eyes down. "You hear about people going missing all the time, but it's in the news, never someone in your own space. It's difficult not to be nervous. And I'm already nervous enough to be here."

TB looked down at her, murmuring against the top of her head. "I've got you, little Flame. I promise. There's no need to be nervous. Just careful."

It was a dual message to her, which she appreciated.

Sylvan looked back to Medusa. "Can I ask you a question?"

"Of course," the woman replied.

"Do you..." She stopped, then restarted. "I'm sorry. This is probably forward of me, but... how does your triad work in public?"

"That is forward, Flame." TB grabbed her chin with his fingers and turned her face to his. "If I have to speak to you again, we're going to have words in private."

"It's okay, Lobo," Medusa assured him.

"I appreciate your openness, Medusa, but she needs to learn what she can and can't say and do here."

Flame nodded at him. Dual message.

Understood. Keep pushing.

"I'm sorry," Sylvan apologized. "I've just never met anyone in an actual triad before. Not judging or offended by it." She offered a smile. "Blame it on all this concern for the missing women. I guess I babble when I'm nervous and don't think things through. I overheard Lobo tell someone all the girls had red hair and, well —" She gestured. "I suggested I color it, and I thought he was going to go through the roof. Men are more touchy about their girlfriend's hair than the women are, I guess."

"It's fine. Really. And yes, they did all have red hair, although oddly enough, Fleur is blonde. Perhaps that was a coincidence up until now."

"As for the relationship," Loki replied, "we work together, so we're always together. Unless we ran into a client here, though, no one would probably be the wiser as to how we're connected." Loki turned intense eyes to Lobo. "Extra eyes on our women is always a good thing, though. Same thing for friends, both here tonight and others farther away. We'll make sure to keep a continued eye out for yours, as we know you would ours."

The three men paused and weighed each other in the silence.

She felt TB tense beside her, and when she looked down, the hand that he'd had resting on the tabletop next to his drink was now clenched into a fist.

TB nodded. "Appreciated."

Gilgamesh picked up his drink and asked a question that seemed to come out of the blue. "Have you ever traveled to Egypt? Particularly Sallum?"

"I was there not long ago on business, but I was focused on Cairo."

Loki waved him off. "Larger cities are no good for seeing the real Egypt. If you really want to get a good feel for the country and what it has to offer, Matruh is the place. We were there in April, as well. It's a Bedouin village just shy of the Libyan border. A fishing village, primarily. One of the oldest ports in the world is my understanding. Nothing of real historical significance other than that, but no tourists floating around clogging up the street life either, so you get a real sense of how things are there. Very interesting."

"Being so close to Libya, I would have thought that was a place tourists would stay away from."

"We had business there, so it was easier for us to move around. It also helps that we didn't stay long. Westerners are always looked at suspiciously in non-tourist cities, but if you take care to blend in, it's easy to move around there."

"And you're in the fishing industry?"

"Our work entails a number of things. Fishing is one of them," Gilgamesh inserted.

"And was the fishing good in Sallum?"

"Most of what we caught wasn't... useful. But we did hear that the season was over for what we were hoping to catch and that the schools had moved on from that area. Since then, we've been traveling the country here, looking for leads on other opportunities."

TB looked hard at them both. "Thank you for the info. Next time I'm in Egypt, I'll have to check it out. Maybe I'll be luckier."

TB lowered his mouth to her ear. "No need to push the questions about the girls. I know what I need to know. Sort of."

With that cryptic comment, the hand around the back of her neck moved to rest around her shoulders, his fingers idly playing with a strand of her hair.

They sat and talked about inconsequential things for a short while longer, and then TB made their excuses. Instead of taking her around the club further, he escorted her out to the parking lot and took her home.

"You didn't need to ask more questions?"

"Not tonight. That triad we spoke to isn't who we think they are, and I didn't want you to ask more questions of them and put them in a bad spot."

"Well, sassafras. I had more questions about triads. And I

didn't get to earn my punishment research either. What a bummer."

He flashed her a look she didn't understand, but it was a moot point anyway. The whole evening seemed rather anticlimactic until they got to her house, and he booted up his laptop, opening a video link. Then she understood why they'd left so early.

"Conversation with the triad came through loud and clear. Interesting discussion," Waters said when he came online.

One by one, the others popped up from their various locations. Waters was driving in his truck. Demon had drawn watch duty tonight and was sitting in his Jeep a short distance from Flame's house. Nemo, dressed all in black, including a balaclava pulled down around his neck, was sitting side-by-side with Midas in the back of a panel van they'd had parked down the street from the club. God's soundwave was present, and who the hell knew where Steel was, but it was pitch black except for the light of his watch screen reflecting up on his face.

TB tagged her around the waist absently and sat her on his lap. Sylvan saw that the others noticed. None of them seemed surprised.

"There are more eyes on the club and these girls than just one undercover cop. I don't know who they are, but Loki, Gilgamesh, and Medusa are clearly not who they say they are. However, they're also not responsible. They're clearly looking for the girls or whoever took them. Their focus was definitely in the bar tonight, though that could have been because they were watching for someone to come in from the outside. They waited specifically for a particular booth to clear, and it was one with a direct line of sight to the main entrance."

"I'm still near the club, and they haven't left yet," Steel piped in. "I'll try to follow them."

"If they split up, follow the woman. She may be posing as the sub, but I'd be willing to bet my paycheck for a year that she's in charge."

"Roger that."

"So we still have nothing?" God asked.

"On the girls, no, but Waters, where's Kubrick?"

"She had a meeting in Napa Valley. What's up?"

"Good. Don't want her to hear this just yet. You catch what I catch?"

"Yeah. A lead on Ka-Bar. It appears your new friends have seen him as recently as April. He was in Sallum, Egypt, just off the border of Libya."

"It's a port," God confirmed. "Whoever has him is moving him somewhere else."

"And maybe moving other things," TB added. "I got the impression that our friendly triad has been casing The Library the same way they've been casing other nightclubs. They mentioned being in some major cities between then and now. They said they were in the fishing business."

"Sounds like they're intel gathering," Steel interjected.

TB agreed. "That's what I thought, too. My guess is they're some sort of mercenaries, like us, but they're following traffic patterns, one in particular that runs through Sallum."

"Sex trafficking?"

"That, and he mentioned they were in the business of other things, as well. I'm guessing any sort of supplies people are trying to move that they don't want out in the open."

Midas chimed in, "I've already got another search running on the dark web for anything and anyone looking for particular traits, like hair color. That's going to be a lot to comb through though."

"Hardee har har, Midas," Nemo said, elbowing his brother. "How long have you been waiting to use that line?"

"About a week."

"Okay, girls," Waters interrupted, "you can joke all you want once our work is done here. All right. We'll get on this from here. Steel, start looking into Sallum. Once we get a handle on that, you and Nemo will go scout it out. For now, Demon, Nemo, and Midas will work with me to watch over you and Flame."

"Copy," each of the men replied before clicking out of the video link.

Flame had been silent the entire time, but now she had questions, most of which she was afraid to ask. "Are you going to tell Kubrick about possibly finding her brother?"

"That's up to Waters. Most likely, he'll tell her there's a lead, but it's likely he's been moved by now."

She nodded. "I think she'd want to know."

"I'm sure she would, princess. Kubrick is pretty tough. The thought that there's any bit of progress would make her feel better. I'm sure Waters will share it with her."

She ran her fingers through his unruly locks up front, trying to smooth them back.

"I have words to finish."

He grabbed her hand as she slid out of his lap, and he kissed her fingertips. "I'll be up shortly. If you want me to, that is."

She smiled. "Silly man. What do you think?" She went upstairs, and he swore her hips were swinging a little wider to the left and right than normal.

He grinned.

Tease.

34

JUNE 18TH

TB

They planned to go to the club again tonight. Tonight's outfit was even hotter. The boots were almost up to the knees, white with zippers up the sides. Her thighs were bare until a pair of white shorts covered her. They weren't hugging her skin or so short that they were indecent, but if she bent over at the waist, he might have gotten the impression that they showed more than they actually did. The blouse was off the shoulder, a white, sheer overlay painted with bright orange flowers.

His hand reached out for her braid, plaited down the side, and thrown over one shoulder, a bright orange ribbon tied in a bow at the end.

She stood on the bottom stair, waiting for him. Her grin was borderline mischievous. Before he realized it, his hands were around her throat, not grabbing but guiding her face closer to his. Her eyes fluttered closed, and he tried to memorize what this moment felt like.

The doorbell rang.

TB yanked his head back with lightning speed, his head turning straight down the hall to the door. His weapon was drawn, and he was motioning with his hand to head back up the stairs.

"Bathroom. Don't leave until I come to get you."

She nodded and flew up the stairs.

Weapon at the ready, TB doused the hall lights and stepped on silent feet toward the front door. A shadow moved across it, almost imperceptibly, but when TB swung the door open wide, no one was there.

Then he looked down at his feet.

"Fuck," he whispered to himself. He lifted his watch to his mouth. "Call Nerdbrain."

The ringtone over his watch went once, then he heard the sounds of huffing and puffing. "Can't talk now, dear. Daddy's working."

"Get that bastard, or you're going back in the locker," TB threatened.

"Yes, honey, I'll pick up milk"—Nemo grunted, sounding like he'd had to jump over something—"on my way home. Gotta go!"

TB barked out another expletive, then reached down and picked up the white box wrapped with a giant red ribbon. With a last look out the door, he brought the box inside and set it on the dining room table. Probably not the smartest move, but whatever was in this box wasn't meant to kill. It was meant to scare.

He pulled a knife from his front pocket, slit the ribbon, and flipped open the lid.

What lay in the box even gave *him* pause.

There was no blood, no tissue, no gore of any kind. Just six braids, each with a different colored silk ribbon at the tail, that had been neatly cut from women's heads. Five red. One blonde.

His heart grabbed at thinking how a seventh braid with a little orange ribbon at the end of the tail could so easily be in this box with the others.

35

———————

JUNE 18TH-19TH

Sylvan

THE MINUTE HE ORDERED HER TO THE BATHROOM, HER EYES FLEW OPEN, and she saw a whole new TB in front of her. The one who earned him his nickname. A total bastard. Cold. Cruel. Emotionless. A killer.

She flew up the stairs, into her room, into her bathroom, shut the door, and locked it. Heart pounding, she stepped into the bathtub, pulled the curtain around her, and made herself into the smallest possible shape she could.

Minutes later, he knocked at the door.

"Flame, it's safe to come out."

She heard him, his voice faint, as if coming down a long hallway, but she couldn't make her body move.

"Flame, open up, it's safe now."

She was so cold. There was more noise, but she was physically locked in place, knees hugged tight to her chest, face planted into the tops of her thighs.

Air rushed past her skin, and she was moving through space without the benefit of her body being in control.

Then she was still, settled into a smaller space, not as tight as she had been in the bathroom but firmly enclosed in warmth. There was a gentle wave of noise in the background, and though it was soothing, it was unintelligible. She felt pressure against the top of her head and something stroking through her hair.

It was some time before she opened her eyes. When she did, she was in her room, but in the extra-wide Victorian armchair in the corner. However, she wasn't sitting directly in the chair. She was in TB's lap, and he was talking to her softly. Nonsense, really. Even though she heard him, she was still too discombobulated to process it. She closed her eyes again and burrowed in closer to his chest, one palm over his heart.

When she swam up to reality the next time, she was in the same place. It must not have been too much later, but she was still embarrassed. "I'm sorry," she apologized, trying to get out of his lap.

He refused to let her go. "Stay." He pressed his lips to the top of her head, and his arms pulled her tighter to him. "It's fine."

"Who was it?" she asked quietly, afraid to hear his answer.

He paused. "No one."

Now she knew she didn't want to know the answer, but she asked anyway. "Then why did the doorbell ring?"

"Someone left a package."

"What was inside it?" Her voice was barely audible.

He hugged her closer still and pressed his lips to the top of her head again, but this time, he left his lips next to her hair as he spoke. "You don't want to know, princess."

Then the tears started. She couldn't stop. If he didn't want to tell her, it was bad. It was really bad. TB had never sugarcoated anything with her. He might not give a lot of details, but he'd never out-and-out refused to tell her anything.

He held her all through the sobs, including the body-wracking ones.

Eventually, she cried herself out. She didn't know how long they sat there, but it was a long time.

"You should get some sleep. You're exhausted. Here or upstairs?"

"Upstairs."

She held her breath in the silence.

"I'll be up in a minute."

This is never going to end.

She had changed into her nightgown and turned on the gas fireplace. It was summer, but she needed the comfort, and it burned without giving off too much heat.

She had just sat down to check her email when she heard him start to come up the stairs. That had been a mistake. The words in front of her blurred. Email after email. All different email addresses. All sinister.

Did you get my present?

They cried.

They screamed.

They begged.

But they weren't you.

This latest one is like you.

She's not afraid.

She'll be a fighter.

I can be patient a little longer.

And eventually, I'll get the real thing.

I'm coming, Jolie.

More and more, all the same type of thing.

It was time to give up.

She wasn't sure if it would help free Fleur, his latest victim, but she couldn't bear it if another girl suffered because of her.

Hopefully, if she gave herself up, it would end. But she needed something first. Something for herself.

TB stood in front of her desk, a concerned look on her face. "Flame?"

She turned her computer around to face him.

He looked over the emails, and she could see that each one made him angrier than the last. He tapped on his watch. "Call Midas."

She heard the phone ring on the other end, and then a groggy voice came over the line. "I'm waiting on the DNA from their hair, TB; I can't make it run any faster. I'll call when something comes through."

Sylvan gasped, her eyes going wide. "Their hair?"

Of course the hair. It was always the hair. Even though you knew it was the hair that called to him, you just couldn't cut it. Now, it's causing that pain to other girls. Your stupid pride!

"I'm not alone, Midas."

"Shit. Sorry, TB. What do you need?"

"I need you to access Flame's emails. He sent a bunch of them, all from different email addresses on Google. Can you trace them?"

"Yes, but if he's bouncing them, which he probably is, it's going to take a while. And even then, it's not a guarantee. If he's smart, he also set them to send at specific times, like a chain. I'm on it."

Midas disconnected, as did TB. He held her gaze. "He cut off their hair. There were six braids in the package."

It's too much.

Strong arms swept her up out of the chair, then laid her in her bed. TB lay between her and the edge of the bed, his arms around her, curling her close to his chest. "I'm not leaving you. With my last breath, remember that."

She snuggled into his chest.

36

JUNE 19TH

TB

THE SUN WAS JUST BEGINNING TO PEEK OVER THE HORIZON. TB's EYES opened quickly and clearly. He hadn't been dreaming as he dozed, but his brain had been processing information. Something had been bothering him. He knew better than to try and tease it forward, so he had let it percolate on its own. In his half-sleep, it came to him.

The sleeves. Why naked except for the sleeves?

His gaze slid over her arm. When he'd taken her to bed, she only had her nightgown on. A nightgown with only the skinniest of straps. Her robe was draped over her chair where she'd put it before catching sight of those emails. She'd been distracted.

Sure enough, no sleeve. The barest, creamiest, softest skin he'd ever touched.

His eyes caught on what looked like a bruise.

Did I do that?

He shouldn't have. It was too high. The other night, he'd wound the belt around her wrists, and this was just under her elbow, almost in the crook of it. And even then, he was extremely careful with his bindings so that they didn't bruise, welt, or cut off blood circulation. In his fog over her, had he miscalculated?

Gently, so as not to wake her, he turned her arm so he could see the underside to make sure there weren't more marks.

His eyes couldn't believe what they were seeing. There wasn't just one mark. Not even just two. There were a series of marks all the way down her arm following the main vein. They were scars —not current. They showed that her use in the past had been often and damaging.

He knew he needed to slow his brain down and think rationally. He really did know it. It hadn't bothered him in the slightest to recover drugs for people during his time as the Collector. It hadn't bothered him that one of his teammates was a recovering user. So why was this so difficult now? It wasn't as if she were currently using.

His brain rewound to when she had insisted that her arms remain covered. She knew what he'd see. Was this what she was so ashamed of that she was afraid to talk about her past? What could be so awful to cause her to hide something like this?

He thought back to everyone pushing him to give her a chance. Steel talking about her truly living in reality. Waters' sanction to pursue her. Kubrick's fierce protectiveness. Was it all bullshit? Had he and his friends been taken in by this seemingly sweet little thing?

Idiot! Don't jump to the wrong conclusions. There are a number of reasons why she wouldn't say. You. Know. Her. Don't get stupid about this.

She lied.

Do you tell everyone about your fuck ups from the past? No. I didn't think so.

I need to think!

He swung out of the bed, his body hunched over his legs, his elbows propped up on his knees, and his head in his hands as his fingers ran through his hair. After a few deep inhales and slow exhales, he stood and began pulling his clothes back on.

37

____

JUNE 19TH

Sylvan

When Sylvan woke, she could tell it was early in the morning. The sky outside her window was still dark, but she could see the beginnings of the blues and purples giving way to the reds and oranges.

Rolling over to get out of bed, she noticed TB's hulking frame in her desk chair. Something about it was off. It wasn't anything she could put her finger on, but she knew that something wasn't right.

She leaned up on one arm. "TB? Is everything okay?"

He didn't speak.

She felt her heart rate accelerate, like the time she'd had too many energy drinks as she was rushing to make a deadline in the wee hours of the morning. Just like then, her heart was pounding so loud she felt like she could hear it, and so fast that if she looked down at her chest, she knew she'd see it pushing at her skin to get out of her body. A cold sweat broke out on her forehead, and her stomach contents were in danger of rising up her throat.

Then she realized how she knew he was upset. He wasn't lounging in the chair. He was sitting straight up in it like it was an electric chair, and his hands curled around and grabbed the ends of the armrests.

"TB?" she tried again, softer this time.

"Who's Jolie?"

Well, sugar.

His voice was hard, and it felt like her eardrums were being pelted with gravel. "Who is Jolie?"

You decided you were going to tell him.

She sighed. "My past."

His jaw was clenched, and she could almost hear his teeth grinding. "I have a job to do. And that job requires getting people to talk. You've been holding out information about your stalker, about your past... including the tracks on your arms."

Her eyes blew wide, and she looked down at the undersides of her forearms. Instantly, she hugged them around her middle. She felt herself shrinking, trying to make herself invisible.

"I'm not a drug user," she whispered.

"Your arms say otherwise, princess. Don't lie to me."

"I'm not lying! It's been a long time, and there hasn't really been a time to just throw that line of conversation out there. All you had to do was ask."

"Really? All I had to do? Correct me if I'm wrong, but I swear we asked you for information about your past, Flame. Two days ago. I seem to recall you tightened up so fast and used every trick you could to not lie but also not give up anything. Why? What could be so awful that you wouldn't want to say?"

"I... I wanted to tell you. I did. I panicked. I worried you'd hate me. Then, I got sick because I realized this was all my fault."

"You know who it is, don't you?"

She sank inside herself. "I started to suspect just before you came here, but I wasn't sure. When the phone call came, I couldn't ignore it anymore or pass things off as coincidence. So, yes," she admitted. "I know now."

"Why not say something last night? I'm trying to understand, but I've got to admit, it feels like you're protecting this shitheel."

"No! Never! I knew I needed to tell you, but I just needed a little more time."

"Time for what?"

"Time to figure out how to tell you. I don't want you to look at me differently."

"Flame"—he crouched down at the side of the bed—"just tell me. I know whatever it is will be bad. You don't need to sugarcoat it or edit your history. Short of you kidnapping the women yourself, I can't imagine what would make me look at you differently."

She hung her head. "You don't know. You can't possibly understand."

"You're right. I can't possibly understand until you tell me what's got you so tied up in knots." He sat on the edge of the bed, his body turned toward her while his feet remained planted on the floor. "Princess, I thought you trusted me to keep you safe? I can't do that when you keep secrets."

"I'm sorry," she whispered.

"So, tell me now. Who is this guy? Why do you think this is your fault?"

She couldn't look at him. Couldn't speak. It was all over. Not only that, but her refusal to open her mouth and tell TB what she knew could easily have gotten those women killed. Her continued silence was practically ensuring their deaths or worse.

Just spit it out! If it's over, it's over. Those women's lives aren't worth it.

He stood up from the bed and paced toward the door, his fingers running through his rumpled hair. When he turned back in her direction, his stare pierced her heart. "I need you to tell me what's going on, Flame. I'm hanging on to my temper by a thread. You can't hold any information to yourself anymore about your past. It's too risky. For you. For them. You've got to tell us what you know."

"I know you probably won't believe me, but I had already decided yesterday to share with you what I know, but I just... I wanted one more night with you where I was still clean in your mind. I've been so scared, TB. So scared I couldn't think straight. The only time I've felt safe is when I've been with you. You said, 'No matter what, I've got you.' 'My last breath,' you said. And I'm about to throw that all away because I was too selfish to speak up sooner. I would have been better off to tell you when it was just a suspicion. But part of me can't regret that I didn't because then I wouldn't have gotten to have you, even for just this little bit of time."

She admitted with defeat, "Yes, I was scared to share my past with you because doing so put me right back into the eye of the storm that my life was until six years ago. I've worked so hard to be at peace with my past. To accept it. To move on.

"But TB, you can't miss the irony in this situation. You make this big deal out of honesty, but you can't even be honest with yourself, let alone me. I thought you honestly felt something for me, even if you were reluctant to feel it. That you would want something with me bad enough to let go of *your* past and fight for it.

"Instead, I discover you don't want anything bad enough except to be the villain in your own story. You use your Total Bastard persona to destroy anything good that comes your way. It's safer to be apart from others because you don't have to feel. It's easier to be your nickname because it discourages people from getting close. Because wanting something, and wanting it badly enough, breaks down the lie you've been telling yourself most, if not all, of your life. You don't just use your anger and your pain to isolate yourself—you revel in it."

She got out of bed, the sheet wound around her like a shroud. Tears threatened to unleash. Her voice was barely above a whisper and on the edge of desperation. "Please understand. I did everything I could to save myself, but now I'm right back in his grasp, and there's going to be no stopping him. I am not something to be bought and sold any more than those women are."

He stalked up to her, his chest heaving. "What are you talking about?"

She could see the confusion warring with the disbelief in his eyes.

"I'll tell your team everything. But you can't be in the room. I can't watch your face. It will kill me."

She was weary. All of this was too much, and she wanted to lock herself away again. Not just physically but mentally and emotionally as well. It had been safer that way.

38

———————

JUNE 19TH

TB

Outside the conference room, TB clutched at Midas' arm to prevent him from going inside. "Midas. I..."

Midas used his free arm to grab TB's opposite shoulder. "I've got her. She'll be fine. Trust me. And while you're on the other side of that screen, figure out your shit. Because this is definitely your point of no return."

A single clap to TB's shoulder and Midas went into the conference room. TB saw Flame in the space between Midas' body, the door, and the door jamb, and then he couldn't see her anymore when the door closed.

Midas had some sort of voodoo magic he did on "good cop" interrogations. No one understood how it worked, even him, so when they had softer targets, he took the lead with his auto-suggestion tactics.

Banished to the security camera room, TB stood in front of the monitors, watching the room. Midas sat at the head. Flame was one seat to his right. The others stood around the room, relaxed yet focused. They were trying not to scare her, but TB knew she was petrified by how her teeth were gnawing on her lip and the tight fists clenched in her lap.

"Everything feels stretched. Like if I lock myself down any harder, I'm going to shatter," he said to himself.

"That's because you know you might not be able to fix this."

TB looked to his right and saw the speaker had a green light on it. God was listening in. TB had known the man would be but hadn't figured he'd be listening in on the security room end as well.

"Let me guess," the voice continued. "Feeling panicked? Angry? Confused? Reliving your argument and realizing all the ways you've fucked up? Wishing you could reverse time?"

TB relived the conversation in her sanctuary.

He *did* always paint himself as a villain.

He *did* destroy things first so that others couldn't.

He *did* hold himself away from others because when they left, it wouldn't hurt.

He *did* see himself as unredeemable.

He *did* see the worst in others because he jumped to the most obvious conclusion, thereby allowing him to let go before they did.

He wanted her so badly, but he truly believed he *didn't* deserve her, so he subconsciously took every opportunity to try to turn her away.

But then he turned around and tried to bind her to him using the only weapon he had, which was her feelings for him.

The poor woman had to feel like she was constantly being whipped around in every direction with him. She had no clue how he felt. And why should she? He'd never told her.

And you can't use the excuse that you didn't know. It was always your way: deny, deny, deny.

"I failed her," TB acknowledged. "I did promise I'd protect her. I may have kept her out of the hands of her stalker, but I didn't protect her from me and my self-destructive nature."

"Finally, he understands," God mumbled.

TB's attention was drawn back to the conference room.

"Who are you, Flame?"

The question came from Midas.

Clearing her throat, her eyes focused on Midas, saying, "What do you want to know?"

Midas had a folder in front of him with her name on the tab. A very thin folder.

Midas opened the folder and looked up at her, his expression blank.

The open folder revealed about a dozen small, stapled sets of paper. Midas laid them out neatly on the table with deliberation, identifying each one as he did so. "Social security number. State I.D. A savings account containing just over eight million dollars. A checking account with over forty thousand dollars in it—only debit card transactions and automatic payments for bills. No credit cards. Five years of tax returns claiming earnings from writing your books—all showing huge amounts of earnings each year—no other declarations. A title on the house, which is paid in full. A history of gas and electric, cell phone, and internet usage. A website and social media accounts dedicated to your twenty-five books, but no personal pages or accounts. That's it. Nothing else. And none of it goes back more than six years. Prior to that, you did not exist."

She did not look down at the papers. She simply stared at Midas.

"I'll ask again. Who are you? Because this"—Midas waved a hand over the papers—"is not a real person."

"My name is Sylvan Jones. You can see I'm exactly who I say I am."

"But only for the past six years. Who were you before that?"

Her gaze was steady on Midas, but TB took in the hard swallow, the pulse beating skittishly in her neck, and the fists clenching and unclenching repeatedly in her lap.

"I was the same person I am now."

Waters broke in. "Let's not play semantics games, Flame.

Characteristics aside, you were most definitely not known by the name you are now. It didn't exist back then."

Midas took back over. "Flame, why did you not exist prior to six years ago?"

Her gaze finally broke, going to her hands in her lap.

Tears threatened to fall from her eyes, and TB felt himself wanting to pull her out of that room and hide her somewhere.

A shape knelt down at her side. Nemo. He turned the chair slightly and reached into her lap, his hands resting over hers. "Flame, look at me."

Liquid emerald eyes looked at the blond playboy.

He smiled gently at her. "While it's entirely possible that what you say is true, we're all in agreement with Waters. You need to tell us. There's very little you could say that we haven't heard before. No one will judge you."

"You can't promise that, Nemo," she whispered as she looked back down at their hands in her lap. "That's already a lie. I can feel his judgment from here."

No one needed to identify whose judgment she was referring to.

He fought the discomfort, locking it down. On the inside— sick to his stomach at whatever was coming. On the outside— badass and pissed. But not for the reasons most people would have guessed.

Nemo reached to tip her chin up so that her eyes met his again, then he raised one of her hands to his mouth, kissing the knuckles, followed by rubbing his thumb across them. He smiled encouragingly at Flame. "We all have secrets. Each and every one of us, including Mr. Totally Stupid. Some of them are worse than others. All of us have felt unredeemable. Some of us still do," he emphasized. "No matter what, we'll protect you. And you know TB has your back, even though he's refusing to admit to his feelings.

"But he's being that way right now because he's scared. When he feels like he can't control things, he lashes out. Some people would say that's immature. That he's throwing a temper tantrum.

But that's not it at all. His brain doesn't process fear like a normal person's. He can only process fear in the form of anger."

Nemo flicked a quick look over her shoulder to the camera embedded in the frame of the painting behind her. TB knew where Nemo was about to go, and his stomach dropped in a real moment of regret.

Don't, Nemo. Let it go.

"Flame, do you know how TB got his name?"

She shook her head. "He just said it was because he was cruel."

Nemo nodded. "He is. But believe me, when he shows that side of himself to someone, you'd best believe they deserve much worse. One of our first jobs, we were hired to track down a drug boss and rescue his daughter. Her mother's family was very wealthy, and it sounded like an easy project. Go in, get the girl, bring her home. What we didn't know until TB caught him in the act was that this particular asshole was shooting up his ten-year-old daughter and selling her to his men. TB went into berserker mode. I've never seen anything like it. None of us have. That man didn't deserve to live after what he'd done to that girl. But what TB did to him? It's probably why he's wanted dead in so many countries."

And I'd fucking do it again.

"That man's daughter was there for the whole thing. Her father had her so brainwashed, she screamed at TB to stop. She called him selfish, cruel, and sadistic. Selfish for taking her father away. Cruel for murdering him in front of the daughter who loved him. Sadistic for causing so much pain. And it *was* painful to watch, let alone for that man to experience.

"But you need to know this, Flame. TB isn't a good man. He's righteous."

What the fuck?

"He'll tell you he isn't worthy of anything good because of the blood on his hands. He believes he has to be alone because his anger at those who hurt others is so terribly strong. But he doesn't see what we see.

"You know why we call him Total Bastard? It's not because he is one, although that's what his pea-brain believes. We call him that because he rids the world *of* Total Bastards. The men who are selfish, who are cruel, who are sadistic."

Flame's tears were free-flowing.

Nemo continued, "So when he pushed you, like he clearly did this morning, it was because his heart cut off all of the blood flow to his brain, making him stupid for a few minutes." Nemo turned her arm over and pushed the sleeve up to the elbow. "He saw this, and I'd bet my life he was suddenly back in that moment when he caught that man, and his men, raping a daughter who should have been loved. Protected."

"So he panicked," Midas piped in. "He feels like he can't protect you because this jackwagon keeps finding ways to reach out to you. Worse yet, he feels like he doesn't deserve you, and that means he's terrified to admit he loves you, Flame, because you might leave him if you ever figure that out. So he keeps pushing you away, even though he has a burning need to pull you closer until you're so bound to him that the two of you become one person."

TB stood frozen, watching his woman's heart break and his friends betray him.

Betrayal? Really?

They had no right to share that story.

Why? It's their story, too. All of them did and saw horrific things on that project. Everyone's soul came back stained, not just yours.

She'll never forgive what I did.

She doesn't have to, dumbass. You need to realize that you saved that child's life. That child hated you then. She might still hate you. But she's alive today because you killed that sonofabitch.

But the way I killed him...

Doesn't matter. It's done. The girl is safe. End of story.

It seemed like the screens stopped recording because there was no sound from the conference room. No one looked as if they were even breathing.

Demon's voice was the first to cut through the silence. "How long, Flame?"

She inhaled, let out a long exhale, and looked to the medic.

He pushed her to speak. "How long have you been free of it?"

"I've been clean since I left... home. Six years."

The word sounded like it tasted funny in her mouth. Almost like it was foreign or not the right word. TB felt his heart speed up.

She shuddered as she took in a deep breath, exhaled long again, and began to talk.

"My parents were addicts. My father was a dealer. My mother was a prostitute."

TB felt his body turning cold. He could feel himself emotionally and psychologically shutting down. Instantly, he pictured that drug boss, but instead of seeing him abuse the little girl, he saw Flame. Pictured her as a teenager.

"My earliest memory in life is walking down the street with a little pink backpack. I was five, maybe? I don't really know. I don't know when my actual birthday is. I can only guess at how old I actually am."

"Jesus," someone whispered. He wasn't sure who.

"My dad sent me on 'errands' every day. A pool hall. A pawnshop. A bodega. A couple of people's homes. At every stop, there would be someone who met me at the door. Each person reached into my backpack and removed something, then placed something inside. And there was always a gift for me. At the pool hall, they'd give me a small cup of soda. The man at the pawnshop gave me little trinkets, probably things he bought off people. I remember a butterfly hair clip one time. The bodega was the only place I was allowed inside, but still, there was the backpack ritual. The girl there was the best. Always any ice cream treat I wanted out of the case."

She offered a sad grin at the simple childhood joy of ice cream. Nemo, still crouched at her side, seemed to understand and gave her a small nod. His thumbs gently rotated circles of calm on the backs of her hands.

"Most places were regular stops, but every once in a while, there would be a new stop. Never more than four or five blocks away, but as young as I was, I'm guessing that's too far for a child of that age to have been walking on their own.

"One day, I went past the local school, and all of the kids were outside playing. They were laughing. Having fun. They didn't have to stay home and run errands for their fathers. I'd never been to school or played with other kids. I remember wanting nothing more than to be on the other side of that playground fence, running and shrieking in joy like they were. When they all went inside, I ran home and told my father I wanted to go where all of those other kids were. I didn't want to run errands anymore."

The tears came. It was a losing battle. There was no way to hold them back now. "He yelled at me. Called me ungrateful. Said there was no way he was going to lose his runner. If he sent me to school, he'd have to run the errands himself, and then bad men—I can only assume he meant the police—would take him away. After all, if they caught me, what would they do to an innocent little kid? And if he were to disappear, he told me, Mother and I would be alone. We'd starve without him." She snorted. "Like he was some great provider. Like he cared what happened to us. Then..." her voice dropped even lower, "he made it very clear that I should never ask again."

Flame pulled her hands from Nemo's grasp, and her arm crossed over her middle to grab the other arm. Her eyes were open, but they had drifted to staring down the expanse of the table, focused on nothing. The right hand rubbed subconsciously at her left forearm. Every time on the downstroke, she winced.

"He beat you?" Midas asked.

She spoke without acknowledging the question. "I cried. I begged him to stop, and that seemed to make him even angrier. He backed me into a corner. I tried to curl into a little ball to protect myself, but he kept hitting me. Then he kicked me. Hard. In the arm, maybe? Must have been, but I don't remember much after that. I guess he knocked me unconscious. When I came to, my arm was swollen and black and blue."

He briefly remembered seeing the weird kink in the belt around her wrist when he bound her hands together, but he'd been so caught up in the moment that he didn't think to look closer. So many dots were connecting now, and a fuller picture was forming.

"I guess it was broken, but I didn't know that, and neither he nor my mother was going to waste their drug money to take me to the hospital. When it didn't heal properly, I made sure it was always covered so that no one could see it.

"He hurt me so badly. I was petrified. And that fucking bastard made me go back out on my errands the next day, broken arm and all."

The profanity from her, where it had never been heard from before, made her pain that much more real. "Oh, princess, I'm so sorry," TB whispered to her image on the screen.

The voice came from the speakers. "It works better if you apologize to the actual person, you know."

TB's eyes never moved from her on the screen. "I didn't know. Waters said it would feel like the world was imploding. It's worse." The last part was whispered.

"I said nothing was ever going to be the same," the voice said with a sigh, as if to himself. "And it hasn't been."

TB didn't know what God was talking about. Truthfully, it didn't matter because all TB was feeling was pain. Pure, unfiltered, unstoppable pain.

Back in the conference room, Waters spoke next. "That explains your childhood but not the new identity. What happened six years ago? California is hell and gone from New York City."

She sat up straight, looking into his hazel eyes. The tears kept falling.

Nemo palmed her cheeks with his large hands, turning her gaze to him, his thumbs swiping away the tears that would not stop. "It's okay, Flame. You're safe here. Whatever it was is in the past and can't hurt you anymore."

"But it's not, Nemo," she told him. "That's just it. The past is why this is all happening now. It's why TB was right to judge me as selfish for not giving you what information I had, even as I denied it mattered."

TB didn't want to hear the rest of this. It could only get worse from here, and he had a feeling the worst he could imagine still wasn't the worst it got.

She sighed and turned her face away from Nemo's gaze. "It was a few years later. Or, at least, I think it was. It's not like we had a calendar on the wall. One night, I came home from my errands, and my parents weren't there. They didn't return that night. It was three days before I accepted that they weren't coming back. That was when he came for me. Gendry."

The way she said his name made TB's heart clench. A name. He had a name. A name for whomever it was that had hurt his woman. Who had frightened her. Who had stolen her life.

"He was my father's boss, and he claimed that my father placed me in his care as he was dying. He claimed my parents died by overdose." She rolled her eyes with an exasperated sigh. "Both? At the same time? Even as a child, I knew that was unlikely. So, I went with him.

"At first, it seemed like things had improved. He was nice to me. He seemed like he cared that I'd had things so rough. I had my own room, nice clothes, good food. He never beat me, which at the time seemed far more important than anything else. I still didn't get to go to school, but he hired a tutor to teach me to read and write. All those things I had wanted but hadn't been allowed to have before.

"I'm not sure exactly how long I was with him, but it was several years. I must have been just into my teens when I noticed his attention toward me began to shift. Maybe it had always been that way, but by then, I realized he was always watching me. I'd enter a room he was in, and I could feel his eyes on me, following me every second. I felt dirty every time.

"People started coming over. Mostly men, but whoever they were, they were clearly higher up the chain than him. I wasn't completely naive. By then, I had figured out how Gendry made his living, but what options did I have? If I ran away, one of his enforcers would just drag me back. If I ran and managed to evade him, how would I support myself? I had no skills to speak of. And even if I went to a police officer, I soon learned the hard way that he had more than a few in his back pocket.

"Sometimes, when I'd walk into the room, conversations would abruptly change. The men would look at me the same way he did. Some of them would be nice to me, but I knew it wasn't really because they wanted to be nice or help me. One or two tried to touch me, but Gendry wouldn't let them. He'd say things like they would owe him for a taste. At first, I didn't understand, but it didn't take long to realize that there could be worse things than beatings."

Her voice cracked, and she began to cough. Demon brought her a bottle of water and encouraged her to drink.

"Somewhere around that same time period, I got sick. It was probably just a cold, but he kept shoving medicine into me. I was so tired all the time, so muzzy-headed. I know now that he was drugging me. That's when the marks began to appear on my arms. If I was aware enough to remember him injecting me, he just kept reassuring me that they were vitamin shots. He was trying to make me well again.

"There are entire periods of time that I have absolutely no memory of, or if I do, it's shadowy. Just fragments of memories. I try not to think about what happened during those times," she whispered.

The men murmured epithets under their breath.

With one swift motion and a growl of pure rage, TB swept the entire contents off the desk in front of the computers, screaming in anger. Before he knew what he was doing, he was out the door, down the hall, and bursting through the conference room. Chest heaving, muscles popped, breath soughing in anger, he could only utter one word.

"Where?"

Flame jumped up from her seat and pulled on his arm. "TB! Stop! It's not worth it! It's over. It was so long ago." She put her hands up to his chest. Her eyes pleaded with him to regain control of his anger. "I'm not worth that rage inside of you."

His eyes went glassy. "Don't you *ever* say that, princess." TB reached up and smoothed the strands of her red hair that had escaped from her braid at the nape of her neck. Then his hands clasped hers and held them tightly between them as if they were praying. "You are worth my rage and so much more."

Waters broke in. "What caused you to decide to run anyway?"

"Gendry was on his way up in the organization. He had a huge client list, and he made good money. Penthouse. Nice car. Designer clothes. The finest of everything. But he also loved his product, and in the drug business, the dealers at the top end never use the product. Gendry didn't have the strength to stop.

"He also had other interests, namely me. My mother had been in his stable of women that he would send out to customers who not only wanted drugs for themselves but also wanted sex. Just normal, everyday guys who made the mistake of contacting a hooker. Gendry would use her to put those men in compromising positions, and he would blackmail them. Not for money—for connections. Places he could funnel the product through. Businesses to launder the money he took in. Obviously, I was much older when I learned this, but a lot more made sense about my parents. In fact, they were probably trapped by him early in their days of using, just like what they were doing to others.

"When he got into a particular bind, either because he was using his own inventory or used the money he owed to his chain of command, he would 'rent' me out to a boss or a boss' visiting client. After the clients left, he'd come into my room, drunk, high, and angry. His mouth would say more than he meant for it to, and one of those nights, I managed to be clear enough to hear him berate me, my mother, and my father for putting him in the position he was in, having to use me to pay off his debts. How my father promised Gendry that he could have me. How he got impatient and purposely overdosed my parents so that he could collect his prize."

"It took two more years to finally get away, and it wasn't easy.

I knew no one who would help me, and I had nowhere to go. But I knew where Gendry kept his extra cash. It wasn't easy, being so drugged up all the time, but I made a concentrated effort to see the combination on his safe.

"As sneaky and smart as he was, I guess he didn't account for the fact that as you use heroin, you become accustomed to it. Like any drug, you need more in order to maintain the high. He never gave me more than what he gave me the first time, so eventually, the effects were less and less. I knew if I was going to get away from him, I couldn't show him that I was capable of making decisions or doing anything without help, so I waited for the right opportunity. There were days when I thought it would never come.

"Then, one night, he left me alone in the apartment. He didn't do it often, and usually, he gave me an extra hit when he left to keep me pretty much comatose. But that particular day, there had been a heated telephone call. Someone was demanding money he didn't have. I think"—she shuddered—"he promised to sell me to them in exchange for whatever he owed. I knew this was my last chance.

"He left. As soon as he was out of the building—I watched him from the balcony—and into the limo waiting, I got into the safe, took what money was there, and I left. I borrowed a black hoodie from his closet, grabbed a T-shirt and jeans from my dresser, stuffed them and the cash into a backpack, and headed to the train station, where I bought a ticket to Florida. I got on the train, found a bathroom where I changed into the T-shirt and jeans, threw my dress in the garbage, put on the hoodie, pulled it over my head, and got off the train, looking like any other homeless vagrant hanging around the station.

"Then I went to the bus station. I asked a young girl there to buy me a ticket to the next city a bus was leaving for, and I ended up in Trenton. Once there, I stole away on a train with a huge family headed to Chicago. How I managed that is beyond me, but from there, it got easier and easier. I rode around to a different city each day, changing directions, backtracking, you name it. Finally, I made it here."

Midas smiled at her. "You're a pretty tough cookie."

Her return smile was wan. "I don't know about that. There were days when I wanted to just stay put. Let Gendry find me. I was so tired. The drugs were clearing my system, and I was very sick the entire time I was trying to get away."

"But you didn't give in," Demon reminded her. "You were strong. You knew it was the only way."

She nodded. "Whenever I felt like giving up, that's what I would remind myself of. But still, there were days when the urge to give up was stronger than the urge to run."

Her shoulders shook with exhaustion. TB felt the vibrations all the way through him as if he were a divining rod. She would crash soon.

"When I arrived and found a shelter to spend the night, I must have slept for two or three days. I woke up to discover that everyone around me was different than who'd been there before. The woman who ran the place, Ms. Monica, said just by looking at me, she saw I was running from something bad. Instead of waking me and kicking me out, she broke the rules and let me stay. Then she really broke the rules and took me home. I stayed with her for almost three months. She was the one who helped me get an I.D. and a social security card. She helped me get an apartment and learn how to use a computer."

"I hate to ask, but your previous life is a long road from spicy romance novels. How the hell did that come about?" Waters asked.

Flame smiled. "Ms. Monica again. She loved them. Had hundreds of them in her house. While I was detoxing and she was working, that's what I did. I read her books. And then I thought, maybe I could do that for a job. When I learned how to read and write, I did it nonstop. Sucked up everything I could find. I certainly couldn't be out and about for Gendry to find. This was something I could do and be anonymous. Apparently, I have a talent for it."

TB pulled her close, his large frame dwarfing her much smaller one. Glaring at his teammates, he growled, "You assholes don't need to read any more of them."

The guys were smirking at his order. He didn't care if he sounded like he'd murder them if they did. These idiots did not need to be seeing what fantasies his woman created in her dirty little mind.

He kissed the top of her head. "I'm so sorry, princess. You shouldn't, but if you forgive me, and if you'll let me, I will protect you. I swear on my life, little Flame, no one will ever touch you again. I promise you will be safe," he whispered. "With my last breath."

Flame's emerald eyes looked soberly up into his. "You still want me, knowing what he did to me? All the things I did?"

"Flame, you are a survivor. You didn't choose that life. Most women wouldn't have had the strength to do what you did. None of us would blame them for staying rather than attempting to break free. Still want you? Of course I do. I've always wanted you," he whispered again, framing her face in his hands, his eyes imploring her to understand. "I wanted you before we even got to our third chat session. I'd never heard your voice. I'd never seen your face. But I wanted to make you mine."

He brought his forehead down to hers and looked her in the eyes as he asked, "The real question is, can you still want me?"

The room went absolutely still as everyone held their breath.

Is this what they mean by a pregnant moment? It feels like the air weighs a hundred pounds. It actually hurts to draw in air.

She burrowed into his chest.

He exhaled in utter relief. Suddenly, the tightness in his chest lessened. His muscles unlocked. His brain booted back into life.

His eyes went to his team. One by one, they nodded their assent. Sylvan had been claimed. She was now tribe.

39

———————

JUNE 19TH

Sylvan

WATERS HAD BEEN THE ONE TO BREAK THE SILENCE THAT HAD infiltrated the room. "Okay, so put two and two together; we get someone named Gendry who is trying to reclaim Flame. Why the other girls, though?"

"Compensation," came the muffled reply.

All heads turned to Sylvan. She unburied her head from TB's chest. "If I'm right, and I was going to be used to pay off his debts, he lost a lot of money when I ran away. People in his line of work —they don't accept mistakes, let alone apologies. Punishment would have been swift and costly. And if he's angry enough to come after me all these years later, my guess is he lost almost everything."

"Could he possibly, in that short amount of time, build himself back up financially to do this?" TB asked.

"It's not impossible," Sylvan hedged. "If he were punished for using the product and skimming from the profits, he would be denied access to inventory and suppliers. If he needed to make up for his losses quickly, running girls would be a fast way to do it. The risk is greater, but so is the reward, and he doesn't need someone to supply him with the product. He can just go out and snatch it off the streets. He's also stupid enough to have sold himself to a boss, especially if that boss supplied him with ways and means that would get him to me faster. It's possible that the other girls were contingency plans to recoup some of his money if he couldn't get to me, or... he could simply be rebuilding his stable of prostitutes."

Waters cleared his throat. "So, that means these girls probably aren't the first. They're just the ones locally, or at least that we know of. Flame, we need you to help Midas. We need as much information as possible on this Gendry asshole. We confirm and reconfirm everything.

"Demon. Inventory the infirmary. Once we find those women, they're likely going to need medical attention. Prepare for drug detox, open wounds from restraints, dehydration, possible broken bones, internal injuries, contusions, anything you can think of. Order whatever supplies you might need and have Cherry get them today if at all possible.

"Steel. Go through the armory. No telling what kind of firepower we're going to need. Make sure everyone has enough extra clips for their personal gear, and then make sure there are enough flash bangs and tear gas canisters and that all the NVGs, masks, and gear are good to go. We're likely going to be working in public areas, so not one speck of skin can show.

"Nemo. You're on the trucks. I want three SUVs and a panel van. Fueled up, cleaned out, inspected, and reloaded. Then I need you to load them with whatever you can think of for a snatch and grab. Water, blankets, med kits, body bags. We know there are six girls, but who knows if there are more, and no clue how many douchebags we'll need to transport.

"I want us to be one hundred percent ready the moment we know where he, or they, are."

God had been inordinately quiet until now. "What about the triad?"

TB scanned the faces of the men around him. "They're not traffickers. They're something… else. Not recovery, not special forces. I don't know. I trust them, but I don't. If they knew Ka-Bar was a captive, they didn't make any effort to retrieve him. However, they clearly know who he is, which means they know who we are and what we do, and they did pass on the information. And it's clear they're scouting out that club for something."

Crinkling plastic could be heard over the speaker. Was that a sigh of reluctance? God's voice, muffled by his caramel apple sucker stuffed in his mouth, gave the order. "Make contact," God ordered. "We have fuck-all idea what we're walking into. This could be the work of one giant asshole, or it could be something much larger. We could use the extra help. If need be, we'll erase any problems after the fact."

"Will do."

TB turned his attention back fully to Flame. "Will you be okay with Midas for a little bit while I track down Loki?"

She nodded but squeezed him tightly.

"I'll be back. As fast as I can. I promise, sweetheart." He returned her embrace by wrapping his arms around her shoulders to pull her closer, and his lips lingered on her forehead. And then he was gone.

She sat with Midas and gave him every scrap of information she could remember about her parents, the drug route, and where they lived. That was hard. But what came after that was worse.

His voice was gentle but firm. "Flame? I don't want to ask you, but I have to. I need everything you can remember about Gendry and your time with him."

She stared at him. Helpless. Panicked. Her head hurt, her stomach churned, and everything felt like it was closing in on her.

"Breathe, Flame. If you pass out on me, TB's going to kill me, and I don't mean figuratively. It'll be death by piñata punching."

"Piñata punching?" she hiccupped.

"Yeah. Nemo has a war going on with TB. No one understands why. My brother is… annoying. I love him, but he marches to his own beat. For some reason he has this need to ambush TB with all kinds of crap. Confetti cannons, water balloons, air horns. It never ends. We're still finding feathers from an incident two years ago. Anyway, he threatened to truss Nemo up like a piñata not too long ago, and he meant it."

The story had its intended effect—light and funny to ease the tension and help her forget she was on the verge of a panic attack.

She considered the scenario. "Yeah. He probably would. Is that why he never calls Nemo by his name?"

"Yup. Always calls him something negative starting with the letter N." Midas snuck a look at her. "Okay, Flame, everything about Gendry. And I mean everything. Height, weight, hair color, body marks like tattoos and scars, you name it. Then, address or description of the part of town. Anything you can remember. After that, associates."

"Okay." Her voice was small and lost. Even she could hear that.

A warm hand reached for hers and clasped it with a reassuring squeeze. "I'm right here. None of them can hurt you anymore. But I'll be honest—we need to get through this part before TB gets back. He's gonna lose his shit as it is. If he has to hear it live… well, let's just make sure he doesn't."

He reached into his desk jar and handed her some mini Snickers bars. "You'll need the sugar. And do me a favor. If Waters comes in, even if you're not hungry, make a big production of eating one."

"Why?"

Midas winked at her. "He'll know why, and that's all that matters."

THERE'D BEEN a lot of tears. Midas had held her through several bouts that were soul-crushing.

There had been a lot of jaw-clenching on Midas' part.

Demon had been in and out to make sure she was hydrated and warm.

Cherry had brought her TB's leather jacket out of his office after the second long crying jag, thinking it would calm her. She'd been right. It smelled like him mixed with the leather, and it made her feel like he was there with her.

Three hours later, they were still in the conference room, just finishing up, when she felt a sizzle go up her spine.

Will I always feel this when he walks into a room?

Leaning in the doorway was TB. "You okay, princess?"

She flew into his arms, his jacket hanging on her small frame like she was playing dress up in an adult's clothes.

He caught her in his arms and lifted her off the floor into a hug, then carried her back inside the room. "You look good in my jacket, princess."

It felt so good to be in his arms. But for how long? Once they caught her stalker, would he leave her like everyone else had? Or would he simply drift away with time?

Could she even hope to be what he needed so that he stuck around permanently?

Not likely.

She registered that somewhere along the line, Midas had snuck past them, leaving them alone in the conference room.

"I didn't thank Midas."

"He hasn't done anything yet to be thanked for," TB grumbled into her neck. "And a nicely addressed envelope sent by mail from your house will be sufficient. If you're feeling especially generous, you can send him a box of Snickers candy bars."

She smiled.

Possessive and jealous. More reasons to be called Total Bastard.

One of TB's hands slid from around her shoulders to her braid, pulling on the end so that her head tilted up to his. Heavens, but she loved when he did that. So powerful, and it seemed to pull at every other part of her insides as well, all the way to her core.

Their eyes met, and all she could do was stare, trying to find the answers to her questions in his eyes. While she surveyed them, as usual, they were devoid of answers.

"TB—"

"Stop. Please." He set her down on the floor, making sure she was steady before taking her hands in his. "There are a lot of things I should say to you right now. But everything's all jumbled up, and I don't even know where to start."

She gripped the front of his shirt so tightly he was likely to have wrinkles from her stretching it. "Just start," she whispered. "I'll listen. I'm smart. I'll figure it out."

He smiled sadly at her, his fingers squeezing hers. "You are. And you will. I just—" He swallowed a huge lump in his throat and looked down at their hands. "I don't think an apology could ever be enough. And what I have to tell you isn't an excuse for my behavior."

He lowered his face to hers, brushing her forehead with his lips, her eyes fluttering closed at his touch. Foreheads touching, the sun coming in through the glass windows, she felt heat surrounding them, but he felt freezing cold despite the warm summer's day.

He'd kept himself from her. But... she had known he was. In a way, she had no right to be mad about that because she had kept herself from him, too. And he hadn't known her secrets. He hadn't known what drove her to bury her past. If she'd just told him, none of this probably would have happened.

But she also knew she wasn't entirely to blame. At least she had been honest with herself that she was keeping him in the dark. TB was so immersed in his false self-identity, he hadn't even consciously known what he was doing.

As he made his confession, his lips remained close to her skin, skimming down to the corner of her eye, to her cheek, and to the corner of her mouth. As if he worried that if they no longer touched her, the words wouldn't be believed.

"There is no excuse for this morning other than Nemo being right on all counts, princess. I'm afraid. Beyond afraid, actually. More like terrified. I haven't been this frightened since I was seven years old." He pulled her tighter to him, his arms banding around her as if afraid she'd run away. "People leave. They don't always mean to, but they do. Sometimes, the reasons why make no sense. You weren't even born yet when it happened. When I was seven, my parents were killed in front of me. Hamas suicide bomber while we were at breakfast. It was a huge story in the news back then.

"Most of that time is a blur. But I remember, even as I held my dead mother's hand, I was alone. Utterly. I was so scared. We had no family. We lived in an over-crowded, near condemnable apartment building where people kept to themselves because it was safer that way. There was no one to come look for me when they died because no one really knew I existed. I doubt it even registered to anyone a family, let alone a child, from the building was no longer around.

"There was a policeman who finally found me. He took me home a few nights to stay with his family. But they lived in a small apartment and didn't have the room for another child, so he left me at an orphanage, hoping, I'm sure, that some family members would eventually come forward and claim me.

"The orphanage was a terrible place. With next to no staff, we basically ran wild. We had to fight for everything, sometimes literally, in order to stay alive. Anything you managed to get ahold of that could be considered your own was a weapon to be used against you. Something to take and use as a bargaining chip. Kids are cruel, but not surprising when you're just trying to survive in a hostile world. I had nothing when I went into the orphanage except the clothes on my body. So I had nothing to take. Therefore, I was isolated from the other kids. I wasn't worth bothering with.

"When I was eighteen, I left and joined the army. Not out of some sense of patriotic duty. It's compulsory for all citizens, but to me, it represented a chance at a family that I'd been missing all those years. I'd find my place again. But that also was taken away.

"Once our initial training was complete, just as I'd begun to feel like I had others I could trust again, I was ripped away from them. Apparently, psychologically, I was the perfect match for the Intelligence Division. A nice way of saying interrogator, which is a professional way of saying torturer. My ability to divorce myself from whatever was going on around me externally made me the perfect choice. And I was oh-so-good at compartmentalizing after eleven years in the orphanage. I felt nothing when working over a suspect.

"I became disillusioned. It was like my heart turned off. Guilt or innocence didn't matter. Only gaining the confession mattered. Motivations, fears, neither of those mattered. Only the result mattered. It was eating away what little humanity remained.

"So one day, I got up and left. Didn't resign. Didn't wait for my tour to be finished. I just disappeared into the desert. Micah Ewen existed no more."

He pulled back just slightly, so she opened her eyes, wanting him to know that she saw him. She understood. Their lives had paralleled each other so closely, except that for her, it had been drugs that stole her parents from her, and for him, it had been a religious and political zealot. Both of them had been abandoned due to forces out of their control. Both had been taught that their lives were worth only what they could bring to other people.

"On my own," he continued, "I became a private contractor. I told you about some of that on your porch. What I didn't tell you was that I was on a self-created path to destruction. I didn't care what jobs I took. I didn't care how dangerous they were. I didn't care if I lived to collect my fee. I was just putting myself in situation after situation, trying to get the world to abandon me altogether. And the worse the job appeared, the more likely I was to take it because perhaps I'd finally be punished for doing something I shouldn't have been doing rather than punishing myself for something I had no control over.

"Waters found me when I had hit the lowest I'd ever been. He hired me to kidnap him. Told me some story about ransoming an American soldier for leverage against the United States and a whole bunch of other stuff I don't even remember. Instead of kidnapping him, I ended up caught in his snare. Took my breath away when I realized he was offering me a job. A way out. A way to rebalance the scales and start over. I don't know that I ever really will. But today, listening to you finally let all that blackness out? I guess it was the wake-up call I needed.

"I have no right to your forgiveness. I have no right to claim any of your goodness as my own. I am still a total bastard for being selfish enough to want you anyway. Cruel enough to do whatever it takes to have you. Sadistic enough to make someone else hurt if it means I can have what I want. And what I want is you. All of you. Every piece."

His forehead touched hers again, and a tortured plea came out. "Please don't take yourself away from me, Flame. I need your light. I need your warmth. They're the only things keeping me tethered to this Earth. The only thing keeping me from completely disappearing."

This beautiful man. Tortured soul that he was, she loved him. It wasn't a choice. She just did.

"TB, I've been yours since the day we met. No matter how infuriating you are, there's no letting you go. We both made terrible decisions by not talking to one another truthfully. If I don't forgive you for being honest, then I can't ever forgive myself for not stepping forward sooner with my part in these women's disappearances. So yes, I forgive you. But only if you forgive yourself."

"That's going to be difficult."

"I'll help you," she promised.

Something shifted in the room. She wasn't sure what happened, but suddenly, the weight on her shoulders lifted off just slightly. She could breathe again. Everything felt closer to normal, but she needed something from him to show her he was willing to let her in. She desperately wanted him to kiss her until she moaned. Touch her skin until she shivered. Love her until she promised him anything.

He smiled softly and murmured, "Princess, we're at my work. You need to not look at me that way, or I just might stop caring about all the cameras in this room and lay you down on this table right here and now."

Her heartbeat sped up at being caught with her thoughts so obvious despite her best efforts. "How do you always know what I'm thinking?"

"Your eyes hide nothing from me. And it doesn't hurt that your pupils are blown wide open," he admitted. "That's always a sure sign of what my little Flame wants."

His hand had let go of her braid, so her head naturally tilted back down to his sternum. Her fingers played with the wrinkles in his T-shirt. Looking at him actually hurt; she loved him so much.

Be brave, Sylvan. You can't even begin to be what he needs if you can't tell him what you want.

With every ounce of courage she possessed, she returned her face to his gaze. "Then take me home, TB. I need to be yours. Only yours."

She felt his breath stop. Then he growled. Literally growled. She felt it in his chest as well as heard it, and it made her heart pound.

Jinkies, that was hot!

"I still don't believe I deserve you. But fuck if I'm not going to take you and spend the rest of my days proving myself wrong. You have never once told me, without prompting, what you wanted. Hot as fuck, little Flame."

Without a word, he pulled his arms from around her waist, grabbed her by the hand, and stalked around the conference room table to the closed door. Down the hall in front of the elevator, he pulled her, then pushed the down button. She swore she heard a chuckle and a murmured "Thank fuck" from one of the offices they passed.

Arriving just after them, Cherry sat down at her desk, not looking up. "I'll mark you out of the office for the rest of the day, shall I?" she asked.

"Fuckin' right," he grumbled loud enough for her to hear. He punched the down key again as if that would help it to arrive faster. Sylvan felt laughter building at his actions, but she worked hard not to let it come out. He wouldn't appreciate the humor in the situation right now.

When the doors finally opened, he went to pull her into the car, and Nemo stood along the wall by the buttons, leaning nonchalantly against the railing, arms crossed loosely over his chest, popping his gum, and grinning like a fool.

"Going down, kids?"

Sylvan worked extra hard not to giggle. He really was incorrigible but in the most adorable way. Some woman was going to be so irritated and yet so full of laughter at the same time when he was finally caught.

"Get out, Neanderthal," TB ordered.

Nemo held up his hands in mock surrender and pushed off the wall. "Good luck getting to the garage, Teeny Bopper." He shoved his hands in his pockets and sauntered out of the elevator, whistling to himself.

As the doors closed, TB muttered something about, "Thankfully, it wasn't a fucking confetti cannon."

"I think this might be worse," Sylvan said, and now the giggles were getting closer to the surface.

40

____

JUNE 19TH

TB

HE LOOKED AT HER QUIZZICALLY, THEN FOLLOWED HER EYE LINE TO THE button panel. "Oh, for fuck's sake. I'm gonna kill him."

Nemo had pushed every button on the panel. All ten of them.

Then he groaned. Not only that, but the elevator was actually going up first, not down. "Definitely going to kill him. Slowly."

The lobby was on floor two, so when the doors opened at floor three, they saw Midas standing there. Unexpectedly, there was an explosive pop. TB automatically sheltered Flame in the corner of the elevator with his body while multi-colored paper showered around them. "Goddammit, Midas!" he thundered.

He felt shaking in his arms, so he quickly turned to the woman he held there. "Princess, I'm so sorry, my team—" He stopped short.

Instead of cowering in his arms, she was actually giggling. She looked up at him, a pink rectangle of paper caught in the top of her hair. "Guess you should be more careful of what you're thankful for."

The doors had closed and were now opening at floor four. Waters stood there. Explosive pop. More confetti.

TB felt Flame peek out from around his arms, and then looked over his shoulder just in time to see Waters wink at her. "Just for that, I'm not coming in tomorrow," TB growled.

"Wasn't expecting you to," his boss replied as the door closed.

Floor five. Doors opened. Steel. More confetti. He saluted TB as the door closed.

Floor six. No one was there.

Thank fuck that's over.

Floor seven. BANG! Demon. "Seriously? He got you in on it?" Demon just shrugged and waved to Flame as the door closed.

By this time, tears were streaming down Flame's face, and she was holding her sides in pain from the laughter.

Floors eight and nine were open doors with no one there.

Floor ten was the penthouse. The elevator moved to the tenth floor and stopped, but the door didn't open.

"No telling what the Big Boss would have done if the door had opened at his apartment."

"It wouldn't have been confetti," came the dark voice over the speaker in the elevator. "I'd have been much more creative."

TB rolled his eyes. "Figures you'd be watching. Just so you know, I'm not cleaning this shit up." The floor was covered with paper, as well as sticking in places to both of them.

"Oh, no. That's Nemo's job."

"You're paying him too much if he can afford all of this crap all the time."

"He doesn't pay for it. I do. We have it built into the annual budget. It amuses the hell out of me to watch his war with you."

"Shithorn. I quit."

God laughed hard at that. "Yeah, right. I'll see you on Monday. Don't you dare come back before then."

He should have known it wasn't over, but he'd forgotten about Nemo. When the door opened in the garage, there he stood with two canons that he let fly. Flame was clinging to him, and she was laughing so hard she could barely stand. TB swept her up in a bridal carry and brushed past his nemesis, heading straight for his Humvee. He grumbled silently in his head, but secretly, he was a little bit amused. His team sure knew how to inaugurate a new person into the fold.

Thank fuck Kubrick isn't here. She would have had Silly String.

Sylvan's house was only about twenty minutes from the office, but for whatever reason, those twenty minutes felt like an hour. He couldn't even blame it on rush hour. It clearly had everything to do with needing to be alone with the woman next to him in the truck.

Fuck "with" her. I need "inside" her. Now!

When they finally arrived, he barely had the vehicle in park in the garage and the garage door down before the vehicle was turned off, and he was sliding out of the seat onto the pavement. He stormed around the back of the truck, yanked her door open, unbuckled her seat belt, and had her over his shoulder, ass in the air.

"TB," she hissed. "You're being a caveman!"

"Don't care," he grunted. "Your steps are too tiny, and I don't want to pull your arm out of the socket."

"Well, if you weren't so Frankenstein-huge, it wouldn't take three of my steps to keep up with one of yours," she shot back.

Swinging the inner door open, he hustled her through, closed the door, locked it tight, put her down, then rearmed the alarm panel. Once he had, he turned to her with an index finger pointed at her. "Upstairs. Now. Clothes off. I'll be there in three minutes, so you had better be ready."

Eyes wide, Flame didn't even hesitate. She turned and flew up the stairs.

The grin on his face was that of a predator who knew his prey was a given. He set his watch for five minutes just to make her wait a little, then began to do a perimeter of the interior of the house, verifying that everything was locked up and the curtains were drawn. Once done, he headed to the kitchen and grabbed several bottles of water because when he was done with her, he knew she would need hydrating.

Just as he closed the refrigerator door, his watch alarm beeped. Turning it off, his smile turned even more wolfish, and he stalked to the stairs, purposefully letting his heavy tread be heard as he climbed.

Navigating the wrought iron spiral staircase to the third floor, he made sure to hit each stair with a heavy step and made sure to climb slowly to increase her awareness of his arrival. His mouth was watering in anticipation of what he was going to find. A small part of him hoped she wasn't quite ready so that he could mete out a little punishment.

The saliva in his mouth dried up in a single second.

Fuck, fuck, fuck!

Late afternoon sunlight shone through the skylight in the center of her sanctuary. In the middle of the pool of light it created, she knelt, completely naked. She was sitting on her heels, hands clasped behind her, gripped at the small of her back, the position forcing her generous breasts forward. Around her eyes was a white silk blindfold, knotted so that she couldn't see a thing. Lying on the floor in front of her was a skein of white silk rope in a loose coil.

"Sylvan," he whispered.

He watched her chest rise and fall, saw her body tremble, and heard the slight gasp that she couldn't contain at hearing him call her by name, something he had never done before.

He crossed over to the bed and set the water bottles in the alcove above the pillows. Then he moved to stand in front of her.

Her braid lay over the front of her shoulder, the end tied with a pink silk ribbon. He fingered the end of it. For a heart-wrenching moment, it reminded him of what he'd found in the box. Five red hair braids and one blonde braid neatly chopped from a young woman's head. Mentally, he shook himself, collecting his wits to find the Dom within.

"Remove my boots, Flame."

She let go of her wrists behind her back and began to undo the laces on his left boot. After loosening them, she gently raised his foot to pull and remove it. Setting it off to the side, she repeated the process on the right foot. Then she returned to her position to await his further instructions.

"Stand." She unfolded her body and stood before him. His hand reached out to touch her side and slid down to her hip. "I'm going to move to the bed. Follow my lead." She did. When he sat on the bed, he spread his legs. "Take two more steps forward, princess." Once she had done so, he closed his legs slightly so that she could feel him hemming her in, the denim coarse on her knees. "Take off my shirt."

Unclasping her arms, she bent at the waist to reach for his tee, and she pulled it free from his pants. The position brought her face perilously close to his, and he struggled not to turn just slightly so that he could kiss her. Instead, he took a deep breath.

Roses and arousal. There is nothing better than her scent. Well, except hearing her soft cries when I'm buried inside her.

As she pulled the tee clear and up his torso, she began to straighten, the material dragging his arms up so that she could pull it free from his body. Once it was off, she turned it right side out, folded it, and stood with it on top of her open palms. He took it from her and tossed it onto the floor at the foot of the bed, uncaring that her neat folding was now wasted in a heap on the floor.

As he stood up, he clasped her backside and hauled her up the front of him. Automatically, her arms wound around his neck, and her legs around his waist. Cradling her close to him, he walked over to press her tight against one of the bookcases. "Hold on tight with those pretty legs, princess."

With her pressed up against the spines of her beloved books, he was able to remove his hands from underneath her. Reaching behind his neck, he took both of her hands in his, stretching them up above her head. His mouth swept down to her ear, nipping the lobe with his front teeth, causing her to hiss. Then he gathered the lobe between his lips, his tongue stroking the bitten area with tenderness, and gently sucked the wounded flesh.

She moaned.

His mouth drifted down her throat, open-mouthed kisses with his tongue flicking against her pulse point, sucking hard on the tendon where her neck met her shoulder.

"Oh, my," she breathed out.

He placed both of her small wrists in the grip of one hand above her head, then he slid his other hand to grasp a breast, kneading it with strong pulls, making sure to pull on her nipple as he narrowed his touch. Afterward, he smoothed over the nipple with his fingertips before grasping her breast fully in his hand again.

"That feels so good," she moaned.

His mouth drifted further down, his hand pushed her breast up toward his mouth, and his lips reached to capture her nipple between his teeth. He bit lightly, causing the flesh to distend further.

Again, she gasped, then sighed as he immediately swirled his tongue around and across the flesh to soothe the stinging.

He pressed up with his hips, her body not moving against the shelves so that she could feel how hard he was for her. "You feel that, little Flame? You do that to me," he murmured against her breast, then moved to give the other the exact same treatment. "Do you know how much I want to fuck you? How much I want to make you scream for mercy as I edge you over and over toward orgasm? I want to hold you down and pound that pussy of yours with my hips so hard I leave bruises on the insides of your thighs, marking you as mine. I want to make you come so hard you pass out with my name on your lips. And then, when you wake up, do it all over again.

"I want to take you from behind, holding onto these beautiful hips so that you feel my balls slap against your clit, triggering it while my cock rasps against your G-spot at the same time so that you flood me with your cum. And then I want to take all that silky fluid and spread it on your asshole, slide my huge dick inside you there, and make sure you know exactly who owns this body. Who owns your orgasms."

He could feel her body shaking at earthquake levels and swept away by a maelstrom of sensations. It was time to blow up everything between them.

He let go of her hands, then allowed her to slide slightly down the front of the bookcase as he kneeled on the floor. Her pussy was lined up exactly to his mouth. "Arms above your head. Do not touch me."

"TB—"

"Please, Flame. If you touch me, I'll never be able to lick this sweet pussy. And I need to do that more than I need air to breathe."

A groan issued out of her mouth, and he waited until she complied with his request to put her hands above her head before he focused his attention back between her thighs. He reached for her leg and put it over his shoulder, opening her further to him. Before she even registered what he was doing, his tongue was swiping between her lower lips, teasing her hole and her clit by brushing from one to the other without stopping. The tang of her fluids on his lips and tongue, he used his hands to press against her pelvic bones, his thumbs stretching her lips open to reveal both spots.

"Need your flames, princess. Need your heat again."

Eyes on her from below, he buried his tongue inside her channel, tasting her straight from the source.

Flame began to beg in earnest for him to hurry up and bring her over the edge. His tongue would pulse in and out of her, mimicking the actions his cock would later use inside her. He swirled it around her insides, pressing the tip against the top wall, then dragging it out hard. As his tongue returned to push back inside her, it met with a powerful flood of her fluids, and at the same time, her body shook so hard that she'd had to grip the shelves as supports in order to stay upright.

Soft swipes of his tongue along her skin helped to ease her body back down, as well as remove most of the stickiness from her orgasm off of her thighs. His hands began to slide up her curves, which eventually forced his mouth to move up the front of her body as well. Kissing the soft skin just above her belly button, TB made sure to do an extra hard pull with his lips, leaving behind a red love bite to mark her as his.

His hands framed her body, his thumbs caressing the under-sides of her breasts, watching the skin pebble and flush at his touch. She was still shaking from his attention, so he worked to relax her again. He smiled evilly against her side as he pressed a kiss to her hip.

All the better to make you explode again, my dear.

One hand reached for her shoulder, gently pulling on it to lower her arm, turned so that the underside was toward his face. He pressed a kiss to each of the permanent bruises it presented. When he reached the top one, he helped her place her arm over his shoulder and around his neck. He repeated the process with the other arm. Once both arms were around his neck, he lifted her up and took her back to the window bed. Gently, he lay her down on tousled sheets and kneeled between her legs as they hung over the edge of the bed.

"Ready, princess?"

She fisted what portion of his hair she could and shoved his head down between her legs with a strength he hadn't known that she had.

"No talking. More licking," she managed to whisper.

"Just licking?" he teased.

"Licking. Sucking. Kissing. Touching. Fucking. You made a to-do list for yourself earlier. Get to it."

He chuckled. "All the better to pleasure you, my dear."

41

JUNE 22ND

Sylvan

Neither TB nor Flame had left the house for two days. Other than to get her something to eat and drink or for one of them to go to the bathroom, TB hadn't left her side, let alone went downstairs. And every time she tried to slip out of bed to work on her book, he'd slide his arms around her, preventing her escape effort, reeling her back into bed, his arms, and loving her thoroughly.

But all good things must come to an end. Waters had finally texted and told him to get his lazy ass out of her bed and get themselves to The Library.

No rest for the wicked.

Tonight was all for TB. Emerald-green silk blouse that was unbuttoned past her cleavage and tucked into skin-tight black pants. A black, lace-covered waist cincher helped to push up the cleavage peeking from the plackets of her blouse. Velvet ankle boots gave her an extra five inches of height. Her hair was in a single, long, thick braid. And the wolf collar was winking in the dance floor lighting all the way here to the bar.

Currently, they stood at the bar. He was tapping at the charm around her throat, and she knew that his locked-in gaze on it was causing him to think about the implications of the collar as well as what had happened the past couple of days. She knew now, beyond the shadow of a doubt. A commitment in words wasn't important to her. She knew he was hers, even if it was never said between them. Even if they were to never see each other again, he was hers, and she was his. No piece of jewelry or conversation was ever going to make it truer than what they knew in their own heads.

She caught his playing finger with her hands. "You're going to hypnotize yourself if you keep that up," she teased.

Grinning, he tipped down and kissed her brow between her eyes. "Too late. The woman wearing it already has me in her power."

Sylvan blushed. TB was starting to have a new meaning—Totally Blindsided.

"I'm going to go use the ladies' room."

"I'll walk you over."

"TB. It's twenty feet away. You can see me the entire way there and back with no obstruction. I think it's safe."

He hesitated. She could actually see him working out the odds in his head, weighing his options, looking for holes in the plan. Reluctantly, he let go of her arm.

"There and back. Quick-like. I don't like it when you're gone from my side."

She gave his cheek a soft stroke with her hand, smiling at his open face. "I don't like it either," she admitted. She went on tiptoe to brush a kiss along his cheek that he had wisely leaned down to her for. "Back in a flash."

Sylvan looked up into the vanity mirror, wondering how things had gotten this far so fast. She was in way over her head.

And you love it.

The door opened behind her, and Tabitha walked in.

"Hello, Sylvan." She came up to the vanity and stood next to her. Leaning over the countertop, she licked the tip of her pinkie finger, then used it to smooth along her immaculately shaped eyebrow. "I see that tall, dark, and grumpy brought you back again tonight." She began to pat down her hair, looking for imaginary wisps that were out of her sleek twist hairdo.

"Yes. I've been meeting a lot of interesting people."

Tabitha checked for lipstick on her teeth. "Gaining characters for your book?"

"I've certainly gotten to see a lot of different types of relationships and characteristics. Those are certainly insightful for character building."

Tabitha stood upright and faced Sylvan. "Yes, I have noticed that since your first night here, you've both been talking to people, not playing."

Sylvan blushed. "I love the scene. The energy is fantastic, and so are the people. But I guess I'm more private when it comes to the physical activity part."

"So you've been playing at home?"

Sylvan noticed that the question didn't come with a smile or a teasing tone. Instead, it was more pointed. Maybe even a bit angry.

"A little."

"Don't you think it's rather dangerous to let him into your home? I mean, you barely know him."

Okay, that's definitely angry.

"Tabitha, I thought you trusted him. You connected us, after all."

"Yes, well, I didn't expect him to engage with you physically. It was just meant to be interviews. I honestly didn't think he would find you to be his type." She turned and faced the mirror again, smoothing nonexistent wrinkles in her dress. "You were supposed to be my insurance policy. By showing him your ridiculous innocence, it was supposed to remind him of what he really needs in a woman. But apparently, the novelty of your inexperience was an attraction to him. It probably wouldn't have lasted long, though, if it had the opportunity."

Tabitha smiled at her in the mirror. It was not the friendly smile Sylvan was used to. It projected superiority and a fountain of information that the recipient knew nothing about.

"Are you...? Were you a couple?" Sylvan asked, confusion clear on her face.

"Before I opened The Library, we played together. He was the one man I could truly be submissive to. With everyone else and everywhere else, I was a Domme through and through. He's the only man I would submit to. Ever.

"When I took over The Library, he refused to scene with me. Said it made him uncomfortable to be in bed, so to speak, with the owner. I decided to bide my time. He'd come around, eventually. Unfortunately, his interest in the club as a whole seemed to fade. I knew I had to do something to regain his attention.

"That's when you fell so conveniently into my hands. I thought the plan was foolproof. You needed to talk to someone about BDSM, and you knew absolutely nothing. I threw you together to show him exactly what he would be missing out on if he walked away from the club, and then I planned to work my way back into his life.

"Turns out it wasn't the club. It was you. The fool went and fell in love with a vanilla innocent who wouldn't know a paddle from a flogger. Now, he wants a happy little family life with his bondage kink thrown in.

"You're in love with TB? I mean, Lobo?"

"TB?" Tabitha scowled. "Is that his real name?"

"It's a nickname."

"Then this is worse than I had imagined if he's sharing personal information." That comment seemed to be aimed more at herself than Sylvan. Like someone flipped a light switch, her face changed to an overly bright, plastic smile. "No matter. Luckily, I've made other arrangements for you. Fate intervened yet again, this time to resolve my problem with you. It was nice meeting you, Sylvan. You had a gift with your storytelling. Too bad this ending won't be a happy ever after." She took several steps toward the door, then looked over her shoulder at Sylvan's frozen form. "Well, not for you."

As Tabitha passed through the doorway into the club, Medusa came into the lounge, a frown on her face. She looked at Sylvan with concern. "Were you alone here with her?"

"I think so," Sylvan replied. "There was no one in here when I first came in, and I didn't hear or see anyone come in here afterward. Should I ask why you want to know?"

Medusa came up close to Sylvan and spoke in a hushed voice. "Don't be alone with her again. She's mixed up somehow with these missing girls. I don't think she was at the start, but something's changed. We found communications between her and a supplier we've been monitoring."

"Gendry," Sylvan whispered, sinking onto one of the padded stools in front of the vanity.

"You know him?"

Sylvan nodded.

"How?"

"It's a long story. Let's just say I thought I'd escaped him six years ago. It looks like he found me again. Someone's been stalking me online, on the phone, at my house. I thought maybe it was him. We confirmed it two days ago."

"You and Lobo?" Medusa asked.

"Yes."

Medusa swore under her breath. "I knew it. You're the target."

Sylvan tried to calm her erratic heartbeat and panicked breathing. This was no time to lose her head and be the too-stupid-to-live girl. Gendry was here. TB was here but across the club. She needed to get to him fast because whatever Tabitha had been referring to sounded like it was happening soon.

"Gendry must have found me. He tracked me to Tabitha and the club. She's got an obsession with Lobo, and she's using him as a way to get rid of me. Claims Lobo is in love with me, and I'm stealing him from her or something. It sounded like she was planning on handing me over to Gendry."

Suddenly, the lights went out. From inside the lounge, they could hear the collective gasp and light screams from the patrons at the surprise, then the general hubbub of people as they stumbled around in the dark. Sylvan felt Medusa grab onto her arm.

"Listen to me very carefully," she whispered. "I want you to go into one of the stalls. Climb up on the toilet. Do not close or lock the door. Do you understand?"

"Yes," Sylvan whispered back.

"Do not make a sound, and no matter what you hear, do not come out of there until the lights come back on. Trust no one except me or Lobo. If anyone comes in and tries to take you out of here other than one of us, don't leave."

"What about you?"

"I'll be fine. Go. Go now!"

Sylvan hurried into the restroom area, went to the second to last stall, and climbed gingerly onto the toilet seat. Luckily, the toilets had tanks on the back, and she was able to sit. If she had to stand in the high-heeled boots she was wearing, it wouldn't be long before her legs gave out or she slipped and fell.

She had no idea how much time had passed. It was probably less than a minute. Maybe two. But it felt like forever.

There was the sound of a door opening, but the noises from inside the club didn't get louder, which was weird.

Please let it be TB! He should have been here by now. He would have known something was wrong when the lights went out, and even if he didn't, he still would have come to make sure I was safe.

Because the lounge was carpeted, she couldn't hear any steps. She did make out some sounds that might have been material rubbing against other material. Pant legs from someone walking, maybe? Whoever it was did not call out, so it was clear they did not have good intentions.

There was a thud, then a grunt, and Sylvan heard grappling noises. It sounded like punches and kicks were being meted out.

One set of noises was clearly uttered by a male. The other was higher pitched and likely female.

Gendry and Medusa?

Sylvan literally bit her lip to keep from crying out to the woman. She was attempting to protect Sylvan despite not knowing her, and she worried that Gendry would be too much for her.

A crash sounded, followed by shattering glass, and a guttural groan escaped whomever had been slammed up against what Sylvan figured were the counter and mirrors. Medusa was little, but she looked like she was wiry and strong. Hopefully, she'd gotten in a good shove to her attacker.

The fighting sounds stopped, and all she could hear was heavy breathing. Looking up over the top of the stall walls, she saw a light reflect off the ceiling. A cell phone flashlight, maybe?

"Bitch. You're going to get more than you bargained for."

Obviously, Medusa had not outwitted her attacker. Sylvan hoped the woman was only knocked out, but she'd recognized that voice hurling the threat at her would-be protector.

Gendry! He's found me.

The flashlight swept around the lounge area as if looking for something. Then she heard the sound of a call being made. The phone on the other end rang once before being picked up.

There was no greeting. "Get in here. We've got an extra prize to take with us." Then he disconnected the call.

Hard-soled shoes began to click on the marble flooring leading to the bathroom stalls, and she held her breath. She was going to get taken. It was inevitable now, so what should she do to help TB find her faster? Because he would come for her. Of that, she was certain. She didn't know why he wasn't here now, but once he realized she was gone, he would burn down the world to find her.

The shoes stopped at the first stall. She heard Gendry push open the stall door to reveal it as completely empty.

The outer door of the lounge opened, and she could hear the noise and see another sweeping light.

"Take the bitch on the floor. I'll handle Jolie."

Silent tears filled her eyes, and she felt her limbs begin to tremble. She wanted so desperately to be brave. She wanted TB to be proud of her for how she handled this moment. She wanted to be the strong woman that he deserved, but in these seconds, she experienced a paralyzing fear.

She heard the door of stall two being pushed open.

Stall three.

This is it.

The door pushed open.

"Hello, Jolie. Long time no see."

42

JUNE 22ND-23RD

TB

TB watched Flame walk away from him toward the ladies' room with a sense of unease. He knew he was smothering her, but until this little fuckgoblin, Gendry, was found and pounded into oblivion, and the other six girls missing were found, his skin would probably continue to crawl.

Shortly after she entered the restroom, he saw Tabitha enter. At least he knew someone she was in there with.

He finished his drink, then watched Medusa enter the ladies' room as Tabitha exited. Both women had odd looks on their faces. Tabitha was thinking furiously. Medusa appeared concerned, then ducked quickly behind the closing door. By that time, Tabitha had pulled out her cell phone and was talking angrily into it.

Cell phones aren't allowed on the floor.

His watch beeped. Frowning, he looked down. "What the fuck?" TB muttered.

In the text was a photo of the club parking lot. It showed a car parked under one of the lot lights, the passenger side door open, and in the passenger seat was Fleur, the most recent of the missing girls. He couldn't tell if she was alive or dead, but they needed to get to her quickly, just in case.

He forwarded the number that the text came from to Midas, and then he voice-activated his earbud. "Midas!"

He didn't bother to greet TB. "I see it, I see it. I'm running the plate and pictures. Steel's on his way to check out the car. Whatever you do, don't leave the bar."

A second text came through. This one showed video footage of the first missing girl. She was in what appeared to be an upright, empty coffin. She could move around slightly, but not enough to stretch out her arms in any direction. She couldn't sit, couldn't lie down.

Suddenly, the club was plunged into darkness.

"Midas!" TB yelled over the shocked gasps of the club members in the bar, "he's here!"

"Fuck! Where's Flame?"

"Ladies' room."

"Can you get there?"

Using the flashlight app on his watch, he began working his way through the crowd, but he was having little success. It was like everyone had been hired to work against him getting across the bar. "It's pandemonium here. You'd think people have never been in a power outage before. It's going to take me a moment. Do you have Flame's tracker online?"

"She's still on the property. Not moving."

"I just saw Medusa go in there with her."

"Stay on target to get to her. I still don't have any information on that crew, so I don't trust them yet."

TB continued to fight his way across the club, but now individuals who had been upstairs in the play portion of the club were adding to the mix of bodies attempting to find a way out.

Steel's voice came over his earbud. "I need Demon. She's unconscious. Pulse thready. Head wound, and I'm pretty sure she's drugged."

"Copy that," Demon replied.

Shoving his way through the final stream of people, TB found himself at the restroom door. He opened the door, walked through it, saw the disaster of the lounge area covered in broken mirror glass and upturned furniture, saw Medusa being hefted over an unknown man's shoulder, and pain exploded across the back of his head. Then nothing.

He had no idea how much later it was, but it probably wasn't more than a few minutes. He groaned. Everything was pitch black, but he could feel his eyelids raising and lowering as he blinked them rapidly to try and clear the fog in his head. He pushed himself up off the floor, his hand reaching up to the back of his head, where he could feel a giant lump forming.

Instantly, everything had clarity.

"Flame!" he bellowed.

Using his flashlight app, he swept the room. While he registered the upheaval he remembered seeing before he had been knocked unconscious, it meant very little to him in the grand scheme of things. Only finding Flame mattered.

"Flame, answer me!"

Nothing. He only heard the muffled voices of those out in the main area of the club as they continued to try and exit in the blackout.

He felt panic rising as he burst into the toilet and sink area of the room. All of the stalls were open and unoccupied. The ladies' room was empty. She was gone.

Up until this moment, TB had blocked out the conversation over his earbud. Now, he interrupted the flow of communication. "Midas! She's gone."

"Thank, fuck, you're back. Yes, that's what I've been trying to tell you. Her tracker is on, but there's something wrong. Where are you?"

"I went through the ladies' room door. Someone had Medusa over their shoulder, and before I could react, I got knocked out from behind. When I came to, everyone was gone." He pushed out into the main room, then followed the flow of people out into the parking lot. As soon as he hit the cool night air, he spoke again, "Tell me you've got her, Midas."

"Wish I could. The signal is good, but it's like it's locked in place. It hasn't moved. I'm calibrating."

"Midas, fucking find her."

"Working on it. Waters didn't hire me for my good looks."

"They're not going to be good much longer if you don't find her."

Another voice, out of breath from running, joined over the earbud. "Don't piss off King Kong, bro. We don't need him climbing a tall building and plummeting to his death."

"Nemo, this is not a time for joking around. I swear to all that's holy in this world—"

"Relax, giant ape-man. If I don't make jokes to redirect your anger, your blood pressure will soar, and then you'll have an embolism. He may not have a trace on her signal, but I've got one better. Midas! Track an Escalade, black, license Whiskey-Zulu-Yankee-Nine-Nine-Foxtrot. Watched them pitch the girls into it and take off like their asses were on fire."

"Thank fuck," TB grounded out. "Which way, Nemo?"

"Just peeled out of the parking lot about two minutes ago. Headed for the I-5. Sorry. I'm fast, but not that fast."

Midas reassured him over the line. "Little bro, you've given me enough. If it's a rental, it'll have GPS I can hack into."

Waters came over the earpiece. "Steel, get the girl back to Tribe. We need her out of there before the boys in blue arrive."

"Demon and I are already on it, bossman."

"Sirens arriving in two, Steel. Gotta hustle," Midas informed him.

"All right, everybody, get your asses back to Tribe. We work from here. If we want to keep on this, we've got to let the blue line do their thing, then come back when they're gone."

TB wanted to follow the vehicle that took Flame and Medusa from the property. It was irrational. He knew there was no way he could actually do so. They were lucky to even get a make of the vehicle, let alone the license plate. He trusted Midas. The hacker would find them. The team would come up with a plan, and then they'd go after Flame and the others.

They would not fail.

They couldn't. Not now. It was official. He loved that woman. She was his, and she would be found so that he could spend the rest of his life figuring out how to keep her from leaving him.

43

JUNE 23RD

TB

Arriving at Tribe Corporation, TB didn't have the patience to wait for an elevator to go the two floors to the lobby. He slammed through the fire stair door, then took the four landings two steps at a time. As he busted through at the lobby level, Waters came barreling out of his office door. "Conference room," was all he said. As the two men took off down the hallway, they heard the ding of the elevator arriving from one of the upper floors onto their floor. Nemo exited and headed their way.

"Sorry. Had a fight with a dumpster and lost. Needed to change."

A third text came in. Missing girl number two came into view. She was in a similar container.

As they entered the conference room, Midas had a link to TB's watch up on the telescreen so that everyone could see what he was receiving.

"How the hell does this fucknut have my number?" TB growled.

"Don't know, don't care right this second. If he didn't, we wouldn't have this video. We'll worry about that mess later."

A fourth text came up on the screen just as Waters was patching God in through the speaker. Third girl.

"Demon and Steel are with Fleur in the infirmary. She's still unconscious. Demon's doing blood work to see what's in her system," Waters told the room.

Fifth text. Fourth girl.

Sixth text. Tilly Moll.

Soon, he had video footage of all of the missing girls and two empty containers. It didn't take a rocket scientist to figure out who was going in those containers.

None of the footage was good. Now they were able to see slightly more than before because the girls were stirring slightly inside the cells. Each of the girls was next to naked. They were clean and didn't appear to be hurt, but they were not fully awake. And there were digital numbers running above their heads.

"Midas," TB choked out.

"Yeah, man, I see it. The numbers are running backward. Lowest countdown is the first girl who went missing. Jesus, this is live footage." TB heard swearing around him. "The footage has no sound, and it's only broadcasting, not receiving. He can't hear us if we speak."

"But we can't hear him, either."

"Fuck." Midas' expletive was beyond angry. "It's an auction. Just found it on the dark web. The timers match the closing of each auction. Bids are closing on girl number one within ten minutes. But this makes no sense. Waters, why would he hold onto these other women so long just to sell them now?"

"I don't know. Would have thought the danger of getting caught, added to the cost of maintaining them, would have been too great. We need to worry about that later, though."

The texts on the screen shrunk to form a banner across the top of the telescreen. The core of the screen became the timer for girl number one and the auction site. The first woman was currently at a bid of just over two million dollars. The bidders were playing with each other, raising the amounts in small increments with each bid, making her life a game.

God piped in. "Can you shut down the auction, Midas?"

"I can, but if I spend my time doing that, I can't find where the women are."

"Keep looking for the women," TB ordered. No way was he going to allow anything to get in the way of finding Flame, even if it meant those other women were "sold." It might make him an asshole, but they could always go after them once Flame was secure.

All of a sudden, there was shadowy movement in the second to last frame. Light flooded one of the empty cells as its door opened. A man's head came into view from underneath the camera. He had Medusa in his arms, unconscious. He leaned her against the wall, then took the wrist shackles and hooked them around her wrists, the arms stretching to their maximum distance. She was basically hanging from her wrists. When she woke up, she would have room to stand, but not much beyond that.

The shackles must have been attached to the timer because as soon as they clicked into place, her countdown started. Three hours. Not a lot of time. But they didn't need a lot of time. Just a location. This prick couldn't be far away since Medusa and Flame had disappeared less than two hours ago.

Once Medusa was secure, the man slapped her face. Hard. She was slow in responding, still clearly under the effects of being out cold, but it was unclear whether it was because he'd knocked her unconscious or because he'd given her some kind of drug. She had cuts, scrapes, and bruises all over her. She'd obviously been in a scuffle. And there was a jagged, oozing cut along the inside of her left forearm. TB remembered all the broken glass from the ladies' room—the shattered vanity mirror—and realized that Medusa had fought to protect Flame.

Her captor hit her again.

This time, she opened her eyes, clearly trying to blink her vision back into focus. She scrambled to get her feet under her and stand. The man must have said something to her, but because there was no audio, all they had was Medusa's responses to gauge what was going on.

She spit at him.

"Thatta girl," Nemo praised.

TB felt incredibly hopeless. He knew what was going to happen next. Another container was going to be filled, and this one would have Flame in it.

Sure enough, seconds after Gendry left Medusa, he showed up in an open cell with Flame in tow. The difference was that she was awake. She wasn't fighting him. She looked terrified.

"Do whatever he tells you to do, sweetheart," TB whispered.

He watched as Gendry yelled at her to do something. He watched as she put her wrists into the cuffs and locked them shut. The bastard was forcing her to put herself in her own prison. Punishment for running away in the first place.

The timer started.

Then Gendry did something TB would not have imagined. He reached up and tilted the camera inside the box so that it caught his face on camera. He smirked into it. Stepping back, he put his arm around Flame's shoulders and turned her to face the camera head-on. TB could feel her fear through the screen and the revulsion as Gendry kissed her cheekbone, one hand squeezing her chin to hold her in place. He laughed, said something to Flame, and then forced his mouth on hers.

When she struggled and tried to avoid the contact, he used his teeth to bite her lower lip, causing her to cry out in pain. He took advantage of her mouth opening and thrust his tongue into her mouth, clenching her chin tighter so that she couldn't close her teeth on his tongue. When he pulled back from her, he looked straight at the camera, winked, and shoved her away from him. His last act was to refocus the camera away from her and directly on her timer.

Three hours, minus seconds. That's what he was reducing his little Flame's life to. Time. It was a taunt. This is how much time you have, and I'm not even going to let you see her.

"Midas," TB growled.

"I know, big guy, I know. I'm working on it. Triangulating is tricky. He's bouncing this fucker all over the place."

Waters clapped him on the back. "Come on. While Midas dominates the zeroes and ones into submission, let's work on location from another angle. Profile him. We know who this fucker is, so let's use what we know and find him. She's not going anywhere right now. And if he's selling her, he's going to want her in perfect shape for the best price, so exhale, take a step back, and think."

TB nodded. "I know. It's just... she's gotta be so fucking scared."

"She knows you're looking for her."

"Yeah, but her tracker's not working. Why?"

"Midas said something's interfering with the signal. Like she's inside something that's thick metal." Waters clapped his shoulder one more time. "I'll say it again. She knows you're looking for her. And she knows you'll burn down the world to find her. So yes, I'm sure she's scared. But she's also smart. She won't panic."

TB's brain was refusing to process. He needed to get in the correct headspace, but all he could think about was that his woman was locked in a tiny box, about to be auctioned and sent who the fuck knew where, and he couldn't get to her.

His eyes went to the screen and watched the numbers tick down second by second.

An alarm went off. The telescreen reduced all the previous video footage to the lower right of the screen and refocused to show the front of the building. Two men—Loki and Gilgamesh— stood in full view of the camera, clearly knowing they had Tribe's attention.

"Nemo, go let them in," God ordered over the speaker.

"Boss—" Waters started.

"Nemo, do as you're told."

"On it." Before leaving for the front door, Nemo bumped TB's shoulder to get his attention. In his hands, he had several folders.

"Midas had me go get this from his cave. It's everything he's got on Gendry, Flame, and her parents." Nemo set the folders down, then took off to let the two strangers inside the sanctum walls.

It was mere moments before the three men were back in the room.

"Your man here says you have a vehicle make, model, and license. If you give it to us, we can work that angle for you."

"Who are you people?" Waters asked. "Why should I give you that info when I have no idea who you are?"

"Because that's our… woman he's got," Loki argued. "And we'll owe you if you help us find her."

TB thought the word choices were off, but he was too border-line panicked to pay it much attention.

"Inject a tracker in them and let them have at it," TB yelled. "At least we'll know where they go if they decide to double-cross us."

"No trackers. We'll take one of your guys with us as insurance for you."

It was a gamble. God's voice bellowed through the speaker. "Steel! Go with them."

Steel considered the two men carefully, then stepped forward. He nodded at Loki and Gilgamesh.

Waters swore. "I don't like this." He hesitated another moment. "Give them earbuds. I want check-ins every five minutes. Miss just one, and I'm coming after Steel with every weapon we possess."

Loki turned on his heel and headed back toward the lobby. Gilgamesh nodded at Waters. "No double-crossing planned. Just need to find our girl and help you get yours back. The other girls getting free is a bonus. C'mon, Steel."

Midas handed earbuds to Steel for the two men, then went back to his computer screens. As Steel left the room on Gilgamesh's heels, he looked to TB and gave a single head nod. Then he was gone.

Nemo was back. He had opened the top folder of intel and started laying items out one by one along the table. TB watched his teammate's face. He was fully concentrating on the task at hand. He wasn't cracking jokes or making lewd remarks. He wasn't cracking his gum or blowing obnoxious bubbles. Hell, he wasn't even chewing gum at all. He wasn't even fully dressed. He'd clearly flown through a shower and thrown on whatever was handy because he was wearing green sweatpants and a navy blue T-shirt, and he had on some sort of dock shoes instead of his normal boots.

Nemo had already started on the second folder. The first one must have been on one of her parents because there was very little there. This second one didn't look like it had much, either.

"Thank you," TB croaked. He cleared his throat. "She's..." He couldn't finish.

Nemo looked up at him. "Yours. I know. I got your back, TB. We'll find her and bring her home." Then he went back to sorting papers.

TB slid the final file folder across the table. It was the thickest one. Gendry. Currently, the dead man walking. Because once TB found him, he would make him dead.

44

———————

JUNE 23RD

Sylvan

Sylvan tried to keep the panic at bay. She drew in a deep breath, closed her eyes, then let the air out. She continued to breathe deeply. Inhale for three counts, hold on the fourth, exhale for three, and hold on the fourth. Repeat. In her mind, she focused on the image of the wolf's head on her missing collar.

Gendry had taken her jewelry from her and checked her obvious pockets when they were in the SUV. The wolf collar with the tracker in it had disappeared into a metal box that had then been ditched to throw TB off the trail if he tried to track her.

Dumbass. The idiot hadn't thought to frisk the rest of her to look for wires or anything like that. It was really amazing to her that this idiot was capable of running a drug and prostitution ring as a middleman and had never been caught. Wasn't frisking for phones Criminal 101 stuff?

Midas had given her a burner phone programmed to TB and him only since he was using her phone to try and gather intel on her stalker's location. Currently, it was in her hidden corset pocket, in silent mode, so even though it was on, it wouldn't ring or vibrate. As long as the man didn't strip her down to nothing, it would stay on her.

Would TB think of that? Would he remember that she always kept it on her person? She hoped so.

She glanced up at the timer. Two hours, fifty-two minutes, and sixteen seconds.

A buzzer sounded far down on her right.

"Flame, you okay?"

The voice came from the container to her immediate right. Medusa.

"Yeah, I'm okay. You?"

"I'm good."

A buzzer sounded down to her right.

"What's that noise?" Sylvan asked.

"That means the countdown is at zero, and the sale is complete."

"Shit," Sylvan whispered.

There was silence for a few minutes.

"I'm sorry I got you into this mess," Sylvan apologized.

"Not your fault, girl. I've been in 'this mess,' as you call it, for a lot longer than you think."

Sylvan stayed silent.

"Flame," Medusa tried again. "Does Lobo have a tracker on you?" Medusa tried again. "I know who he is, what he does. We're very familiar with Tribe, even though they are not familiar with us."

"You? You mean you, Loki, and Gilgamesh?"

"Yes. It's a long story. Look, I know you don't know me from anyone, but I need to know. Does he have a way to track you?"

"Well, no. I mean, he did. But it was in the collar I was wearing. There's another way he could find me. He'd have to remember some information to do it, though."

"Will he remember it?"

"Yes. Eventually. I don't know. Possibly. Hopefully."

There was a sigh. "Well, that sucks. Not for you!" the woman corrected. "For me."

"I don't understand."

"Sorry. You wouldn't. We were just so damn close. I have a tracker on me, but they weren't going to be coming for me. Not yet, anyway. And even with you being taken as well, I don't know if they'd have come after us."

"What are you talking about?"

"You weren't part of the plan. We were hoping to follow the pipeline the girls are moving through."

"You *wanted* to be caught?"

What the flim-flam was the matter with this woman?! Who wants to be taken by sex traffickers, even if you're trying to catch them?

"Yes, that was the plan. You've sort of complicated things here without meaning to. We need Gendry alive and working. We've been trying to redirect things, but it's difficult to do when you also don't want to out yourself. But since he took you, Lobo's going to take care of that, and we'll be back at square one."

"I can't believe they'd just let you be taken."

"Risks are necessary sometimes."

"You mean sacrifices. You're sacrificing yourself, and they're letting you."

There was a rustling noise as if Medusa were trying to finagle her way into a position besides standing up and some faint scraping noises. There was a muffled curse and a sigh, then a pointed inhale and exhale as if Medusa were trying to center herself.

"Flame, some things are bigger than one person. Do you know how many people are trafficked every year? Last year, it was over twenty-seven million. Mostly women and girls. Some of it's labor-related, but a large portion of it is sexual slavery. The conditions are… well, let's just say most don't make it out alive. And of those who do, it's not even a half-life."

"But if they don't step in, you'll be sent to who knows where."

"Flame, I wasn't planning on being rescued."

Sylvan let that sink in. "They'll…"

"Yes. Probably."

"You're crazy! How can you want that to happen?"

"I don't *want* it to. And I'm certainly not going to simply let it happen. I'll fight every step of the way. But the only way to cut down these pipelines is to blow them up from within. I'm willing to make the sacrifice to put a major dent in the numbers."

"And your men are willing to allow that to happen?"

"They're not *my* men. Not like you're thinking. The triad thing is just a cover so we could move about the club together and not have to involve other members."

"But still," Sylvan argued. "To allow any woman to sacrifice herself to sex traffickers is hardly appropriate." She stopped herself. "That sounded stupid."

Medusa laughed. "I get it. And normally I would agree. What kind of man allows that? But Loki and Gil have their own connections to all of this, both incredibly ugly, and they're not really thinking all that clearly about it. Otherwise, I doubt it would have been 'allowed' as you call it."

"And what about you?"

"Why am I willing to sacrifice myself, you mean?" Medusa paused. "Let's just say that I'm not entirely innocent in all of this. It's my way to atone for my unwitting part in it."

Another buzzer sounded. Girl number three had just been sold.

"That's the third girl," Sylvan whispered. "There'll be two more before you. He said those five women were fifteen minutes apart."

"If I lose this opportunity, we may never get another chance to shut this shit down. What is your countdown at?"

Sylvan looked up at the digital timer. "Two hours and six minutes."

She heard a lot of swearing and puffing coming from Medusa's box. There was the rattling of the handcuffs and then an elongated hiss followed by a squeal and a sudden jerk. Metal jangled against itself.

"I'm out of my cuffs. I'm going to switch boxes with one of the two remaining girls."

"Won't he see you?"

"I don't know. I hope not. I'm hoping he's taking care of money transfers and shipping details and won't be paying attention. If he does see me, we'll know. But I need to try and make sure I get through the pipeline to the destination for one of the women. If I wait to let my own sale go through, I may lose my chance because it allows more time for Lobo and his band of merry men to get here."

"Medusa, don't do this!" Sylvan hissed.

"I don't have a choice."

"There's always a choice. There's always another way."

"Stay quiet, Flame. Even if you're sold, Lobo will still come for you. They likely know I'm gone as well, or will be soon, because Loki and Gil will tell them if they don't already know. I'm going to place another tracker on the outside of your container. It will give them another avenue to track you.

"But, Flame, this next part is super important. Do whatever you're told to do. Do whatever it takes to stay alive. Alive and damaged is better than dead. And if you do as you're told, if you accept it and keep hold of the fact that Lobo will find you, the damage will be less no matter what physically occurs to you."

"Medusa, no!"

Sylvan heard a cracking noise and what sounded like the tinkling of something small and made of glass breaking. "That was my camera. I don't have long. Stay alive, Flame."

The sound of a metal door softly opening and closing could be heard, and then a soft groan and a murmur. Moments later, Sylvan heard the whisper of the door opening again, a whimper, and a shushing sound, followed by a closing door, and then silence. Medusa had effectively switched out one of the girls for herself, then gone to put herself in the other girl's box.

Another ten minutes passed. A buzzer sounded.

Fifteen minutes passed. Another buzzer.

A short time later, Sylvan heard sounds like squeaky wheels and metal being moved. The sold girls were being relocated. Her stomach turned at the thought.

Hurry, TB!

45

JUNE 23RD

"W HAT HAVE WE GOT?" W ATERS ASKED AS HE ROUNDED UP THE TROOPS.

Nemo was looking at the tabletop where Flame's purse contents were strewn about because he'd turned it upside down, dumped everything out, and was pawing through them. His expression looked pained.

TB asked him, "What are you looking for?"

"This is Flame's purse, right? The one she was carrying the other day when you two flew out of here?"

"Yes, but nothing in there's going to help us find her."

"Where's her phone?"

"She doesn't carry it in her purse. She carries it on her at all times. Woman actually has a pocket sewn into each one of her outfits..." His voice trailed off.

Nemo looked at him.

"I'm a fucking moron. Midas!" TB bellowed. "Trace her fucking phone. She has it on her."

"What? How do you know?"

"I just do. Trace it!"

TB heard keys clicking over the speaker. "Got a signal. You gotta be shitting me. No one ever still has their phone on them when they get kidnapped," he murmured.

"I'm heading for the armory. Patch into my watch. Where is she?"

Midas' voice came across the watch's speakers. "You're not going to believe this. She's at The Library."

Waters ran to TB's side, Nemo following closely behind them. "That's not possible," Waters replied.

"Well, her phone is if she's not. But the signal's goofy."

Waters looked at TB. "What's under the club?"

"Under it? Nothing. I mean, there's a basement, but it's just storage of liquor and foodstuffs. Air conditioner and furnace. That kind of stuff. I've only been in it once or twice, but it's pretty much an empty room."

"Is there anything under that?"

"Nothing that I'm aware of."

Midas called over the line, "Well, according to the GPS, her phone is literally in the middle of the dance floor."

"It's definitely not there. We didn't step foot out onto that floor tonight. We were in the bar only, and then she went into the lounge, which is where she was taken from."

They were in the armory and loading up their personal weapons. "Hate to ask this, man, but what if Gendry's working with someone from the club?"

"Impossible. I questioned everyone. They all read clear."

Waters looked at him pointedly. "Everyone?"

"Every bartender, every monitor, even the new door guardian." He stopped. "No. Not everyone." He turned his gaze to Waters. "It never once occurred to me to question one person."

THE VEHICLE WAS silent as TB, Nemo, and Demon checked their weapons. Waters was behind the wheel. Steel had checked in moments ago, letting them know they were in the back alley behind The Library where the abandoned Escalade now sat.

Gendry, the fucker had tried to throw them off with taking her jewelry off and dumping it near the freeway entrance, then circled back with them to the club. But because he didn't know about the phone in Flame's secret pocket, he was clueless that TB and friends were about to rain down destruction on him.

"Midas has looped the security cameras, so we're clear here and inside," Nemo informed them after receiving a text from his brother.

"Feckin' unbelievable," Demon commented with a shake of his head. "No wonder it was so easy for any of the girls to disappear from here. They never left the feckin' building in the first place."

"Makes you wonder," Waters chimed in. "How many others might have gone missing without us having a hint. Think about it. A nightclub is the perfect front for trafficking. People get overly intoxicated, solicitous staff 'help' them home, then poof. Nowhere to be found, and who knows how long before people notice or how long before connections get made. Most people don't tell others when they're going to a kink club, I'm guessing."

"Those in the lifestyle don't hide it, but they don't broadcast it. And people who are new to it, they're usually overly cautious," TB agreed.

There was silence in the car.

"I don't even begin to know how to do this."

Waters shifted the conversation. He lowered his voice to try and give the moment a semblance of being more private, but both knew that the guys in the back would be able to hear them.

"Do what?" Waters asked.

"Love her."

A smack came to the back of his head. "Dude, you just do it. There's no technique to it."

TB turned around on Nemo. "All those women in your life, and that's your answer?"

Nemo scoffed. "That's just sex. That requires technique. Choices made. Skills learned. I'm talking about loving her. There's no one way to do it. It's an instinct. A drive." He shrugged and looked out the passenger window. "You can't stop it even if you try."

TB looked at Waters. The blond in the driver seat mouthed, "Meow," then went back to focusing on negotiating the sharp turn into the narrow alley.

Hmm. Apparently, that little cat burglar was still living rent-free in Nemo's headspace after their run-in four years ago.

Looking out the window, TB saw that Steel, Loki, and Gilgamesh were parked with them nose-to-nose on either end of the Escalade. No one would be getting out this way.

When the vehicle came to a halt, everyone checked their weapons one last time. TB could feel anger burning inside of him. Anger that was so hot it was cold fire licking at every one of his veins. He knew he needed to harness that anger, but he honestly wasn't sure how to do it. Never in his life had he felt a strong emotion during a project—not even when he'd rescued his team leader from captivity.

"Waters," TB started. He inhaled, then exhaled. "Nemo needs to lead. I can't—"

"Not a problem. I anticipated that. When we get inside, focus on getting to Flame. That's your whole job. We've got everything else."

"But—"

"But nothing, Total Beanstalk," Nemo cut in. "I've got you. I've got you both. Just get your girl and be done with it."

TB swallowed hard. He needed to have a conversation with Nemo when this was all over. He was an absolute asshole to this guy on a regular basis, and Nemo could totally leave him stranded over this, but he wasn't going to. Hadn't once the entire time he'd been watching over the two of them.

"Nemo—"

Another smack to the back of the head was paired with, "Don't." TB looked over his shoulder. Bright blue eyes stared back at him. "Dude. I know."

There was a double clap down on his shoulder from the back seat and then Nemo was out the door and ready to breach the back entrance on Waters' signal.

TB remained frozen in his seat a few moments longer, watching Waters talk with Steel, Loki, and Gilgamesh, when another voice came from the back seat.

"Nemo's not nearly as shallow as everyone thinks he is."

"Yeah, I'm beginning to realize that."

"Good," Demon grunted. "The persona he projects is not who he is. Because that man would die to protect any one of us or, by extension, someone we love. Especially you. Don't take that for granted." With that, the medic exited the truck.

TB inhaled deeply, then exhaled, finally exiting the truck himself.

I'm coming, little Flame. Just hold on.

46

____

JUNE 23RD

Sylvan

*M*Y FEET ARE KILLING ME.

She snorted at the stupid thought her brain wanted to complain about. She had much more serious issues than sore feet. Had someone told her she was going to be kidnapped today, she would have worn flats. But no. Her vain self chose high-heeled boots to distract TB with, so now, if she took them off, her toes wouldn't even reach the floor. She was stuck.

A slightly hysterical giggle escaped at the thought, but she managed to smother it quickly.

"Gotta keep it together. TB is coming," she reminded herself. She refused to accept any other option.

There had been a long period of time with no buzzers for a while. So when the noise suddenly sounded directly next to her, she jumped.

That's Medusa's box! Will he look inside before he moves it? He didn't seem to check earlier for whichever box she switched into, so maybe he won't notice. Oh, freakazoid! Hurry, TB, hurry!

She looked up at her timer. Just under fifteen minutes.

Suddenly, someone pounded three times on the door of her box. She yelped in fright.

"Tsk, tsk, tsk, no need to shout, Jolie."

She shivered.

Gendry.

For the first year or so after escaping, she'd heard his voice daily in her head. Every voice sounded like him. Every stranger's face in the crowd had been his. Slowly, and with Ms. Monica's help, his voice had faded. Seven months ago, when all of the stalking behavior started, memories of his voice began to slowly leak back into her mind. Today, it was like all those years of freedom were washed away with simply the sound of his actual voice.

"What do you want, Gendry?"

"Oh, the fair maiden speaks! I thought for sure you'd try to play dumb. Pretend you weren't yourself. Try to convince me I have the wrong woman."

"What would be the point? You know it's me. I ran away. I just wanted away from you."

"But here's the thing, Red. I didn't want you away from me. I wanted you by my side."

"You were going to sell me to the highest bidder, you slime bucket. You killed my parents, you basically kidnapped me, you addicted me to drugs, then hired me out as payment to your bosses, and then you were going to try and use me to solve your money issues."

"Yes, well, sometimes we don't always get what we want."

"And what about what I wanted?"

Gendry laughed. "Since when has what you wanted ever mattered to anyone?"

Since TB. He says the choices are always mine.

"My choices are mine, Gendry. It's always about what I want. You may have me in a box right now. You may think you're going to win, but TB will come for you. And he will destroy you for what you've done."

Gendry's laugh became louder. "Brave words for a little girl locked up in a box. You have no choices, Jolie. You never did. You never will. In about ten minutes, you'll have even less choice because where you're going, you'll be lucky to last ten months with what's in store for you. The men bidding on you right now think they're playing a game they might win. But the man who's going to win your auction, he can't possibly lose. He has more money than most countries put together, and he's wanted you for a long time. And once he has what he needs from you, you'll be erased from this planet as if you never existed. Not that you ever really did."

He slapped the door of the box again. "I'd love to stay and chat. Better yet, I'd love to have a last taste of you. But, sadly, we're out of time. And you were hardly worth it anyway. Not enough fight in you. Goodbye, Jolie. I win."

Sylvan raged inside the box, pulling and yanking on the chains keeping her from searching for a way to break through the door. Logically, she knew she was locked in and wouldn't be able to escape, but that didn't mean she wasn't going to try.

"I got away from you once, Gendry. I can do it again."

Gendry's laughter grew fainter and fainter as it echoed through the warehouse space. "Not likely, Red."

47

JUNE 23RD

TB

THE CLUB WAS EERILY QUIET WHEN THEY ENTERED FROM THE ALLEY entrance. Instead of the bar being to their left upon entry, it was straight ahead and on their right. To their immediate left was the pool and the small stage. To their right was the door to the upstairs playrooms. Weapons drawn and NVGs in place, they entered the club and split into three groups. Steel, Loki, and Gilgamesh went to clear upstairs. Demon and Waters went to clear the main floor and bar. Nemo and TB went to the restrooms.

"Clear," Nemo called out from the women's toilets.

"Clear," TB returned from the men's.

When they stepped out into the main area, Demon and Waters were returning from clearing the bar and front entryway. Tables were overturned, broken glass was strewn everywhere, and personal items of all sorts were left behind from the power failure. Everyone still had their weapons drawn, and they were still on alert, but the weapons were now pointed at the floor rather than outward as coverage.

"Bar and front entry are clear," Waters informed them. "Tabitha's office looks undisturbed."

Please let that mean she's not involved.

TB knew that was false hope talking, but it didn't hurt to voice it inside his head. There was no way she could be uninvolved if activities of trafficking were happening on the property.

Nemo asked, "Where's the door to the basement, TB?"

"Go through the door where Steel and the guys went. It's directly to the left as you go over the threshold."

Quickly, quietly, and attentively, the four men crossed to the door and went through it. Steel, Loki, and Gilgamesh were just coming down the stairs from the private rooms.

"Everything's clear upstairs. No one's here."

TB nodded to the door on the left side of the hallway. "That goes to the storage and utilities. You'll be able to see where the dance floor is when you get down there. There are a series of box structures that hold lights in them that flash up into the club. She's got to be right under there somewhere."

Nemo took the flexi cam tubing and slid it gently under the door. After moving it gently as far left and right as he could, he looked to Waters.

"No one in sight," their team leader said. "There's a landing that's about three feet wide and two feet deep once the door opens. Metal stairs, eighteen of them, to the floor. Metal rails on both sides."

"Cool. A slide." The smirk on Nemo's face showed that despite the seriousness of the situation, he enjoyed the hunt.

"It's all yours, Nemo. You have point," Waters ordered.

The men's weapons went into position. Nemo flattened himself against the wall to the left of the closed door, Waters was flattened to the wall to its right, his hand on the door knob. Loki and Gilgamesh were standing at the ready, in the high and low positions to protect Nemo.

Waters began the countdown on his fingers. When his hand went to a fist, he flung the door open. Nemo threw himself through the entryway, launched himself to a sitting position on the stair rails, and slid down to the bottom of the steps, his gun pointed in front of him.

Loki and Gilgamesh stepped through and positioned themselves over each rail at the top of the flight, their guns aimed to the left and right of the landing. Demon was flat on the landing, covering Nemo's slide.

"Clear, bossman," Nemo said.

With stealth and precision, the men went down the stairs and fanned out in all directions. It didn't take more than a few seconds. The basement was wide open and there was nowhere to hide. There was also no sign of Flame's phone on the floor of the basement where the GPS locator said it currently was.

"It should be right here," TB stated the obvious.

"There has to be another level to the basement," Waters surmised. "Everybody look around."

It took only moments for the men to survey the walls and flooring, but there were no other doorways.

TB could feel his frustration bubbling to the surface. "She has to be here!"

"The entrance must be somewhere else," Steel gathered. "A doorway elsewhere in the club. And they were snatched from the restrooms. Something over that direction maybe?"

"Midas, do you copy?"

"I read you loud and clear, boss. I just hacked into the city mainframe, and I'm looking at building specs. There are no permits or plans on file to build onto the building."

"Fuck!" TB swore.

"Patience, my young padawan, you didn't let me finish. There *is* a permit for the business next door to finish the original basement on that building, which happens to go down an additional sixty feet below this one. AND... they used to own this business as well until it was sold to the current owners of The Library—who, at that time, filled in the connecting sections of the two buildings and covered all the subflooring so that the two no longer shared the space twenty feet below you."

"Awesome work, Midas," Waters called out. "But now we

need a way over there. Do we have to enter from the other building?"

"Nope. Believe it or not, there's an unfinished space between the ladies' room and the building next door. There must be an easy way to pop the wall in there."

"The supply closet," TB monotoned. "There's a door by the toilets. I bet the entrance is somehow through there."

As one, the group hustled back up the stairs and out into the main area of the club, then headed straight into the ladies' room lounge. The supply closet was locked, so Nemo went to work with his lock picks. Within seconds the door was open, the overhead light was on... but all they were faced with were shelves.

"This is so bullshit," Nemo fussed. "One of these walls moves, pure and simple." He started pulling on the metal shelving, ripping it from its anchors on the wall, until finally there was a scraping noise, and he was able to pull an entire section of a wall loose to reveal a walkway between framed portions of the two buildings. Not only that, but it was on a gentle incline.

"Behold, gentlemen."

Loki grunted. "Talk about a valley of death."

"Yeah," Waters agreed. "Suddenly I'm back in Afghanistan in a boxed-in convoy. Easy to get mowed down in here."

"We go in twos," Loki offered. "Ten seconds apart with a stop at any corner to clear the way. That way we have room to back up if need be. Gilgamesh and I will offer to go first."

Waters considered. "Agreed. Nemo and Steel will follow. Demon, TB, and I will bring up the rear."

"On my mark. Go." Loki and Gilgamesh took off at a brisk pace until they hit the turn. Once they reached it, one took the high, the other took the low, and they made a swift turn around the wall. "Looks like it's a continuation of switchbacks," Loki said over the earbuds.

"Sending Nemo and Steel down."

"Copy."

Waters waved the two men down to provide cover fire as the two men made the turn in the switchbacks. After a few moments,

Nemo gave Waters the "approach" signal, and the three remaining men came down to them. From that point on, they proceeded to move down the ramps like a snake undulating along its course until they reached the bottom, emptying out into a cavernous warehouse.

"Who would have thought there'd be this much room down here?" Gilgamesh whispered.

Loki grunted. "This must be one of the new satellite locations." His sarcasm was clear. Everything in the warehouse was new. The air was permeated with the smell of fresh concrete and construction. Lighting was sparse yet, but in the distance they could see a series of coffin-sized boxes lined up to be loaded onto a mechanized conveyor headed up to the surface.

"You've seen this before?" Waters asked.

Loki nodded. "Looks like several others we've run across. Welcome to the future of sex trafficking, my new friends. Think of it like a distribution center. Central order hub takes the clients' orders. Those are distributed out to satellite locations who fill the orders, then ship the product."

TB was vibrating with a need to find Flame. "Can we discuss the details later? If we don't move quickly, Flame, Medusa, and those other girls are going to disappear, and we'll never find them."

Loki and Gilgamesh shared a look, then turned their eyes back to the action in the distance. "Your girl will likely be the last box. You take care of the girls you can get to. Loki and I will handle the two goons."

As the men did a weapons check, TB growled, "Gendry is mine."

Nemo responded, "Focus on Flame, TB. I'll make sure the asshole is secured and ready for playtime back at Tribe."

TB had never seen such a serious expression on the playboy's face nor heard such a murderous tone in his voice. TB gave him a nod, and they went back to work.

On Waters' signal, they quickly fanned out to reach the action in front of them. Because they were quiet, they got closer than they should have. However, because there was next to nothing in the facility, they didn't get close enough before they were noticed.

Tabitha stood with Gendry behind a bank of computers and monitors. He wore an expensive gray suit, a lighter gray button-down shirt, and a thin burgundy tie. In his late thirties, he had a distinctly European air about him. Hawk-like features, naturally tan skin, and shoulder-length curly hair brushed straight back from his face. He was clearly talking to someone on the other side of his computer screen, which was why they were able to sneak in as close as they did. Between the noise of the conveyors, the focus of his two goons on ensuring the boxes were neatly loaded, and his focus on the conversation that was happening, the men made it to within twenty-five feet before weapons were needed.

When they were finally noticed, it was by one of the goons supervising the box loading. In a flash, his weapon was drawn from inside his suit coat, but it was too late. TB, his teammates, and Medusa's men were already in shooting mode. Goon number one went down in a heap before he could take aim.

Goon number two whirled around at the sound of bullets. He barely had a chance to register what he was seeing before he went down to the ground in a heap.

Loki and Gilgamesh sprinted toward the conveyors, slamming the emergency off switch.

Gendry had pulled a gun from inside his jacket, as well, and managed to squeeze off a couple of shots. TB felt a burning sensation along his bicep, but he kept moving forward to the last box that was at the foot of the conveyor. Behind him, his teammates were securing Gendry and Tabitha.

Loki and Gilgamesh had reversed the conveyor and were systematically unloading the boxes, readying them to be opened to free the girls inside.

"Flame, can you hear me?"

"TB?"

"Can you squeeze yourself into the left corner of the box? I need to shoot off the lock. Close your eyes, princess. Turn your head to the side."

Hoping that she'd followed his directions, he aimed his gun at the lock, and took his shot. As soon as the door splintered, he was ripping it open. Inside, Flame was shuddering in the corner, tears streaming down her face. Instantly he was half inside with her, gathering her close. Squeezing her tight, he took a giant inhale of her scent, the sweet smell of roses clinging to her skin and hair. "Are you hurt?"

"No," came her muffled voice from where her face was buried in his chest. "I knew you'd come for me, but I was still afraid—"

"I'm so sorry, sweetheart. I'm gonna get you out of here."

He knew he needed to get her out of the shackles overhead, but he was afraid to let go of her. Afraid she'd disappear if he did.

Someone tapped him on the shoulder. He ignored them. Just kept squeezing Flame to him, taking in her scent and reassuring himself she was alive and unhurt.

"TB, I pulled the key for the shackles off of Gendry. We've got him and Tabitha secure. The other girls are all unlocked and ready to leave. Free your woman and let's go."

TB turned his head to see Waters standing behind him, holding out a key. "I can't let go of her. You do it."

Waters gave him a smile, then reached over the couple to unlock the cuffs. Once they opened, Flame's arms clutched TB's neck in desperation. "I've got you, princess. I've got you."

Finally some part of his brain switched back on. TB wasted no time sweeping Flame off of her feet, hugging her tight to his chest, and moving toward the ramps and to the exit with purpose. He was not letting her spend one more minute in this space.

48

JUNE 23RD-24TH

TB

THUD! THUD! THUD-THUD-THUD! THUD! THUD-THUD!

The sounds of flesh meeting flesh stopped, but it was evident that the pain from the contact did not. Gendry's head was lolling to the right, his breathing full-on wheezing, his face drawn tight in pain.

"Had enough?" TB asked.

The man's response whistled through his missing teeth. "Not even close."

A single naked lightbulb burned in the room that was bare except for a single metal chair. Bound to the chair, Gendry bled out on his Armani suit. His left eye was swollen shut, and the right was on its way to looking the same. His nose was off center, dried rivers of blood caking his top lip, painting over and around his mouth. His upper lip was split, adding blood to his chin and neck. Overall, the flesh of his face was bruised and cut from the punches he'd endured.

In addition to the badly battered face, the man's left shoulder was clearly out of the socket and had to be excruciatingly painful, being wrenched back behind the chair where his hands were zip-tied. His once crisp, white thousand-dollar dress shirt was showing signs of being saturated with sweat and blood, covering what was surely to be an entire torso of bruised ribs. His kidneys were likely severely damaged. His ankles were bound to the legs of the chair with zip-ties tied too tightly, cutting off circulation to the point where his feet were swelling and turning blue-black.

In the shadows, TB leaned himself against the wall in the upper right corner of the room, his hands behind his back, flat to the wall. His ankles were crossed. His eyes were hooded, gaze straight out at the wall across the room. His demeanor was that of a man who had all the time in the world to wait.

"Where do you send the girls?" The giant's tone was one of boredom, as if he'd asked this question hundreds of times already.

"Fuck you," the man snapped.

"Wrong answer. Care to try again?" TB's response showed no emotion whatsoever.

"Fuck. You." The man pushed out the sound louder and clearer, as if he thought TB was hard of hearing. Both men knew that not to be true, just as they knew the second command was a taunt.

"I applaud your strategy, but your tactic won't work."

The man gave a snort of derision. "And what strategy is that?"

TB stepped away from the wall and sauntered over to stand in front of the bound man. "You're hoping that you can make me mad. Make me seethe in a red rage, maybe make a mistake, and attack in anger. You're hoping that will give you an opening to escape. But it won't happen."

The bound man's lips suddenly curled up into a pitiful smile, and a whistling sound escaped as his body shook with laughter. "Everyone has a trigger. Jolie is yours."

"Jolie is nothing to me. She died the day Sylvan escaped you. And since Sylvan is safe, I can't be triggered into making a mistake. But I don't have what I need. The girls were clearly all headed to another place, and they were headed there together. Since that's the case, that means they go somewhere else before being distributed to their owners. What I need is the next stop on the itinerary for the girls you've been selling. So I ask again, where?"

The man's lips turned up slightly, causing the scab on his lip to split open and begin bleeding again. A gurgling sound began from deep within him. As the sound grew, his shoulders began to shake, eventually revealing laughter. The sound that issued from him resembled something like a mad scientist in a bad science fiction movie. His face became even more gruesome as the smile on it broke into a mouth of teeth stained red. What teeth he had left, anyway.

His smile fell, the laughter clearly painful, as he broke into a fit of coughing, which had to be even more tortuous. Minutes later, when the coughing stopped, blood bubbled at the corner of his mouth. He ran his tongue around the inside of his mouth, then spat blood and a tooth to the floor. Three other teeth were already there to greet it.

Another smile formed on the man's crooked mouth. "I'll never tell you."

"We'll see," TB replied with a lack of concern.

His step seemed dismissive of his victim as he moved to his right side. Without warning, he delivered a brutal punch to the man's chin, snapping his head back. That was followed up with a barrage of quick, sharp jabs that pummeled his ribs. There was a distinct snapping sound as another one broke.

The victim muttered, "Mother-fucking asshole," through a groan of pain. "You better hope I don't get free of this chair. Because if I do, I'll kill you."

"Brave words for a man who's about to see what's on the other side."

"Not brave," the man gurgled. "True. I will gut you like a pig."

Standing behind the man and just to his right, TB leaned down to rumble in his ear. "You hear that gurgling sound when you speak or breathe? What you're hearing is the blood collecting in your lungs. I snapped another rib to go with the other three I broke earlier. Right now, the greenstick fractures are turning into shards, puncturing your lungs with little tiny holes. The shattered bits are traveling through your body, and once they make contact with your other organs, your veins, and even your bones, they will burrow their way in, poisoning your body by releasing toxins those organs hold and letting them loose into your body cavity. It will be a long, painful death. Many hours… maybe even days… while you slowly drown in your own blood and bacteria. Even if you got free from that chair, you wouldn't make it two steps before you collapsed."

"You don't scare me."

TB grinned to himself and stood up straight. "Then you're even dumber than I figured."

"Without me, you've got nothing. You won't kill me."

A glint of light blurred in front of the prisoner, and he felt the cold, sharp edge of a blade against the skin of his neck. "Oh, I will kill you. There's no other outcome for you regarding that. The question will be, do you make it easy on yourself, giving me the information I want so that I end you quickly? Or do you continue to resist and eventually die in pain like a wounded animal?"

Choking against the blade, a trickle of blood joining the rest, the man croaked out, "Fuck. You."

TB whirled, grabbing the man by his shoulder-length hair, pulling his head back as far as he could.

Bound, in pain, and dying, Gendry found the energy to smile with perverse glee. His breaths came out in pants. "Not too smart despite all your toys and skills, are you?"

"Tell me or you'll wish you had never met me," TB growled.

A cough that expressed blood came forth. The man closed his eyes, and TB twisted the hair in his grasp and yanked, a chunk of hair and skin coming free in his hand. It made a slapping noise as he threw it to the floor.

The giant reached into a toolbox on the floor, withdrawing a syringe, a vial of clear liquid, and a rubber tourniquet. He approached the prisoner and set down the items on the floor.

Removing his knife from his sheath once again, he sliced through the jacket sleeve and shirt sleeve, revealing the man's arm. He tied the tourniquet around his upper arm. A vein began to swell to the surface almost immediately. Holding the vial upside down and to the light, he jabbed the syringe into the bottle, drawing liquid into the reservoir.

TB flicked the syringe, then located the popped vein. "Let's see if we can't augment that pain. Maybe you'll be more cooperative when you start hallucinating your worst nightmares."

Without consideration of the pain he created, he pressed the needle into the vein, depressed the plunger, and when it was empty, released the tourniquet.

The captive hissed at the injection, swearing violently when his captor yanked the needle out of the vein. "Fucking asshole!"

"That would be me." TB cleaned up his materials, then circled around to face his prisoner. "That injection is a special creation of mine. A mixture of heroin, ketamine, and some other surprises. It should take effect in a few minutes. When it does, a friend of mine is going to spend some time with you. He's exceptionally talented with suggestion and other psychological games. If you don't give him what I want, eventually you'll pass out since the primary side effect of my masterpiece is sedation. Impossible to escape the nightmares he'll create for you."

TB turned and walked to the door. When he reached it, he threw over his shoulder, "Resist, and I'll be back with a larger dose. Overdose, and I'll Narcan your ass right back to me until I get what I want. We'll see how long you last. The record is four days before my worst case begged me to kill him. He took another day or two to cough up the information. By then sepsis had settled in from the dirty needles I used. When the pain became too great, he spilled his guts.

"You decide if you want to hold the Guinness World Record or if you'd rather just throw in the towel and go peacefully."

With that, he opened the door. Waiting on the threshold was Midas. TB stepped back, allowing the other man into the room. "He's all yours."

As TB closed the door, he heard his replacement begin. "So. I'm going to tell you a story about a man who visited hell while still alive. Shall we begin? Once upon a time, there was a scumbag who kidnapped a beautiful, red-haired princess..."

In the men's room, TB had just finished washing his hands and was drying them when he was hit with a sudden wave of nausea. It built within him, and he could feel his stomach contents threatening to surge up into his esophagus and spew through his mouth. Locking his elbows, he leaned on the sink's edge, staring down at the countertop, willing his body to maintain control of its systems.

He couldn't unsee it. All his brain could process was the sight of Flame, shackled inside that metal coffin, tears streaming down her cheeks, trying so hard to hold onto her anger and be brave but finally succumbing to the relief that he had reached her in time.

It was no use. He spat bile into the sink, no longer able to keep the rush of the acid from rising.

When he finally felt as if he had some semblance of control again, he turned on the faucet, cupped his hands beneath it to collect water, and then brought his hands to his mouth to take in the water, swish it around in his mouth to rinse out the bitter aftertaste, then spit the tainted water into the sink. He repeated the process three times until, finally, only the barest trace of it remained in the back of his throat.

He washed his hands. Turning off the faucet, he grabbed several paper towels from the dispenser and dried them, as well as swiped a towel across his lips to wipe away the last vestiges of the water he'd splashed on his face. He was just throwing the towels in the garbage can when he heard the door open quietly behind him, then swish shut on its hinges.

He didn't turn around. Instead, he looked into the mirror to see Midas standing behind him. His tag team interrogation partner simply stood in the background, leaning against the wall, arms crossed, studying TB's reflection.

"Well?" TB asked.

"Waters and Steel double-teamed Tabitha and got her whole sordid story. She thought she could use Flame's inexperience to pull you back to her. When it had the opposite effect, she started hatching another plan. That never came to fruition because Gendry waltzed in with an offer to cut her in on the sales of the girls if she helped him secure Flame. She leapt at that opportunity, hoping that her disappearance might drive you back into her arms."

TB snorted. "Would never have happened. Knew somehow that woman was poison." Silence hung between the two men. Finally, TB asked, "What is Waters going to do with her?"

"Waters? Nothing. He left her with Steel in the other interrogation room. When he went back fifteen minutes later, both Steel and the woman were gone, and he took Demon along for disposal."

TB looked down into the sink. He wished he could feel some sympathy for Tabitha's demise, but it just wouldn't come. Instead, he felt bad for the sharks. Hopefully none of them choked on her in their feeding frenzy.

I'm truly a terrible human being.

Midas broke through his musing. "I've got something. No idea what. It doesn't make sense. He said, 'Salieri.'"

"The composer?"

"I don't think that's how he meant it. But I'll be digging."

TB nodded. "Ready for me to take out the trash?"

"I've got what I need. You okay, or do you want Nemo to take care of it?"

"Nah, that fucker's mine." He sighed. "Will she hate me for this?"

"TB, she knows you're not squeaky clean. She hasn't run screaming for the hills yet. Just don't tell her details. But ridding the world of that assnozzle is not going to change the fact that she loves you."

"I don't deserve her."

"Yeah, you do." Midas pushed off the wall and stepped up to him. In his hand, he held a piece of paper. "I did some unsolicited research for you. Check them out." Then he exited the restroom.

TB looked at the piece of paper with only a web address on it. When he looked at it closer, he didn't recognize the business, but it was clear what type of business it was. Did he dare?

Whatever the answer to that question was, it would have to wait. Pocketing the paper, he looked up at his reflection and ran his fingers through his hair. Time to do some waste management.

49

JUNE 25TH

TB

WHY AM I SO GODDAMN TIRED?

Everyone was waiting for him when TB entered the conference room, including Steel and Demon back from their own garbage run. He looked at Waters. "It's done."

There was a look of concern on his team leader's face, but he said nothing to him. Instead, he spoke to the group as a whole. "Now that we're all here, our friends have some more direct information for us on our missing SEAL." He locked down the room's security measures through the starfish and turned to the telescreen where Loki sat. The background looked like he might have been on a corporate jet of some sort.

"Loki. Thank you, again, for your help with recovering Flame and the other women. Extra hands are appreciated."

"No problem. He had our girl, Medusa, so it was a no-brainer."

Stepping forward, TB added, "She defended my woman. She has my marker anytime she needs it."

Loki gave a head nod. "I'll be sure to tell her. She may need it someday."

Waters added, "My boss said no markers needed. Any of you, anytime, anyplace, we'll be there."

"As will we. I've given your computer guru a way to contact us should you need. But right now, I have something you want more than a marker." Loki shared his screen. On it were photos of two Egyptian men in designer suits, each with a hand on the arm of a tall, blond-haired man who'd clearly seen better days. He was wearing casual clothes as if he were an underling or even a client of the men escorting him, but closer observation revealed an almost healed black eye and several scabbed-over cuts on his face and forearms.

"Lose something?" Loki asked.

"Ka-Bar," Steel confirmed.

"These photos were taken in Sallum back in April when we were there. He was taken into a warehouse that's listed as an import/export company. Chances are they've moved him, but it's a place to start."

"Any chance you know who the two suits are?" Waters asked.

"Hemeda and Pilis Kader. The warehouse is owned by the family business."

Waters looked to Midas for confirmation. "Zahra's brother and a cousin," the computer tech replied.

Loki chimed in, "I take it you're familiar with them?"

"Only by name. Our man has connections to Hemeda's sister."

"I assume they're close connections," Loki surmised.

"Very. Anything else you can tell us?"

They watched as Loki glanced quickly off-camera. He gave off an air of being in charge, but the glance looked as if he were seeking permission to divulge information. TB knew a beta in a pack when he saw one.

He must have received permission to give them another breadcrumb. "Rumor has it that a supplier is using the port of Sallum for an expansion pipeline for moving merchandise. Everything from Egyptian artifacts to designer knockoffs, drugs to slaves. We believe that location is where the bookkeeping is, and maybe some other inconsequential things. We didn't see evidence of any product being moved through there. That would require much higher security and would stand out to both local law officials and the general public."

Midas asked, "Does this have to do with something called 'Salieri'?"

Loki didn't flinch or look off screen, but his nostrils gave the slightest of flares. "Where did you hear that name?"

"Gendry gave up the name just before we set him free."

"You let him go?" Loki asked.

"Hell, I did," TB grunted. "I set him free from his body."

Waters cut straight to the point. "How does Gendry fit into this, and why would he have held onto these women until he had access to Flame?"

Again, Loki's eye was drawn off camera and TB wondered who was directing the conversation. It could be Gilgamesh, but he was willing to bet it was Medusa.

"The supply chain we've been following is trying to expand. Your man, Gendry, became a new contractor for the supply chain. He came in at a very low and very local level. He was being fast-tracked through the chain's system for the past two years.

"Ten years ago, he was moving drugs for another organization, one based in New York City. He'd made quite a name for himself there, but then just as quickly as he rose in the cartel's ranks, he began to fall out of favor. Fell in love with the lifestyle a little too much, including the product, and started to become unreliable. He was cut loose six years ago when over ten million in drug funds disappeared. Word was he'd managed to cover his losses, and then something went wrong and the money couldn't be paid back. How he wasn't killed for that, I've no idea. I'm wondering if Sylvan Jones doesn't figure into that somehow since she's the common denominator between his two jobs."

TB turned to Waters. "That matches up with what Flame told us. She thought she was being used to cover his debt. But ten million? That's high for a single girl."

"She worth that to you?" Waters snarked.

TB rolled his eyes. "Worth any price to me, but to some guy just out to buy a toy to play with? Too high. I worked the skin trade a time or two as part of my contractor business. Nothing I ever collected even came close to that price."

"He's right, Waters," Loki confirmed. "Ten million for a single girl in 2016? Way too high, no matter who she was. A million, maybe two, if she was virgin and ticked a bunch of other specific boxes for someone. There was something about your girl that the buyer wanted. Fast forward and someone is after her again, through the same seller?"

"This isn't just any supply chain anymore, gentlemen," God interrupted. "This is something bigger. Something far worse than simple trafficking for labor and sex slaves."

Loki nodded. "As I mentioned earlier, the location under the club looked as if it was going to be used for a shipping point. We've seen others, but not ones nearly this sophisticated. This looked new and in the early stages of set up. There weren't nearly enough sarcophagi for it to be an established point of sale. Slime bucket that he was, Gendry's instincts were good, which is probably part of why he was on the fast-track.

"The location is pretty sweet. Easy access to all the main freeways, highways, a small airstrip, and the docks. Not to mention, it's within easy driving of the California border in a pinch. Plus, the location itself is a good hunting ground, but only if used wisely. Too many people go missing directly from there, it would be noticed. However, moving product through that area would have been easy as there are a lot of trendy clubs and businesses in the area. Dressed the part properly, a procurer would be difficult to spot.

"As to why he was holding onto the girls, Gendry needed to test the auction service as well as the supply line. He had a very specific order with an open-ended shipping date: Sylvan Jones. He was also asked to provide proof that the digital system and its pipeline could move multiple persons through it undetected. So, while he waited for the perfect opportunity, he collected a few other samples of his work to run the test. Then your BDSM giant shows up unexpectedly, and his timeline gets all thrown to shit. Gendry was forced to improvise.

"You've stumbled into something we've been tracking through its growth for years. Place an order through a buyer, guaranteed shipping, warehouses of supplies to be shipped internationally. Welcome to the funhouse, gentlemen." Someone offscreen slid Loki a piece of paper. After glancing at it, he looked up and said, "I have to sign off as we're about to go dark. If you need a helping hand in the future, you know how to find us."

The telescreen went dark.

"Wow. They definitely went dark," Midas said.

"What do you mean?" Waters asked.

"I mean, they're nowhere. Usually, I can back channel and see where they are. But I can't see anything. It's like they never were on our server."

"We record everything, though."

"Yeah, well…" Midas clicked a few keys, and static appeared on the screen. "Ghosts in the machine. No recording exists."

"That's ridiculous. It's not possible."

"Well, they found a way."

Waters' brow furrowed. "Keep searching for them in the background. They may be friends right now, but that doesn't mean they couldn't become foes. I want to know who they are."

"Got it."

TB looked at Waters. "We going to Sallum?"

Waters shook his head. "I'm going to send Nemo and Steel as planned. No sense tripping unseen wires before we mean to be seen. Two are easier to hide than six. Until we know where he is, I'm reluctant to go anywhere full force."

Waters clicked out of the security protocols and looked around the table. "Forty-eight hours off for all but Demon and me. We'll be settling, debriefing, and reacclimating the women into everyday life. Midas, keep your programs running, but get some rest. If there's an emergency, I'll text." The men began to file out of the room, chattering as they did so.

TB remained behind looking out the window, considering his next moves. His life was now in such uncharted territory that he had no idea how to proceed.

It was silent in the room for a long time, the sun setting over the city skyline. When he turned, he expected to see Waters or even Steel, but it was neither.

Nemo.

That I did not expect.

TB was wary, but Nemo was standing at the head of the conference room table with a serious expression on his face, holding up his hands like he was being confronted by a man with a gun. "I come in peace," he intoned. Hoisting himself up on the conference table, he locked his elbows and curled his fingers around the edge. "I figured you'd be the first one out the door with Waters' orders. Why are you still here?"

TB shrugged. "She's home, resting. Kubrick's with her."

"That's not an answer to the question. Why are you still here?"

TB opened his mouth to answer, reconsidered, and closed his mouth. He tried a second time but was no more successful. Finally, he settled on, "She's vulnerable. Even though she knew she was a target before I came into the picture, she has been living on fumes. She needs sleep. Quiet."

"She'd probably sleep and rest better knowing you're close."

"Now that Gendry and the danger are gone, she may discover that I'm not nearly as attractive to her."

"That's bullshit, and you know it. She was in love with you before she even met you."

"How would you know?" TB asked, suspiciously.

"The day we set up her house? In the doorway? The whisper? I asked her if she was in love with you. She can't hide anything, which is refreshing, to be honest. There's no subterfuge or masking with her. She shows you everything she's feeling."

TB felt panic pooling in his gut. "I'm going to hurt her. I won't be able to help it. Somewhere, somehow, I'm going to fuck it all up because I have no clue what the fuckall I'm doing."

Nemo laughed. "Dude, no man knows what he's doing when it comes to women. Even I don't, and I've slept with more women than even I can count." He pulled a piece of gum out of his pocket, unwrapped it, popped it in his mouth, and pocketed the wrapper. "It's obvious you care about her. What's the hang up?"

"Caring about her, wanting to be in a relationship with her, and loving her are three very different things. I don't think you get it."

Nemo hummed to himself. "It's interesting to me that you jumped to the end option of loving her. So, ask me again how I know you want a relationship with this woman." He winked. "Look, just tell her what she needs to hear, which is the truth. Tell her you love her and you're never going to let her go."

That's it? I can do that.

TB was thinking hard. "She knows I've never been part of a couple. How do I make her believe I'm serious?"

"Take a piece of advice from her books. Make a grand gesture. Put yourself in a vulnerable position. You're such a big badass; showing her your belly, so to speak, will be a dead giveaway."

"How do I know what will work for this grand gesture?"

Nemo laughed good-naturedly. "You're the interrogator, dumbass. It's the same thing but without the torture angle. Don't watch her. *See* her. Who she really is. Listen to her. Not just what she is saying, but what she *isn't*. Should be child's play for you."

"Examples," TB prompted.

His teammate sighed in exasperation. "I don't know. Most of it's instinctual. Do things she needs done, but even she doesn't know she needs done. Button her coat. Read to her. Braid her hair."

"I don't know how to braid hair."

"It's called YouTube. Tons of videos for anything you want. How do you think I learned to tie a tie? But you know, since you are an interrogator with a penchant for restraints, maybe some torture techniques wouldn't be out of the question."

"What the fuck?"

"Not those kinds of torture techniques! Jesus, you really are obtuse sometimes. Your skills. The *other* ones." Nemo raised his eyebrows at TB and lowered his chin.

TB was quiet for a moment. Then his eyes opened wider in understanding. "Oh." He considered Nemo's words. "Oh." Although the word was quieter, it held much more meaning the second time. And the epiphany of what gesture would reach her came in like a tsunami: fast, fierce, and forceful.

Nemo blew a bubble with his gum, and when it popped, he winked. "Now you've got it."

50

———————

JUNE 25TH

Sylvan

Soothing creaking noises came from the porch swing as Kai's foot gently powered it back and forth, her arm around Sylvan's shoulders. Kai's hand gently smoothed up and down Sylvan's bicep, her head tilted and resting on Sylvan's head.

"Syl, talk to me," Kai pleaded.

Sylvan sat in silence. Exhaustion seeped through every pore of her body, but she couldn't shut her brain down. While she'd been locked up in the box waiting for TB to rescue her, she'd obviously been afraid, but now she was still afraid, which made no sense to her. She was home. Gendry was gone.

Gone? Try dead. You know TB won't let him live.

"Syl?"

She knew she should respond. She felt bad because she knew Kai needed reassurance that her friend was okay, but Sylvan was so not okay. She needed TB. She needed him now. He'd have to come to the house at some point to collect his things. The question was, would he leave or would he stay?

"He'll be here, Syl. He's not going anywhere."

Sylvan smiled against Kai's shoulder. Kai always could read her mind.

Almost immediately, there was the sound of a car pulling into the garage. After it shut off, there was the sound of a door opening and closing, of boots crossing the hardwood floors, and then of the patio door sliding open.

"Flame?"

Her head didn't move, but her eyes looked up through her lashes at his concerned face.

He flicked a look at Kai, then he looked back at Sylvan. "Princess?" His boots clicked against the deck flooring, and he crouched down in front of her. The hand in her lap was engulfed in his, the thumb rubbing across her knuckles. "Princess, I need to hear how you're feeling. Demon said you weren't hurt, but that's just the outside. I need to know about the inside."

She still didn't speak.

Why can't you speak? They're going to worry there's something really wrong with you when the truth is even you don't know what's wrong.

Well, that was a lie. Ironically, it had nothing to do with Gendry, being kidnapped, and possibly being sold. It had everything to do with him. And her. And what happened with them now since the stalker situation was resolved.

Kai hugged Sylvan with her one arm and kissed the top of her head. "I'll leave you two alone. I'm guessing you have things to talk about."

Once Kai had passed back into the living room and closed the door behind her, TB took her place on the swing. Immediately he gathered her in his arms and pulled her into his lap, tucking her under his chin. His legs picked up a slow, steady rhythm of pushing the swing, and he held her close. Incredible warmth flooded her body. But more importantly, she felt safe.

Time had no meaning as they sat there, rocking amid the summer breeze. The sun was beginning to set when she finally felt herself rallying. "TB?"

"What can I do for you, Flame? How can I help you? What do you need?"

"I just need you," she replied. "Are you going or staying?"

"I'd like to stay if that's okay. If you'd prefer I go—"

"No!" She put a hand to his chest as if that would somehow stop him. "I want you to stay." Her eyes stared at his chest. "But how long will you stay?"

Her heart hammered in her chest. She both needed an answer and didn't want to hear it.

"I've been ordered to stay away from Tribe for forty-eight hours. Then I go back to work."

She sighed and nodded. "Where are you going?"

"Going? I just said. To work."

"I meant, where are they sending you for work?"

Curled fingers reached under her chin and tipped her eyes up to his. "Tribe, princess. I'm not going overseas. At least, not that I know of. I suppose anything could happen, but there's no plan to be anywhere but in L.A. for right now."

"So you'll stay with me?" She hoped her voice didn't sound as needy to him as it did to her.

"I'll stay with you as long as you want me." A kiss to the forehead sealed the promise. "I'm not going anywhere, princess. I'm in this all the way."

Sylvan slid her arms up around TB's neck and squeezed tight, her face buried under his chin. "Thank you."

"For what, little Flame?"

"For talking to me about my research. For the night at the club. For rescuing me. For everything."

"No need to thank me, sweetheart. I wanted to do it all and more. I still do. And I'll tell you a secret." A kiss to the shell of her ear, his warm breath followed. "I don't want to stop."

They sat on the porch swing long into the evening, wrapped around each other, not talking. Just being.

51

JULY 15TH

TB

UNTIL RECENTLY, IT HAD BEEN A LONG TIME SINCE HE HAD FELT FEAR. THE night Flame had been taken had been the first day since the death of his parents that he'd allowed that emotion any power over him. Tonight, however, he was petrified. How was it possible for one tiny little woman, one who was scared of her own shadow at times, one who trusted no one, to trust him? A man who had nothing to offer her but off-the-charts sex and a surly temper. He doubted the former could even begin to make up for the latter.

He had always believed that nothing could make him run. Oh, what a lie that was. He had always been running. Running from his grief over his parents. Running from the restraint of the army. Running from the law. Running from his team. Running from himself.

There would be no more running. Not anymore. And definitely not from her.

The past few weeks had been eye-opening ones for him.

He'd never lived with anyone before. Not like this. The over-crowded rooms of the orphanage, the tents and barracks of the army, were not like this. In those places, there had been no privacy. Not even enough to sit and think quietly. Here? He was with her whenever he wasn't at Tribe, but he didn't feel crowded. Even if he sat with her all night in her sanctuary, he never felt like his privacy was invaded.

He had tried to stay at Tribe one night the first week. He spent a long time explaining to her why he was leaving. Giving her space. Not wanting to invade. Taking things slow. He should have saved himself the hours of time he used to plot and plan the delivery of his reasoning because it didn't work. He got to the apartment, wandered around for a while, then got back in his truck, went to her house, and slid into bed beside her. She hadn't said a word.

The next night, he tried again. He didn't even make it six blocks before he turned around to get back to her.

He hadn't gone back to his apartment since, except to pick up his few belongings, which now hung in a closet in "his" room from when he was protecting her. They kept their things in their individual rooms but ate together when he got home, they sat together while she worked, and they slept together in the window bed every night.

He wouldn't have it any other way.

Two weeks ago, Nemo had advised him to make a grand gesture that would show Flame he meant to stay. A gesture that would be the ultimate gift so that she would want to bind herself to him permanently. He'd known since that day what he needed to do, but emotionally, she had been nowhere near ready for it. Today, she was.

The stair creaked behind him, and his hand reflexively went to rub at his chest as he turned.

Is it going to be like this every time she walks down those fucking stairs?

She took his breath away. The clothes weren't even revealing most of the time. It was just something about the whole situation. The sound of her arrival. The scent of her perfume. The sight of all that innocence, sass, and sexiness all wrapped up in one. The anticipation of meeting her at the bottom of the stairs. Her on the bottom step, him flat on the floor, and looking into her eyes. He didn't think it could ever get old because every time that damn stair creaked from her stepping on it, he'd be transported back to these moments of wonder and anticipation.

He met her at the bottom step. He still had to look down at her, but tonight was a little less than usual. She wore the black coat dress like a steampunk goddess. It was all form-fitted sleeves and bodice, but once the waistline hit, all bets were off. The skirt flared out, with flounced layers underneath, and the buttons down the front stopped functioning just below the juncture where her legs met, revealing a creamy expanse of thigh until black velvet over-the-knee boots that were her standard five-inch heel. Added bonus? She had these fake tinted eyeglasses, small and round in shape, making her look like a scientist and a librarian all in one. Smart woman that she was, she knew his weakness and exploited that by piling her red hair high on her head in some sort of creative top knot and leaving stray strands down and curling around her face. He'd be playing with one or more of those curls all night long, and she knew it.

"You look gorgeous, princess," he told her as he leaned down to kiss her cheek. "You make a very suitable steampunk librarian for Tripoli's theme night at the grand re-opening of The Library."

Her hands went to his chest and rested there. "You're not so bad yourself. But you are not exactly in keeping with the theme," she chastised as she gestured to his everyday outfit of a black dress shirt, black jeans, and black cowboy boots.

He grunted. "Not big into dress up. At least, not for myself."

"Mmm. That's all right. I've always been partial to your bad wolf persona," she teased, reaching out to smooth down his shirt collar. Her attention was caught by his newest tattoo on the side of his neck—a red wolf with emerald-green eyes.

His hand reached up to take her hand in his, which he brought to his mouth and kissed her fingertips. He caught the scent of roses on her wrist, where she had dabbed her favorite perfume.

He breathed her in, then he pulled her close, hugging her tightly to him, wishing he could wrap up this moment like he was wrapping her up in his arms. They stood there, just holding one another in the quiet of the house.

"I have something for you," he said as he pulled away.

He turned and walked over to the dining room table, where a black gift bag sat. From out of the bag, he pulled a jewelry box from the store Midas had researched and given to him on the day they rescued Flame. It clearly held some type of necklace. He exhaled slowly, the weight of the box in his hand translating into a grip tightening around his lungs.

Will she understand what it means?

Slowly, he turned to face her. She stood where he'd left her, her bottom lip trapped beneath her top front teeth.

She's nervous because she can tell that you're nervous. Relax!

The space between them was less than twenty feet, but it felt like they were at two ends of a black tunnel. One that was closing in on them with each step he took back toward her.

Once back in front of her, he held out the box to her.

She looked at him, confused.

"Open it." Technically, it may have been a command, but his voice was soft and filled with trepidation.

Cautiously, she reached for the box and opened the hinged lid. She couldn't help but give a soft gasp at what was inside, and her eyes opened wider. She put her hand out to touch it but then pulled back at the last second, grabbing her throat with that same hand.

Inside the velvet box was a strand of twelve teardrop gems attached to a chainmail collar. And in the center of the collar was a silver wolf's head inside the O-ring, its head thrown back in a howl for its mate. At the back was a small silver lock with a key inside it.

"It's beautiful," she whispered. She looked closer. "Are... are those diamonds?"

He shrugged. His nerves were jangling.

"I don't know what to say."

"Say you'll wear it for me. Please."

She looked at him, her eyes shining. "You've never said 'please' before."

"This is important.

She chewed on her bottom lip. "This isn't just a collar for nights out at The Library."

"No, it's not," he confirmed. "This is permanent. This is something you'd give someone for a collaring ceremony." He sighed. "I'm not doing this right."

"There's no right or wrong way, TB. It's just your way. Think of it like when you ask me to spell out my limits bluntly. I need your words clearly on this so that I know where your head is. You're not exactly Mr. Expressive. And we definitely don't want misconceptions on this."

He smiled. "No. No, we do not."

"So, just tell me. No frills or fancy speeches. Just say what you need to say."

Centering his breathing helped him clear his cluttered brain. "I love you, Sylvan. I honestly never believed I'd find someone I wanted permanently in my life, but I've discovered that now I do. You are all the pieces of me that are missing. I want to make our arrangement permanent. I know it's probably not the type of arrangement you've dreamed of, but to me, it's far stronger of a bond than a marriage would be. I can't marry you. Not in a traditional sense, because I technically don't exist. But this I can do.

"As for the lock, it's a reminder. Not for you. For me. Not that I really need it, but it's a reminder of the gift you're giving me. A reminder to take care of you. Because if you don't take care of something—if you just lock it away, it withers and dies."

Her palm cradled the side of his face. "I would be honored to wear it."

He exhaled in relief.

"Turn around, Sylvan."

As she turned her back to him, with shaking hands, he removed the collar from the white silk bed it lay upon. He closed the box, tossed it on the landing, took each end, raised it up over her head, then lowered it down in front of her face. He placed it at her throat just above the hollow he loved to kiss so much. With a quiet click, he locked the collar in place. He kissed the back of her head, then gently turned her on the stair to face him.

She stepped down off the stairs and went to stand in front of the mirror in the hallway. She reached up to touch the gems that dangled from the chainmail links. He stepped up behind her—his hands on her shoulders, his head bent down to rest his lips next to her ear. Their eyes caught in the mirror, and he was reminded of the first night they met at the club when he showed through the mirror exactly the beauty that she was. The flush on her chest, neck, and cheeks told him she was remembering as well.

"It's beautiful on you," he assured her. "I knew it would be."

"It's more than I deserve."

Shaking his head, he turned her to face him, arms banding gently around her waist. "No. In fact, I have one more gift for you. That is if you don't mind being late to the party tonight."

"Hmm." She pretended to consider the option. "Does this gift include multiple toe-curling orgasms? Because if it does, we probably will never make it to the party at all. I don't think you want Tripoli mad at you."

Normally, he would have chuckled at her playfulness, but the collar was only the first half of what he'd been fearing tonight. Now, he needed to give her the second half.

"I have a sneaking suspicion he'd understand." He thought about what he'd just said and then about his plan. "Then again, he probably wouldn't."

Do I dare?

Can you do it?

For her, yes. I can give her this. And if I do, it means I'm giving her everything. Everything she wants. Everything she needs.

Everything I need.

"If I didn't know better, I'd think my big, badass interrogator was nervous," she teased.

"Worse. Terrified."

"What could scare you?"

Releasing her waist, he dragged his arms from around her, snagging her forearms as he backed up. When his hands reached hers, they gripped them tightly. "Come with me."

With a gentle tug, he pulled her to the stairs. Together, they walked side-by-side up to the second floor, then down the hall to the staircase to the third floor. A hand on her lower back, he urged her to climb the spiral staircase ahead of him. When they reached the top, she turned to ask him what was going on, but her eye was caught by something in her peripheral vision. A double take clarified what she had seen.

A white, silk blindfold.

A short coil of white silk rope.

Grinning, she crossed over to the bed and picked the items up, modeling one in each hand, her hip cocked and a sultry smile on her face. "Are we taking them with or putting them to use now?"

Without a smile in response, he crossed the room to stand in front of her, his fingers deftly unbuttoning his dress shirt and untucking it from the waist of his jeans. "Now." He dropped the shirt on the floor at the foot of the bed.

Standing shirtless before her, he removed the wire-rimmed glasses perched on the end of her nose, folded the arms, and set them on the bookcase at the foot of the bed.

One by one, he began pulling her hairpins free, placing them neatly on top of the bookshelf. Once he thought he had them all removed and her hair hung loose down her back, his hands threaded through the long tresses, ensuring all of the pins were gone and that the tangles were combed out.

God, I love her hair. Totally obsessed with it.

He took one step back from her, leaving her standing with the blindfold and rope still in her hands and her lip being worried by her front teeth. Reaching out, he rescued the lip from being wounded.

With a smile of reassurance, he sat on the edge of the bed to pull his boots off. Standing again, his hands reached for his belt. He pulled the loose end with his right hand, flipped the buckle with his left, and slid the leather from the prong. With one pull, he slipped the belt from the loops of his jeans, then threw it to join his shirt. When the metal clinked against the floor, he saw her jump slightly, and her skin rose in gooseflesh. He wanted to pull her close to warm her, but he was afraid if he did, he wouldn't continue with his plan.

He unbuttoned his jeans and slid the zipper down, the rasp of the metal teeth loud in the quiet. Her breaths were beginning to speed up, her chest rising and falling in awareness of what was coming.

He slid the jeans down gently past his hips. Once he'd cleared his hips, he shoved the denim down to his ankles in an impatient push. He removed the pants from his legs, throwing them to his clothing pile, and also pulled his socks from his feet. Shoving them in his boots, he then tossed the boots over to the pile as well. She definitely jumped at their thunk.

His hand was shaking as it raised to hers holding the blindfold. After taking it from her, he reached back up to her face and stroked the back of his hand down her cheek, the white silk strand trailing along her side.

"So beautiful. So trusting. You undo me, Sylvan." He ran his hands up and down her arms to try and chase some of the gooseflesh away.

Draping the blindfold around his neck, he took the rope from her hand and laid it on the bed, then began the sensual assault of undressing her. With every button he slipped, every tie he loosened, every zipper he released, he made sure to kiss the inch of skin it revealed. With every piece of clothing he took off of her, his hands smoothed over the flushed skin. When he knelt at her feet to remove her boots, he heard her whimper.

When she was bared to him, his hands curved around the back of her thighs, and he looked up at her. "It's time."

She picked up the rope again and held it out to him. His smile was a mere ghost of humor while curling her fingers around it. He shook his head. "No, Sylvan. Not this time."

She furrowed her brow. "But—"

He stopped her question with a finger pressed to his lips. "It's not for you, princess. It's for me."

Her confusion remained. "I don't understand."

"I know. That's why I'm telling you. The rope isn't to restrain you. It's to restrain me. Do you understand?"

Her gaze was curious. Understanding dawned in a flash, her eyes widening in surprise, her mouth dropping open, her cheeks blushing deep. "But... you're a Dom."

"And what is a Dom's job?"

"To take care of their sub's needs."

"Correct, princess."

"But I don't need this. I don't need to tie you up."

"Not specifically, maybe. But you need me to give myself to you, and this is the best way I can do that. If I make myself vulnerable to you, it is a clear statement that I trust you implicitly. That I'm choosing you. That I'm giving you everything."

Her eyes swam with tears. "Everything?" she whispered.

"Everything, Sylvan. Every broken, grumpy piece of me. I'm yours. Always."

Her hands smoothed across his forehead, down his cheeks, and rested there. She bent down and pressed her lips to his forehead. When she stood upright, there were tears falling from her eyes.

"Why are you crying? Aren't you happy?"

She nodded. "So happy."

He pulled the blindfold from around his neck and held it up to her. "Do your worst, princess."

"The gesture is enough."

Shaking his head, he reassured her. "No. I want this. I want you to have this."

Now, it was her hands shaking as they reached out to take it from his hand. The exchange was far more symbolic than he had imagined it would be.

No going back now. And dammit, I don't want to go back.

52

———————

JULY 15TH

Sylvan

Holy sugar on saltines!

Tentatively, she placed the blindfold over his eyes, wrapping it around his head, and tied it in a flat knot behind his head. Adjusting it to ensure it was over his eyes, she checked to make sure it was tight enough to prevent it from coming off. "Can you see?" she asked.

"No."

"Is it uncomfortable?"

She watched him swallow. "No."

"Okay." She withdrew her hands and placed one over her stomach to quell the butterflies. "Lie back on the bed with your head on the pillow."

Hands behind him on the edge of the bed, he hoisted himself onto the bed, then slid back on the covers so that he was lying in the center.

Gingerly, she climbed up onto the bed next to him, rope in hand, then straddled him, careful to avoid sitting on his jutting cock. Afraid she would refuse to follow through, she let the rope unwind, its length laying loosely on his chest and trailing off the side closest to the floor. Gathering his hands in hers, she put them together, wrist to wrist, and wound the rope several times around them. Gently, she guided his arms above his head and helped him find the center post behind the pillows and part of the book-shelves' support system. Once his hands had gripped the post, she tied off the ends, draping the excess length on the bookshelf, then slid her fingers between the rope and his skin to make sure that it was tight enough not to slip loose, but also not too tight to abrade his skin, just like he had always done with her.

"If you feel any numbness, tingling, or pain, you tell me immediately."

He licked his lips, which were just short of a grimace, but he nodded.

"Words, TB."

He chuckled tightly. "Well played, princess. It's uncomfort-able. But no more so than it was for you, I imagine. I haven't been in this spot since I joined my first kink club."

Jealousy reared hard. "You've been tied before?"

"It made sense to me that anything I intended to do to a submissive, I needed to experience myself. I wanted to under-stand what she would feel."

"Everything?" she squeaked.

He smiled again. "Yes. Everything," he emphasized to her. "But you can put the green-eyed monster away, princess. It was one time for each of those things, and not with anyone I was attracted to. Being dominated by a Domme is not something I wish to repeat," he admitted. "I would only do this again for you."

She pitched forward with a speed she didn't know she possessed and slammed her lips down onto his. Hungrily, she swept her tongue over the seam of his lips, forcing it into his mouth. She flicked his tongue with the tip of hers, then slid it along his.

She could feel him vibrating beneath her. He was trying to remain submissive to her, but he was struggling.

This man. To have him at her whims? For him to allow her to have this unprecedented control over his pleasure? This truly was *everything* that he could give her.

"You trust me, don't you, TB?" Flame asked.

"I would never put myself in this position with you if I didn't. But I would like to make one request."

Even when he asks for something, he doesn't phrase it as a question. Dominant to his core.

"Which is?"

"Call me Micah."

He wants me to use his real name. Oh, sassafras!

From her perch astride him, she leaned down, bringing her lips to barely brush against the hollow in his throat. "Micah." His name came from her mouth like a sigh, and his body seemed to relax a fraction.

Sylvan found herself at a loss. What should she do with him? This was so much easier when she just had to exist. He was responsible for all decisions, and she had only to experience. But now she was expected to lead, and she felt awkward despite being given free rein to do with him whatever she liked.

She returned her mouth to the hollow of his throat, this time pressing a kiss there. The tip of her tongue slipped between her lips to taste his skin. It was warm and tasted slightly of salt. Sweat from nerves at being restrained? She felt her power increase.

Emboldened by his taste, she dragged the point of her tongue across his clavicle, then down to his nipple. Her tongue traced a circle around the disk, and when it had made an entire journey of three hundred and sixty degrees, she used her front teeth to ever-so-gently grip the nipple and tug.

He hissed, and his back arched slightly off of the mattress. "Fuck, Sylvan. Again."

"What do you say, Micah?"

"Please," he gritted out through his teeth.

"Very well done. I guess I have to reward you for that."

She crossed over to the other nipple and repeated the process.

But before she bit and tugged this time, she whispered, "We can't have this nipple feeling neglected, now can we?"

His groan at the pulling from her mouth was part laugh. "You're enjoying using my words and tactics against me way too much. Use this opportunity wisely, young lady. You will never get it again."

"Mmmmmm," she hummed as her tongue licked a path back up to his throat, where she latched on like a nursing kitten. "Never say never," she mumbled against his skin, then went back to sucking lightly at the spot.

Sylvan wiggled her way back along Micah's torso until she felt the gentle nudge of the tip of his cock against her ass. She felt a slight wetness against her skin from him, and she smiled to herself.

Get ready, my lovely giant. I'm going to rock your world.

He was hissing slightly again, so she looked up at him from her sprawled position. She placed a well-manicured finger against his lips. "One more sound out of you, young man, and I'll stop what I'm about to do."

She knew he couldn't see her face, but it amused her to imagine what he'd picture in his own head at what she was doing or going to be doing. Rising onto her knees, she took her weight off of his chest and hips. The only place they were now touching was the insides of her knees and calves to his hips and thighs. Placing her hands wide of his body on the bed, she swung her left leg over him so that she was kneeling on the outside of the bed at his hip.

He didn't speak, but she could tell by the clenched jaw that he desperately wanted to give her a command. One that likely held the threat of a spanking if she didn't comply with what he wanted, and quickly. His hips even rose slightly off the mattress as if trying to follow her body.

"No, no, no, Micah. Your job is to simply lie there. Your pleasure is my responsibility now."

"That's mean, Sylvan."

"Oh, so it's not mean when you say that to me?" she teased.

"No, it's not. You need me to tell you that, or you don't get the maximum amount of pleasure out of our time together. You rush toward your pleasure. My job is to make sure you savor it, even when it's passionate. Even when it's quick, you can't rush it. There's a difference."

"Well, don't 'rush' me by thrusting your hips into the air like that. We'll get there," she repeated yet another of his phrases, trying desperately not to giggle at his frustration.

"Woman, I am so going to paddle your ass when I get loose."

"Perhaps I should keep you tied up permanently, then, hmmm?"

Facing the foot of the bed, she pressed her lips to his right hip, at the very start of the V-cut to his groin. Her tongue slipped out between her lips again, and she traced the cut all the way to his cock. Then she snaked her tongue back into her mouth but drew her index finger up the wet stripe she had drawn from cock to hip.

She placed that same index finger into her mouth and began to suck on it, gathering her saliva onto the digit. When she let it go, she made a popping sound so that Micah would hear it and wonder what she was doing.

"Sylvan?" he questioned.

"Quiet, Micah. You'll like this."

Taking her wet finger, she touched it to the root of his cock and drew it to the underside of the mushroom cap at its tip. With the last of her wetness there, she circled around the cap, then stroked it to the tip, which was weeping precum. She swirled it lightly around the tip of his cock, then took what remained on the tip of her finger, opened her mouth, and proceeded to clean her finger off by dragging closed lips from the webbing of her fingers until the tip exited her mouth, again with a pop.

"You taste so good, Micah. I think I need some more."

Still facing the foot of the bed, she placed her left hand on the top of his left thigh. Her right hand on top of his right thigh. Then agonizingly slowly, she began to lower her mouth to his hard cock. She stopped just short of the tip, so close he'd feel the heat of her breath but far enough that he'd be desperate for her to finish the connection.

"Do you want me to taste your cock before I fuck you, Micah?"

"Ex-xcuse me?" he asked.

"I'm sorry, wasn't I speaking loudly enough?" she teased. Raising her voice in volume just a little, she repeated, "Do you want me to taste your cock before I fuck you, Micah?"

"Holy shit," he whispered on a groan. "You did not just say those words."

"What words?" she asked innocently.

She was hovering just over the tip, precum still leaking from it, the head growing a darker red with each passing moment.

"You said the words 'cock' and 'fuck.' I've only ever heard you swear once. My little Flame doesn't swear, let alone say dirty words during sex."

"Well, I can stop if you'd prefer."

"Stop what? Stop talking dirty? Or stop having sex? Don't you dare stop either, or I'll spank your ass raw."

"Well, I think you'd have a very difficult time doing that, Micah. After all, you're all tied up and can't touch me. I can basically do whatever I want. And I want to taste my cock. And it is mine, Micah. Make no mistake."

Wasting no more time, in one swift movement, she swung her leg back over Micah's body, but this time with her legs on either side of his head and her mouth hovering over his cock. "Less talking and more licking, Micah."

She heard a groan from Micah and felt the brush of his hair against the insides of her thighs. His firm tongue muscle slid between her folds, gathering up the arousal that had already been forming and escaping her body. She mimicked his movements by swiping up the fluid his body was releasing, recognizing that eventually, he would need to be slick to enter her.

Sylvan found herself lost in the sensation of his skin under her tongue and the ghost of response he made against hers. She heard a low moan, at first not realizing it was her. Her lips were wrapped around the head of his cock, her tongue cradling his tip, and she felt saliva pooling in her cheeks. As slow as she could manage, she slid down his length, keeping her tongue connected to his shaft until her lips reached contact with his groin.

Perspiration popped from her skin at the strain of holding back. Tears leaked from her eyes. Her mouth ached with the stretch around him, and his head lodged in her throat, but she was not letting him go because when her lips met his skin, the most amazing feeling began inside her. He had responded in kind by making his tongue a long, stiffened point, and he buried it inside her channel as deep as he could. He began using it to scrape along the roof of her walls, and she felt her insides trembling, tickling, curling up, burning, and then releasing in a tidal wave against his mouth.

An involuntary muffled shriek issued from deep inside her, and she forced herself down his cock just a bit further before she swallowed around the head of it. His body reacted in kind by jerking further into her mouth, releasing what felt like a flood of cum, and his own muffled groans over the sensation. Both refused to withdraw their mouths from the other until their bodies stopped twitching in response.

Sylvan pulled her core up from Micah's mouth and her mouth from his cock. Not bothering to wipe her mouth from the last of his fluids, she swung herself around one hundred eighty degrees so that she was now facing him. His breath was sawing in and out, his lips and face shiny from her, and she knew that she would look similar. They both would look as if they'd been thoroughly fucked, but they weren't done yet.

Her hand grasped for his cock, which was still hard despite his orgasm, and she slid herself down its length until she was fully seated, her walls twitching with aftershocks.

"Sylvan," he groaned. "Need your mouth, princess."

Hands on his shoulders, she eased down so that their mouths meshed. The kisses lacked finesse, both still grappling with trying to breathe normally. But neither one of them cared because each breath meant moving bodies, and moving bodies meant friction of skin on skin. His cock was still pulsing, her walls were still twitching, and both were desperate to feel that hot rush of pleasure run through their bodies again.

Using her grip on his shoulders as leverage, she raised her weight off of him, sliding up his cock, hesitated at the top, then slid back down and ground her clit against him as she rotated her hips. She repeated the movements, trying to establish a rhythm, chasing the electric tingles pulsing through her bloodstream. Micah was in perfect sync with her—his knees bent to form a V for her body to feel saddled to him and to keep her feeling caged in, his heels digging into the mattress so that he could punch his hips up to meet hers thrusting down.

Sensation after sensation bombarded her. He was the one bound and blindfolded, but suddenly, she was the one who felt restrained. Despite his closeness and feeling safe, she still felt panicked inside. Sylvan collapsed onto his chest, her forehead to his, her hair forming a curtain to block out everything around them. "Micah," she pleaded, her whisper trembling on her lips.

"Sylvan? What's wrong?"

She didn't want to answer. She tried to hold back, but she couldn't. "Yellow."

A sudden twist of his hands above his head, his muscles bulged, and there was a ripping sound. Then his hands were free, and he was tearing the blindfold from his eyes. Immediately, he jackknifed upright, swept an arm underneath her backside, and clutched her tightly to him without dislodging himself from inside her.

"Wrap around me, sweetheart."

53

JULY 15TH

TB

HIS LITTLE FLAME DIDN'T NEED TO BE ASKED TWICE. SHE CLENCHED HIM tight around the neck with her arms, burying her face in his neck. Her legs wrapped around his waist, her thighs gripping his hips.

"What is it, Sylvan?" His hands stroked down her hair, his lips pressing to the top of her head. "Why 'yellow'?"

"It's too much." She admitted the truth. "I should feel free, empowered, but instead, I can't breathe."

Gripping her hair in his fingers, he wound it around his fist, tightly but gently, so that eventually she was forced to tip her head back to look in his eyes. "I've got you, princess."

"How do you stand it? I felt so free when we were together before. Like I was flying. It was exciting, at first, to have you at my mercy. But suddenly, I felt weighed down. Oppressed. Weak."

"Oh, princess, you are the strong one. *You*. And it has always been you that has had the control." Smoothing the hair back from her face, he kissed her forehead, a smile on his face. "All the decisions… all the power… it's always been yours. It has nothing to do with the ropes, or belts, or the control of the orgasms. That just means I listen to you and to your body to know how to give you pleasure. That I'm capable of delivering what you need from me physically.

"Dominance and submission are about trust. That's why it's called a power exchange. The Dominant is always the one who is caged because he or she is bound by the promise. The promise to make decisions that keep the submissive happy, cared for, and safe. The promise to fulfill the submissive's needs, not the needs of the self. Our pleasure is found in fulfilling the promise.

"The submissive is the one who is free. By becoming my submissive, you trust me to see to your happiness, your needs, your safety. And when I no longer meet that purpose, you have the control to end everything. I am the weak one because my entire life is devoted to serving *you*."

Another kiss to her forehead, and then he buried his head in her hair. "Do you understand, Sylvan? I'm giving you *everything* that I can, *everything that I am*. It is why I've never entered into a contract with a submissive before because I could never make that promise."

Lifting his head. "Unwind from me, monkey."

Slowly, reluctantly, Sylvan let go of her stranglehold on TB, and he leaned over the edge of the bed to swipe his pants from the pile on the floor. He dug in the right-hand pocket. Once he found what he needed, he dropped the pants back on the floor, grabbed her hand, and placed the delicate key for the collar in her palm. Gently, he folded her fingers around it.

"All the choices are always yours," he whispered.

Sylvan pressed the closed fist to her heart, her other hand covering her mouth. She was trying not to cry, so he did the only thing he knew to keep that from happening. He kissed her. Hard. A hand curled up around the back of her neck, and an arm curled around her waist, both pressing her as close to him as possible.

His hands framed her face. "I love you, Sylvan. Always. Forever. With every breath until my last."

She repeated, "I love you, Micah. Always. Forever. With every breath until my last."

ALSO BY NICOLE CRAIG

Good Enough: The Deadman's Tribe Book 1 – B0CJFSW6LZ

Team Leader, Waters, hires on to consult on a movie about Navy SEALs. Director Kai Serrano not only needs his expertise, but also needs his protection as the men of Tribe Corporation search for her missing brother.

Bad Enough: The Deadman's Tribe Book 2 – B0CTHZPN6Y

Interrogator and all-around bad boy TB has been talking in secret to romance novelist Sylvan Jones about the BDSM lifestyle as part of her research for a new novel. But when secrets from Sylvan's past come back to haunt her, the bad boy is forced into the good girl's real world, and he'll burn the world down to protect her.

Never Enough: The Deadman's Tribe Book 3 – B0CZ339NWF

Thief and playboy Nemo partners up with fellow thief Haskell to trace a cache of conflict diamonds through Africa. Will the playboy have his heart stolen by Le Chatte Noire, or will he resist being caught for life?

Strong Enough: The Deadman's Tribe Book 4 – B0F1RBGWHF

Twenty-six years ago, Cherry's father was kidnapped and never found. Her entire life has been a search for those who took him. After all this time, she finally has a lead. Posing as newlyweds, she and Demon, Tribe's medic, travel to the Caribbean, where they uncover ancient secrets that are tied to his disappearance. Those same secrets now endanger the attraction they've finally decided to explore.

The Lucky Rabbit: A prequel spin-off to the series Six Paths to Justice
— B0D777NVR5

A short story in *The Lucky in Love* charity anthology. Cosmos, member and part owner of a BDSM club called The Library, meets a woman who intrigues him more than any other woman has. After a memorable night together, he gets called away on an emergency, and their newfound relationship hangs in the balance. (This story is a prequel to a spin-off series from *Bad Enough,* and will connect to the *Operation Alpha: Police & Fire* world of Susan Stoker.)

Justice for Francesca: Six Paths to Justice Book 1 (Operation Alpha: Police & Fire) — B0DTV65N4V

Tripoli and Fleur's story (seen in *Bad Enough)*

Ethan "Tripoli" Evans met FBI agent Francesca McCabe while she was undercover. When her case exploded around her, she was forced to leave the investigation without notice, leaving him hurt and confused. It's now two years later, there's a murdered woman in his nightclub, and Francesca has been assigned to investigate. Tripoli is not about to allow his second chance to pass him by.

<u>Up Next</u>

Midas's Story: The Deadman's Tribe Book 5

RELEASES OCTOBER 2025!

ABOUT THE AUTHOR

At ten years old, Nicole Craig snuck into a secret box of her mother's books filled with mysteries and romances. Since that day, she has a book (or five) available at all times. At the age of thirty, her husband encouraged her to try her hand at writing. It only took another twenty-five years of teaching high school and a pandemic to do it, creating the types of books she found in that magical box.

Nicole lives in Southeastern Wisconsin. She is a devout Milwaukee Brewers fan, mother of three furry feline children, and married to The One. After twenty-five years as a high school English teacher, she decided to retire to spin fantastic tales, travel, and live the ultimate fantasy: reading a book a day until the end of time.

Please consider leaving a review on Amazon or Goodreads. It's one of the best ways to thank a writer (besides buying their books!) for the work they've done.

Check out her Facebook Reader Group or any of her social media links to get the latest updates on The Deadman's Tribe series or other upcoming projects.

Facebook Reader Group: Nicole Craig's Tribe
Website: https://nicolecraigauthor.com/
Instagram: https://www.instagram.com/nicolecraigauthor/
Newsletter: https://dl.bookfunnel.com/aoslx3def0

I had no idea what these past six months were going to bring me. I was certainly proud of my accomplishments with Book 1. What I was not prepared for was the crippling anxiety that would come with Book 2. Would it be "good enough" to stand alongside its predecessor? (Sorry. Couldn't resist.) After what felt like months of editing, and tearing it apart, and putting it back together, only to tear it apart again… probably times five… I've been told to quit worrying. Thank you to the following individuals for their continued support. Who knew that most of them would become therapists through Direct Messaging?

Mr. C–You are a fabulous alpha reader. I love that you're not afraid to tell me "This is not making sense" and still feel comfortable falling asleep next to me at night. I've never watched you eat up a book as fast as this one. I won't tell Lee Child you're cheating on him if you don't.

Isabelle Peterson–I've so enjoyed getting to know you since the Superfan podcast on Kennedy L. Mitchell. Your perspective is welcome anytime, and I look forward to our upcoming project.

Allyson Mingo–Thank you for the awesome graphics for *Good Enough*. You have a golden heart that more people should be blessed to know and experience.

Friday Night Crew–There are people who come into your life and you have no idea how important they are going to become. Then suddenly, something happens, and they become your biggest cheerleaders. They sell copies of your books to complete strangers in bars and in cities you don't live in. They let you ramble on about shit that no one cares about but you, and yeah, they tease you about which of them were the inspiration for the main characters, but you know they love this for you. (Just make sure it stays that way or someone with your name is going to die in one of my books.)

Anna Blakely & Mr. B–You are truly a Tier One Author and her Consort. Your support for me and my work, as well as how you extend your knowledge to other new authors, and the love you have for your fans (especially the Talk Tuesday crowd) make you the First Couple of Romantic Suspense.

Ryleigh Sloan–I'm still picturing that gorge with a Tribe couple swinging up above hungry crocodiles. Thank you for breaking my Candy Crush addiction.

Terrie-Lee Olivier and Megan Van Rooyen (Book Besties Long Distanceship Podcast)–Thank you for having me on your show. It was fabulous, and my cheeks are STILL hurting five hours later after recording our episode. I'd be on the next plane to South Africa if I could.

SJ Higgins, Stef White, Vanessa Esquibel, Kelly Finley, and Kat Wyeth–The Hot Mess Express is forever in your debt once again.

Nicole Craig's Tribe–Thank you for being a part of my reader group. We are small, but we are tribe.

My ARC Tribe–Thank you for taking some of your valuable time to read and review my novel. I know it's not an easy job. I appreciate your honest reviews.

To Anyone Who Reads This Book–Thank you. TB and Sylvan thank you, as well. And remember: anything is possible if you want it bad enough.

To my colleagues of the past 25 years–Whether it was for one year, or for all twenty-five. Whether it was side-by-side in the classroom or just a nod as we passed in the hallways. It was my pleasure and privilege to work by your side. Teaching is not a job. It is not even a career. It is a calling. Do not allow those who have never run a classroom tell you how easy you have it. There is NOT A DAMN THING that's easy about teaching. It's messy. It's painful. It's heart-breaking. It's soul-crushing. And that's just the part that involves trying to help our students be better human beings. The pay is never worth what we do to our health, our home-lives, and our personal well-being. But that's not why we do it. We do it because someone needs to. And if not us, then who?